THE TWELVE DANCING PRINCESSES

There was a king who had twelve beautiful daughters. They slept in twelve beds all in one room; and when they went to bed, the doors were shut and locked up; but every morning their shoes were found to be quite worn through as if they had been danced in all night; and yet nobody could find out how it happened, or where they had been.

Then the king made it known to all the land, that if any person could discover the secret, and find out where it was that the princesses danced in the night, he should have the one he liked best for his wife, and should be king after his death; but whoever tried and did not succeed, after three days and nights, should be put to death.

A king's son soon came. He was well entertained, and in the evening was taken to the chamber next to the one where the princesses lay in their twelve beds. There he was to sit and watch where they went to dance; and, in order that nothing might pass without his hearing it, the door of his chamber was left open. But the king's son soon fell asleep; and when he awoke in the morning he found that the princesses had all been dancing, for the soles of their shoes were full of holes. The same thing happened the second and third night: so the king ordered his head to be cut off. After him came several others; but they had all the same luck, and all lost their lives in the same manner.

Now it chanced that an old soldier, who had been wounded in battle and could fight no longer, passed through the country where this king reigned: and as he was travelling through a wood, he met an old woman, who asked him where he was going. "I hardly know where I am going, or what I had better do," said the soldier; "but I think I should like very well to find out where it is that the princesses dance, and then in time I might be a king." "Well," said the old dame, "that is no very hard task: only take care not to drink any of the wine which one of the princesses will bring to you in the evening; and as soon as she leaves you pretend to be fast asleep."

Then she gave him a cloak, and said, "As soon as you put that on you will become invisible, and you will then be able to follow the princesses wherever they go." When the soldier heard all this good counsel, he determined to try his luck: so he went to the king, and said he was willing to undertake the task.

He was as well received as the others had been, and the king ordered fine royal robes to be given him; and when the evening came he was led to the outer chamber. Just as he was going to lie down, the eldest of the princesses brought him a cup of wine; but the soldier threw it all away secretly, taking care not to drink a drop. Then he laid himself down on his bed, and in a little while began to snore very loud as if he was fast asleep. When the twelve princesses heard this they laughed heartily; and the eldest said, "This fellow too might have done a wiser thing than lose his life in this way!" Then they rose up and opened their drawers and boxes, and took out all their fine clothes, and dressed themselves at the glass, and skipped about as if they were eager to begin dancing. But the youngest said, "I don't know how it is, while you are so happy I feel very uneasy; I am sure some mischance will befall us." "You simpleton," said the eldest, "you are always afraid; have you forgotten how many kings' sons have already watched us in vain? And as for this soldier, even if I had not given him his sleeping draught, he would have slept soundly enough."

When they were all ready, they went and looked at the soldier; but he snored on, and did not stir hand or foot: so they thought they were quite safe; and the eldest went up to her own bed and clapped her hands, and the bed sunk into the floor and a trap-door flew open. The soldier saw them going down through the trap-door one after another, the eldest leading the way; and thinking he had no time to lose, he jumped up, put on the cloak which the old woman had given him, and followed them; but in the middle of the stairs he trod on the gown of the youngest princess, and she cried out to her sisters, "All is not right; some one took hold of my gown." "You silly creature!" said the eldest, "it is nothing but a nail in the wall." Then down they all went, and at the bottom they found themselves in a most delightful grove of trees; and the leaves were all of silver, and glittered and sparkled beautifully. The soldier wished to take away some token of the place; so he broke off a little branch, and there came a loud noise from the tree. Then the youngest daughter said again, "I am sure all is not right—did not you hear that noise? That never happened before." But the eldest said, "It is only our princes, who are shouting for joy at our approach."

Then they came to another grove of trees, where all

3

the leaves were of gold; and afterwards to a third, where the leaves were all glittering diamonds. And the soldier broke a branch from each; and every time there was a loud noise, which made the youngest sister tremble with fear; but the eldest still said, It was only the princes, who were crying for joy. So they went on till they came to a great lake; and at the side of the lake there lay twelve little boats with twelve handsome princes in them, who seemed to be waiting there for the princesses.

One of the princesses went into each boat, and the soldier stepped into the same boat with the youngest. As they were rowing over the lake, the prince who was in the boat with the youngest princess and the soldier said, "I do not know why it is, but though I am rowing with all my might we do not get on so fast as usual, and I am quite tired: the boat seems very heavy to-day." "It is only the heat of the weather," said the princess; "I feel it very warm too."

On the other side of the lake stood a fine illuminated castle, from which came the merry music of horns and trumpets. There they all landed, and went into the castle, and each prince danced with his princess; and the soldier, who was all the time invisible, danced with them too; and when any of the princesses had a cup of wine set by her, he drank it all up, so that when she put the cup to her mouth it was empty. At this, too, the youngest sister was terribly frightened, but the eldest always silenced her. They danced on till three o'clock in the morning, and then all their shoes were worn out, so that they were obliged to leave off. The princes rowed them back again over the lake; (but this time the soldier placed himself in the boat with the eldest princess;) and on the opposite shore they took leave of each other, the princesses promising to come again the next night.

When they came to the stairs, the soldier ran on before the princesses, and laid himself down; and as the twelve sisters slowly came up very much tired, they heard him snoring in his bed; so they said, "Now all is quite safe;" then they undressed themselves, put away their fine clothes, pulled off their shoes, and went to bed. In the morning the soldier said nothing about what had happened, but determined to see more of this strange adventure, and went again the second and third night; and every thing happened just as before; the princesses danced each time till their shoes were worn to pieces, and then returned home. However, on the third night the soldier carried away one of the golden cups as a token of where he had been.

As soon as the time came when he was to declare the secret, he was taken before the king with the three branches and the golden cup; and the twelve princesses stood listening behind the door to hear what he would say. And when the king asked him. "Where do my twelve daughters dance at night?" he answered, "With twelve princes in a castle under ground." And then he told the king all that had happened, and showed him the three branches and the golden cup which he had brought with him. Then the king called for the princesses, and asked them whether what the soldier said was true: and when they saw that they were discovered, and that it was of no use to deny what had happened, they confessed it all. And the king asked the soldier which of them he would choose for his wife; and he answered, "I am not very young; so I will have the eldest."—And they were married that very day, and the soldier was chosen to be the king's heir.

TOM THUMB

There was once a poor woodman sitting by the fire in his cottage, and his wife sat by his side spinning. "How lonely it is," said he, "for you and me to sit here by ourselves without any children to play about and amuse us, while other people seem so happy and merry with their children!" "What you say is very true," said the wife, sighing and turning round her wheel, "how happy should I be if I had but one child! and if it were ever so small, nay, if it were no bigger than my thumb, I should be very happy, and love it dearly." Now it came to pass that this good woman's wish was fulfilled just as she desired; for, some time afterwards, she had a little boy who was quite healthy and strong, but not much bigger than my thumb. So they said, "Well, we cannot say we have not got what we wished for, and, little as he is, we all love him dearly;" and they called him Tom Thumb.

They gave him plenty of food, yet he never grew bigger, but remained just the same size as when he was born; still his eyes were sharp and sparkling, and he soon showed himself to be a clever little fellow, who always knew well what he was about. One day, as the woodman was getting ready to go into the wood to cut fuel, he said, "I wish I had some one to bring the cart after me, for I want to make haste." "O father!" cried Tom, "I will take care of that; the cart shall be in the wood by the time you want it." Then the woodman laughed, and said, "How can that be? you cannot reach up to the horse's bridle." "Never mind that, father," said Tom; "if my mother will only harness the horse, I will get into his ear and tell him which way to go." "Well," said the father, "we will try for once."

When the time came, the mother harnessed the horse to the cart, and put Tom into his ear; and as he sat there, the little man told the beast how to go, crying out, "Go on," and "Stop," as he wanted; so the horse went on just as if the woodman had driven it himself into the wood. It happened that, as the horse was going a little too fast, and Tom was calling out "Gently! gently!" two strangers came up. "What an odd thing that is!" said one, "there is a cart going along and I hear a carter talking to the horse, but can see no one." "That is strange," said the other; "let us follow the cart and see where it goes." So they went on into the wood, till at last they came to the place where the woodman was. Then Tom Thumb, seeing his father, cried out, "See, father, here I am, with the cart, all right and safe; now take me down." So his father took hold of the horse with one hand, and with the other took his son out of the ear; then he put him down upon a straw, where he sat as merry as you please. The two strangers were all this time looking on, and did not know what to say for wonder. At last one took the other aside and said, "That little urchin will make our fortune if we can get him and carry him about from town to town as a show: we must buy him." So they went to the woodman and asked him what he would take for the little man: "He will be better off," said they, "with us than with you." "I won't sell him at all," said the father, "my own flesh and blood is dearer to me than all the silver and gold in the world." But Tom, hearing of the bargain they wanted to make, crept up his father's coat to his shoulder, and whispered in his ear, "Take the money, father, and let them have me, I'll soon come back to you."

So the woodman at last agreed to sell Tom to the strangers for a large piece of gold. "Where do you like to sit?" said one of them. "Oh! put me on the rim of your hat, that will be a nice gallery for me; I can walk about there, and see the country as we go along." So they did as he wished; and when Tom had taken leave of his father, they took him away with them. They journeyed on till it began to be dusky, and then the little man said, "Let me get down, I'm tired." So the man took off his hat and set him down on a clod of earth in a ploughed field by the side of the road. But Tom ran about amongst the furrows, and at last slipt into an old mouse-hole. "Good night, masters," said he, "I'm off! mind and look sharp after me the next time." They ran directly to the place, and poked the ends of their sticks into the mouse-hole, but all in vain; Tom only crawled farther and farther in, and at last it became quite dark, so that they were obliged to go their way without their prize, as sulky as you please.

When Tom found they were gone, he came out of his hiding-place. "What dangerous walking it is," said he, "in this ploughed field! If I were to fall from one of these great clods, I should certainly break my neck." At last, by good luck, he found a large empty snail-shell. "This is lucky," said he, "I can sleep here very well," and in he crept. Just as he was falling asleep he heard two men passing, and one said to the other, "How shall we manage to steal that rich parson's silver and gold?" "I'll tell you," cried Tom. "What noise was that?" said the thief, frightened, "I am sure I heard some one speak." They stood still listening, and Tom said, "Take me with you, and I'll soon show you how to get the parson's money." "But where are you?" said they. "Look about on the ground," answered he, "and listen where the sound comes from." At last the thieves found him out, and lifted him up in their hands. "You little urchin!" said they, "what can you do for us?" "Why I can get between the iron window-bars of the parson's house, and throw you out whatever you want." "That's a good thought," said the thieves, "come along, we shall see what you can do."

When they came to the parson's house, Tom slipt through the window-bars into the room, and then called out as loud as he could bawl, "Will you have all that is here?" At this the thieves were frightened, and said, "Softly, softly! Speak low, that you may not awaken any body." But Tom pretended not to understand them, and bawled out again, "How much will you have? Shall I throw it all out?" Now the cook lay in the next room, and hearing a noise she raised herself in her bed and listened. Meantime the thieves were frightened, and ran off to a little distance; but at last they plucked up courage, and said, "The little urchin is only trying to make fools of us." So they came back and whispered softly to him, saying, "Now let us have no more of your jokes, but throw out some of the money." Then Tom called out as loud as he could, "Very well: hold your hands, here it comes." The cook heard this quite plain, so she sprang out of bed and ran to open the door. The thieves ran off as if a wolf was at their tails; and the maid, having groped about and found nothing,

9

went away for a light. By the time she returned, Tom had slipt off into the barn; and when the cook had looked about and searched every hole and corner, and found nobody, she went to bed, thinking she must have been dreaming with her eyes open. The little man crawled about in the hay-loft, and at last found a glorious place to finish his night's rest in; so he laid himself down, meaning to sleep till day-light, and then find his way home to his father and mother. But, alas! how cruelly was he disappointed! what crosses and sorrows happen in this world! The cook got up early before day-break to feed the cows: she went straight to the hay-loft, and carried away a large bundle of hay with the little man in the middle of it fast asleep. He still, however, slept on, and did not awake till he found himself in the mouth of the cow, who had taken him up with a mouthful of hay: "Good lack-a-day!" said he, "how did I manage to tumble into the mill?" But he soon found out where he really was, and was obliged to have all his wits about him in order that he might not get between the cow's teeth, and so be crushed to death. At last down he went into her stomach. "It is rather dark here," said he; "they forgot to build windows in this room to let the sun in: a candle would be no bad thing."

Though he made the best of his bad luck, he did not like his quarters at all; and the worst of it was, that more and more hay was always coming down, and the space in which he was became smaller and smaller. At last he cried out as loud as he could, "Don't bring me any more hay! Don't bring me any more hay!" The maid happened to be just then milking the cow, and hearing some one speak and seeing nobody, and yet being quite sure it was the same voice that she had heard in the night, she was so frightened that she fell off her stool and overset the milk-pail. She ran off as fast as she could to her master the parson, and said, "Sir, sir, the cow is talking!" But the parson said, "Woman, thou art surely mad!" However, he went with her into the cow-house to see what was the matter. Scarcely had they set their foot on the threshold, when Tom called out, "Don't bring me any more hay!" Then the parson himself was frightened; and thinking the cow was surely bewitched, ordered that she should be killed directly. So the cow was killed, and the stomach, in which Tom lay, was thrown out upon a dunghill.

Tom soon set himself to work to get out, which was not a very easy task; but at last, just as he had made room to get his head out, a new misfortune befell him: a hungry wolf sprang out, and swallowed the whole stomach with Tom in it at a single gulp, and ran away. Tom, however, was not disheartened; and, thinking the wolf would not dislike having some chat with him as he was going along, he called out, "My good friend, I can show you a famous treat." "Where's that?" said the wolf. "In such and such a house," said Tom, describing his father's house, "you can crawl through the drain into the kitchen, and there you will find cakes, ham, beef, and every thing your heart can desire." The wolf did not want to be asked twice; so that very night he went to the house and crawled through the drain into the kitchen, and ate and drank there to his heart's content. As soon as he was satisfied, he wanted to get away, but he had eaten so much that he could not get out the same way that he came in. This was just what Tom had reckoned upon; and he now began to set up a great shout, making all the noise he could. "Will you be quiet?" said the wolf:

"you'll awaken every body in the house." "What's that to me?" said the little man: "you have had your frolic, now I've a mind to be merry myself;" and he began again singing and shouting as loud as he could.

The woodman and his wife, being awakened by the noise, peeped through a crack in the door; but when they saw that the wolf was there, you may well suppose that they were terribly frightened; and the woodman ran for his axe, and gave his wife a scythe.—"Now do you stay behind," said the woodman; "and when I have knocked him on the head, do you rip up his belly for him with the scythe." Tom heard all this, and said, "Father, father! I am here, the wolf has swallowed me:" and his father said, "Heaven be praised! we have found our dear child again;" and he told his wife not to use the scythe, for fear she should hurt him. Then he aimed a great blow, and struck the wolf on the head, and killed him on the spot; and when he was dead they cut open his body and set Tommy free. "Ah!" said the father, "what fears we have had for you!" "Yes, father," answered he, "I have travelled all over the world, since we parted, in one way or other; and now I am very glad to get fresh air again." "Why, where have you been?" said his father. "I have been in a mouse-hole, in a snail-shell, down a cow's throat, and in the wolf's belly; and yet here I am again safe and sound." "Well," said they "we will not sell you again for all the riches in the world." So they hugged and kissed their dear little son, and gave him plenty to eat and drink, and fetched new clothes for him, for his old ones were quite spoiled on his journey.

KING GRISLY-BEARD

A great king had a daughter who was very beautiful, but so proud and haughty and conceited, that none of the princes who came to ask her in marriage were good enough for her, and she only made sport of them.

Once upon a time the king held a great feast, and invited all her suitors; and they sat in a row according to their rank, kings and princes and dukes and earls. Then the princess came in and passed by them all, but she had something spiteful to say to every one. The first was too fat: "He's as round as a tub," said she. The next was too tall: "What a maypole!" said she. The next was too short: "What a dumpling!" said she. The fourth was too pale, and she called him "Wallface." The fifth was too red, so she called him "Cockscomb." The sixth was not straight enough, so she said he was like a green stick that had been laid to dry over a baker's oven. And thus she had some joke to crack upon every one: but she laughed more than all at a good king who was there. "Look at him," said she, "his beard is like an old mop, he shall be called Grisly-beard." So the king got the nickname of Grisly-beard.

But the old king was very angry when he saw how his daughter behaved, and how she ill-treated all his guests; and he vowed that, willing or unwilling, she should marry the first beggar that came to the door.

Two days after there came by a travelling musician, who began to sing under the window, and beg alms: and when the king heard him, he said, "Let him come in." So they brought in a dirty-looking fellow; and when he had sung before the king and the princess, he begged a boon. Then the king said, "You have sung so well, that I will give you my daughter for your wife." The princess begged and prayed; but the king said, "I have sworn to give you to the first beggar, and I will keep my word." So words and tears were of no avail; the parson was sent for, and she was married to the musician. When this was over, the king said, "Now get ready to go; you must not stay here; you must travel on with your husband."

Then the beggar departed, and took her with him; and they soon came to a great wood. "Pray," said she, "whose is this wood?" "It belongs to king Grisly-beard," answered he; "hadst thou taken him, all had been thine." "Ah! unlucky wretch that I am!" sighed she, "would that I had married king Grisly-beard!" Next they came to some fine meadows. "Whose are these beautiful green meadows?" said she. "They belong to king Grisly-beard; hadst thou taken him, they had all been thine." "Ah! unlucky wretch that I am!" said she, "would that I had married king Grisly-beard!"

Then they came to a great city. "Whose is this noble city?" said she. "It belongs to king Grisly-beard; hadst thou taken him, it had all been thine." "Ah! miserable wretch that I am!" sighed she, "why did I not marry king Grisly-beard?" "That is no business of mine," said the musician; "why should you wish for another husband? am not I good enough for you?"

At last they came to a small cottage. "What a paltry place!" said she; "to whom does that little dirty hole belong?" The musician answered, "That is your and my house, where we are to live." "Where are your servants?" cried she. "What do we want with servants?"

said he, "you must do for yourself whatever is to be done. Now make the fire, and put on water and cook my supper, for I am very tired." But the princess knew nothing of making fires and cooking, and the beggar was forced to help her. When they had eaten a very scanty meal they went to bed; but the musician called her up very early in the morning to clean the house. Thus they lived for two days: and when they had eaten up all there was in the cottage, the man said, "Wife, we can't go on thus, spending money and earning nothing. You must learn to weave baskets." Then he went out and cut willows and brought them home, and she began to weave: but it made her fingers very sore. "I see this work won't do," said he, "try and spin; perhaps you will do that better." So she sat down and tried to spin; but the threads cut her tender fingers till the blood ran. "See now," said the musician, "you are good for nothing, you can do no work;—what a bargain I have got! However, I'll try and set up a trade in pots and pans, and you shall stand in the market and sell them." "Alas!" sighed she, "when I stand in the market and any of my father's court pass by and see me there, how they will laugh at me!"

But the beggar did not care for that; and said she must work, if she did not wish to die of hunger. At first the trade went well; for many people, seeing such a beautiful woman, went to buy her wares, and paid their money without thinking of taking away the goods. They lived on this as long as it lasted, and then her husband bought a fresh lot of ware, and she sat herself down with it in a corner of the market; but a drunken soldier soon came by, and rode his horse against her stall and broke all her goods into a thousand pieces. Then she began to weep, and knew not what to do. "Ah! what will become of me!" said she; "what will my husband say?" So she ran home and told him all. "Who would have thought you would have been so silly," said he, "as to put an earthenware stall in the corner of the market, where every body passes?—But let us have no more crying; I see you are not fit for this sort of work: so I have been to the king's palace, and asked if they did not want a kitchen-maid, and they have promised to take you, and there you will have plenty to eat."

Thus the princess became a kitchen-maid, and helped the cook to do all the dirtiest work: she was allowed to carry home some of the meat that was left, and on this she and her husband lived.

She had not been there long, before she heard that the king's eldest son was passing by, going to be married, and she went to one of the windows and looked out. Every thing was ready, and all the pomp and splendour of the court was there. Then she thought with an aching heart on her own sad fate, and bitterly grieved for the pride and folly which had brought her so low. And the servants gave her some of the rich meats, which she put into her basket to take home.

All on a sudden, as she was going out, in came the king's son in golden clothes: and when he saw a beautiful woman at the door, he took her by the hand, and said she should be his partner in the dance: but she trembled for fear, for she saw that it was king Grisly-beard, who was making sport of her. However, he kept fast hold and led her in; and the cover of the basket came off, so that the meats in it fell all about. Then every body laughed and jeered at her; and she was so abashed that she wished herself a thousand feet deep in

16

the earth. She sprang to the door to run away; but on the steps king Grisly-beard overtook and brought her back, and said, "Fear me not! I am the musician who has lived with you in the hut: I brought you there because I loved you. I am also the soldier who overset your stall. I have done all this only to cure you of pride, and to punish you for the ill-treatment you bestowed on me. Now all is over; you have learnt wisdom, your faults are gone, and it is time to celebrate our marriage feast!"

Then the chamberlains came and brought her the most beautiful robes: and her father and his whole court were there already, and congratulated her on her marriage. Joy was in every face. The feast was grand, and all were merry; and I wish you and I had been of the party.

THE ELVES AND THE SHOEMAKER

There was once a shoemaker who worked very hard and was very honest; but still he could not earn enough to live upon, and at last all he had in the world was gone, except just leather enough to make one pair of shoes. Then he cut them all ready to make up the next day, meaning to get up early in the morning to work. His conscience was clear and his heart light amidst all his troubles; so he went peaceably to bed, left all his cares to heaven, and fell asleep. In the morning, after he had said his prayers, he set himself down to his work, when, to his great wonder, there stood the shoes, all ready made, upon the table. The good man knew not what to say or think of this strange event. He looked at the workmanship; there was not one false stitch in the

17

whole job; and all was so neat and true, that it was a complete masterpiece.

That same day a customer came in, and the shoes pleased him so well that he willingly paid a price higher than usual for them; and the poor shoemaker with the money bought leather enough to make two pairs more. In the evening he cut out the work, and went to bed early that he might get up and begin betimes next day: but he was saved all the trouble, for when he got up in the morning the work was finished ready to his hand. Presently in came buyers, who paid him handsomely for his goods, so that he bought leather enough for four pairs more. He cut out the work again over night, and found it finished in the morning as before; and so it went on for some time: what was got ready in the evening was always done by daybreak, and the good man soon became thriving and prosperous again.

One evening about Christmas time, as he and his wife were sitting over the fire chatting together, he said to her, "I should like to sit up and watch to-night, that we may see who it is that comes and does my work for me." The wife liked the thought; so they left a light burning, and hid themselves in the corner of the room behind a curtain that was hung up there, and watched what should happen.

As soon as it was midnight, there came two lit- tle naked dwarfs; and they sat themselves upon the shoemaker's bench, took up all the work that was cut out, and began to ply with their little fingers, stitching and rapping and tapping away at such a rate, that the shoemaker was all amazement, and could not take his eyes off for a moment. And on they went till the job was quite finished, and the shoes stood ready for use upon the table. This was long before daybreak; and then they bustled away as quick as lightning.

The next day the wife said to the shoemaker, "These little wights have made us rich, and we ought to be thankful to them, and do them a good office in return. I am quite vexed to see them run about as they do; they have nothing upon their backs to keep off the cold. I'll tell you what, I will make each of them a shirt, and a coat and waistcoat, and a pair of pantaloons into the bargain; do you make each of them a little pair of shoes."

The thought pleased the good shoemaker very much; and one evening, when all the things were ready, they laid them on the table instead of the work that they used to cut out, and then went and hid themselves to watch what the little elves would do. About midnight they came in, and were going to sit down to their work as usual; but when they saw the clothes lying for them, they laughed and were greatly delighted. Then they dressed themselves in the twinkling of an eye, and danced and capered and sprang about as merry as could be, till at last they danced out at the door over the green; and the shoemaker saw them no more: but every thing went well with him from that time forward, as long as he lived.

THE KING OF
THE GOLDEN MOUNTAIN

A certain merchant had two children, a son and daughter, both very young, and scarcely able to run alone. He had two richly laden ships then making a voyage upon the seas, in which he had embarked all his property, in the hope of making great gains, when the news came that they were lost. Thus from being a rich man he became very poor, so that nothing was left him but one small plot of land; and, to relieve his mind a little of his trouble, he often went out to walk there.

One day, as he was roving along, a little rough-looking dwarf stood before him, and asked him why he was so sorrowful, and what it was that he took so deeply to heart. But the merchant replied, "If you could do me any good, I would tell you." "Who knows but I may?" said the little man; "tell me what is the matter, and perhaps I can be of some service." Then the merchant told him how all his wealth was gone to the bottom of the sea, and how he had nothing left except that little plot of land. "Oh! trouble not yourself about that," said the dwarf; "only promise to bring me here, twelve years hence, whatever meets you first on your return home, and I will give you as much gold as you please." The merchant thought this was no great request; that it would most likely be his dog, or something of that sort, but forgot his little child: so he agreed to the bargain, and signed and sealed the engagement to do what was required.

But as he drew near home, his little boy was so pleased to see him, that he crept behind him and laid fast hold of his legs. Then the father started with fear, and saw what it was that he had bound himself to do; but as no gold was come, he consoled himself by thinking that it was only a joke that the dwarf was playing him.

About a month afterwards he went up stairs into an old lumber room to look for some old iron, that he might sell it and raise a little money; and there he saw a large pile of gold lying on the floor. At the sight of this he was greatly delighted, went into trade again, and became a greater merchant than before.

Meantime his son grew up, and as the end of the twelve years drew near, the merchant became very anxious and thoughtful; so that care and sorrow were written upon his face. The son one day asked what was the matter: but his father refused to tell for some time; at last however he said that he had, without knowing it, sold him to a little ugly-looking dwarf for a great quantity of gold; and that the twelve years were coming round when he must perform his agreement. Then the son said, "Father, give yourself very little trouble about that; depend upon it I shall be too much for the little man."

When the time came, they went out together to the appointed place; and the son drew a circle on the ground, and set himself and his father in the middle. The little dwarf soon came, and said to the merchant, "Have you brought me what you promised?" The old man was silent, but his son answered, "What do you want here?" The dwarf said, "I come to talk with your father, not with you" "You have deceived and betrayed my father," said the son; "give him up his bond." "No,"

21

replied the other, "I will not yield up my rights." Upon this a long dispute arose; and at last it was agreed that the son should be put into an open boat, that lay on the side of a piece of water hard by, and that the father should push him off with his own hand; so that he should be turned adrift. Then he took leave of his father, and set himself in the boat; and as it was pushed off it heaved, and fell on one side into the water: so the merchant thought that his son was lost, and went home very sorrowful.

But the boat went safely on, and did not sink; and the young man sat securely within, till at length it ran ashore upon an unknown land. As he jumped upon the shore, he saw before him a beautiful castle, but empty and desolate within, for it was enchanted. At last, however, he found a white snake in one of the chambers.

Now the white snake was an enchanted princess; and she rejoiced greatly to see him, and said, "Art thou at last come to be my deliverer? Twelve long years have I waited for thee, for thou alone canst save me. This night twelve men will come: their faces will be black, and they will be hung round with chains. They will ask what thou dost here; but be silent, give no answer, and let them do what they will—beat and torment thee. Suffer all, only speak not a word, and at twelve o'clock they must depart. The second night twelve others will come; and the third night twenty-four, who will even cut off thy head; but at the twelfth hour of that night their power is gone, and I shall be free, and will come and bring thee the water of life and health." And all came to pass as she had said; the merchant's son spoke not a word, and the third night the princess appeared, and fell on his neck and kissed him; joy and gladness burst forth throughout the castle; the wedding was celebrated, and he was king of the Golden Mountain.

They lived together very happily, and the queen had a son. Eight years had passed over their heads when the king thought of his father: and his heart was moved, and he longed to see him once again. But the queen opposed his going, and said, "I know well that misfortunes will come." However, he gave her no rest till she consented. At his departure she presented him with a wishing-ring, and said, "Take this ring, and put it on your finger; whatever you wish it will bring you: only promise that you will not make use of it to bring me hence to your father's." Then he promised what she asked, and put the ring on his finger, and wished himself near the town where his father lived. He found himself at the gates in a moment; but the guards would not let him enter, because he was so strangely clad. So he went up to a neighbouring mountain where a shepherd dwelt, and borrowed his old frock, and thus passed unobserved into the town. When he came to his father's house, he said he was his son; but the merchant would not believe him, and said he had had but one son, who he knew was long since dead; and as he was only dressed like a poor shepherd, he would not even offer him any thing to eat. The king however persisted that he was his son, and said, "Is there no mark by which you would know if I am really your son?" "Yes," observed his mother, "our son has a mark like a raspberry under the right arm." Then he showed them the mark, and they were satisfied that what he had said was true. He next told them how he was king of the Golden Mountain, and was married to a princess, and had a son seven years old. But the merchant said, "That can never be true; he must be a fine king truly who travels about in a shepherd's frock." At this the son was very angry; and, forgetting his promise, turned his ring, and wished for his queen and son. In an instant they stood before him; but the queen wept, and said he had broken his word, and misfortune would follow. He did all he could to soothe her, and she at last appeared to be appeased; but she was not so in reality, and only meditated how she should take her revenge.

One day he took her to walk with him out of the town, and showed her the spot where the boat was turned adrift upon the wide waters. Then he sat himself down, and said, "I am very much tired; sit by me, I will rest my head in your lap, and sleep a while." As soon as he had fallen asleep, however, she drew the ring from his finger, and crept softly away, and wished herself and her son at home in their kingdom. And when the king awoke, he found himself alone, and saw that the ring was gone from his finger. "I can never return to my father's house," said he; "they would say I am a sorcerer; I will journey forth into the world till I come again to my kingdom."

So saying, he set out and travelled till he came to a mountain, where three giants were sharing their inheritance; and as they saw him pass, they cried out and said, "Little men have sharp wits; he shall divide the inheritance between us." Now it consisted of a sword that cut off an enemy's head whenever the wearer gave the words "Heads off!"—a cloak that made the owner invisible, or gave him any form he pleased; and a pair of boots that transported the person who put them on wherever he wished. The king said they must first let him try these wonderful things, that he might know how to set a value upon them. Then they gave him the cloak, and he wished himself a fly, and in a moment he was a fly. "The cloak is very well," said he; "now give me the sword." "No," said they, "not unless you promise not to say 'Heads off!' for if you do, we are all dead men." So they gave it him on condition that he tried its virtue only on a tree. He next asked for the boots also; and the moment he had all three in his possession he wished himself at the Golden Mountain; and there he was in an instant. So the giants were left behind with no inheritance to divide or quarrel about.

As he came near to the castle he heard the sound of merry music; and the people around told him that his queen was about to celebrate her marriage with another prince. Then he threw his cloak around him, and passed through the castle, and placed himself by the side of his queen, where no one saw him. But when any thing to eat was put upon her plate, he took it away and ate it himself; and when a glass of wine was handed to her, he took and drank it: and thus, though they kept on serving her with meat and drink, her plate continued always empty.

Upon this, fear and remorse came over her, and she went into her chamber and wept; and he followed her there. "Alas!" said she to herself, "did not my deliverer come? why then doth enchantment still surround me?"

"Thou traitress!" said he, "thy deliverer indeed came, and now is near thee: has he deserved this of thee?" And he went out and dismissed the company, and said the wedding was at an end, for that he was returned to his kingdom: but the princes and nobles and counsellors mocked at him. However, he would enter into no parley with them, but only demanded whether they would depart in peace, or not. Then they turned and tried to seize him; but he drew his sword, and, with a word, the traitors' heads fell before him; and he was once more king of the Golden Mountain.

THE GOLDEN GOOSE

There was a man who had three sons. The youngest was called Dummling, and was on all occasions despised and ill-treated by the whole family. It happened that the eldest took it into his head one day to go into the wood to cut fuel; and his mother gave him a delicious pasty and a bottle of wine to take with him, that he might refresh himself at his work. As he went into the wood, a little old man bid him good day, and said, "Give me a little piece of meat from your plate, and a little wine out of your bottle; I am very hungry and thirsty." But this clever young man said, "Give you my meat and wine! No, I thank you; I should not have enough left for myself:" and away he went. He soon began to cut down a tree; but he had not worked long before he missed his stroke, and cut himself, and was obliged to go home to have the wound dressed. Now it was the little old man that caused him this mischief.

Next went out the second son to work; and his mother gave him too a pasty and a bottle of wine. And the same little old man met him also, and asked him for something to eat and drink. But he too thought himself vastly clever, and said, "Whatever you get, I shall lose;

so go your way!" The little man took care that he should have his reward; and the second stroke that he aimed against a tree, hit him on the leg; so that he too was forced to go home.

Then Dummling said, "Father, I should like to go and cut wood too." But his father answered, "Your brothers have both lamed themselves; you had better stay at home, for you know nothing of the business." But Dummling was very pressing; and at last his father said, "Go your way; you will be wiser when you have suffered for your folly." And his mother gave him only some dry bread, and a bottle of sour beer; but when he went into the wood, he met the little old man, who said, "Give me some meat and drink, for I am very hungry and thirsty." Dummling said, "I have only dry bread and sour beer; if that will suit you, we will sit down and eat it together." So they sat down; and when the lad pulled out his bread, behold it was turned into a capital pasty, and his sour beer became delightful wine. They ate and drank heartily; and when they had done, the little man said, "As you have a kind heart, and have been willing to share every thing with me, I will send a blessing upon you. There stands an old tree; cut it down, and you will find something at the root." Then he took his leave, and went his way.

Dummling set to work, and cut down the tree; and when it fell, he found in a hollow under the roots a goose with feathers of pure gold. He took it up, and went on to an inn, where he proposed to sleep for the night. The landlord had three daughters; and when they saw the goose, they were very curious to examine what this wonderful bird could be, and wished very much to pluck one of the feathers out of its tail. At last the eldest said, "I must and will have a feather." So she waited till his back was turned, and then seized the goose by the wing; but to her great surprise there she stuck, for neither hand nor finger could she get away again. Presently in came the second sister, and thought to have a feather too; but the moment she touched her sister, there she too hung fast. At last came the third, and wanted a feather; but the other two cried out, "Keep away! for heaven's sake, keep away!" However, she did not understand what they meant. "If they are there," thought she, "I may as well be there too." So she went up to them; but the moment she touched her sisters she stuck fast, and hung to the goose as they did. And so they kept company with the goose all night.

The next morning Dummling carried off the goose under his arm; and took no notice of the three girls, but went out with them sticking fast behind; and wherever he travelled, they too were obliged to follow, whether they would or no, as fast as their legs could carry them.

In the middle of a field the parson met them; and when he saw the train, he said, "Are you not ashamed of yourselves, you bold girls, to run after the young man in that way over the fields? is that proper behaviour?" Then he took the youngest by the hand to lead her away; but the moment he touched her he too hung fast, and followed in the train. Presently up came the clerk; and when he saw his master the parson running after the three girls, he wondered greatly, and said, "Hollo! hollo! your reverence! whither so fast? there is a christening to-day." Then he ran up, and took him by the gown, and in a moment he was fast too. As the five were thus trudging along, one behind another, they met two labourers with their mattocks coming from work; and the parson cried out to them to set him free. But scarcely had they touched him, when they too fell into the ranks, and so made seven, all running after Dummling and his goose.

At last they arrived at a city, where reigned a king who had an only daughter. The princess was of so thoughtful and serious a turn of mind that no one could make her laugh; and the king had proclaimed to all the world, that whoever could make her laugh should have her for his wife. When the young man heard this, he went to her with his goose and all its train; and as soon as she saw the seven all hanging together, and running about, treading on each other's heels she could not help bursting into a long and loud laugh. Then Dummling claimed her for his wife; the wedding was celebrated, and he was heir to the kingdom, and lived long and happily with his wife.

HANSEL AND GRETTEL

Hansel one day took his sister Grettel by the hand, and said, "Since our poor mother died we have had no happy days; for our new mother beats us all day long and when we go near her, she pushes us away. We have nothing but hard crusts to eat; and the little dog that lies by the fire is better off than we; for he sometimes has a nice piece of meat thrown to him. Heaven have mercy upon us! O if our poor mother knew how we are used! Come, we will go and travel over the wide world.' They went the whole day walking over the fields, till in the evening they came to a great wood; and then they were so tired and hungry that they sat down in a hollow tree and went to sleep.

In the morning when they awoke, the sun had risen high above the trees, and shone warm upon the hollow tree. Then Hansel said, "Sister, I am very thirsty; if I could find a brook, I would go and drink, and fetch you some water too. Listen, I think I hear the sound of one." Then Hansel rose up and took Grettel by the hand and went in search of the brook. But their cruel step-mother was a fairy, and had followed them into the wood to work them mischief: and when they had found a brook that ran sparkling over the pebbles, Hansel wanted to drink; but Grettel thought she heard the brook, as it babbled along, say, "Whoever drinks here will be turned into a tiger." Then she cried out, "Ah, brother! do not drink, or you will be turned into a wild beast and tear me to pieces." Then Hansel yielded, although he was parched with thirst. "I will wait," said he, "for the next brook." But when they came to the next, Grettel listened again, and thought she heard, "Whoever drinks here will become a wolf." Then she cried out, "Brother, brother, do not drink, or you will become a wolf and eat me." So he did not drink, but said, "I will wait for the next brook; there I must drink, say what you will, I am so thirsty."

As they came to the third brook, Grettel listened, and heard, "Whoever drinks here will become a fawn." "Ah, brother!" said she, "do not drink, or you will be turned into a fawn and run away from me." But Hansel had already stooped down upon his knees, and the moment he put his lips into the water he was turned into a fawn.

Grettel wept bitterly over the poor creature, and the tears too rolled down his eyes as he laid himself beside her. Then she said, "Rest in peace, dear fawn, I will never never leave thee." So she took off her golden necklace and put it round his neck, and plucked some rushes and plaited them into a soft string to fasten to it; and led the poor little thing by her side farther into the wood.

After they had travelled a long way, they came at last to a little cottage; and Grettel, having looked in and seen that it was quite empty, thought to herself, "We can stay and live here." Then she went and gathered leaves and moss to make a soft bed for the fawn: and every morning she went out and plucked nuts, roots, and berries for herself, and sweet shrubs and tender grass for her companion; and it ate out of her hand, and was pleased, and played and frisked about her. In the evening, when Grettel was tired, and had said her prayers, she laid her head upon the fawn for her pillow, and slept: and if poor Hansel could but have his right form again, they thought they should lead a very happy life.

They lived thus a long while in the wood by themselves, till it chanced that the king of that country came to hold a great hunt there. And when the fawn heard all around the echoing of the horns, and the baying of the dogs, and the merry shouts of the huntsmen, he wished very much to go and see what was going on. "Ah sister! sister!" said he, "let me go out into the wood, I can stay no longer." And he begged so long, that she at last agreed to let him go. "But," said she, "be sure to come to me in the evening: I shall shut up the door to keep out those wild huntsmen; but if you tap at it, and say, "Sister, let me in," I shall know you; but if you don't speak, I shall keep the door fast." Then away sprang the fawn, and frisked and bounded along in the open air. The king and his huntsmen saw the beautiful creature, and followed but could not overtake him; for when they thought they were sure of their prize, he sprung over the bushes and was out of sight in a moment.

As it grew dark he came running home to the hut, and tapped, and said "Sister, sister, let me in." Then she opened the little door, and in he jumped and slept soundly all night on his soft bed.

Next morning the hunt began again; and when he heard the huntsmen's horns, he said, "Sister, open the door for me, I must go again." Then she let him out, and said, "Come back in the evening, and remember what you are to say." When the king and the huntsmen saw the fawn with the golden collar again, they gave him chase; but he was too quick for them. The chase lasted the whole day; but at last the huntsmen nearly surrounded him, and one of them wounded him in the foot, so that he became sadly lame and could hardly crawl home. The man who had wounded him followed close behind, and hid himself, and heard the little fawn say, "Sister, sister, let me in:" upon which the door opened and soon shut again. The huntsman marked all well, and went to the king and told him what he had seen and heard; then the king said, "To-morrow we will have another chase."

Grettel was very much frightened when she saw that her dear little fawn was wounded; but she washed the blood away and put some healing herbs on it, and said, "Now go to bed, dear fawn, and you will soon be well again." The wound was so small, that in the morning there was nothing to be seen of it; and when the horn blew, the little creature said, "I can't stay here, I must go and look on; I will take care that none of them shall catch me." But Grettel said, "I am sure they will kill you this time, I will not let you go." "I shall die of vexation," answered he, "if you keep me here; when I hear the horns, I feel as if I could fly." Then Grettel was forced to let him go; so she opened the door with a heavy heart, and he bounded out gaily into the wood.

When the king saw him, he said to his huntsman, "Now chase him all day long till you catch him; but let none of you do him any harm." The sun set, however, without their being able to overtake him, and the king called away the huntsmen, and said to the one who had watched, "Now come and show me the little hut." So they went to the door and tapped, and said, "Sister, sister, let me in." Then the door opened and the king went in, and there stood a maiden more lovely than any he had ever seen. Grettel was frightened to see that it was not her fawn, but a king with a golden crown, that was come into her hut: however, he spoke kindly to her, and took her hand, and said, "Will you come with me to my castle and be my wife?" "Yes," said the maiden; "but my fawn must go with me, I cannot part with that." "Well," said the king, "he shall come and live with you all your life, and want for nothing." Just at that moment in sprung the little fawn; and his sister tied the string to his neck, and they left the hut in the wood together.

Then the king took Grettel to his palace, and celebrated the marriage in great state. And she told the king all her story; and he sent for the fairy and punished her: and the fawn was changed into Hansel again, and he and his sister loved one another, and lived happily together all their days.

THE FROG-PRINCE

One fine evening a young princess went into a wood, and sat down by the side of a cool spring of water. She had a golden ball in her hand, which was her favourite plaything, and she amused herself with tossing it into the air and catching it again as it fell. After a time she threw it up so high that when she stretched out her hand to catch it, the ball bounded away and rolled along upon the ground, till at last it fell into the spring. The princess looked into the spring after her ball; but it was very deep, so deep that she could not see the bottom of it. Then she began to lament her loss, and said, "Alas! if I could only get my ball again, I would give all my fine clothes and jewels, and every thing that I have in the world." Whilst she was speaking a frog put its head out of the water, and said, "Princess, why do you weep so bitterly?" "Alas!" said she, "what can you do for me, you nasty frog? My golden ball has fallen into the spring." The frog said, "I want not your pearls and jewels and fine clothes; but if you will love me and let me live with you, and eat from your little golden plate, and sleep upon your little bed, I will bring you your ball again." "What nonsense," thought the princess," this silly frog is talking! He can never get out of the well: however, he may be able to get my ball for me; and therefore I will promise him what he asks." So she said to the frog, "Well, if you will bring me my ball, I promise to do all you require." Then the frog put his head down, and dived deep under the water; and after a little while he came up again with the ball in his mouth, and threw it on the ground. As soon as the young princess saw her ball, she ran to pick it up, and was so overjoyed to have it in her hand again, that she never thought of the frog, but ran home with it as fast as she could. The frog called after her, "Stay, princess, and take me with you as you promised;" but she did not stop to hear a word.

The next day, just as the princess had sat down to dinner, she heard a strange noise, tap-tap, as if somebody was coming up the marble staircase; and soon afterwards something knocked gently at the door, and said,

> "Open the door, my princess dear,
> Open the door to thy true love here!
> And mind the words that thou and I said
> By the fountain cool in the greenwood shade."

Then the princess ran to the door and opened it, and there she saw the frog, whom she had quite forgotten; she was terribly frightened, and shutting the door as fast as she could, came back to her seat. The king her father asked her what had frightened her. "There is a nasty frog," said she, "at the door, who lifted my ball out of the spring this morning: I promised him that he should live with me here, thinking that he could never get out of the spring; but there he is at the door and wants to come in!" While she was speaking the frog knocked again at the door, and said,

> "Open the door, my princess dear,
> Open the door to thy true love here!
> And mind the words that thou and I said
> By the fountain cool in the greenwood shade."

The king said to the young princess, "As you have made a promise, you must keep it; so go and let him in." She did so, and the frog hopped into the room, and came up close to the table. "Pray lift me upon a chair," said he to the princess, "and let me sit next to you." As soon as she had done this, the frog said, "Put your plate closer to me that I may eat out of it." This she did, and when he had eaten as much as he could, he said, "Now I am tired; carry me up stairs and put me into your little bed." And the princess took him up in her hand and put him upon the pillow of her own little bed, where he slept all night long. As soon as it was light he jumped up, hopped down stairs, and went out of the house. "Now," thought the princess, "he is gone, and I shall be troubled with him no more."

But she was mistaken; for when night came again, she heard the same tapping at the door, and when she opened it, the frog came in and slept upon her pillow as before till the morning broke: and the third night he did the same; but when the princess awoke on the following morning, she was astonished to see, instead of the frog, a handsome prince gazing on her with the most beautiful eyes that ever were seen, and standing at the head of her bed.

He told her that he had been enchanted by a malicious fairy, who had changed him into the form of a frog, in which he was fated to remain till some princess should take him out of the spring and let him sleep upon her bed for three nights. "You," said the prince, "have broken this cruel charm, and now I have nothing to wish for but that you should go with me into my father's kingdom, where I will marry you, and love you as long as you live."

The young princess, you may be sure, was not long in giving her consent; and as they spoke a splendid carriage drove up with eight beautiful horses decked with plumes of feathers and golden harness, and behind rode the prince's servant, the faithful Henry, who had bewailed the misfortune of his dear master so long and bitterly that his heart had well nigh burst. Then all set out full of joy for the Prince's kingdom; where they arrived safely, and lived happily a great many years.

RUMPEL-STILTS-KIN

In a certain kingdom once lived a poor miller who had a very beautiful daughter. She was moreover exceedingly shrewd and clever; and the miller was so vain and proud of her, that he one day told the king of the land that his daughter could spin gold out of straw. Now this king was very fond of money; and when he heard the miller's boast, his avarice was excited, and he ordered the girl to be brought before him. Then he led her to a chamber where there was a great quantity of straw, gave her a spinning-wheel, and said, "All this must be spun into gold before morning, as you value your life." It was in vain that the poor maiden declared that she could do no such thing, the chamber was locked and she remained alone.

She sat down in one corner of the room and began to lament over her hard fate, when on a sudden the door opened, and a droll-looking little man hobbled in, and said, "Good morrow to you, my good lass, what are you weeping for?" "Alas!" answered she, "I must spin this straw into gold, and I know not how." "What will you give me," said the little man, "to do it for you?" "My necklace," replied the maiden. He took her at her word, and sat himself down to the wheel; round about it went merrily, and presently the work was done and the gold all spun.

When the king came and saw this, he was greatly astonished and pleased; but his heart grew still more greedy of gain, and he shut up the poor miller's daughter again with a fresh task. Then she knew not what to do, and sat down once more to weep; but the little man presently opened the door, and said, "What will you give me to do your task?" "The ring on my finger," replied she. So her little friend took the ring, and began to work at the wheel, till by the morning all was finished again.

The king was vastly delighted to see all this glittering treasure; but still he was not satisfied, and took the miller's daughter into a yet larger room, and said, "All this must be spun to-night; and if you succeed, you shall be my queen." As soon as she was alone the dwarf came in, and said, "What will you give me to spin gold for you this third time?" "I have nothing left," said she. "Then promise me," said the little man, "your first little child when you are queen." "That may never be," thought the miller's daughter; and as she knew no other way to get her task done, she promised him what he asked, and he spun once more the whole heap of gold. The king came in the morning, and finding all he wanted, married her, and so the miller's daughter really became queen.

At the birth of her first little child the queen rejoiced very much, and forgot the little man and her promise; but one day he came into her chamber and reminded her of it. Then she grieved sorely at her misfortune, and offered him all the treasures of the kingdom in exchange; but in vain, till at last her tears softened him, and he said, "I will give you three days' grace, and if during that time you tell me my name, you shall keep your child."

Now the queen lay awake all night, thinking of all the odd names that she had ever heard, and dispatched messengers all over the land to inquire after new ones. The next day the little man came, and she began with Timothy, Benjamin, Jeremiah, and all the names she could remember; but to all of them he said, "That's not my name."

The second day she began with all the comical names she could hear of, Bandy-legs, Hunch-back, Crook-shanks, and so on, but the little gentleman still said to every one of them, "That's not my name."

The third day came back one of the messengers, and said, "I can hear of no one other name; but yesterday, as I was climbing a high hill among the trees of the forest where the fox and the hare bid each other good night, I saw a little hut, and before the hut burnt a fire, and round about the fire danced a funny little man upon one leg, and sung

> "Merrily the feast I'll make,
> Today I'll brew, to-morrow bake;
> Merrily I'll dance and sing,
> For next day will a stranger bring:
> Little does my lady dream
> Rumpel-Stilts-Kin is my name!"

When the queen heard this, she jumped for joy, and as soon as her little visitor came, and said, "Now, lady, what is my name?" "Is it John?" asked she. "No!" "Is it Tom?" "No!"

> "Can your name be Rumpel-Stilts-Kin?"

"Some witch told you that! Some witch told you that!" cried the little man, and dashed his right foot in a rage so deep into the floor, that he was forced to lay hold of it with both hands to pull it out. Then he made the best of his way off, while every body laughed at him for having had all his trouble for nothing.

THE FISHERMAN AND HIS WIFE

There was once a fisherman who lived with his wife in a ditch, close by the sea-side. The fisherman used to go out all day a-fishing; and one day, as he sat on the shore with his rod, looking at the shining water and watching his line, all on a sudden his float was dragged away deep under the sea: and in drawing it up he pulled a great fish out of the water. The fish said to him, "Pray let me live: I am not a real fish; I am an enchanted prince, put me in the water again, and let me go." "Oh!" said the man, "you need not make so many words about the matter; I wish to have nothing to do with a fish that can talk; so swim away as soon as you please." Then he put him back into the water, and the fish darted straight down to the bottom, and left a long streak of blood behind him.

When the fisherman went home to his wife in the ditch, he told her how he had caught a great fish, and how it had told him it was an enchanted prince, and that on hearing it speak he had let it go again. "Did you not ask it for any thing?" said the wife. "No," said the man, "what should I ask for?" "Ah!" said the wife, "we live very wretchedly here in this nasty stinking ditch; do go back, and tell the fish we want a little cottage."

The fisherman did not much like the business: however, he went to the sea, and when he came there the water looked all yellow and green. And he stood at the water's edge, and said,

"O man of the sea!
Come listen to me,
For Alice my wife,
The plague of my life,
Has sent me to beg a boon of thee!"

Then the fish came swimming to him, and said, "Well, what does she want?" "Ah!" answered the fisherman, "my wife says that when I had caught you, I ought to have asked you for something before I let you go again; she does not like living any longer in the ditch, and wants a little cottage." "Go home, then," said the fish, "she is in the cottage already." So the man went home, and saw his wife standing at the door of a cottage. "Come in, come in," said she; "is not this much better than the ditch?" And there was a parlour, and a bed-chamber, and a kitchen; and behind the cottage there was a little garden with all sorts of flowers and fruits, and a court-yard full of ducks and chickens. "Ah!" said the fisherman, "how happily we shall live!" "We will try to do so at least," said his wife.

Every thing went right for a week or two, and then Dame Alice said, "Husband, there is not room enough in this cottage, the court-yard and garden are a great deal too small; I should like to have a large stone castle to live in; so go to the fish again, and tell him to give us a castle." "Wife," said the fisherman, "I don't like to go to him again, for perhaps he will be angry; we ought to be content with the cottage." "Nonsense!" said the wife; "he will do it very willingly; go along, and try."

The fisherman went; but his heart was very heavy: and when he came to the sea, it looked blue and

gloomy, though it was quite calm, and he went close
to it, and said,

> "O man of the sea!
> Come listen to me,
> For Alice my wife,
> The plague of my life,
> Hath sent me to beg a boon of thee!"

"Well, what does she want now?" said the fish. "Ah!"
said the man very sorrowfully, "my wife wants to live
in a stone castle." "Go home then," said the fish, "she
is standing at the door of it already." So away went the
fisherman, and found his wife standing before a great
castle. "See," said she, "is not this grand?" With that
they went into the castle together, and found a great
many servants there, and the rooms all richly furnished
and full of golden chairs and tables; and behind the
castle was a garden, and a wood half a mile long, full
of sheep, and goats, and hares, and deer; and in the
court-yard were stables and cow-houses. "Well," said
the man, "now will we live contented and happy in
this beautiful castle for the rest of our lives." "Perhaps
we may," said the wife; "but let us consider and sleep
upon it before we make up our minds:" so they went
to bed.

The next morning, when Dame Alice awoke, it was
broad day-light, and she jogged the fisherman with her
elbow, and said, "Get up, husband, and bestir yourself,
for we must be king of all the land." "Wife, wife," said
the man, "why should we wish to be king? I will not be
king." "Then I will," said Alice. "But, wife," answered
the fisherman, "how can you be king? the fish cannot

make you a king." "Husband," said she, "say no more about it, but go and try; I will be king!" So the man went away, quite sorrowful to think that his wife should want to be king. The sea looked a dark grey colour, and was covered with foam as he cried out,

> "O man of the sea!
> Come listen to me,
> For Alice my wife,
> The plague of my life,
> Hath sent me to beg a boon of thee!"

"Well, what would she have now?" said the fish. "Alas!" said the man, "my wife wants to be king." "Go home," said the fish; "she is king already."

Then the fisherman went home; and as he came close to the palace, he saw a troop of soldiers, and heard the sound of drums and trumpets; and when he entered in, he saw his wife sitting on a high throne of gold and diamonds, with a golden crown upon her head; and on each side of her stood six beautiful maidens, each a head taller than the other. "Well, wife," said the fisherman, "are you king?" "Yes," said she, "I am king." And when he had looked at her for a long time, he said, "Ah, wife! what a fine thing it is to be king! now we shall never have any thing more to wish for." "I don't know how that may be," said she; "never is a long time. I am king, 'tis true, but I begin to be tired of it, and I think I should like to be emperor." "Alas, wife! why should you wish to be emperor?" said the fisherman. "Husband," said she, "go to the fish; I say I will be emperor." "Ah, wife!" replied the fisherman, "the fish cannot make an emperor, and I should not like to ask for such a thing." "I am king," said Alice, "and you are my slave, so go directly!" So the fisherman was obliged to go; and he muttered as he went along. "This will come to no good, it is too much to ask, the fish will be tired at last, and then we shall repent of what we have done." He soon arrived at the sea, and the water was quite black and muddy, and a mighty whirlwind blew over it; but he went to the shore, and said,

> "O man of the sea!
> Come listen to me,
> For Alice my wife,
> The plague of my life,
> Hath sent me to beg a boon of thee!"

"What would she have now!" said the fish. "Ah!" said the fisherman, "she wants to be emperor." "Go home," said the fish; "she is emperor already."

So he went home again; and as he came near he saw his wife sitting on a very lofty throne made of solid gold, with a great crown on her head full two yards high, and on each side of her stood her guards and attendants in a row, each one smaller than the other, from the tallest giant down to a little dwarf no bigger than my finger. And before her stood princes, and dukes, and earls: and the fisherman went up to her and said, "Wife, are you emperor?" "Yes," said she, "I am emperor." "Ah!" said the man as he gazed upon her, "what a fine thing it is to be emperor!" "Husband," said she, "why should we stay at being emperor; I will be pope next." "O wife, wife!" said he, "how can you be pope? there is but one pope at a time in Christendom." "Husband," said she, "I will be pope this very day." "But," replied the husband, "the fish cannot make you pope." "What nonsense!" said she, "if he can make an emperor, he can make a pope, go and try him." So the fisherman went. But when he came to the shore the wind was raging, and the sea was tossed up and down like boiling water, and the ships were in the greatest distress and danced upon the waves most fearfully; in the middle of the sky there was a little blue, but towards the south it was all red as if a dreadful storm was rising. At this the fisherman was terribly frightened, and trembled, so that his knees knocked together: but he went to the shore and said,

> "O man of the sea!
> Come listen to me,
> For Alice my wife,
> The plague of my life,
> Hath sent me to beg a boon of thee!"

"What does she want now?" said the fish. "Ah!" said the fisherman, "my wife wants to be pope." "Go home," said the fish, "she is pope already."

Then the fisherman went home, and found his wife sitting on a throne that was two miles high; and she had three great crowns on her head, and around stood all the pomp and power of the Church; and on each side were two rows of burning lights, of all sizes, the greatest as large as the highest and biggest tower in the world, and the least no larger than a small rushlight. "Wife," said the fisherman as he looked at all this grandeur, "Are you pope?" "Yes," said she, "I am pope." "Well, wife," replied he, "it is a grand thing to be pope; and now you must be content, for you can be nothing greater." "I will consider of that," said the wife. Then they went to bed:

but Dame Alice could not sleep all night for thinking what she should be next. At last morning came, and the sun rose. "Ha!" thought she as she looked at it through the window, "cannot I prevent the sun rising?" At this she was very angry, and she wakened her husband, and said, "Husband, go to the fish and tell him I want to be lord of the sun and moon." The fisherman was half asleep, but the thought frightened him so much, that he started and fell out of bed. "Alas, wife!" said he, "cannot you be content to be pope?" "No," said she, "I am very uneasy, and cannot bear to see the sun and moon rise without my leave. Go to the fish directly."

Then the man went trembling for fear; and as he was going down to the shore a dreadful storm arose, so that the trees and the rocks shook; and the heavens became black, and the lightning played, and the thunder rolled; and you might have seen in the sea great black waves like mountains with a white crown of foam upon them; and the fisherman said,

> "O man of the sea!
> Come listen to me,
> For Alice my wife,
> The plague of my life,
> Hath sent me to beg a boon of thee!"

"What does she want now?" said the fish. "Ah!" said he, "she wants to be lord of the sun and moon." "Go home," said the fish, "to your ditch again!" and there they live to this very day.

THE GOLDEN BIRD

A certain king had a beautiful garden, and in the garden stood a tree which bore golden apples. These apples were always counted, and about the time when they began to grow ripe it was found that every night one of them was gone. The king became very angry at this, and ordered the gardener to keep watch all night under the tree. The gardener set his eldest son to watch; but about twelve o'clock he fell asleep, and in the morning another of the apples was missing. Then the second son was ordered to watch; and at midnight he too fell asleep, and in the morning another apple was gone. Then the third son offered to keep watch; but the gardener at first would not let him, for fear some harm should come to him: however, at last he consented, and the young man laid himself under the tree to watch. As the clock struck twelve he heard a rustling noise in the air, and a bird came flying that was of pure gold; and as it was snapping at one of the apples with its beak, the gardener's son jumped up and shot an arrow at it. But the arrow did the bird no harm; only it dropped a golden feather from its tail, and then flew away. The golden feather was brought to the king in the morning, and all the council was called together. Every one agreed that it was worth more than all the wealth of the kingdom: but the king said, "One feather is of no use to me, I must have the whole bird."

Then the gardener's eldest son set out and thought to find the golden bird very easily; and when he had gone but a little way, he came to a wood, and by the side of the wood he saw a fox sitting; so he took his bow and made ready to shoot at it. Then the fox said, "Do not shoot me, for I will give you good counsel; I know what your business is, and that you want to find the golden bird. You will reach a village in the evening; and when you get there, you will see two inns opposite to each other, one of which is very pleasant and beautiful to look at: go not in there, but rest for the night in the other, though it may appear to you to be very poor and mean." But the son thought to himself, "What can such a beast as this know about the matter?" So he shot his arrow at the fox; but he missed it, and it set up its tail above its back and ran into the wood. Then he went his way, and in the evening came to the village where the two inns were; and in one of these were people singing, and dancing, and feasting; but the other looked very dirty, and poor. "I should be very silly," said he, "if I went to that shabby house, and left this charming place;" so he went into the smart house, and ate and drank at his ease, and forgot the bird, and his country too.

Time passed on; and as the eldest son did not come back, and no tidings were heard of him, the second son set out, and the same thing happened to him. He met the fox, who gave him the same good advice: but when he came to the two inns, his eldest brother was standing at the window where the merrymaking was, and called to him to come in; and he could not withstand the temptation, but went in, and forgot the golden bird and his country in the same manner.

Time passed on again, and the youngest son too wished to set out into the wide world to seek for the golden bird; but his father would not listen to it for a long while, for he was very fond of his son, and was afraid that some ill luck might happen to him also, and prevent his coming back. However, at last it was agreed he should go, for he would not rest at home; and as he came to the wood, he met the fox, and heard the same good counsel. But he was thankful to the fox, and did not attempt his life as his brothers had done; so the fox said, "Sit upon my tail, and you will travel faster." So he sat down, and the fox began to run, and away they went over stock and stone so quick that their hair whistled in the wind.

When they came to the village, the son followed the fox's counsel, and without looking about him went to the shabby inn and rested there all night at his ease. In the morning came the fox again and met him as he was beginning his journey, and said, "Go straight forward, till you come to a castle, before which lie a whole troop of soldiers fast asleep and snoring: take no notice of them, but go into the castle and pass on and on till you come to a room, where the golden bird sits in a wooden cage; close by it stands a beautiful golden cage; but do not try to take the bird out of the shabby cage and put it into the handsome one, otherwise you will repent it." Then the fox stretched out his tail again, and the young man sat himself down, and away they went over stock and stone till their hair whistled in the wind.

Before the castle gate all was as the fox had said: so the son went in and found the chamber where the golden bird hung in a wooden cage, and below stood the golden cage, and the three golden apples that had been lost were lying close by it. Then thought he to himself, "It will be a very droll thing to bring away such a fine bird in this shabby cage;" so he opened the door and took hold of it and put it into the golden cage. But the bird set up such a loud scream that all the soldiers awoke, and they took him prisoner and carried him before the king. The next morning the court sat to judge him; and when all was heard, it sentenced him to die, unless he should bring the king the golden horse which could run as swiftly as the wind; and if he did this, he was to have the golden bird given him for his own.

So he set out once more on his journey, sighing, and in great despair, when on a sudden his good friend the fox met him, and said, "You see now what has happened on account of your not listening to my counsel. I will still, however, tell you how to find the golden horse, if you will do as I bid you. You must go straight on till you come to the castle where the horse stands in his stall: by his side will lie the groom fast asleep and snoring: take away the horse quietly, but be sure to put the old leathern saddle upon him, and not the golden one that is close by it." Then the son sat down on the fox's tail, and away they went over stock and stone till their hair whistled in the wind.

All went right, and the groom lay snoring with his hand upon the golden saddle. But when the son looked at the horse, he thought it a great pity to put the leathern saddle upon it. "I will give him the good one," said he; "I am sure he deserves it." As he took up the golden saddle the groom awoke and cried out so loud, that all the guards ran in and took him prisoner, and in the morning he was again brought before the court to be judged, and was sentenced to die. But it was agreed, that, if he could bring thither the beautiful princess, he should live, and have the bird and the horse given him for his own.

Then he went his way again very sorrowful; but the old fox came and said, "Why did not you listen to me? If you had, you would have carried away both the bird and the horse; yet will I once more give you counsel. Go straight on, and in the evening you will arrive at a castle. At twelve o'clock at night the princess goes to the bathing-house: go up to her and give her a kiss, and she will let you lead her away; but take care you do not suffer her to go and take leave of her father and mother." Then the fox stretched out his tail, and so away they went over stock and stone till their hair whistled again.

As they came to the castle, all was as the fox had said, and at twelve o'clock the young man met the princess going to the bath and gave her the kiss, and she agreed to run away with him, but begged with many tears that he would let her take leave of her father. At first he refused, but she wept still more and more, and fell at his feet, till at last he consented; but the moment she came to her father's house the guards awoke and he was taken prisoner again.

Then he was brought before the king, and the king said, "You shall never have my daughter unless in eight days you dig away the hill that stops the view from my window." Now this hill was so big that the whole world could not take it away: and when he had worked for seven days, and had done very little, the fox came and said, "Lie down and go to sleep; I will work for you." And in the morning he awoke and the hill was gone; so he went merrily to the king, and told him that now that it was removed he must give him the princess.

Then the king was obliged to keep his word, and away went the young man and the princess; and the fox came and said to him, "We will have all three, the princess, the horse, and the bird." "Ah!" said the young man, "that would be a great thing, but how can you contrive it?"

"If you will only listen," said the fox, "it can soon be done. When you come to the king, and he asks for the beautiful princess, you must say, "Here she is!" Then he will be very joyful; and you will mount the golden horse that they are to give you, and put out your hand to take leave of them; but shake hands with the princess last. Then lift her quickly on to the horse behind you; clap your spurs to his side, and gallop away as fast as you can."

All went right: then the fox said, "When you come to the castle where the bird is, I will stay with the princess at the door, and you will ride in and speak to the king; and when he sees that it is the right horse, he will bring out the bird; but you must sit still, and say that you want to look at it, to see whether it is the true golden bird; and when you get it into your hand, ride away."

This, too, happened as the fox said; they carried off the bird, the princess mounted again, and they rode on to a great wood. Then the fox came, and said, "Pray kill me, and cut off my head and my feet." But the young man refused to do it: so the fox said, "I will at any rate give you good counsel: beware of two things; ransom no one from the gallows, and sit down by the side of no river." Then away he went. "Well," thought the young man, "it is no hard matter to keep that advice."

He rode on with the princess, till at last he came to the village where he had left his two brothers. And there he heard a great noise and uproar; and when he asked what was the matter, the people said, "Two men are going to be hanged." As he came nearer, he saw that the two men were his brothers, who had turned robbers; so he said, "Cannot they in any way be saved?" But the people said "No," unless he would bestow all his money upon the rascals and buy their liberty. Then he did not stay to think about the matter, but paid what was asked, and his brothers were given up, and went on with him towards their home.

And as they came to the wood where the fox first met them, it was so cool and pleasant that the two brothers said, "Let us sit down by the side of the river, and rest a while, to eat and drink." So he said, "Yes," and forgot the fox's counsel, and sat down on the side of the river; and while he suspected nothing, they came behind, and threw him down the bank, and took the princess, the horse, and the bird, and went home to the king their master, and said, "All this have we won by our labour." Then there was great rejoicing made; but the horse would not eat, the bird would not sing, and the princess wept.

The youngest son fell to the bottom of the river's bed: luckily it was nearly dry, but his bones were almost broken, and the bank was so steep that he could find no way to get out. Then the old fox came once more, and scolded him for not following his advice; otherwise no evil would have befallen him: "Yet," said he, "I cannot leave you here, so lay hold of my tail and hold fast." Then he pulled him out of the river, and said to him, as he got upon the bank, "Your brothers have set watch to kill you, if they find you in the kingdom." So he dressed himself as a poor man, and came secretly to the king's court, and was scarcely within the doors when the horse began to eat, and the bird to sing, and the princess left off weeping. Then he went to the king, and told him all his brothers' roguery; and they were seized and punished, and he had the princess given to him again; and after the king's death he was heir to his kingdom.

A long while after, he went to walk one day in the wood, and the old fox met him, and besought him with tears in his eyes to kill him, and cut off his head and feet. And at last he did so, and in a moment the fox was changed into a man, and turned out to be the brother of the princess, who had been lost a great many many years.

THE TRAVELLING MUSICIANS

An honest farmer had once an ass, that had been a faithful servant to him a great many years, but was now growing old and every day more and more unfit for work. His master therefore was tired of keeping him and began to think of putting an end to him; but the ass, who saw that some mischief was in the wind, took himself slyly off, and began his journey towards the great city, "for there," thought he, "I may turn musician."

After he had travelled a little way, he spied a dog lying by the road-side and panting as if he were very tired. "What makes you pant so, my friend?" said the ass. "Alas!" said the dog, "my master was going to knock me on the head, because I am old and weak, and can no longer make myself useful to him in hunting; so I ran away: but what can I do to earn my livelihood?" "Hark ye!" said the ass, "I am going to the great city to turn musician: suppose you go with me, and try what you can do in the same way?" The dog said he was willing, and they jogged on together.

They had not gone far before they saw a cat sitting in the middle of the road and making a most rueful face. "Pray, my good lady," said the ass, "what's the matter with you? you look quite out of spirits!" "Ah me!" said the cat, "how can one be in good spirits when one's life is in danger? Because I am beginning to grow old, and had rather lie at my ease by the fire than run about the house after the mice, my mistress laid hold of me, and was going to drown me; and though I have been lucky enough to get away from her, I do not know what I am to live upon." "O!" said the ass, "by all means go with us to the great city; you are a good night singer, and may make your fortune as a musician." The cat was pleased with the thought, and joined the party.

Soon afterwards, as they were passing by a farmyard, they saw a cock perched upon a gate, and screaming out with all his might and main. "Bravo!" said the ass; "upon my word you make a famous noise; pray what is all this about?" "Why," said the cock, "I was just now saying that we should have fine weather for our washing-day, and yet my mistress and the cook don't thank me for my pains, but threaten to cut off my head tomorrow, and make broth of me for the guests that are coming on Sunday" "Heaven forbid" said the ass; "come with us, Master Chanticleer; it will be better, at any rate, than staying here to have your head cut off! Besides, who knows? If we take care to sing in tune, we may get up some kind of a concert: so come along with us." "With all my heart," said the cock: so they all four went on jollily together.

They could not, however, reach the great city the first day; so when night came on, they went into a wood to sleep. The ass and the dog laid themselves down under a great tree, and the cat climbed up into the branches; while the cock, thinking that the higher he sat the safer he should be, flew up the very top of the tree, and then, according to his custom, before he went to sleep, looked out on all sides of him to see that every thing was well. In doing this, he saw afar off something bright and shining; and calling to his companions said, "There must be a house no great way off, for I see a light." "If that be the case," said the ass, "we had better change our quarters, for our lodging is not the best in the world!" "Besides," added the dog, "I should not be the worse for a bone or two, or a bit of meat." So they walked off together towards the spot where Chanticleer had seen the light; and as they drew near, it became larger and brighter, till they at last came close to a house in which a gang of robbers lived.

The ass, being the tallest of the company, marched up to the window and peeped in. "Well, Donkey," said Chanticleer, "what do you see?" "What do I see?" replied the ass, "why I see a table spread with all kinds of good things, and robbers sitting round it making merry." "That would be a noble lodging for us," said the cock. "Yes," said the ass, "if we could only get in:" so they consulted together how they should contrive to get the robbers out; and at last they hit upon a plan. The ass placed himself upright on his hind-legs, with his fore-feet resting against the window; the dog got upon his back; the cat scrambled up to the dog's shoulders, and the cock flew up and sat upon the cat's head. When all was ready, a signal was given, and they began their music. The ass brayed, the dog barked, the cat mewed, and the cock screamed; and then they all broke through the window at once, and came tumbling into the room, amongst the broken glass, with a most hideous clatter! The robbers, who had been not a little frightened by the opening concert, had now no doubt that some frightful hobgoblin had broken in upon them, and scampered away as fast as they could.

The coast once clear, our travellers soon sat down, and dispatched what the robbers had left, with as much eagerness as if they had not expected to eat again for a month. As soon as they had satisfied themselves, they put out the lights, and each once more sought out a resting-place to his own liking. The donkey laid himself down upon a heap of straw in the yard; the dog stretched himself upon a mat behind the door; the cat rolled herself up on the hearth before the warm ashes; and the cock perched upon a beam on top of the house; and, as they were all rather tired with their journey, they soon fell asleep.

But about midnight, when the robbers saw from afar that the lights were out and that all seemed quiet, they began to think that they had been in too great a hurry to run away; and one of them, who was bolder than the rest, went to see what was going on. Finding every thing still, he marched into the kitchen, and groped about till he found a match in order to light a candle; and then, espying the glittering fiery eyes of the cat, he mistook them for live coals, and held the match to them to light it. But the cat, not understanding this joke, sprung at his face, and spit, and scratched at him. This frightened him dreadfully, and away he ran to the back door; but there the dog jumped up and bit him in the leg; and as he was crossing over the yard the ass kicked him; and the cock, who had been awakened by the noise, crowed with all his might. At this the robber ran back as fast as he could to his comrades, and told the captain "how a horrid witch had got into the house, and had spit at him and scratched his face with her long bony fingers; how a man with a knife in his hand had hidden himself behind the door, and stabbed him in the leg; how a black monster stood in the yard and struck him with a club, and how the devil sat upon the top of the house and cried out, "Throw the rascal up here!" After this the robbers never dared to go back to the house: but the musicians were so pleased with their quarters, that they took up their abode there; and there they are, I dare say, at this very day.

HANS IN LUCK

Hans had served his master seven years, and at last said to him, "Master, my time is up, I should like to go home and see my mother; so give me my wages." And the master said, "You have been a faithful and good servant, so your pay shall be handsome." Then he gave him a piece of silver that was as big as his head.

Hans took out his pocket-handkerchief, put the piece of silver into it, threw it over his shoulder, and jogged off homewards. As he went lazily on, dragging one foot after another, a man came in sight, trotting along gaily on a capital horse. "Ah!" said Hans aloud, "what a fine thing it is to ride on horseback! there he sits as if he was at home in his chair; he trips against no stones, spares his shoes, and yet gets on he hardly knows how." The horseman heard this, and said, "Well, Hans, why do you go on foot then?" "Ah!" said he, "I have this load to carry; to be sure it is silver, but it is so heavy that I can't hold up my head, and it hurts my shoulder sadly." "What do you say to changing?" said the horseman; "I will give you my horse, and you shall give me the silver." "With all my heart," said Hans: "but I tell you one thing,—you'll have a weary task to drag it along." The horseman got off, took the silver, helped Hans up, gave him the bridle into his hand, and said, "When you want to go very fast, you must smack your lips loud, and cry 'Jip'."

Hans was delighted as he sat on the horse, and rode merrily on. After a time he thought he should like to go a little faster, so he smacked his lips, and cried "Jip". Away went the horse full gallop; and before Hans knew what he was about, he was thrown off, and lay in a ditch by the roadside; and his horse would have run off, if a shepherd who was coming by, driving a cow, had not stopt it. Hans soon came to himself, and got upon his legs again. He was sadly vexed, and said to the shepherd, "This riding is no joke when a man gets on a beast like this, that stumbles and flings him off as if he would break his neck. However, I'm off now once for all: I like your cow a great deal better; one can walk along at one's leisure behind her, and have milk, butter, and cheese, every day into the bargain. What would I give to have such a cow!" "Well," said the shepherd, "if you are so fond of her, I will change my cow for your horse." "Done!" said Hans merrily. The shepherd jumped upon the horse, and away he rode.

Hans drove off his cow quietly, and thought his

bargain a very lucky one. "If I have only a piece of bread (and I certainly shall be able to get that), I can, whenever I like, eat my butter and cheese with it; and when I am thirsty I can milk my cow and drink the milk: what can I wish for more?" When he came to an inn, he halted, ate up all his bread, and gave away his last penny for a glass of beer: then he drove his cow towards his mother's village; and the heat grew greater as noon came on, till at last he found himself on a wide heath that would take him more than an hour to cross, and he began to be so hot and parched that his tongue clave to the roof of his mouth. "I can find a cure for this," thought he, "now will I milk my cow and quench my thirst;" so he tied her to the stump of a tree, and held his leathern cap to milk into; but not a drop was to be had.

While he was trying his luck and managing the matter very clumsily, the uneasy beast gave him a kick on the head that knocked him down, and there he lay a long while senseless. Luckily a butcher soon came by driving a pig in a wheel-barrow. "What is the matter with you?" said the butcher as he helped him up. Hans told him what had happened, and the butcher gave him a flask, saying. "There, drink and refresh yourself; your cow will give you no milk, she is an old beast good for nothing but the slaughterhouse." "Alas, alas! said Hans, "who would have thought it? If I kill her, what will she be good for? I hate cow-beef, it is not tender enough for me. If it were a pig now, one could do something with it, it would at any rate make some sausages." "Well," said the butcher, "to please you, I'll change, and give you the pig for the cow." "Heaven reward you for your kindness!" said Hans as he gave the butcher the cow, and took the pig off the wheel-barrow, and drove it off, holding it by the string that was tied to its leg.

So on he jogged, and all seemed now to go right with him; he had met with some misfortunes, to be sure; but he was now well repaid for all. The next person he met was a countryman carrying a fine white goose under his arm. The countryman stopped to ask what was o'clock; and Hans told him all his luck, and how he had made so many good bargains. The countryman said he was going to take the goose to a christening; "Feel," said he, "how heavy it is, and yet it is only eight weeks old. Whoever roasts and eats it may cut plenty of fat off it, it has lived so well!" "You're right," said Hans as he weighed it in his hand; "but my pig is no trifle." Meantime the countryman began to look grave, and shook his head. "Hark ye," said he, "my good friend; your pig may get you into a scrape; in the village I just come from, the squire has had a pig stolen out of his stye. I was dreadfully afraid, when I saw you, that you had got the squire's pig; it will be a bad job if they catch you; the least they'll do, will be to throw you into the horsepond."

Poor Hans was sadly frightened. "Good man," cried he, "pray get me out of this scrape; you know this country better than I, take my pig and give me the goose." "I ought to have something into the bargain," said the countryman; "however, I will not bear hard upon you, as you are in trouble." Then he took the string in his hand, and drove off the pig by a side path; while Hans went on the way homewards free from care. "After all," thought he, "I have the best of the bargain: first there will be a capital roast; then the fat will find me in goose grease for six months; and then there are all the beautiful white feathers; I will put them into my pillow, and then I am sure I shall sleep soundly without rocking. How happy my mother will be!"

As he came to the last village, he saw a scissor-grinder, with his wheel, working away, and singing

O'er hill and o'er dale so happy I roam,
Work light and live well, all the world is my home;
Who so blythe, so merry as I?

Hans stood looking for a while, and at last said, "You must be well off, master grinder, you seem so happy at your work." "Yes," said the other, "mine is a golden trade; a good grinder never puts his hand in his pocket without finding money in it:—but where did you get that beautiful goose?" "I did not buy it, but changed a pig for it." "And where did you get the pig?" "I gave a cow for it." "And the cow?" "I gave a horse for it." "And the horse?" "I gave a piece of silver as big as my head for that." "And the silver?" "Oh! I worked hard for that seven long years." "You have thriven well in the world hitherto," said the grinder; "now if you could find money in your pocket whenever you put your hand into it, your fortune would be made." "Very true: but how is that to be managed?" "You must turn grinder like me," said the other; "you only want a grindstone; the rest will come of itself. Here is one that is a little the worse for wear: I would not ask more than the value of your goose for it;—will you buy?" "How can you ask such a question?" replied Hans; "I should be the happiest man in the world, if I could have money whenever I put my hand in my pocket; what could I want more? there's the goose!" "Now," said the grinder, as he gave him a common rough stone that lay by his side, "this is a most capital stone; do but manage it cleverly, and you can make an old nail cut with it."

Hans took the stone and went off with a light heart: his eyes sparkled for joy, and he said to himself, "I must have been born in a lucky hour; every thing that I want or wish for comes to me of itself."

Meantime he began to be tired, for he had been travelling ever since day-break; he was hungry too, for he had given away his last penny in his joy at getting the cow. At last he could go no farther, and the stone tired him terribly; he dragged himself to the side of a pond, that he might drink some water, and rest a while; so he laid the stone carefully by his side on the bank: but as he stooped down to drink, he forgot it, pushed it a little, and down it went plump into the pond. For a while he watched it sinking in the deep clear water, then sprang up for joy, and again fell upon his knees, and thanked heaven with tears in his eyes for its kindness in taking away his only plague, the ugly heavy stone. "How happy am I!" cried he: "no mortal was ever so lucky as I am." Then up he got with a light and merry heart and walked on free from all his troubles, till he reached his mother's house.

THE TOM-TIT AND THE BEAR

One summer day, as the wolf and the bear were walking together in a wood, they heard a bird singing most delightfully. "Brother," said the bear, "what can that bird be that is singing so sweetly?" "O!" said the wolf, "that is his majesty the king of the birds, we must take care to show him all possible respect." (Now I should tell you that this bird was after all no other than the tom-tit.) "If that is the case," said the bear, "I should like to see the royal palace; so pray come along and show it to me." "Gently, my friend," said the wolf, "we cannot see it just yet, we must wait till the queen comes home."

Soon afterwards the queen came with food in her beak, and she and the king began to feed their young ones. "Now for it!" said the bear; and was about to follow them, to see what was to be seen. "Stop a little, master Bruin," said the wolf, "we must wait now till their majesties are gone again." So they marked the hole where they had seen the nest, and went away. But the bear, being very eager to see the royal palace, soon came back again, and peeping into the nest, saw five or six young birds lying at the bottom of it. "What nonsense!" said Bruin, "this is not a royal palace: I never saw such a filthy place in my life; and you are no royal children, you little base-born brats!" As soon as the young tom-tits heard this they were very angry, and screamed out, "We are not base-born, you stupid bear! our father and mother are honest good sort of people: and depend upon it you shall suffer for your insolence!" At this the wolf and the bear grew frightened, and ran away to their dens. But the young tom-tits kept crying and screaming; and when their father and mother came home and offered them food, they all said, "We will not touch a bit; no, not the leg of a fly, though we should die of hunger, till that rascal Bruin has been punished for calling us base-born brats." "Make yourselves easy, my darlings," said the

65

old king, "you may be sure he shall meet with his deserts."

So he went out and stood before the bear's den, and cried out with a loud voice, "Bruin the bear! thou hast shamefully insulted our lawful children: we therefore hereby declare bloody and cruel war against thee and thine, which shall never cease until thou hast been punished as thou so richly deservest." Now when the bear heard this, he called together the ox, the ass, the stag, and all the beasts of the earth, in order to consult about the means of his defence. And the tom-tit also enlisted on his side all the birds of the air, both great and small, and a very large army of hornets, gnats, bees, and flies, and other insects.

As the time approached when the war was to begin, the tom-tit sent out spies to see who was the commander-in-chief of the enemy's forces; and the gnat, who was by far the cleverest spy of them all, flew backwards and forwards in the wood where the enemy's troops were, and at last hid himself under a leaf on a tree, close by which the orders of the day were given out. And the bear, who was standing so near the tree that the gnat could hear all he said, called to the fox and said, "Reynard, you are the cleverest of all the beasts; therefore you shall be our general and lead us to battle: but we must first agree upon some signal, by which we may know what you want us to do." "Behold," said the fox, "I have a fine, long, bushy tail, which is very like a plume of red feathers, and gives me a very warlike air: now remember, when you see me raise up my tail, you may be sure that the battle is won, and you have then nothing to do but to rush down upon the enemy with all your force. On the other hand, if I drop my tail, the

day is lost, and you must run away as fast as you can."
Now when the gnat had heard all this, he flew back to
the tom-tit and told him every thing that had passed.

At length the day came when the battle was to be
fought; and as soon as it was light, behold! the army of
beasts came rushing forward with such a fearful sound
that the earth shook. And his majesty the tom-tit, with
his troops, came flying along in warlike array, flapping
and fluttering, and beating the air, so that it was quite
frightful to hear; and both armies set themselves in
order of battle upon the field. Now the tom-tit gave
orders to a troop of hornets that at the first onset they
should march straight towards Captain Reynard, and
fixing themselves about his tail, should sting him with
all their might and main. The hornets did as they were
told: and when Reynard felt the first sting, he started
aside and shook one of his legs, but still held up his
tail with wonderful bravery; at the second sting he was
forced to drop his tail for a moment; but when the third
hornet had fixed itself, he could bear it no longer, but
clapped his tail between his legs and scampered away
as fast as he could. As soon as the beasts saw this, they
thought of course all was lost, and scoured across the
country in the greatest dismay; leaving the birds masters
of the field.

And now the king and queen flew back in triumph
to their children, and said, "Now, children, eat, drink,
and be merry, for the victory is ours!" But the young
birds said, "No; not till Bruin has humbly begged our
pardon for calling us base-born." So the king flew back
to the bear's den, and cried out, "Thou villain bear!
come forthwith to my abode, and humbly beseech my
children to forgive thee the insult thou hast offered

them; for, if thou wilt not do this, every bone in thy wretched body shall be broken to pieces." So the bear was forced to crawl out of his den very sulkily, and do what the king bade him: and after that the young birds sat down together, and ate and drank and made merry till midnight.

ROSE-BUD

Once upon a time there lived a king and queen who had no children; and this they lamented very much. But one day as the queen was walking by the side of the river, a little fish lifted its head out of the water, and said, "Your wish shall be fulfilled, and you shall soon have a daughter." What the little fish had foretold soon came to pass; and the queen had a little girl that was so very beautiful that the king could not cease looking on it for joy, and determined to hold a great feast. So he invited not only his relations, friends, and neighbours, but also all the fairies, that they might be kind and good to his little daughter. Now there were thirteen fairies in his kingdom, and he had only twelve golden dishes for them to eat out of, so that he was obliged to leave one of the fairies without an invitation. The rest came, and after the feast was over they gave all their best gifts to the little princess: one gave her virtue, another beauty, another riches, and so on till she had all that was excellent in the world. When eleven had done blessing her, the thirteenth, who had not been invited, and was very angry on that account, came in, and determined to take her revenge. So she cried out, "The king's daughter shall in her fifteenth year be wounded by a spindle, and fall down dead." Then the twelfth, who had not yet given her gift, came forward and said that the bad wish must be fulfilled, but that she could soften it, and that the king's daughter should not die, but fall asleep for a hundred years.

But the king hoped to save his dear child from the threatened evil, and ordered that all the spindles in the kingdom should be bought up and destroyed. All the fairies' gifts were in the mean time fulfilled; for the princess was so beautiful, and well-behaved, and amiable, and wise, that every one who knew her loved her. Now it happened that on the very day she was fifteen years old the king and queen were not at home, and she was left alone in the palace. So she roved about by herself, and looked at all the rooms and chambers, till at last she came to an old tower, to which there was a narrow staircase ending with a little door. In the door there was a golden key, and when she turned it the door sprang open, and there sat an old lady spinning away very busily. "Why, how now, good mother," said the princess, "what are you doing there?" "Spinning," said the old lady, and nodded her head. "How prettily that little thing turns round!" said the princess, and took the spindle and began to spin. But scarcely had she touched it, before the prophecy was fulfilled, and she fell down lifeless on the ground.

However, she was not dead, but had only fallen into a deep sleep; and the king and the queen, who just then came home, and all their court, fell asleep too; and the horses slept in the stables, and the dogs in the court, the pigeons on the house-top and the flies on the walls. Even the fire on the hearth left off blazing, and went to sleep; and the meat that was roasting stood still; and the cook, who was at that moment pulling the kitchen-boy by the hair to give him a box on the ear for something he had done amiss, let him go, and both fell asleep; and so every thing stood still, and slept soundly.

A large hedge of thorns soon grew round the palace, and every year it became higher and thicker, till at last the whole palace was surrounded and hid, so that not even the roof or the chimneys could be seen. But there went a report through all the land of the beautiful sleeping Rose-Bud (for so was the king's daughter called); so that from time to time several kings' sons came, and tried to break through the thicket into the palace. This they could never do; for the thorns and bushes laid hold of them as it were with hands, and there they stuck fast and died miserably.

After many many years there came a king's son into that land, and an old man told him the story of the thicket of thorns, and how a beautiful palace stood behind it, in which was a wondrous princess, called Rose-Bud, asleep with all her court. He told, too, how he had heard from his grandfather that many many princes had come, and had tried to break through the thicket, but had stuck fast and died. Then the young prince said, "All this shall not frighten me, I will go and see Rose-Bud." The old man tried to dissuade him, but he persisted in going.

Now that very day were the hundred years completed; and as the prince came to the thicket, he saw nothing but beautiful flowering shrubs, through which he passed with ease, and they closed after him as firm as ever. Then he came at last to the palace, and there in the court lay the dogs asleep, and the horses in the stables, and on

70

the roof sat the pigeons fast asleep with their heads under their wings; and when he came into the palace, the flies slept on the walls, and the cook in the kitchen was still holding up her hand as if she would beat the boy, and the maid sat with a black fowl in her hand ready to be plucked.

Then he went on still farther, and all was so still that he could hear every breath he drew; till at last he came to the old tower and opened the door of the little room in which Rose-Bud was, and there she lay fast asleep, and looked so beautiful that he could not take his eyes off, and he stooped down and gave her a kiss. But the moment he kissed her she opened her eyes and awoke, and smiled upon him. Then they went out together, and presently the king and queen also awoke, and all the court, and they gazed on each other with great wonder. And the horses got up and shook themselves, and the dogs jumped about and barked; the pigeons took their heads from under their wings, and looked about and flew into the fields; the flies on the walls buzzed away; the fire in the kitchen blazed up and cooked the dinner, and the roast meat turned round again; the cook gave the boy the box on his ear so that he cried out, and the maid went on plucking the fowl. And then was the wedding of the prince and Rose-Bud celebrated, and they lived happily together all their lives long.

THE THREE CHILDREN OF FORTUNE

Once upon a time a father sent for his three sons, and gave to the eldest a cock, to the second a scythe, and to the third a cat. "I am now old," said he, "my end is approaching, and I would fain provide for you before I die. Money I have none, and what I now give you seems of but little worth; yet it rests with yourselves alone to turn my gifts to good account. Only seek out for a land where what you have is as yet unknown, and your fortune is made."

After the death of the father, the eldest set out with his cock: but wherever he went, in every town he saw from afar off a cock sitting upon the church steeple, and turning round with the wind. In the villages he always heard plenty of them crowing, and his bird was therefore nothing new; so there did not seem much chance of his making his fortune. At length it happened that he came to an island where the people who lived there had never heard of a cock, and knew not even how to reckon the time. They knew, indeed, if it were morning or evening; but at night, if they lay awake, they had no means of knowing how time went. "Behold," said he to them, "what a noble animal this is! how like a knight he is! he carries a bright red crest upon his head, and spurs upon his heels; he crows three times every night, at stated hours, and at the third time the sun is about to rise. But this is not all; sometimes he screams in broad day-light, and then you must take warning, for the weather is surely about to change." This pleased the natives mightily; they kept awake one whole night, and heard, to their great joy, how gloriously the cock called the hour, at two, four, and six o'clock. Then they asked him whether the bird was to be sold, and how much he would sell it for. "About as much gold as an ass can carry," said he. "A very fair price for such an animal," cried they with one voice; and agreed to give him what he asked.

When he returned home with his wealth, his brothers wondered greatly; and the second said, "I will now set forth likewise, and see if I can turn my scythe to as good an account." There did not seem, however, much likelihood of this; for go where he would, he was met by peasants who had as good a scythe on their shoulders as he had. But at last, as good luck would have it, he came to an island where the people had never heard of a scythe: there, as soon as the corn was ripe, they went into the fields and pulled it up; but this was very hard work, and a great deal of it was lost. The man then set to work with his scythe; and mowed down their whole crop so quickly, that the people stood staring open-mouthed with wonder. They were willing to give him what he asked for such a marvellous thing: but he only took a horse laden with as much gold as it could carry.

Now the third brother had a great longing to go and see what he could make of his cat. So he set out: and at first it happened to him as it had to the others, so long as he kept upon the main land, he met with no success; there were plenty of cats every where, indeed too many, so that the young ones were for the most part, as soon as they came into the world, drowned in the water. At last he passed over to an island, where, as it chanced most luckily for him, nobody had ever seen a cat; and they were overrun with mice to such a degree, that the little wretches danced upon the tables and chairs, whether the master of the house were at home or not. The people complained loudly of this grievance; the king himself knew not how to rid himself of them in his palace; in every corner mice were squeaking, and they gnawed everything that their teeth could lay hold of. Here was a fine field for Puss—she soon began her chase, and had cleared two rooms in the twinkling of an eye; when the people besought their king to buy the wonderful animal, for the good of the public, at any price. The king willingly gave what was asked,—a mule laden with gold and jewels; and thus the third brother returned home with a richer prize than either of the others.

Meantime the cat feasted away upon the mice in the royal palace, and devoured so many that they were no longer in any great numbers. At length, quite spent and tired with her work, she became extremely thirsty; so she stood still, drew up her head, and cried, "Miau, Miau!" The king gathered together all his subjects when they heard this strange cry, and many ran shrieking in a great fright out of the palace. But the king held a great council below as to what was best to be done; and it was at length fixed to send a herald to the cat, to warn her to leave the castle forthwith, or that force would be used to remove her. "For," said the counsellors, "we would far more willingly put up with the mice (since we are used to that evil), than get rid of them at the risk of our lives." A page accordingly went, and asked the cat "whether she were willing to quit the castle?" But Puss, whose thirst became every moment more and more pressing, answered nothing but "Miau! Miau!" which the page interpreted to mean "No! No!" and therefore carried this answer to the king. "Well," said the counsellors, "then we must try what force will do." So the guns were planted, and the palace was fired upon from all sides. When the fire reached the room where the cat was, she sprang out of the window and ran away; but the besiegers did not see her, and went on firing until the whole palace was burnt to the ground.

FREDERICK AND CATHERINE

There was once a man called Frederick: he had a wife whose name was Catherine, and they had not long been married. One day Frederick said, "Kate! I am going to work in the fields; when I come back I shall be hungry, so let me have something nice cooked, and a good draught of ale." "Very well," said she, "it shall all be ready." When dinner-time drew nigh, Catherine took a nice steak, which was all the meat she had, and put it on the fire to fry. The steak soon began to look brown, and to crackle in the pan; and Catherine stood by with a fork and turned it: then she said to herself, "The steak is almost ready, I may as well go to the cellar for the ale." So she left the pan on the fire, and took a large jug and went into the cellar and tapped the ale cask. The beer ran into the jug, and Catherine stood looking on. At last it popped into her head, "The dog is not shut up—he may be running away with the steak; that's well thought of." So up she ran from the cellar; and sure enough the rascally cur had got the steak in his mouth, and was making off with it.

Away ran Catherine, and away ran the dog across the field! but he ran faster than she, and stuck close to the steak. "It's all gone, and 'what can't be cured must be endured,'" said Catherine. So she turned round; and as she had run a good way and was tired, she walked home leisurely to cool herself.

Now all this time the ale was running too, for Catherine had not turned the cock; and when the jug was full the liquor ran upon the floor till the cask was empty. When she got to the cellar stairs she saw what had happened. "My stars!" said she, "what shall I do to keep Frederick from seeing all this slopping about?" So she thought a while; and at last remembered that there was a sack of fine meal bought at the last fair, and that if she sprinkled this over the floor it would suck up the ale nicely. "What a lucky thing," said she, "that we kept that meal! we have now a good use for it." So away she went for it: but she managed to set it down just upon the great jug full of beer, and upset it; and thus all the ale that had been saved was set swimming on the floor also. "Ah! well," said she, "when one goes, another may as well follow." Then she strewed the meal all about the cellar, and was quite pleased with her cleverness, and said, "How very neat and clean it looks!"

At noon Frederick came home. "Now, wife," cried he, "what have you for dinner?" "O Frederick!" answered she, "I was cooking you a steak; but while I went down to draw the ale, the dog ran away with it; and while I ran after him, the ale all ran out; and when I went to dry up the ale with the sack of meal that we got at the fair, I upset the jug: but the cellar is now quite dry, and looks so clean!" "Kate, Kate," said he, "how could you do all this? Why did you leave the steak to fry, and the ale to run, and then spoil all the meal?" "Why, Frederick," said she, "I did not know I was doing wrong, you should have told me before."

The husband thought to himself, If my wife manages matters thus, I must look sharp myself. Now he had a good deal of gold in the house: so he said to Catherine, "What pretty yellow buttons these are! I shall put them into a box and bury them in the garden; but take care that you never go near or meddle with them." "No, Frederick," said she, "that I never will." As soon as he was gone, there came by some pedlars with earthenware plates and dishes, and they asked her whether she would buy. "Oh dear me, I should like to buy very much, but I have no money: if you had any use for yellow buttons, I might deal with you." "Yellow buttons!" said they: "let us have a look at them." "Go into the garden and dig where I tell you, and you will find the yellow buttons: I dare not go myself." So the rogues went: and when they found what these yellow buttons were, they took them all away, and left her plenty of plates and dishes. Then she set them all about the house for a show: and when Frederick came back, he cried out, "Kate, what have you been doing?" "See," said she, "I have bought all these with your yellow buttons: but I did not touch them myself; the pedlars went themselves and dug them up." "Wife, wife," said Frederick, "what a pretty piece of work you have made! those yellow buttons were all my money: How came you to do such a thing?" "Why," answered she, "I did not know there was any harm in it; you should have told me."

Catherine stood musing for a while, and at last said to her husband, "Hark ye, Frederick, we will soon get the gold back: let us run after the thieves." "Well, we will try," answered he; "but take some butter and cheese with you, that we may have something to eat by the way." "Very well," said she; and they set out: and as Frederick walked the fastest, he left his wife some way behind. "It does not matter," thought she: "when we turn back, I shall be so much nearer home than he."

Presently she came to the top of a hill; down the side of which there was a road so narrow that the cart-wheels always chafed the trees on each side as they passed. "Ah, see now," said she, "how they have bruised and wounded those poor trees; they will never get well." So she took pity on them, and made use of the butter to grease them all, so that the wheels might not hurt them so much. While she was doing this kind office, one of her cheeses fell out of the basket, and rolled down the hill. Catherine looked, but could not see where it was gone; so she said, "Well, I suppose the other will go the same way and find you; he has younger legs than I have." Then she rolled the other cheese after it; and away it went, nobody knows where, down the hill. But she said she supposed they knew the road, and would follow her, and she could not stay there all day waiting for them.

At last she overtook Frederick, who desired her to give him something to eat. Then she gave him the dry bread. "Where are the butter and cheese?" said he. "Oh!" answered she, "I used the butter to grease those poor trees that the wheels chafed so: and one of the cheeses ran away, so I sent the other after it to find it, and I suppose they are both on the road together somewhere." "What a goose you are to do such silly things!" said the husband. "How can

78

you say so?" said she; "I am sure you never told me not."

They ate the dry bread together; and Frederick said, "Kate, I hope you locked the door safe when you came away." "No," answered she, "you did not tell me." "Then go home, and do it now before we go any farther," said Frederick, "and bring with you something to eat."

Catherine did as he told her, and thought to herself by the way, "Frederick wants something to eat; but I don't think he is very fond of butter and cheese: I'll bring him a bag of fine nuts, and the vinegar, for I have often seen him take some."

When she reached home, she bolted the back door, but the front door she took off the hinges, and said, "Frederick told me to lock the door, but surely it can no where be so safe as if I take it with me." So she took her time by the way: and when she overtook her husband she cried out, "There, Frederick, there is the door itself, now you may watch it as carefully as you please." "Alas! alas!" said he, "what a clever wife I have! I sent you to make the house fast, and you take the door away, so that every body may go in and out as they please:—however, as you have brought the door, you shall carry it about with you for your pains." "Very well," answered she, "I'll carry the door; but I'll not carry the nuts and vinegar bottle also,—that would be too much of a load; so, if you please, I'll fasten them to the door."

Frederick of course made no objection to that plan, and they set off into the wood to look for the thieves; but they could not find them: and when it grew dark, they climbed up into a tree to spend the night there.

Scarcely were they up, than who should come by but the very rogues they were looking for. They were in truth great rascals, and belonged to that class of people who find things before they are lost: they were tired; so they sat down and made a fire under the very tree where Frederick and Catherine were. Frederick slipped down on the other side, and picked up some stones. Then he climbed up again, and tried to hit the thieves on the head with them: but they only said, "It must be near morning, for the wind shakes the fir-apples down."

Catherine, who had the door on her shoulder, began to be very tired; but she thought it was the nuts upon it that were so heavy: so she said softly, "Frederick, I must let the nuts go." "No," answered he, "not now, they will discover us." "I can't help that, they must go." "Well then, make haste and throw them down, if you will." Then away rattled the nuts down among the boughs; and one of the thieves cried. "Bless me, it is hailing."

A little while after, Catherine thought the door was still very heavy: so she whispered to Frederick, "I must throw the vinegar down." "Pray don't," answered he, "it will discover us." "I can't help that," said she, "go it must." So she poured all the vinegar down; and the thieves said, "What a heavy dew there is!"

At last it popped into Catherine's head that it was the door itself that was so heavy all the time: so she whispered Frederick, "I must throw the door down soon." But he begged and prayed her not to do so, for he was sure it would betray them. "Here goes, however," said she: and down went the door with such a clatter upon the thieves, that they cried out "Murder!" and not knowing what was coming, ran away as fast as they could, and left all the gold. So when Frederick and Catherine came down, there they found all their money safe and sound.

THE DOG AND THE SPARROW

A shepherd's dog had a master who took no care of him, but often let him suffer the greatest hunger. At last he could bear it no longer; so he took to his heels, and off he ran in a very sad and sorrowful mood. On the road he met a sparrow, that said to him, "Why are you so sad, my friend?" "Because," said the dog, "I am very very hungry, and have nothing to eat." "If that be all," answered the sparrow, "come with me into the next town, and I will soon find you plenty of food." So on they went together into the town: and as they passed by a butcher's shop, the sparrow said to the dog, "Stand there a little while, till I peck you down a piece of meat." So the sparrow perched upon the shelf: and having first looked carefully about her to see if any one was watching her, she pecked and scratched at a steak that lay upon the edge of the shelf, till at last down it fell. Then the dog snapped it up, and scrambled away with it into a corner, where he soon ate it all up. "Well," said the sparrow, "you shall have some more if you will; so come with me to the next shop, and I will peck you down another steak." When the dog had eaten this too, the sparrow said to him, "Well, my good friend, have you had enough now?" "I have had plenty of meat," answered he, "but I should like to have a piece of bread to eat after it." "Come with me then," said the sparrow, "and you shall soon have that too." So she took him to a baker's shop, and pecked at two rolls that lay in the window, till they fell down: and as the dog still wished for more, she took him to another shop and pecked down some more for him. When that was eaten, the sparrow asked him whether he had had enough now. "Yes," said he; "and now let us take a walk a little way out of the town." So they both went out upon the high road: but as the weather was warm, they had not gone far before the dog said, "I am very much tired,—I should like to take a nap." "Very well," answered the sparrow, "do so, and in the meantime I will perch upon that bush." So the dog stretched himself out on the road, and fell fast asleep. Whilst he slept there came by a carter with a cart drawn by three horses, and loaded with two casks of wine. The sparrow, seeing that the carter did not turn out of the way, but would go on in the track in which the dog lay, so as to drive over him, called out, "Stop! stop! Mr Carter, or it shall be the worse for you." But the carter, grumbling to himself, "You make it the worse for me, indeed! what can you do!" cracked his whip, and drove his cart over the poor dog, so that the wheels crushed him to death. "There," cried the sparrow, "thou cruel villain, thou hast killed my friend the dog. Now mind what I say. This deed of thine shall cost thee all thou art worth." "Do your worst, and welcome," said the brute, "what harm can you do me?" and passed on. But the sparrow crept under the tilt of the cart, and pecked at the bung of one of the casks till she loosened it; and then all the wine ran out, without the carter seeing it. At last he looked round, and saw that the cart was dripping, and the cask quite empty. "What an unlucky wretch I am!" cried he. "Not wretch enough yet!" said the sparrow, as she alighted upon the head of one of the horses, and pecked at him till he reared up and kicked. When the carter saw this, he drew out his hatchet and aimed a blow at the sparrow, meaning to kill her; but she flew away, and the blow fell upon the poor horse's head with such force, that he fell down dead. "Unlucky wretch that I am!" cried he. "Not wretch enough yet!" said the sparrow. And as the carter went on with the other two horses, she again crept under the tilt of the cart, and pecked out the bung of the second cask, so that all the wine ran out. When the carter saw this, he again cried out, "Miserable wretch that I am!" But the sparrow answered, "Not wretch enough yet!" and perched on the head of the second horse, and pecked at him too. The carter ran up and struck at her again with his hatchet; but away she flew, and the blow fell upon the second horse and killed him on the spot. "Unlucky wretch that I am!" said he. "Not wretch enough yet!" said the sparrow; and perching upon the third horse, she began to peck him too. The carrier was mad with fury; and without looking about him, or caring what he was about, struck again at the sparrow; but killed his third horse as he had done the other two. "Alas! miserable wretch that I am!" cried he. "Not wretch enough yet!" answered the sparrow as she flew away; "now will I plague and punish thee at thy own house." The carter was forced at last to leave his cart behind him, and to go home overflowing with rage and vexation. "Alas!" said he to his wife, "what ill luck has befallen me!—my wine is all spilt, and my horses all three dead." "Alas! husband," replied she, "and a wicked bird has come into the house, and has brought with her all the birds in the world, I am sure, and they have fallen upon our corn in the loft, and are eating it up at such a rate!" Away ran the husband up stairs, and saw thousands of birds sitting upon the floor eating up his corn, with the sparrow in the midst of them. "Unlucky wretch that I am!" cried the carter; for he saw that the corn was almost all gone. "Not wretch enough yet!" said the sparrow; "thy cruelty shall cost thee thy life yet!" and away she flew.

The carter seeing that he had thus lost all that he had, went down into his kitchen; and was still not sorry for what he had done, but sat himself angrily and sulkily in the chimney corner. But the sparrow sat on the outside of the window, and cried "Carter! thy cruelty shall cost thee thy life!" With that he jumped up in a rage, seized his hatchet, and threw it at the sparrow; but it missed her, and only broke the window. The sparrow now hopped in, perched upon the window-seat, and cried, "Carter! it shall cost thee thy life!" Then he became mad and blind with rage, and struck the window seat with such force that he cleft it in two: and as the sparrow flew from place to place, the carter and his wife were so furious, that they broke all their furniture, glasses, chairs, benches, the table, and at last the walls, without touching the bird at all. In the end, however, they caught her: and the wife said, "Shall I kill her at once?" "No," cried he, "that is letting her off too easily: she shall die a much more cruel death; I will eat her." But the sparrow began to flutter about, and stretched out her neck and cried, "Carter! it shall cost thee thy life yet!" With that he could wait no longer: so he gave his wife the hatchet, and cried, "Wife, strike at the bird and kill her in my hand." And the wife struck; but she missed her aim, and hit her husband on the head so that he fell down dead, and the sparrow flew quietly home to her nest.

THE QUEEN BEE

Two king's sons once upon a time went out into the world to seek their fortunes; but they soon fell into a wasteful foolish way of living, so that they could not return home again. Then their young brother, who was a little insignificant dwarf, went out to seek for his brothers: but when he had found them they only laughed at him, to think that he, who was so young and simple, should try to travel through the world, when they, who were so much wiser, had been unable to get on. However, they all set out on their journey together, and came at last to an ant-hill. The two elder brothers would have pulled it down, in order to see how the poor ants in their fright would run about and carry off their eggs. But the little dwarf said, "Let the poor things enjoy themselves, I will not suffer you to trouble them."

So on they went, and came to a lake where many many ducks were swimming about. The two brothers wanted to catch two, and roast them. But the dwarf said, "Let the poor things enjoy themselves, you shall not kill them." Next they came to a bees' nest in a hollow tree, and there was so much honey that it ran down the trunk; and the two brothers wanted to light a fire under the tree and kill the bees, so as to get their honey. But the dwarf held them back, and said, "Let the pretty insects enjoy themselves, I cannot let you burn them."

At length the three brothers came to a castle: and as they passed by the stables they saw fine horses standing there, but all were of marble, and no man was to be seen. Then they went through all the rooms, till they came to a door on which were three locks: but in the middle of the door there was a wicket, so that they could look into the next room. There they saw a little grey old man sitting at a table; and they called to him once or twice, but he did not hear: however, they called a third time, and then he rose and came out to them.

He said nothing, but took hold of them and led them to a beautiful table covered with all sorts of good things: and when they had eaten and drunk, he showed each of them to a bedchamber.

The next morning he came to the eldest and took him to a marble table, where were three tablets, containing an account of the means by which the castle might be disenchanted. The first tablet said—"In the wood, under the moss, lie the thousand pearls belonging to the king's daughter; they must all be found: and if one be missing by set of sun, he who seeks them will be turned into marble."

The eldest brother set out, and sought for the pearls the whole day; but the evening came, and he had not found the first hundred: so he was turned into stone as the tablet had foretold.

The next day the second brother undertook the task; but he succeeded no better than the first; for he could only find the second hundred of the pearls; and therefore he too was turned into stone.

At last came the little dwarf's turn: and he looked in the moss; but it was so hard to find the pearls, and the job was so tiresome!—so he sat down upon a stone and

86

cried. And as he sat there, the king of the ants (whose life he had saved) came to help him, with five thousand ants; and it was not long before they had found all the pearls and laid them in a heap.

The second tablet said—"The key of the princess's bed-chamber must be fished up out of the lake." And as the dwarf came to the brink of it, he saw the two ducks whose lives he had saved swimming about; and they dived down and soon brought up the key from the bottom.

The third task was the hardest. It was to choose out the youngest and the best of the king's three daughters. Now they were all beautiful, and all exactly alike: but he was told that the eldest had eaten a piece of sugar, the next some sweet syrup, and the youngest a spoonful of honey; so he was to guess which it was that had eaten the honey.

Then came the queen of the bees, who had been saved by the little dwarf from the fire, and she tried the lips of all three; but at last she sat upon the lips of the one that had eaten the honey; and so the dwarf knew which was the youngest. Thus the spell was broken, and all who had been turned into stones awoke, and took their proper forms. And the dwarf married the youngest and the best of the princesses, and was king after her father's death; but his two brothers married the other two sisters.

THE WONDERFUL MUSICIAN

There was once a capital musician who played delightfully on the fiddle, and he went rambling in a forest in a merry mood. Then he said to himself, "Time goes rather heavily on, I must find a companion." So he took up his fiddle, and fiddled away till the wood resounded with his music.

Presently up came a wolf. "Dear me! there's a wolf coming to see me," said the musician. But the wolf came up to him, and said, "How very prettily you play! I wish you would teach me." "That is easily done," said the musician, "if you will only do what I bid you." "Yes," replied the wolf, "I shall be a very apt scholar." So they went on a little way together, and came at last to an old oak tree that was hollow within, and had a large crack in the middle of the trunk. "Look there," said the musician, "if you wish to learn to fiddle, put your fore feet into that crack." The wolf did as he was bid: but the musician picked up a large stone and wedged both his forefeet fast into the crack, so as to make him a prisoner. "Now be so good as to wait there till I come back," said he, and jogged on.

After a while, he said again to himself, "Time goes very heavily, I must find another companion." So he took his fiddle, and fiddled away again in the wood. Presently up came a fox that was wandering close by. "Ah! there is a fox," said he. The fox came up and said, "You delightful musician, how prettily you play! I must and will learn to play as you do." "That you may soon do," said the musician, "if you do as I tell you." "That I will," said the fox. So they travelled on together till they came to a narrow footpath with high bushes on each side. Then the musician bent a stout hazel stem down to the ground from one side of the path, and set his foot on the top, and held it fast; and bent another from the other side, and said to the fox, "Now, pretty fox, if you want to fiddle, give me hold of your left paw." So the fox gave him his paw; and he tied it fast to the top of one of the hazel stems. "Now give me your right," said he; and the fox did as he was told: then the musician tied that paw to the other hazel; and took off his foot, and away up flew the bushes, and the fox too, and hung sprawling and swinging in the air. "Now be so kind as to stay there till I come back," said the musician, and jogged on.

But he soon said to himself, "Time begins to hang heavy, I must find a companion." So he took up his fiddle and fiddled away divinely. Then up came a hare running along. "Ah! there is a hare," said the musician. And the hare said to him, "You fine fiddler, how beautifully you play! will you teach me?" "Yes," said the musician, "I will soon do that, if you will follow my orders." "Yes," said the hare, "I shall make a good scholar." Then they went on together very well for a long while, till they came to an open space in the wood. The musician tied a string round the hare's neck, and fastened the other end to the tree. "Now," said he, "pretty hare, quick, jump about, run round the tree twenty times." So the silly hare did as she was bid: and when she had run twenty times round the tree, she had twisted the string twenty times round the trunk, and was fast prisoner; and she might pull and pull away as long as she pleased, and only pulled the string faster about her neck. "Now wait there till I come back," said the musician.

But the wolf had pulled and bitten and scratched at the stone a long while, till at last he had got his feet out and was at liberty. Then he said in a great passion, "I will run after that rascally musician and tear him in pieces." As the fox saw him run by, he said, "Ah, brother wolf, pray let me down, the musician has played tricks with me." So the wolf set to work at the bottom of the hazel stem, and bit it in two; and away went both together to find the musician: and as they came to the hare, she cried out too for help. So they went and set her free, and all followed the enemy together.

Meantime the musician had been fiddling away, and found another companion; for a poor woodcutter had been pleased with the music, and could not help following him with his axe under his arm. The musician was pleased to get a man for his companion, and behaved very civilly to him, and played him no tricks, but stopped and played his prettiest tunes till his heart overflowed for joy. While the woodcutter was standing listening, he saw the wolf, the fox, and the hare coming, and knew by their faces that they were in a great rage, and coming to do some mischief. So he stood before the musician with his great axe, as much as to say, No one shall hurt him as long as I have this axe. And when the beasts saw this, they were so frightened that they ran back into the wood. Then the musician played the woodcutter one of his best tunes for his pains, and went on with his journey.

JORINDA AND JORINDEL

There was once an old castle that stood in the middle of a large thick wood, and in the castle lived an old fairy. All the day long she flew about in the form of an owl, or crept about the country like a cat; but at night she always became an old woman again. When any youth came within a hundred paces of her castle, he became quite fixed, and could not move a step till she came and set him free: but when any pretty maiden came within that distance, she was changed into a bird; and the fairy put her into a cage and hung her up in a chamber in the castle. There were seven hundred of these cages hanging in the castle, and all with beautiful birds in them.

Now there was once a maiden whose name was Jorinda: she was prettier than all the pretty girls that ever were seen; and a shepherd whose name was Jorindel was very fond of her, and they were soon to be married. One day they went to walk in the wood, that they might be alone: and Jorindel said, "We must take care that we don't go too near to the castle." It was a beautiful evening; the last rays of the setting sun shone bright through the long stems of the trees upon the green underwood beneath, and the turtledoves sang plaintively from the tall birches.

Jorinda sat down to gaze upon the sun; Jorindel sat by her side; and both felt sad, they knew not why; but it seemed as if they were to be parted from one another for ever. They had wandered a long way; and when they looked to see which way they should go home, they found themselves at a loss to know what path to take.

The sun was setting fast, and already half of his circle had disappeared behind the hill: Jorindel on a sudden looked behind him, and as he saw through the bushes that they had, without knowing it, sat down close under the old walls of the castle, he shrank for fear, turned pale, and trembled. Jorinda was singing,

"The ring-dove sang from the willow spray,
    Well-a-day! well-a-day!
He mourn'd for the fate
Of his lovely mate,
    Well-a-day!"

The song ceased suddenly. Jorindel turned to see the reason, and beheld his Jorinda changed into a nightingale; so that her song ended with a mournful *jug, jug.* An owl with fiery eyes flew three times round them, and three times screamed *Tu whu! Tu whu! Tu whu!* Jorindel could not move: he stood fixed as a stone, and could neither weep, nor speak, nor stir hand or foot. And now the sun went quite down; the gloomy night came; the owl flew into a bush; and a moment after the old fairy came forth, pale and meagre, with staring eyes, and a nose and chin that almost met one another.

She mumbled something to herself, seized the nightingale, and went away with it in her hand. Poor Jorindel saw the nightingale was gone,—but what could he do? he could not move from the spot where he stood. At last the fairy came back, and sung with a hoarse voice,

"Till the prisoner's fast,
And her doom is cast,
    There stay! Oh, stay!
When the charm is around her,
And the spell has bound her,
    Hie away! away!"

On a sudden Jorindel found himself free. Then he fell
on his knees before the fairy, and prayed her to give him
back his dear Jorinda: but she said he should never see
her again, and went her way.

He prayed, he wept, he sorrowed, but all in vain.
"Alas!" he said, "what will become of me?"

He could not return to his own home, so he went to a
strange village, and employed himself in keeping sheep.
Many a time did he walk round and round as near to
the hated castle as he dared go. At last he dreamt one
night that he found a beautiful purple flower, and in
the middle of it lay a costly pearl; and he dreamt that he
plucked the flower, and went with it in his hand into the
castle, and that every thing he touched with it was disenchanted, and that there he found his dear Jorinda again.

In the morning when he awoke, he began to search
over hill and dale for this pretty flower; and eight long
days he sought for it in vain: but on the ninth day early
in the morning he found the beautiful purple flower;
and in the middle of it was a large dew drop as big as
a costly pearl.

Then he plucked the flower, and set out and travelled
day and night till he came again to the castle. He walked
nearer than a hundred paces to it, and yet he did not
become fixed as before, but found that he could go close
up to the door.

Jorindel was very glad to see this: he touched the door with the flower, and it sprang open, so that he went in through the court, and listened when he heard so many birds singing. At last he came to the chamber where the fairy sat, with the seven hundred birds singing in the seven hundred cages. And when she saw Jorindel she was very angry, and screamed with rage; but she could not come within two yards of him; for the flower he held in his hand protected him. He looked around at the birds, but alas! there were many many nightingales, and how then should he find his Jorinda? While he was thinking what to do, he observed that the fairy had taken down one of the cages, and was making her escape through the door. He ran or flew to her, touched the cage with the flower,—and his Jorinda stood before him. She threw her arms round his neck and looked as beautiful as ever, as beautiful as when they walked together in the wood.

Then he touched all the other birds with the flower, so that they resumed their old forms; and took his dear Jorinda home, where they lived happily together many years.

THE GRATEFUL BEASTS

A certain man, who had lost almost all his money, resolved to set off with the little that was left him, and travel into the wide world. Then the first place he came to was a village, where the young people were running about crying and shouting. "What is the matter?" asked he. "See here," answered they, "we have got a mouse that we make dance to please us. Do look at him: what a droll sight it is! how he jumps about!" But the man pitied the poor little thing, and said, "Let the mouse go, and I will give you money." So he gave them some, and took the mouse and let him run; and he soon jumped into a hole that was close by, and was out of their reach.

Then he travelled on and came to another village, and there the children had got an ass that they made stand on its hind legs and tumble, at which they laughed and shouted, and gave the poor beast no rest. So the good man gave them also some money to let the poor ass alone.

At the next village he came to, the young people had got a bear that had been taught to dance, and they were plaguing the poor thing sadly. Then he gave them too some money to let the beast go, and the bear was very glad to get on his four feet, and seemed quite happy.

But the man had now given away all the money he had in the world, and had not a shilling in his pocket. Then said he to himself, "The king has heaps of gold in his treasury that he never uses; I cannot die of hunger, I hope I shall be forgiven if I borrow a little, and when I get rich again I will repay it all."

Then he managed to get into the treasury, and took a very little money; but as he came out the king's guards saw him; so they said he was a thief, and took him to the Judge, and he was sentenced to be thrown into the water in a box. The lid of the box was full of holes to let in air, and a jug of water and a loaf of bread were given him.

Whilst he was swimming along in the water very sorrowfully, he heard something nibbling and biting at the lock; and all of a sudden it fell off, the lid flew open, and there stood his old friend the little mouse, who had done him this service. And then came the ass and the bear, and pulled the box ashore; and all helped him because he had been kind to them.

But now they did not know what to do next, and began to consult together; when on a sudden a wave threw on the shore a beautiful white stone that looked like an egg. Then the bear said, "That's a lucky thing: this is the wonderful stone, and whoever has it may have every thing else that he wishes." So the man went and picked up the stone, and wished for a palace and a garden, and a stud of horses; and his wish was fulfilled as soon as he had made it. And there he lived in his castle and garden, with fine stables and horses; and all was so grand and beautiful, that he never could wonder and gaze at it enough.

After some time, some merchants passed by that way. "See," said they, "what a princely palace! The last time we were here, it was nothing but a desert waste." They were very curious to know how all this had happened; so they went in and asked the master of the palace how it had been so quickly raised. "I have done nothing myself," answered he, "it is the wonderful stone that did all."—"What a strange stone that must be!" said they: then he invited them in and showed it to them. They asked him whether he would sell it, and offered him all their goods for it; and the goods seemed so fine and costly, that he quite forgot that the stone would bring him in a moment a thousand better and richer things, and he agreed to make the bargain.

Scarcely was the stone, however, out of his hands before all his riches were gone, and he found himself sitting in his box in the water, with his jug of water and loaf of bread by his side. The grateful beasts, the mouse, the ass, and the bear, came directly to help him; but the mouse found she could not nibble off the lock this time, for it was a great deal stronger than before. Then the bear said, "We must find the wonderful stone again, or all our endeavours will be fruitless."

The merchants, meantime, had taken up their abode in the palace; so away went the three friends, and when they came near, the bear said, "Mouse, go in and look through the key-hole and see where the stone is kept: you are small, nobody will see you." The mouse did as she was told, but soon came back and said, "Bad news! I have looked in, and the stone hangs under the looking-glass by a red silk string, and on each side of it sits a great cat with fiery eyes to watch it."

Then the others took council together and said, "Go back again, and wait till the master of the palace is in bed asleep, then nip his nose and pull his hair." Away went the mouse, and did as they directed her; and the master jumped up very angry, and rubbed his nose, and cried, "Those rascally cats are good for nothing at all, they let the mice eat my very nose and pull the hair off my head." Then he hunted them out of the room; and so the mouse had the best of the game.

Next night as soon as the master was asleep, the mouse crept in again, and nibbled at the red silk string to which the stone hung, till down it dropped, and she rolled it along to the door; but when it got there, the poor little mouse was quite tired; so she said to the ass, "Put in your foot, and lift it over the threshold." This was soon done: and they took up the stone, and set off for the water side. Then the ass said, "How shall we reach the box?" But the bear answered, "That is easily managed; I can swim very well, and do you, donkey, put your fore feet over my shoulders;—mind and hold fast, and take the stone in your mouth: as for you, mouse, you can sit in my ear."

It was all settled thus, and away they swam. After a time, the bear began to brag and boast: "We are brave fellows, are not we, ass?" said he; "what do you think?" But the ass held his tongue, and said not a word. "Why don't you answer me?" said the bear, "you must be an ill-mannered brute not to speak when you're spoken to." When the ass heard this, he could hold no longer; so he opened his mouth, and dropped the wonderful stone. "I could not speak," said he; "did not you know I had the stone in my mouth? now 'tis lost, and that's your fault." "Do but hold your tongue and be quiet," said the bear; "and let us think what's to be done."

Then a council was held: and at last they called together all the frogs, their wives and families, relations and friends, and said: "A great enemy is coming to eat you all up; but never mind, bring us up plenty of stones, and we'll build a strong wall to guard you." The frogs hearing this were dreadfully frightened, and set to work, bringing up all the stones they could find. At last came a large fat frog pulling along the wonderful stone by the silken string: and when the bear saw it, he jumped for joy, and said, "Now we have found what we wanted." So he released the old frog from his load, and told him to tell his friends they might go about their business as soon as they pleased.

Then the three friends swam off again for the box; and the lid flew open, and they found that they were but just in time, for the bread was all eaten, and the jug almost empty. But as soon as the good man had the stone in his hand, he wished himself safe and sound in his palace again; and in a moment there he was, with his garden and his stables and his horses; and his three faithful friends dwelt with him, and they all spent their time happily and merrily as long as they lived.

SNOW-DROP

It was in the middle of winter, when the broad flakes of snow were falling around, that a certain queen sat working at a window, the frame of which was made of fine black ebony; and as she was looking out upon the snow, she pricked her finger, and three drops of blood fell upon it. Then she gazed thoughtfully upon the red drops which sprinkled the white snow, and said, "Would that my little daughter may be as white as that snow, as red as the blood, and as black as the ebony window-frame!" And so the little girl grew up: her skin was as white as snow, her cheeks as rosy as the blood, and her hair as black as ebony; and she was called Snow-drop.

But this queen died; and the king soon married another wife, who was very beautiful, but so proud that she could not bear to think that any one could surpass her. She had a magical looking-glass, to which she used to go and gaze upon herself in it, and say,

"Tell me, glass, tell me true!
 Of all the ladies in the land,
 Who is the fairest? tell me who?"

And the glass answered,

"Thou, queen, art fairest in the land."

But Snow-drop grew more and more beautiful; and when she was seven years old, she was as bright as the day, and fairer than the queen herself. Then the glass one day answered the queen, when she went to consult it as usual,

"Thou, queen, may'st fair and beauteous be,
But Snow-drop is lovelier far than thee!"

When she heard this, she turned pale with rage and envy; and called to one of her servants and said, "Take Snow-drop away into the wide wood, that I may never see her more." Then the servant led her away; but his heart melted when she begged him to spare her life, and he said, "I will not hurt thee, thou pretty child." So he left her by herself; and though he thought it most likely that the wild beasts would tear her in pieces, he felt as if a great weight were taken off his heart when he had made up his mind not to kill her, but leave her to her fate.

Then poor Snow-drop wandered along through the wood in great fear; and the wild beasts roared about her, but none did her any harm. In the evening she came to a little cottage, and went in there to rest herself, for her little feet would carry her no farther. Every thing was spruce and neat in the cottage: on the table was spread a white cloth, and there were seven little plates with seven little loaves, and seven little glasses with wine in them; and knives and forks laid in order; and by the wall stood seven little beds. Then, as she was very hungry, she picked a little piece off each loaf, and drank a very little wine out of each glass; and after that she thought she would lie down and rest. So she tried all the little beds; and one was too long, and another was too short, till at last the seventh suited her; and there she laid herself down, and went to sleep.

Presently in came the masters of the cottage, who were seven little dwarfs that lived among the mountains, and dug and searched for gold. They lighted up their seven lamps, and saw directly that all was not right. The first said, "Who has been sitting on my stool?" The second, "Who has been eating off my plate?" The third, "Who has been picking my bread?" The fourth, "Who has been meddling with my spoon?" The fifth, "Who has been handling my fork?" The sixth, "Who has been cutting with my knife?" The seventh, "Who has been drinking my wine?" Then the first looked round and said, "Who has been lying on my bed?" And the rest came running to him, and every one cried out that somebody had been upon his bed. But the seventh saw Snow-drop, and called all his brethren to come and see her; and they cried out with wonder and astonishment, and brought their lamps to look at her, and said, "Good heavens! what a lovely child she is!" And they were delighted to see her, and took care not to wake her; and the seventh dwarf slept an hour with each of the other dwarfs in turn, till the night was gone.

In the morning, Snow-drop told them all her story; and they pitied her, and said if she would keep all things in order, and cook and wash, and knit and spin for them, she might stay where she was, and they would take good care of her. Then they went out all day long to their work, seeking for gold and silver in the mountains; and Snow-drop remained at home: and they warned her, and said, "The queen will soon find out where you are, so take care and let no one in."

But the queen, now that she thought Snow-drop was dead, believed that she was certainly the handsomest lady in the land; and she went to her glass and said,

> "Tell me, glass, tell me true!
> Of all the ladies in the land,
> Who is the fairest? tell me who?"

And the glass answered,

> 'Thou, queen, art the fairest in all this land;
> But over the hills, in the greenwood shade,
> Where the seven dwarfs their dwelling have made,
> There Snow-drop is hiding her head, and she
> Is lovelier far, O queen! than thee."

Then the queen was very much alarmed; for she knew that the glass always spoke the truth, and was sure that the servant had betrayed her. And she could not bear to think that any one lived who was more beautiful than she was; so she disguised herself as an old pedlar, and went her way over the hills to the place where the dwarfs dwelt. Then she knocked at the door, and cried "Fine wares to sell!" Snowdrop looked out at the window, and said, "Good-day, good-woman; what have you to sell?" "Good wares, fine wares," said she; "laces and bobbins of all colours." "I will let the old lady in; she seems to be a very good sort of body," thought Snow-drop; so she ran down, and unbolted the door. "Bless me!" said the old woman, "how badly your stays are laced! Let me lace them up with one of my nice new laces." Snow-drop did not dream of any mischief; so she stood up before the old woman; but she set to work so nimbly, and pulled the lace so tight, that Snow-drop lost her breath, and fell down as if she were dead. "There's an end of all thy beauty," said the spiteful queen, and went away home.

In the evening the seven dwarfs returned; and I need not saw how grieved they were to see their faithful Snow-drop stretched upon the ground motionless, as if she were quite dead. However, they lifted her up, and when they found what was the matter, they cut the lace; and in a little time she began to breathe, and soon came to life again. Then they said, "The old woman was the queen herself; take care another time, and let no one in when we are away."

When the queen got home, she went straight to her glass, and spoke to it as usual; but to her great surprise it still said,

"Thou, queen, art the fairest in all this land;
But over the hills, in the greenwood shade,
Where the seven dwarfs their dwelling have made,
There Snow-drop is hiding her head; and she
Is lovelier far, O queen! than thee."

Then the blood ran cold in her heart with spite and malice to see that Snow-drop still lived; and she dressed herself up again in a disguise, but very different from the one she wore before, and took with her a poisoned comb. When she reached the dwarfs' cottage, she knocked at the door, and cried "Fine wares to sell!" But Snow-drop said, "I dare not let any one in." Then the queen said, "Only look at my beautiful combs;" and gave her the poisoned one. And it looked so pretty that she took it up and put it into her hair to try it; but the moment it touched her head the poison was so powerful that she fell down senseless. "There you may lie," said the queen, and went her way. But by good luck the dwarfs returned very early that evening; and when they saw Snow-drop lying on the ground, they thought what had happened, and soon found the poisoned comb. And when they took it away, she recovered, and told them all that had passed; and they warned her once more not to open the door to any one.

Meantime the queen went home to her glass, and trembled with rage when she received exactly the same answer as before; and she said, "Snow-drop shall die, if it costs me my life." So she went secretly into a chamber, and prepared a poisoned apple: the outside looked very rosy and tempting, but whoever tasted it was sure to die. Then she dressed herself up as a peasant's wife, and travelled over the hills to the dwarfs' cottage, and knocked at the door; but Snow-drop put her head out of the window and said, "I dare not let any one in, for the dwarfs have told me not." "Do as you please," said the old woman, "but at any rate take this pretty apple; I will make you a present of it." "No," said Snow-drop, "I dare not take it." "You silly girl!" answered the other, "what are you afraid of? do you think it is poisoned? Come! do you eat one part, and I will eat the other." Now the apple was so prepared that one side was good, though the other side was poisoned. Then Snow-drop was very much tempted to taste, for the apple looked exceedingly nice; and when she saw the old woman eat, she could refrain no longer. But she had scarcely put the piece into her mouth, when she fell down dead upon the ground. "This time nothing will save thee," said the queen; and she went home to her glass, and at last it said

"Thou, queen, art the fairest of all the fair."

And then her envious heart was glad, and as happy as such a heart could be.

When evening came, and the dwarfs returned home, they found Snow-drop lying on the ground: no breath passed her lips, and they were afraid that she was quite dead. They lifted her up, and combed her hair, and washed her face with wine and water; but all was in vain, for the little girl seemed quite dead. So they laid her down upon a bier, and all seven watched and bewailed her three whole days; and then they proposed to bury her: but her cheeks were still rosy, and her face looked just as it did while she was alive; so they said, "We will never bury her in the cold ground." And they made a coffin of glass, so that they might still look at her, and wrote her name upon it, in golden letters, and that she was a king's daughter. And the coffin was placed upon the hill, and one of the dwarfs always sat by it and watched. And the birds of the air came too, and bemoaned Snow-drop: first of all came an owl, and then a raven, but at last came a dove.

And thus Snow-drop lay for a long long time, and still only looked as though she were asleep; for she was even now as white as snow, and as red as blood, and as black as ebony. At last a prince came and called at the dwarfs' house; and he saw Snow-drop, and read what was written in golden letters. Then he offered the dwarfs money, and earnestly prayed them to let him take her away; but they said, "We will not part with her for all the gold in the world." At last however they had pity on him, and gave him the coffin: but the moment he lifted it up to carry it home with him, the piece of apple fell from between her lips, and Snow-drop awoke, and said, "Where am I?" And the prince answered, "Thou art safe with me." Then he told her all that had happened, and said, "I love you better than all the world: come with me to my father's palace, and you shall be my wife." And Snow-drop consented, and went home with the prince; and every thing was prepared with great pomp and splendour for their wedding.

To the feast was invited, among the rest, Snow-drop's old enemy the queen; and as she was dressing herself in fine rich clothes, she looked in the glass, and said,

> "Tell me, glass, tell me true!
> Of all the ladies in the land,
> Who is fairest? tell me who?"

And the glass answered,

> "Thou, lady, art loveliest *here*, I ween;
> But lovelier far is the new-made queen."

When she heard this, she started with rage; but her envy and curiosity were so great, that she could not help setting out to see the bride. And when she arrived, and saw that it was no other than Snow-drop, who, as she thought, had been dead a long while, she choked with passion, and fell ill and died; but Snow-drop and the prince lived and reigned happily over that land many many years.

THE ADVENTURES OF CHANTICLEER AND PARTLET

1. How they went to the Mountains to eat Nuts

"The nuts are quite ripe now," said Chanticleer to his wife Partlet, "suppose we go together to the mountains, and eat as many as we can, before the squirrel takes them all away." "With all my heart," said Partlet, "let us go and make a holiday of it together." So they went to the mountains; and as it was a lovely day they stayed there till the evening. Now, whether it was that they had eaten so many nuts that they could not walk, or whether they were lazy and would not, I do not know: however, they took it into their heads that it did not become them to go home on foot. So Chanticleer began to build a little carriage of nut-shells: and when it was finished, Partlet jumped into it and sat down, and bid Chanticleer harness himself to it and draw her home. "That's a good joke!" said Chanticleer; "no, that will never do; I had rather by half walk home; I'll sit on the box and be coachman, if you like, but I'll not draw." While this was passing, a duck came quacking up, and cried out, "You thieving vagabonds, what business have you in my grounds; I'll give it you well for your insolence!" and upon that she fell upon Chanticleer most lustily. But Chanticleer was no coward, and returned the duck's blows with his sharp spurs so fiercely, that she soon began to cry out for mercy; which was only granted her upon condition that she would draw the carriage home for them. This she agreed to do; and Chanticleer got upon the box, and drove, crying. "Now, duck, get on as fast as you can." And away they went at a pretty good pace.

After they had travelled along a little way, they met a needle and a pin walking together along the road: and the needle cried out, "Stop! stop!" and said it was so dark that they could hardly find their way, and such dirty walking they could not get on at all: he told them that he and his friend, the pin, had been at a public house a few miles off, and had sat drinking till they had forgotten how late it was; he begged therefore that the travellers would be so kind as to give them a lift in their carriage. Chanticleer, observing that they were but thin fellows, and not likely to take up much room, told them they might ride, but made them promise not to dirty the wheels of the carriage in getting in, nor to tread on Partlet's toes.

Late at night they arrived at an inn; and as it was bad travelling in the dark, and the duck seemed much tired, and waddled about a good deal from one side to the other, they made up their minds to fix their quarters there: but the landlord at first was unwilling, and said his house was full, thinking they might not be very respectable company: however, they spoke civilly to him, and gave him the egg which Partlet had laid by the way, and said they would give him the duck, who was in the habit of laying one every day: so at last he let them come in, and they bespoke a handsome supper, and spent the evening very jollily.

Early in the morning, before it was quite light, and when no body was stirring in the inn, Chanticleer awakened his wife, and, fetching the egg, they pecked a hole in it, ate it up, and threw the shells into the fire-place: they then went to the pin and needle, who were fast asleep, and, seizing them by their heads, stuck one into the landlord's easy chair, and the other into his handkerchief; and having done this, they crept away as softly as possible. However, the duck, who slept in the open air in the yard, heard them coming, and jumping into the brook which ran close by the inn, soon swam out of their reach.

An hour or two afterwards the landlord got up, and took his handkerchief to wipe his face, but the pin ran into him and pricked him: then he walked into the kitchen to light his pipe at the fire, but when he stirred it up the egg-shells flew into his eyes, and almost blinded him. "Bless me!" said he, "all the world seems to have a design against my head this morning:" and so saying, he threw himself sulkily into his easy chair; but, oh dear! the needle ran into him; and this time the pain was not in his head. He now flew into a very great passion, and, suspecting the company who had come in the night before, he went to look after them, but they were all off; so he swore that he never again would take in such a troop of vagabonds, who ate a great deal, paid no reckoning, and gave him nothing for his trouble but their apish tricks.

2. How Chanticleer and Partlet went to visit Mr Korbes

Another day, Chanticleer and Partlet wished to ride out together; so Chanticleer built a handsome carriage with four red wheels, and harnessed six mice to it; and then he and Partlet got into the carriage, and away they drove. Soon afterwards a cat met them, and said, "Where are you going?" And Chanticleer replied,

> "All on our way
> A visit to pay
> To Mr Korbes, the fox, today."

Then the cat said, "Take me with you." Chanticleer said, "With all my heart: get up behind, and be sure you do not fall off."

> "Take care of this handsome coach of mine,
> Nor dirty my pretty red wheels so fine!
>   Now, mice, be ready,
>   And, wheels, run steady!
> For we are going a visit to pay
> To Mr Korbes, the fox, today."

Soon after came up a mill-stone, an egg, a duck, and a pin; and Chanticleer gave them all leave to get into the carriage and go with them.

When they arrived at Mr Korbes's house, he was not at home; so the mice drew the carriage into the coach-house, Chanticleer and Partlet flew upon a beam, the cat sat down in the fire-place, the duck got into the washing cistern, the pin stuck himself into the bed pillow, the mill-stone laid himself over the house door, and the egg rolled herself up in the towel.

When Mr Korbes came home he went to the fire-place to make a fire; but the cat threw all the ashes in his eyes: so he ran to the kitchen to wash himself; but there the duck splashed all the water in his face; and when he tried to wipe himself, the egg broke to pieces in the towel all over his face and eyes. Then he was very angry, and went without his supper to bed; but when he laid his head on the pillow the pin ran into his cheek: at this he became quite furious, and, jumping up, would have run out of the house; but when he came to the door the mill-stone fell down on his head and killed him on the spot.

3. How Partlet died and was buried and how Chanticleer died of grief

Another day Chanticleer and Partlet agreed to go again to the mountains to eat nuts; and it was settled that all the nuts which they found should be shared equally between them. Now Partlet found a very large nut; but she said nothing about it to Chanticleer, and kept it all to herself: however, it was so big that she could not swallow it, and it stuck in her throat. Then she was in a great fright, and cried out to Chanticleer, "Pray run as fast as you can, and fetch me some water, or I shall be choked." Chanticleer ran as fast as he could to the river, and said, "River, give me some water, for Partlet lies on the mountain, and will be choked by a great nut." The river said, "Run first to the bride, and ask her for a silken cord to draw up the water." Chanticleer ran to the bride, and said, "Bride, you must give me a silken cord, for then the river will give me water, and the water I will carry to Partlet, who lies on the mountain, and will be choked by a great nut." But the bride said, "Run first and bring me my garland that is hanging on a willow in the garden." Then Chanticleer ran to the garden, and took the garland from the bough where it hung, and brought it to the bride; and then the bride gave him the silken cord, and he took the silken cord to the river, and the river gave him water, and he carried the water to Partlet; but in the mean time she was choked by the great nut, and lay quite dead, and never moved any more.

Then Chanticleer was very sorry, and cried bitterly; and all the beasts came and wept with him over poor Partlet. And six mice built a little hearse to carry her to her grave; and when it was ready they harnessed themselves before it, and Chanticleer drove them. On the way they met the fox. "Where are you going, Chanticleer?" said he. "To bury my Partlet," said the other, "May I go with you?" said the fox. "Yes; but you must get up behind, or my horses will not be able to draw you." Then the fox got up behind; and presently the wolf, the bear, the goat, and all the beasts of the wood, came and climbed upon the hearse.

So on they went till they came to a rapid stream. "How shall we get over?" said Chanticleer. Then said a straw, "I will lay myself across, and you may pass over upon me." But as the mice were going over, the straw slipped away and fell into the water, and the six mice all fell in and were drowned. What was to be done? Then a large log of wood came and said, "I am big enough; I will lay myself across the stream, and you shall pass over upon me." So he laid himself down; but they managed so clumsily, that the log of wood fell in and was carried away by the stream. Then a stone, who saw what had happened, came up and kindly offered to help poor Chanticleer by laying himself across the stream; and this time he got safely to the other side with the hearse, and managed to get Partlet out of it; but the fox and the other mourners, who were sitting behind, were too heavy, and fell back into the water and were all carried away by the stream, and drowned.

Thus Chanticleer was left alone with his dead Partlet; and having dug a grave for her, he laid her in it, and made a little hillock over her. Then he sat down by the grave, and wept and mourned, till at last he died too: and so all were dead.

THE MISER IN THE BUSH

A farmer had a faithful and diligent servant, who had worked hard for him three years, without having been paid any wages. At last it came into the man's head that he would not go on thus without pay any longer; so he went to his master, and said, "I have worked hard for you a long time, I will trust to you to give me what I deserve to have for my trouble." The farmer was a sad miser, and knew that his man was very simple-hearted; so he took out threepence, and gave him for every year's service a penny. The poor fellow thought it was a great deal of money to have, and said to himself, "Why should I work hard, and live here on bad fare any longer? I can now travel into the wide world, and make myself merry." With that he put his money into his purse, and set out, roaming over hill and valley.

As he jogged along over the fields, singing and dancing, a little dwarf met him, and asked him what made him so merry. "Why, what should make me down-hearted?" said he; "I am sound in health and rich in purse, what should I care for? I have saved up my three years' earnings and have it all safe in my pocket." "How much may it come to?" said the little man. "Full threepence," replied the countryman. "I wish you would give them to me," said the other; "I am very poor." Then the man pitied him, and gave him all he had; and the little dwarf said in return, "As you have such a kind honest heart, I will grant you three wishes—one for every penny; so choose whatever you like." Then the countryman rejoiced at his good luck, and said, "I like many things better than money: first, I will have a bow that will bring down every thing I shoot at; secondly, a fiddle that will set every one dancing that hears me play upon it; and thirdly, I should like that every one should grant what I ask." The dwarf said he should have his three wishes; so he gave him the bow and fiddle, and went his way.

Our honest friend journeyed on his way too; and if he was merry before, he was now ten times more so. He had not gone far before he met an old miser: close by them stood a tree, and on the topmost twig sat a thrush singing away most joyfully. "Oh, what a pretty bird!" said the miser; "I would give a great deal of money to have such a one." "If that's all," said the countryman, "I will soon bring it down." Then he took up his bow, and down fell the thrush into the bushes at the foot of the tree. The miser crept into the bush to find it; but directly he had got into the middle, his companion took up his fiddle and played away, and the miser began to dance and spring about, capering higher and higher in the air. The thorns soon began to tear his clothes till they all hung in rags about him, and he himself was all scratched and wounded, so that the blood ran down. "Oh, for heaven's sake!" cried the miser, "master! master! pray let the fiddle alone. What have I done to deserve this?" "Thou hast shaved many a poor soul close enough," said the other; "thou art only meeting thy reward:" so he played up another tune. Then the miser began to beg and promise, and offered money for his liberty; but he did not come up to the musician's price for some time, and he danced him along brisker and brisker, and the miser bid higher and higher, till at last he offered a round hundred of florins that he had in his purse, and had just gained by cheating some poor fellow. When the countryman saw so much money, he said, "I will agree to your proposal." So he took the purse, put up his fiddle, and travelled on very well pleased with his bargain.

Meanwhile the miser crept out of the bush half-naked and in a piteous plight, and began to ponder how he should take his revenge, and serve his late companion some trick. At last he went to the judge, and complained that a rascal had robbed him of his money, and beaten him into the bargain; and that the fellow who did it carried a bow at his back and a fiddle hung round his neck. Then the judge sent out his officers to bring up the accused wherever they should find him; and he was soon caught and brought up to be tried.

The miser began to tell his tale, and said he had been robbed of his money. "No, you gave it me for playing a tune to you," said the countryman; but the judge told him that was not likely, and cut the matter short by ordering him off to the gallows.

So away he was taken; but as he stood on the steps he said, "My Lord Judge, grant me one last request." "Any thing but thy life," replied the other. "No," said he, "I do not ask my life; only to let me play upon my fiddle for the last time." The miser cried out, "Oh, no!

no! for heaven's sake don't listen to him! don't listen to him!" But the judge said, "It is only this once, he will soon have done." The fact was, he could not refuse the request, on account of the dwarf's third gift.

Then the miser said, "Bind me fast, bind me fast, for pity's sake." But the countryman seized his fiddle, and struck up a tune, and at the first note judge, clerks, and jailer were in motion; all began capering, and no one could hold the miser. At the second note the hangman let his prisoner go, and danced also, and by the time he had played the first bar of the tune, all were dancing together—judge, court, and miser, and all the people who had followed to look on. At first the thing was merry and pleasant enough; but when it had gone on a while, and there seemed to be no end of playing or dancing, they began to cry out, and beg him to leave off; but he stopt not a whit the more for their entreaties, till the judge not only gave him his life, but promised to return him the hundred florins.

Then he called to the miser, and said, "Tell us now, you vagabond, where you got that gold, or I shall play on for your amusement only." "I stole it," said the miser in the presence of all the people; "I acknowledge that I stole it and that you earned it fairly." Then the countryman stopt his fiddle, and left the miser to take his place at the gallows.

THE LADY AND THE LION

A merchant, who had three daughters, was once setting out upon a journey; but before he went he asked each daughter what gift he should bring back for her. The eldest wished for pearls; the second for jewels; but the third said, "Dear father, bring me a rose." Now it was no easy task to find a rose, for it was the middle of winter; yet, as she was the fairest daughter, and was very fond of flowers, her father said he would try what he could do. So he kissed all three, and bid them good-bye. And when the time came for his return, he had bought pearls and jewels for the two eldest, but he had sought every where in vain for the rose; and when he went into any garden and inquired for such a thing, the people laughed at him, and asked him whether he thought roses grew in snow. This grieved him very much, for his third daughter was his dearest child; and as he was journeying home, thinking what he should bring her, he came to a fine castle; and around the castle was a garden, in half of which it appeared to be summer time, and in the other half winter. On one side the finest flowers were in full bloom, and on the other every thing looked desolate and buried in snow. "A lucky hit!" said he as he called to his servant, and told him to go to a beautiful bed of roses that was there, and bring him away one of the flowers. This done, they were riding away well pleased, when a fierce lion sprang up, and roared out, "Whoever dares to steal my roses shall be eaten up alive." Then the man said, "I knew not that the garden belonged to you;

117

can nothing save my life?" "No!" said the lion, "nothing, unless you promise to give me whatever meets you first on your return home; if you agree to this, I will give you your life, and the rose too for your daughter." But the man was unwilling to do so, and said, "It may be my youngest daughter, who loves me most, and always runs to meet me when I go home." Then the servant was greatly frightened, and said, "It may perhaps be only a cat or a dog." And at last the man yielded with a heavy heart, and took the rose; and promised the lion whatever should meet him first on his return.

And as he came near home, it was his youngest and dearest daughter that met him; she came running and kissed him, and welcomed him home; and when she saw that he had brought her the rose, she rejoiced still more. But her father began to be very melancholy, and to weep, saying, "Alas! my dearest child! I have bought this flower dear, for I have promised to give you to a wild lion, and when he has you, he will tear you in pieces, and eat you." And he told her all that had happened; and said she should not go, let what would happen.

But she comforted him, and said, "Dear father, what you have promised must be fulfilled; I will go to the lion, and soothe him, that he may let me return again safe home."

The next morning she asked the way she was to go, and took leave of her father, and went forth with a bold heart into the wood. But the lion was an enchanted prince, and by day he and all his court were lions, but in the evening they took their proper forms again. And when the lady came to the castle, he welcomed her so courteously that she consented to marry him.

The wedding-feast was held, and they lived happily together a long time. The prince was only to be seen as soon as evening came, and then he held his court; but every morning he left his bride, and went away by himself, she knew not whither, till night came again.

After some time he said to her, "To-morrow there will be a great feast in your father's house, for your eldest sister is to be married; and, if you wish to go to visit her, my lions shall lead you thither." Then she rejoiced much at the thoughts of seeing her father once more, and set out with the lions; and every one was overjoyed to see her, for they had thought her dead long since. But she told them how happy she was; and stayed till the feast was over, and then went back to the wood.

Her second sister was soon after married; and when she was invited to the wedding, she said to the prince, "I will not go alone this time; you must go with me." But he would not, and said that would be a very hazardous thing, for if the least ray of the torch light should fall upon him, his enchantment would become still worse, for he should be changed into a dove, and be obliged to wander about the world for seven long years. However, she gave him no rest, and said she would take care no light should fall upon him. So at last they set out together, and took with them their little child too; and she chose a large hall with thick walls, for him to sit in while the wedding torches were lighted; but unluckily no one observed that there was a crack in the door. Then the wedding was held with great pomp; but as the train came from the church, and passed with the torches before the hall, a very small ray of light fell upon the prince. In a moment he disappeared; and when his wife came in, and sought him, she found only a white dove. Then he said to her, "Seven years must I fly up and down over the face of the earth; but every now and then I will let fall a white feather, that shall show you the way I am going; follow it, and at last you may overtake and set me free."

This said, he flew out at the door, and she followed; and every now and then a white feather fell, and showed her the way she was to journey. Thus she went roving on through the wide world, and looked neither to the right hand nor to the left, nor took any rest for seven years. Then she began to rejoice, and thought to herself that the time was fast coming when all her troubles should cease; yet repose was still far off: for one day as she was travelling on, she missed the white feather, and when she lifted up her eyes she could no where see the dove. "Now," thought she to herself, "no human aid can be of use to me;" so she went to the sun, and said, "Thou shinest every where, on the mountain's top, and the valley's depth; hast thou any where seen a white dove?" "No," said the sun, "I have not seen it; but I will give thee a casket—open it when thy hour of need comes." So she thanked the sun, and went on her way till eventide; and when the moon arose, she cried unto it, and said, "Thou shinest through all the night, over field and grove: hast thou no where seen a white dove?" "No," said the moon, "I cannot help thee; but I will give thee an egg—break it when need comes." Then she thanked the moon, and went on till the night-wind blew; and she raised up her voice to it, and said, "Thou blowest through every tree and under every leaf: hast thou not seen the white dove?" "No," said the night-wind; "but I will ask three other winds; perhaps they have seen it." Then the east wind and the west wind came, and said they too had not seen it; but the south wind said, "I have seen the white dove; he has fled to the Red Sea, and is changed once more into a lion, for the seven years are passed away; and there he is fighting with a dragon, and the dragon is an enchanted princess, who seeks to separate him from you." Then the night-wind said, "I will give thee counsel: go to the Red Sea; on the right shore stand many rods; number them, and when thou comest to the eleventh, break it off and smite the dragon with it; so the lion will have the victory, and both of them will appear to you in their human forms. Then instantly set out with thy beloved prince, and journey home over sea and land."

So our poor wanderer went forth, and found all as the night-wind had said; and she plucked the eleventh rod, and smote the dragon, and immediately the lion became a prince and the dragon a princess again. But she forgot the counsel which the night-wind had given; and the false princess watched her opportunity, and took the prince by the arm, and carried him away.

Thus the unfortunate traveller was again forsaken and forlorn; but she took courage and said, "As far as the wind blows, and so long as the cock crows, I will journey on till I find him once again." She went on for a long way, till at length she came to the castle whither the princess had carried the prince; and there was a feast prepared, and she heard that the wedding was about to be held. "Heaven aid me now!" said she; and she took the casket that the sun had given her, and found that within it lay a dress as dazzling as the sun itself. So she put it on, and went into the palace; and all the people gazed upon her; and the dress pleased the bride so much that she asked whether it was to be sold: "Not for gold and silver," answered she; "but for flesh and blood." The princess asked what she meant; and she said, "Let me speak with the bridegroom this night in his chamber, and I will give thee the dress." At last the princess agreed; but she told her chamberlain to give the prince a sleeping-draught, that he might not hear or see her. When evening came, and the prince had fallen asleep, she was led into his chamber, and she sat herself down at his feet and said, "I have followed thee seven years; I have been to the sun, the moon, and the night-wind, to seek thee; and at last I have helped thee to overcome the dragon. Wilt thou then forget me quite?" But the prince slept so soundly that her voice only passed over him, and seemed like the murmuring of the wind among the fir-trees.

Then she was led away, and forced to give up the golden dress; and when she saw that there was no help for her, she went out into a meadow and sat herself down and wept. But as she sat she bethought herself of the egg that the moon had given her; and when she broke it, there ran out a hen and twelve chickens of pure gold, that played about, and then nestled under the old one's wings, so as to form the most beautiful sight in the world. And she rose up, and drove them before her till the bride saw them from her window, and was so pleased that she came forth, and asked her if she would sell the brood. "Not for gold or silver; but for flesh and blood: let me again this evening speak with the bridegroom in his chamber."

Then the princess thought to betray her as before, and agreed to what she asked; but when the prince went to his chamber, he asked the chamberlain why the wind had murmured so in the night. And the chamberlain told him all; how he had given him a sleeping-draught, and a poor maiden had come and spoken to him in his chamber, and was to come again that night. Then the prince took care to throw away the sleeping-draught; and when she came and began again to tell him what woes had befallen her, and how faithful and true to him she had been, he knew his beloved wife's voice, and sprung up, and said, "You have awakened me as from a dream; for the strange princess had thrown a spell around me, so that I had altogether forgotten you: but heaven hath sent you to me in a lucky hour."

And they stole away out of the palace by night secretly (for they feared the princess), and journeyed home; and there they found their child, now grown comely and fair, and lived happily together to the end of their days.

OLD SULTAN

A shepherd had a faithful dog, called Sultan, who was grown very old, and had lost all his teeth. And one day when the shepherd and his wife were standing together before the house, the shepherd said, "I will shoot old Sultan to-morrow morning, for he is of no use now." But his wife said, "Pray let the poor faithful creature live; he has served us well a great many years, and we ought to give him a livelihood for the rest of his days." "But what can we do with him?" said the shepherd, "he has not a tooth in his head, and the thieves don't care for him at all; to be sure he has served us, but then he did it to earn his livelihood; to-morrow shall be his last day, depend upon it."

Poor Sultan, who was lying close by them, heard all that the shepherd and his wife said to one another, and was very much frightened to think to-morrow would be his last day; so in the evening he went to his good friend the wolf, who lived in the wood, and told him all his sorrows, and how his master meant to kill him in the morning. "Make yourself easy," said the wolf, "I will give you some good advice. Your master, you know, goes out every morning very early with his wife into the field; and they take their little child with them, and lay it down behind the hedge in the shade while they are at work. Now do you lie down close by the child, and pretend to be watching it, and I will come out of the wood and run away with it: you must run after me as fast as you can, and I will let it drop; then you may carry it back, and they will think you have saved their child, and will be so thankful to you that they will take care of you as long as you live." The dog liked this plan very well; and accordingly so it was managed. The wolf ran with the child a little way; the shepherd and his wife screamed out; but Sultan soon overtook him, and carried the poor little thing back to his master and mistress. Then the shepherd patted him on the head, and said, "Old Sultan has saved our child from the wolf, and therefore he shall live and be well taken care of, and have plenty to eat. Wife, go home, and give him a good dinner, and let him have my old cushion to sleep on as long as he lives." So from this time forward Sultan had all that he could wish for.

Soon afterwards the wolf came and wished him joy, and said, "Now, my good fellow, you must tell no tales, but turn your head the other way when I want to taste one of the old shepherd's fine fat sheep." "No," said

Sultan; "I will be true to my master." However, the wolf thought he was in joke, and came one night to get a dainty morsel. But Sultan had told his master what the wolf meant to do; so he laid wait for him behind the barn-door, and when the wolf was busy looking out for a good fat sheep, he had a stout cudgel laid about his back, that combed his locks for him finely.

Then the wolf was very angry, and called Sultan "an old rogue", and swore he would have his revenge. So the next morning the wolf sent the boar to challenge Sultan to come into the wood to fight the matter out. Now Sultan had no body he could ask to be his second but the shepherd's old three-legged cat; so he took her with him, and as the poor thing limped along with some trouble, she stuck up her tail straight in the air.

The wolf and the wild boar were first on the ground; and when they espied their enemies coming, and saw the cat's long tail standing straight in the air, they thought she was carrying a sword for Sultan to fight with; and every time she limped, they thought she was picking up a stone to throw at them; so they said they should not like this way of fighting, and the boar lay down behind a bush, and the wolf jumped up into a tree. Sultan and the cat soon came up, and looked about, and wondered that no one was there. The boar, however, had not quite hidden himself, for his ears stuck out of the bush; and when he shook one of them a little, the cat, seeing something move, and thinking it was a mouse, sprang upon it, and bit and scratched it, so that the boar jumped up and grunted, and ran away, roaring out, "Look up in the tree, there sits the one who is to blame." So they looked up, and espied the wolf sitting amongst the branches; and they called him a cowardly rascal, and would not suffer him to come down till he was heartily ashamed of himself, and had promised to be good friends again with old Sultan.

THE TURNIP

There were two brothers who were both soldiers; the one was rich and the other poor. The poor man thought he would try to better himself; so, pulling off his red coat, he became a gardener, and dug his ground well, and sowed turnips.

When the seed came up, there was one plant bigger than all the rest; and it kept getting larger and larger, and seemed as if it would never cease growing; so that it might have been called the prince of turnips for there never was such a one seen before, and never will again. At last it was so big that it filled a cart, and two oxen could hardly draw it; and the gardener knew not what in the world to do with it, nor whether it would be a blessing or a curse to him. One day he said to himself, "What shall I do with it? if I sell it, it will bring no more than another; and for eating, the little turnips are better than this; the best thing perhaps is to carry it and give it to the king as a mark of respect."

Then he yoked his oxen, and drew the turnip to the Court, and gave it to the king. "What a wonderful thing!" said the king; "I have seen many strange things, but such a monster as this I never saw. Where did you get the seed? or is it only your good luck? If so, you are a true child of fortune." "Ah, no!" answered the gardener, "I am no child of fortune; I am a poor soldier, who never

126

could get enough to live upon; so I laid aside my red coat, and set to work, tilling the ground. I have a brother, who is rich, and your majesty knows him well, and all the world knows him; but because I am poor, every body forgets me."

The king then took pity on him, and said, "You shall be poor no longer. I will give you so much that you shall be even richer than your brother." Then he gave him gold and lands and flocks, and made him so rich that his brother's fortune could not at all be compared with his.

When the brother heard of all this, and how a turnip had made the gardener so rich, he envied him sorely, and bethought himself how he could contrive to get the same good fortune for himself. However, he determined to manage more cleverly than his brother, and got together a rich present of gold and fine horses for the king; and thought he must have a much larger gift in return: for if his brother had received so much for only a turnip, what must his present be worth?

The king took the gift very graciously, and said he knew not what to give in return more valuable and wonderful than the great turnip; so the soldier was forced to put it into a cart, and drag it home with him. When he reached home, he knew not upon whom to vent his rage and spite; and at length wicked thoughts came into his head, and he resolved to kill his brother.

So he hired some villains to murder him; and having shown them where to lie in ambush, he went to his brother, and said, "Dear brother, I have found a hidden treasure; let us go and dig it up, and share it between us." The other had no suspicions of his roguery: so they went out together, and as they were travelling along, the murderers rushed out upon him, bound him, and were going to hang him on a tree.

But whilst they were getting all ready, they heard the trampling of a horse at a distance, which so frightened them that they pushed their prisoner neck and shoulders together into a sack, and swung him up by a cord to the tree, where they left him dangling, and ran away. Meantime he worked and worked away, till he made a hole large enough to put out his head.

When the horseman came up, he proved to be a student, a merry fellow, who was journeying along on his nag, and singing as he went. As soon as the man in the sack saw him passing under the tree, he cried out, "Good morning! good morning to thee, my friend!" The student looked about every where; and seeing no one, and not knowing where the voice came from, cried out, "Who calls me?"

Then the man in the tree answered, "Lift up thine eyes, for behold here I sit in the sack of wisdom; here have I, in a short time, learned great and wondrous things. Compared to this seat, all the learning of the schools is as empty air. A little longer, and I shall know all that man can know, and shall come forth wiser than the wisest of mankind. Here I discern the signs and motions of the heavens and the stars; the laws that control the winds; the number of the sands on the sea-shore; the healing of the sick; the virtues of all simples, of birds, and of precious stones. Wert thou but once here, my friend, thou wouldst feel and own the power of knowledge."

The student listened to all this and wondered much; at last he said, "Blessed be the day and hour when I found you; cannot you contrive to let me into the sack for a little while?" Then the other answered, as if very unwillingly,."A little space I may allow thee to sit here, if thou wilt reward me well and entreat me kindly; but thou must tarry yet an hour below, till I have learnt some little matters that are yet unknown to me."

So the student sat himself down and waited a while; but the time hung heavy upon him, and he begged earnestly that he might ascend forthwith, for his thirst of knowledge was great. Then the other pretended to give way, and said, "Thou must let the sack of wisdom descend, by untying yonder cord, and then thou shalt enter." So the student let him down, opened the sack, and set him free. "Now then," cried he, "let me ascend quickly." As he began to put himself into the sack heels first, "Wait a while," said the gardener, "that is not the way." Then he pushed him in head first, tied up the sack, and soon swung up the searcher after wisdom dangling in the air. "How is it with thee, friend?" said he, "dost thou not feel that wisdom comes unto thee? Rest there in peace, till thou art a wiser man than thou wert."

So saying, he trotted off on the student's nag, and left the poor fellow to gather wisdom till somebody should come and let him down.

MRS FOX

There was once a sly old fox with nine tails, who was very curious to know whether his wife was true to him: so he stretched himself out under a bench, and pretended to be as dead as a mouse.

Then Mrs Fox went up into her own room and locked the door: but her maid, the cat, sat at the kitchen fire cooking; and soon after it became known that the old fox was dead, some one knocked at the door, saying,

"Miss Pussy! Miss Pussy! how fare you today?
Are you sleeping or watching the time away?"

Then the cat went and opened the door, and there stood a young fox; so she said to him,

"No, no, Master Fox, I don't sleep in the day,
I'm making some capital white wine whey.
Will your honour be pleased to dinner to stay?"

"No, I thank you," said the fox; "but how is poor Mrs Fox?" Then the cat answered,

"She sits all alone in her chamber up stairs,
And bewails her misfortune with floods of tears:
She weeps till her beautiful eyes are red;
For, alas! alas! Mr Fox is dead."

"Go to her," said the other, "and say that there is a young fox come, who wishes to marry her."

Then up went the cat,—trippety trap,
And knocked at the door,—tippety tap;
"Is good Mrs Fox within?" said she.
"Alas! my dear, what want you with me?"
"There waits a suitor below at the gate."

Then said Mrs Fox,

> "How looks he, my dear? is he tall and straight?
> Has he nine good tails? There must be nine,
> Or he never shall be a suitor of mine."

"Ah!" said the cat, "he has but one." "Then I will never have him," answered Mrs Fox.

So the cat went down, and sent this suitor about his business. Soon after, some one else knocked at the door; it was another fox that had two tails, but he was not better welcomed than the first. After this came several others, till at last one came that had really nine tails just like the old fox.

When the widow heard this, she jumped up and said,

> "Now, Pussy, my dear, open windows and doors,
> And bid all our friends at our wedding to meet;
> And as for that nasty old master of ours,
> Throw him out of the window, Puss, into the street."

But when the wedding feast was all ready, up sprung the old gentleman on a sudden, and taking a club, drove the whole company, together with Mrs Fox, out of doors.

*

After some time, however, the old fox really died; and soon afterwards a wolf came to pay his respects, and knocked at the door.

Wolf. "Good day, Mrs Cat, with your whiskers so trim;
How comes it you're sitting alone so prim?
What's that you are cooking so nicely, I pray?"
Cat. "O, that's bread and milk for my dinner today.
Will your worship be pleased to stay and dine,
Or shall I fetch you a glass of wine?"

"No, I thank you! Mrs Fox is not at home, I suppose?"

Cat. "She sits all alone,
   Her griefs to bemoan;
   For, alas! alas! Mr Fox is gone."
Wolf. "Ah! dear Mrs Puss! that's a loss indeed:
D'ye think she'd take *me* for a husband instead?"
Cat. "Indeed, Mr Wolf, I don't know but she may
If you'll sit down a moment, I'll step up and see."
So she gave him a chair, and shaking her ears,
She very obligingly tripped it up stairs.
She knocked at the door with the rings on her toes,
And said, "Mrs Fox, you're within, I suppose?"
"O yes," said the widow, "pray come in, my dear,
And tell me whose voice in the kitchen I hear."
"It's a wolf," said the cat, "with a nice smooth skin,
Who was passing this way, and just stepped in
To see (as old Mr Fox is dead)
If you like to take him for a husband instead."

"But," said Mrs Fox, "has he red feet and a sharp snout?" "No," said the cat. "Then he won't do for me."
Soon after the wolf was sent about his business, there came a dog, then a goat, and after that a bear, a lion,

and all the beasts, one after another. But they all wanted something that old Mr Fox had, and the cat was ordered to send them all away. At last came a young fox, and Mrs Fox said, "Has he four red feet and a sharp snout?" "Yes," said the cat.

"Then, Puss, make the parlour look clean and neat,
And throw the old gentleman into the street;
A stupid old rascal! I'm glad that he's dead,
Now I've got such a charming young fox instead."
So the wedding was held, and the merry bells rung,
And the friends and relations they danced and they
    sung,
And feasted and drank, I can't tell how long.

THE GIANT WITH THE
THREE GOLDEN HAIRS

There was once a poor man who had an only son born to him. The child was born under a lucky star; and those who told his fortune said that in his fourteenth year he would marry the king's daughter. It so happened that the king of that land soon after the child's birth passed through the village in disguise, and asked whether there was any news. "Yes," said the people, "a child has just been born, that they say is to be a lucky one, and when he is fourteen years old, he is fated to marry the king's daughter." This did not please the king; so he went to the poor child's parents and asked them whether they would sell him their son? "No," said they; but the stranger begged very hard and offered a great deal of money, and they had scarcely bread to eat, so at last they consented, thinking to themselves, he is a luck's child, he can come to no harm.

The king took the child, put it into a box, and rode away; but when he came to a deep stream, he threw it into the current, and said to himself, "That young gentleman will never be my daughter's husband." The box however floated down the stream; some kind spirit watched over it so that no water reached the child, and at last about two miles from the king's capital it stopt at the dam of a mill. The miller soon saw it, and took a long pole, and drew it towards the shore, and finding it heavy, thought there was gold inside; but when he opened it, he found a pretty little boy, that smiled upon him merrily. Now the miller and his wife had no children, and therefore rejoiced to see their prize, saying, "Heaven has sent it to us;" so they treated it very kindly, and brought it up with such care that every one admired and loved it.

About thirteen years passed over their heads, when the king came by accident to the mill, and asked the miller if that was his son. "No," said he, "I found him when a babe in a box in the mill-dam." "How long ago?" asked the king. "Some thirteen years," replied the miller. "He is a fine fellow," said the king, "can you spare him to carry a letter to the queen? it will please me very much, and I will give him two pieces of gold for his trouble." "As your majesty pleases," answered the miller.

Now the king had soon guessed that this was the child whom he had tried to drown; and he wrote a letter by him to the queen, saying, "As soon as the bearer of this arrives let him be killed and immediately buried, so that all may be over before I return."

The young man set out with this letter, but missed his way, and came in the evening to a dark wood. Through the gloom he perceived a light at a distance, towards which he directed his course, and found that it proceeded from a little cottage. There was no one within except an old woman, who was frightened at seeing him, and said, "Why do you come hither, and whither are you going?" "I am going to the queen, to whom I was to have delivered a letter; but I have lost my way, and shall be glad if you will give me a night's rest." "You are very unlucky," said she, "for this is a robbers' hut, and if the band returns while you are do here it may be worse for you." "I am so tired, however," replied he, "that I must take my chance, for I can go no farther;" so he laid the letter on the table, stretched himself out upon a bench, and fell asleep.

When the robbers came home and saw him, they asked the old woman who the strange lad was. "I have given him shelter for charity," said she; "he had a letter to carry to the queen, and lost his way." The robbers took up the letter, broke it open and read the directions which it contained to murder the bearer. Then their leader tore it, and wrote a fresh one desiring the queen, as soon as the young man arrived, to marry him to the king's daughter. Meantime they let him sleep on till morning broke, and then showed him the right way to the queen's palace; where, as soon as she had read the letter, she had all possible preparations made for the wedding; and as the young man was very beautiful, the princess took him willingly for her husband.

After a while the king returned; and when he saw the prediction fulfilled, and that this child of fortune was, notwithstanding all his cunning, married to his daughter, he inquired eagerly how this had happened, and what were the orders which he had given. "Dear husband," said the queen, "here is your letter, read it for yourself." The king took it, and seeing that an exchange had been made, asked his son-in-law what he had done with the letter which he had given him to carry. "I know nothing of it," answered he; "it must have been taken away in the night while I slept." Then the king was very wroth, and said, "No man shall have my daughter who does not descend into the wonderful cave and bring me three golden hairs from the head of the giant king who reigns there; do this and you shall have my consent." "I will soon manage that," said the youth;—so he took leave of his wife and set out on his journey.

At the first city that he came to, the guard of the gate stopt him, and asked what trade he followed and what he knew. "I know every thing," said he. "If that be so," replied they, "you are just the man we want; be so good as to tell us why our fountain in the market-place is dry and will give no water; find out the cause of that, and we will give you two asses loaded with gold." "With all my heart," said he, "when I come back."

Then he journeyed on and came to another city, and there the guard also asked him what trade he followed, and what he understood. "I know every thing," answered he. "Then pray do us a piece of service," said they, "tell us why a tree which used to bear us golden apples, now does not even produce a leaf." "Most willingly," answered he, "as I come back."

At last his way led him to the side of a great lake of water over which he must pass. The ferryman soon began to ask, as the others had done, what was his trade, and what he knew. "Every thing," said he. "Then," said the other, "pray inform me why I am bound for ever to ferry over this water, and have never been able to get my liberty; I will reward you handsomely." "I will tell you all about it," said the young man, "as I come home."

When he had passed the water, he came to the wonderful cave, which looked terribly black and gloomy. But the wizard king was not at home, and his grandmother sat at the door in her easy chair. "What do you seek?" said she. "Three golden hairs from the giant's head," answered he. "You run a great risk," said she, "when he returns home; yet I will try what I can do for you." Then she changed him into an ant, and told him to hide himself in the folds of her cloak. "Very well," said he: "but I want also to know why the city fountain is dry, why the tree that bore golden apples is now leafless, and what it is that binds the ferry-man to his post." "Those are three puzzling questions," said the old dame; "but lie quiet and listen to what the giant says when I pull the golden hairs."

Presently night set in and the old gentleman returned home. As soon as he entered he began to snuff up the air, and cried, "All is not right here: I smell man's flesh." Then he searched all round in vain, and the old dame scolded, and said, "Why should you turn every thing topsy-turvy? I have just set all in order." Upon this he laid his head in her lap and soon fell asleep. As soon as he began to snore, she seized one of the golden hairs and pulled it out. "Mercy!" cried he, starting up, "what are you about?" "I had a dream that disturbed me," said she, "and in my trouble I seized your hair: I dreamt that the fountain in the market-place of the city was become dry and would give no water; what can be the cause?"

"Ah! if they could find that out, they would be glad," said the giant: "under a stone in the fountain sits a toad; when they kill him, it will flow again."

This said, he fell asleep, and the old lady pulled out another hair. "What would you be at?" cried he in a rage. "Don't be angry," said she, "I did it in my sleep; I dreamt that in a great kingdom there was a beautiful tree that used to bear golden apples, and now has not even a leaf upon it; what is the reason of that?" "Aha!" said the giant, "they would like very well to know that secret: at the root of the tree a mouse is gnawing; if they were to kill him, the tree would bear golden apples again; if not, it will soon die. Now let me sleep in peace; if you wake me again, you shall rue it."

Then he fell once more asleep; and when she heard him snore she pulled out the third golden hair, and the giant jumped up and threatened her sorely; but she soothed him, and said, "It was a strange dream: methought I saw a ferryman who was fated to ply backwards and forwards over a lake, and could never be set at liberty; what is the charm that binds him?" "A silly fool!" said the giant; "if he were to give the rudder into the hand of any passenger, he would find himself at liberty, and the other would be obliged to take his place. Now let me sleep."

In the morning the giant arose and went out; and the old woman gave the young man the three golden hairs, reminded him of the answers to his three questions, and sent him on his way.

He soon came to the ferryman, who knew him again, and asked for the answer which he had promised him. "Ferry me over first," said he, "and then I will tell you." When the boat arrived on the other side, he told him to give the rudder to any of his passengers, and then he might run away as soon as he pleased. The next place he came to was the city where the barren tree stood: "Kill the mouse," said he, "that gnaws the root, and you will have golden apples again." They gave him a rich present, and he journeyed on to the city where the fountain had dried up, and the guard demanded his answer to their question. So he told them how to cure the mischief, and they thanked him and gave him the two asses laden with gold.

And now at last this child of fortune reached home. and his wife rejoiced greatly to see him, and to hear how well everything had gone with him. He gave the three golden hairs to the king, who could no longer raise any objection to him, and when he saw all the treasure, cried out in a transport of joy, "Dear son, where did you find all this gold?" "By the side of a lake," said the youth, "where there is plenty more to be had." "Pray, tell me," said the king, "that I may go and get some too." "As much as you please," replied the other; "you will see the ferryman on the lake, let him carry you across, and there you will see gold as plentiful as sand upon the shore."

Away went the greedy king; and when he came to the lake, he beckoned to the ferryman, who took him into his boat, and as soon as he was there gave the rudder into his hand, and sprung ashore, leaving the old king to ferry away as a reward for his sins.

"And is his majesty plying there to this day?" You may be sure of that, for nobody will trouble himself to take the rudder out of his hands.

CHERRY, OR THE FROG-BRIDE

There was once a king who had three sons. Not far from his kingdom lived an old woman who had an only daughter called Cherry. The king sent his sons out to see the world, that they might learn the ways of foreign lands, and get wisdom and skill in ruling the kingdom that they were one day to have for their own. But the old woman lived at peace at home with her daughter, who was called Cherry, because she liked cherries better than any other kind of food, and would eat scarcely any thing else. Now her poor old mother had no garden, and no money to buy cherries every day for her daughter; and at last there was no other plan left but to go to a neighbouring nunnery-garden and beg the finest she could get of the nuns; for she dared not let her daughter go out by herself, as she was very pretty, and she feared some mischance might befall her. Cherry's taste was, however, very well known; and as it happened that the abbess was as fond of cherries as she was, it was soon found out where all the best fruit went; and the holy mother was not a little angry at missing some of her stock and finding whither it had gone.

The princes while wandering on came one day to the town where Cherry and her mother lived; and as they passed along the street saw the fair maiden standing at the window, combing her long and beautiful locks of hair. Then each of the three fell deeply in love with her, and began to say how much he longed to have her for his wife! Scarcely had the wish been spoken, when all drew their swords, and a dreadful battle began; the fight lasted long, and their rage grew hotter and hotter, when at last the abbess hearing the uproar came to the gate. Finding that her neighbour was the cause, her old spite against her broke forth at once, and in her rage she wished Cherry turned into an ugly frog, and sitting in the water under the bridge at the world's end. No sooner said than done; and poor Cherry became a frog, and vanished out of their sight. The princes had now nothing to fight for; so sheathing their swords again, they shook hands as brothers, and went on towards their father's home.

The old king meanwhile found that he grew weak and ill-fitted for the business of reigning: so he thought of giving up his kingdom; but to whom should it be? This was a point that his fatherly heart could not settle; for he loved all his sons alike. "My dear children," said he, "I grow old and weak, and should like to give up my kingdom; but I cannot make up my mind which of you to choose for my heir, for I love you all three; and besides, I should wish to give my people the cleverest and best of you for their king. however, I will give you three trials, and the one who wins the prize shall have the kingdom. The first is to seek me out one hundred ells of cloth, so fine that I can draw it through my golden ring." The sons said they would do their best, and set out on the search.

The two eldest brothers took with them many followers, and coaches and horses of all sorts, to bring home all the beautiful clothes which they should find; but the youngest went alone by himself. They soon came to where the roads branched off into several ways; two ran through smiling meadows, with smooth paths and shady groves, but the third looked dreary and dirty, and went over barren wastes. The two eldest chose the pleasant ways; and the youngest took his leave and whistled along over the dreary road. Whenever fine linen was to be seen, the two elder brothers bought it, and bought so much that their coaches and horses bent under their burthen. The youngest, on the other hand, journeyed on many a weary day, and found not a place where he could buy even one piece of cloth that was at all fine and good. His heart sunk beneath him, and every mile he grew more and more heavy and sorrowful. At last he came to a bridge over a stream, and there he sat himself down to rest and sigh over his bad luck, when an ugly-looking frog popped its head out of the water, and asked, with a voice that had not at all a harsh sound to his ears, what was the matter. The prince said in a pet, "Silly frog! thou canst not help me." "Who told you so?" said the frog; "tell me what ails you." After a while the prince opened the whole story, and told why his father had sent him out. "I will help you," said the frog; so it jumped back into the stream and soon came back dragging a small piece of linen not bigger than one's hand, and by no means the cleanest in the world in its look. However, there it was, and the prince was told to take it away with him. He had no great liking for such a dirty rag; but still there was something in the frog's speech that pleased him much, and he thought to himself, "It can do no harm, it is better than nothing;" so he picked it up, put it in his pocket, and thanked the frog, who dived down again, panting and quite tired, as it seemed, with its work. The farther he went the heavier he found to his great joy the pocket grow, and so he turned himself homewards, trusting greatly in his good luck.

He reached home nearly about the same time that his brothers came up, with their horses and coaches all heavily laden. Then the old king was very glad to see his children again, and pulled the ring off his finger to try who had done the best; but in all the stock which the two eldest had brought there was not one piece a tenth part of which would go through the ring. At this they were greatly abashed; for they had made a laugh of their brother, who came home, as they thought, empty-handed. But how great was their anger, when they saw him pull from his pocket a piece that for softness, beauty, and whiteness, was a thousand times better than any thing that was ever before seen! It was so fine that it passed with ease through the ring; indeed, two such pieces would readily have gone in together. The father embraced the lucky youth, told his servants to throw the coarse linen into the sea, and said to his children, "Now you must set about the second task which I am to set you;—bring me home a little dog, so small that it will lie in a nut-shell."

His sons were not a little frightened at such a task; but they all longed for the crown, and made up their minds to go and try their hands, and so after a few days they set out once more on their travels. At the cross-ways they parted as before, and the youngest chose his old dreary rugged road with all the bright hopes that his former good luck gave him. Scarcely had he sat himself down again at the bridge foot, when his old friend the frog jumped out, set itself beside him, and as before opened its big wide mouth, and croaked out, "What is the matter?" The prince had this time no doubt of the frog's power, and therefore told what he wanted. "It shall be done for you," said the frog; and springing into the stream it soon brought up a hazel-nut, laid it at his feet, and told him to take it home to his father, and crack it gently, and then see what would happen. The prince went his way very well pleased, and the frog, tired with its task, jumped back into the water.

His brothers had reached home first, and brought with them a great many very pretty little dogs. The old king, willing to help them all he could, sent for a large walnutshell and tried it with every one of the little dogs; but one stuck fast with the hind-foot out, and another with the head, and a third with the forefoot, and a fourth with its tail,—in short, some one way and some another; but none was at all likely to sit easily in this new kind of kennel. When all had been tried, the youngest made his father a dutiful bow, and gave him the hazel-nut, begging him to crack it very carefully: the moment this was done out ran a beautiful little white dog upon the king's hand, wagged its tail, fondled his new master, and soon turned about and barked at the other little beasts in the most graceful manner, to the delight of the whole court. The joy of every one was great; the old king again embraced his lucky son, told his people to drown all the other dogs in the sea, and said to his children, "Dear sons! your weightiest tasks are now over; listen to my last wish; whoever brings home the fairest lady shall be at once the heir to my crown."

The prize was so tempting and the chance so fair for all, that none made any doubts about setting to work, each in his own way, to try and be the winner. The youngest was not in such good spirits as he was the last time; he thought to himself, "The old frog has been able to do a great deal for me: but all its power must be nothing to me now, for where should it find me a fair maiden, still less a fairer maiden than was ever seen at my father's court? The swamps where it lives have no living things in them, but toads, snakes, and such vermin." Meantime he went on, and sighed as he sat down again with a heavy heart by the bridge. "Ah frog!" said he, "this time thou canst do me no good." "Never mind," croaked the frog: "only tell me what is the matter now." Then the prince told his old friend what trouble had now come upon him. "Go thy ways home," said the frog; "the fair maiden will follow hard after; but take care and do not laugh at whatever may happen!" This said, it sprang as before into the water and was soon out of sight. The prince still sighed on, for he trusted very little this time to the frog's word; but he had not set many steps towards home before he heard a noise behind him, and looking round saw six large water rats dragging along a large pumpkin like a coach, full trot. On the box sat an old fat toad as coachman, and behind stood two little frogs as footmen, and two fine mice with stately whiskers ran before as outriders; within sat his old friend the frog, rather misshapen and unseemly to be sure, but still with somewhat of a graceful air as it bowed to him in passing. Much too deeply wrapt in thought as to his chance of finding the fair lady whom he was seeking, to take any heed of the strange scene before him, the prince scarcely looked at it, and had still less mind to laugh. The coach passed on a little way, and soon turned a corner that hid it from his sight; but how astonished was he, on turning the corner himself, to find a handsome coach and six black horses standing

145

there, with a coachman in gay livery, and within, the most beautiful lady he had ever seen, whom he soon knew to be the fair Cherry, for whom his heart had so long ago panted! As he came up, the servants opened the coach door, and he was allowed to seat himself by the beautiful lady.

They soon came to his father's city, where his brothers also came, with trains of fair ladies; but as soon as Cherry was seen, all the court gave her with one voice the crown of beauty. The delighted father embraced his son, and named him the heir to his crown, and ordered all the other ladies to be thrown like the little dogs into the sea and drowned. Then the prince married Cherry, and lived long and happily with her, and indeed lives with her still—if he be not dead.

Hans Christian Andersen's
Fairy Tales

Fairy Tales

PARRAGON

Hans Christian Anderson's Fairy Tales
A Parragon Classic

First published between 1835 and 1872

This is a Siena book
Siena is an imprint of Parragon

This edition published in 1998 by
Parragon
13 Whiteladies Road
Clifton
Bristol BS8 1PB

Printed and bound in the UK

THE RED SHOES

There was once a little girl, very pretty and delicate, but so poor that in summer time she always went barefoot, and in winter wore large wooden shoes, so that her little ankles grew quite red and sore.

In the village dwelt the shoemaker's mother. She sat down one day and made out of some old pieces of red cloth a pair of little shoes; they were clumsy enough, certainly, but they fitted the little girl tolerably well, and she gave them to her. The little girl's name was Karen.

It was the day of her mother's funeral when the red shoes were given to Karen; they were not at all suitable for mourning, but she had no others, and in them she walked with bare legs behind the miserable straw bier.

Just then a large old carriage rolled by; in it sat a large old lady; she looked at the little girl and pitied her, and she said to the priest, "Give me the little girl and I will take care of her."

And Karen thought it was all for the sake of the red shoes that the old lady had taken this fancy to her, but the old lady said they were frightful, and they were burnt. And Karen was dressed very neatly; she was taught to read and to work; and people told her she was pretty—but the mirror said, "Thou art more than pretty, thou art beautiful!"

It happened one day that the Queen travelled through that part of the country with her little daughter, the Princess; and all the people, Karen amongst them, crowded in front of the palace, whilst the little Princess stood, dressed in white, at a window, for everyone to see her. She wore neither train nor gold crown; but on her feet were pretty red morocco shoes, much prettier ones indeed than those the shoemaker's mother had made for little Karen. Nothing in the world could be compared to these red shoes.

Karen was now old enough to be confirmed, she was to have both new frock and new shoes. The rich shoemaker in the town took the measure of her little foot. Large glass cases full of neat shoes and shining boots were fixed round the room; however, the old lady's sight was not very good, and, naturally enough, she had not so much pleasure in looking at them as Karen had. Amongst the shoes was a pair of red ones, just like those worn by the Princess. How gay they were! The shoemaker said they had been made for a count's daughter, but had not quite fitted her.

"They are of polished leather," said the old lady, "see how they shine!"

"Yes, they shine beautifully!" exclaimed Karen. And as the shoes fitted her, they were bought; but the old lady did not know that they were red, for she would never have suffered Karen to go to confirmation in red shoes. But Karen did so. Everybody looked at her feet, and as she walked up the nave to the chancel, it seemed to her that even the antique sculptured figures on the monuments, with their stiff ruffs and long black robes, fixed their eyes on her red shoes. Of them only she thought when the Bishop laid his hand on her head, when he spoke of Holy Baptism, of her covenant with God, and how she must now be a full-grown Christian. The organ sent forth its deep, solemn tones, the children's sweet voices mingled with those of the choristers, but Karen still thought only of her red shoes.

That afternoon, when the old lady was told that Karen had worn red shoes at her confirmation, she was much vexed, and told Karen that they were quite unsuitable, and that, henceforward, whenever she went to church, she must wear black shoes, were they ever so old.

Next Sunday was the communion day. Karen looked first at the red shoes, then at the black ones, then at the red again, and—put them on.

It was beautiful sunshiny weather; Karen and the old lady walked to church through the cornfields; the path was very dusty.

At the church door stood an old soldier; he was leaning on crutches, and had a marvellously long beard, not white, but reddish-hued, and he bowed almost to the earth, and asked the old lady if he might wipe the dust off her shoes. And Karen put out her little foot also. "Oh, what pretty dancing-shoes!" quoth the old soldier; "take care, and mind you do not let them slip off when you dance;" and he passed his hands over them.

The old lady gave the soldier a halfpenny, and then went with Karen into church.

And every one looked at Karen's red shoes; and all the carved figures, too, bent their gaze upon them; and when Karen knelt before the altar, the red shoes still floated before her eyes, she thought of them and of them only, and she forgot to join in the hymn of praise—she forgot to repeat "Our Father."

At last all the people came out of church, and the old lady got into her carriage. Karen was just lifting her foot to follow her, when the old soldier standing in the porch exclaimed, "Only look, what pretty dancing-shoes!" And Karen could not help it, she felt she must make a few of her dancing steps; and after she had once begun, her feet continued to move, just as though the shoes had received power over them; she danced round the churchyard, she could not stop. The coachman was obliged to run after her; he took hold of her and lifted her into the carriage, but the feet still continued to dance, so as to kick the good old lady most cruelly. At last the shoes were taken off, and the feet had the rest which they needed.

And now the shoes were put away in a press, but Karen could not help going to look at them every now and then.

The old lady lay ill in bed; the doctor said she could not live much longer. She certainly needed careful nursing, and who should be her nurse and constant attendant but Karen? But there was to be a grand ball in the town, Karen was invited; she looked at the old lady, who was almost dying—she looked at the red shoes—she put them on, there could be no harm in doing that, at least; she went to the ball, and began to dance. But when she wanted to move to the right, the shoes bore her to the left; and when she would dance up the room, the shoes danced down the room, danced down the stairs, through the streets, and through the gates of the town. Dance she did, and dance she must, straight out into the dark wood.

Something all at once shone through the trees. She thought at first it must be the moon's bright face, shining blood-red through the night mists; but no, it was the old soldier with the red beard—he sat there, nodding at her, and repeating, "Only look, what pretty dancing-shoes!"

She was very much frightened, and tried to throw off her red shoes, but could not unclasp them. She hastily tore off her stockings, but the shoes she could not get rid of—they had, it seemed, grown on to her feet. Dance she did, and dance she must, over field and meadow, in rain and in sunshine, by night and by day—by night! that was most horrible! She danced into the lonely churchyard, but the dead there danced not, they were at rest. She would fain have sat down on the poor man's grave, where the bitter tansy grew, but for her there was neither rest nor respite. She danced past the open church door; there she saw an angel, clad in long white robes, and with wings that reached from his shoulders to the earth; his countenance was grave and stern, and in his hand he held a broad glittering sword.

"Dance thou shalt," said he; "dance on, in thy red shoes, till thou art pale and cold, and thy skin shrinks and crumples up like a skeleton's! Dance thou shalt still, from door to door, and wherever proud, vain children live thou shalt knock, so that they may hear thee and fear! Dance shalt thou, dance on——"

"Mercy!" cried Karen; but she heard not the angel's answer, for the shoes carried her through the gate, into the fields, along highways and byways, and still she must dance.

One morning she danced past a door she knew well; she heard psalm-singing from within, and presently a coffin, strewn with flowers, was borne out. Then Karen knew that the good old lady was dead, and she felt herself a thing forsaken by all mankind, and accursed by the Angel of God.

Dance she did, and dance she must, even through the dark night; the shoes bore her continually over thorns and briers, till her limbs were torn and bleeding. Away she danced over the heath to a little solitary house; she knew that the headsman dwelt there, and she tapped with her fingers against the panes, crying—

"Come out! come out!—I cannot come in to you, I am dancing."

And the headsman replied, "Surely thou knowest not who I am. I cut off the heads of wicked men, and my axe is very sharp and keen."

"Cut not off my head!" said Karen, "for then I could not live to repent of my sin; but cut off my feet with the red shoes."

And then she confessed to him all her sin, and the headsman cut off her feet with the red shoes on them; but even after this the shoes still danced away with those little feet over the fields, and into the deep forests.

And the headsman made her a pair of wooden feet, and hewed down some boughs to serve her as crutches, and he taught her the psalm which is always repeated by criminals, and she kissed the hand that had guided the axe, and went her way over the heath. "Now I have certainly suffered quite enough through the red shoes," thought Karen, "I will go to church and let people see me once more!" and she went as fast as she could to the

9

church porch, but as she approached it, the red shoes danced before her, and she was frightened and turned her back.

All that week through she endured the keenest anguish and shed many bitter tears; however, when Sunday came, she said to herself, "Well, I must have suffered and striven enough by this time, I dare say I am quite as good as many of those who are holding their heads so high in church." So she took courage and went there, but she had not passed the churchyard gate before she saw the red shoes again dancing before her, and in great terror she again turned back, and more deeply than ever bewailed her sin.

She then went to the pastor's house, and begged that some employment might be given her, promising to work diligently and do all she could; she did not wish for any wages, she said, she only wanted a roof to shelter her, and to dwell with good people. And the pastor's wife had pity on her, and took her into her service. And Karen was grateful and industrious.

Every evening she sat silently listening to the pastor, while he read the Holy Scriptures aloud. All the children loved her, but when she heard them talk about dress and finery, and about being as beautiful as a queen, she would sorrowfully shake her head.

Again Sunday came, all the pastor's household went to church, and they asked her if she would not go too, but she sighed and looked with tears in her eyes upon her crutches.

When they were all gone, she went into her own little, lowly chamber—it was but just large enough to contain a bed and chair—and there she sat down with her psalm-book in her hand, and whilst she was meekly and devoutly reading in it, the wind wafted the tones of the organ from the church into her room, and she lifted up her face to heaven and prayed, with tears, "Oh, God, help me!"

10

Then the sun shone brightly, so brightly!—and behold! close before her stood the white-robed Angel of God, the same whom she had seen on that night of horror at the church porch, but his hand wielded not now, as then, a sharp, threatening sword—he held a lovely green bough, full of roses. With this he touched the ceiling, which immediately rose to a great height, a bright gold star spangling on the spot where the Angel's green bough had touched it. And he touched the walls, whereupon the room widened, and Karen saw the organ, the old monuments, and the congregation all sitting in their richly-carved seats and singing from their psalm-books.

For the church had come home to the poor girl in her narrow chamber, or rather the chamber had grown, as it were, into the church; she sat with the rest of the pastor's household, and, when the psalm was ended, they looked up and nodded to her, saying, "Thou didst well to come, Karen!"

"This is mercy!" said she.

And the organ played again, and the children's voices in the choir mingled so sweetly and plaintively with it! The bright sunbeams streamed warmly through the windows upon Karen's seat; her heart was so full of sunshine, of peace and gladness, that it broke; her soul flew upon a sunbeam to her Father in heaven, where not a look of reproach awaited her, not a word was breathed of the red shoes.

THE TINDER-BOX

A soldier was marching along the high-road—right, left! right, left! He had his knapsack on his back and a sword by his side, for he had been to the wars, and was now returning home. And on the road he met an old witch; a horrid-looking creature she was, her lower lip hung down almost to her neck.

"Good-evening, soldier!" she said. "What a bright sword, and what a large knapsack you have, my fine fellow! I'll tell you what; you shall have as much money for your own as you can wish!"

"Thanks, old witch!" cried the soldier.

"Do you see yonder large tree?" said the witch, pointing to a tree that stood close by the wayside. "It is quite hollow within. Climb up to the top, and you will find a hole large enough for you to creep through, and thus you will get down into the tree. I will tie a rope round your waist, so that I can pull you up again when you call me."

"But what am I to do down in the tree?" asked the soldier.

"What are you to do?" repeated the witch; "why, fetch money, to be sure! As soon as you get to the bottom, you will find yourself in a wide passage; it is quite light, more than a hundred lamps are burning there. Then you will see three doors; you can open them, the keys are in the locks. On opening the first door you will enter a room. In the midst of it, on the floor, lies a large chest; a dog is seated on it, his eyes are as large as teacups; but never you mind, don't trouble yourself about him! I will lend you my blue apron; you must spread it out on the floor, then go briskly up to the dog, seize him, and set him down on it; and after that is done, you can open the chest, and take as much money out of it as you please. That chest contains none but copper coins; but if you like silver better, you have only to go into the next room; there you will find a dog with eyes as large as mill-wheels, but don't be afraid of him; you have only to set him down on my apron, and then rifle the chest at your leisure. But if you would rather have gold than either silver or copper, that is to be had too, and as much of it as you can carry, if you

12

pass on into the third chamber. The dog that sits on this third money-chest has two eyes, each as large as the Round Tower. A famous creature he is, as you may fancy; but don't be alarmed, just set him down on my apron, and then he will do you no harm, and you can take as much golden treasure from the chest as you like."

"Not a bad plan that, upon my word!" said the soldier. "But how much of the money am I to give you, old woman? For you'll want your full share of the plunder, I've a notion!"

"Not a penny will I have," returned the witch. "The only thing I want you to bring me is an old tinder-box which my grandmother left there by mistake last time she was down in the tree."

"Well then, give me the rope to tie round my waist, and I'll be gone," said the soldier.

"Here it is," said the witch, "and here is my blue apron."

So the soldier climbed the tree, let himself down through the hole in the trunk, and suddenly found himself in the wide passage, lighted up by many hundred lamps, as the witch had described.

He opened the first door. Bravo! There sat he dog with eyes as large as teacups, staring at him as though in utter amazement.

"There's a good creature!" quoth the soldier, as he spread the witch's apron on the floor, and lifted the dog upon it. He then filled his pockets with the copper coins in the chest, shut the lid, put the dog back into his place, and passed on into the second apartment.

Huzza! There sat the dog with eyes as large as mill-wheels.

"You had really better not stare at me so," remarked the soldier; "it will make your eyes weak!" and herewith he set the dog down on the witch's apron. But when, on raising the lid of the chest, he beheld the vast quantity of silver money it contained, he threw all his pence away in disgust, and hastened to fill his pockets and his knapsack with the pure silver. And he passed on into the third chamber. Now, indeed, that was terrifying! The dog in this chamber actually had a pair of eyes each as large as the Round Tower, and they kept rolling round and round in his head like wheels.

"Good-evening!" said the soldier, and he lifted his cap respectfully, for such a monster of a dog as this he had never in his life before seen or heard of. He stood still for a minute or two, looking at him, then thinking, "the sooner it's done the better!" He took hold of the immense creature, removed him from the chest to the floor, and raised the lid of the chest. Oh, what a sight of gold was there! enough to buy not only all Copenhagen, but all the cakes and sugar-plums, all the tin soldiers, whips and rocking-horses in the world! Yes, he must be satisfied now. Hastily the soldier threw out all the silver money he had stuffed into his pockets and knapsack, and took gold instead; not only his pockets and knapsack, but his soldier's cap and boots he crammed full of gold, bright gold! heavy gold! he could hardly walk for the weight he carried. He lifted the dog on the chest again, banged the door of the room behind him, and called out through the tree:

"Hullo, you old witch! pull me up again!"

"Have you got the tinder-box?" asked the witch.

"Upon my honour, I'd quite forgotten it!" shouted the soldier, and back he went to fetch it. The witch then drew him up through the tree, and now he again stood in the high road, his pockets, boots, knapsack, and cap, stuffed with gold pieces.

"Just tell me now, what are you going to do with the tinder-box?" inquired the soldier.

"That's no concern of yours," returned the witch. "You've got your money; give me my tinder-box this instant!"

"Well, take your choice," said the soldier. "Either tell me at once what you want with the tinder-box, or I draw my sword, and cut off your head."

"I won't tell you!" screamed the witch.

So the soldier drew his sword and cut off her head. There she lay; but he did not waste time in looking at what he had done; he made haste to knot all his money securely in the witch's blue apron, made a bundle of it, and slung it across his back, put the tinder-box into his pocket, and went straight to the nearest town.

It was a large, handsome town; a city, in fact. He walked into the first hotel in the place, called for the best rooms, and ordered the choicest and most expensive dishes for his supper, for he was now a rich man, with plenty of gold to spend.

The servant who cleaned the boots could not help thinking they were disgracefully shabby and worn to belong to such a grand gentleman; however, next day he provided himself with new boots and very gay clothes besides. Our soldier was now a great man, and the people of the hotel were called in to give him information about all the places of amusement in the city, and about their King, and the beautiful Princess, his daughter.

"I should rather like to see her!" observed the soldier; "just tell me when I can?"

"No one can see her at all," was the reply; "she dwells in a great copper palace, with ever so many walls and towers round it. No one but the King may go and visit her there, because it has been foretold that she will marry a common soldier, and our King would not like that at all."

"Shouldn't I like to see her though, just for once!" thought the soldier, but it was of no use for him to wish it.

And now he lived such a merry life! went continually to the theatre, drove out in the Royal Gardens, and gave

15

so much money in alms to the poor—to all, in fact, who asked him. And this was well done in him; to be sure, he knew by past experience how miserable it was not to have a shilling in one's pocket. He was always gaily dressed, and had such a crowd of friends, who, one and all, declared he was a most capital fellow, a real gentleman; and that pleased our soldier uncommonly. But, as he was now giving and spending every day, and never received anything in return, his money began to fail him, and at last he had only twopence left, and was forced to remove from the splendid apartments where he had lodged hitherto, and take refuge in a little bit of an attic-chamber, where he had to brush his boots and darn his clothes himself, and where none of his friends ever came to see him, because there were so many stairs to go up, it was quite fatiguing.

It was a very dark evening, and he could not afford to buy himself as much as a rushlight; however, he remembered, all at once, that there were a few matches lying in the tinder-box that the old witch had bade him fetch out of the hollow tree. So he brought out this tinder-box and began to strike a light; but no sooner had he rubbed the flint-stone and made the sparks fly out than the door burst suddenly open, and the dog with eyes as large as teacups, and which he had seen in the cavern beneath the tree, stood before him and said, "What commands has my master for his slave?"

"Upon my honour, this is a pretty joke!" cried the soldier; "a fine sort of tinder-box this is, if it will really provide me with whatever I want. Fetch me some money this instant!" said he to the dog; whereupon the creature vanished, and lo! in half a minute he was back again, holding in his mouth a large bag full of pence.

So now the soldier understood the rare virtue of this charming tinder-box. If he struck the flint only once, the dog that sat on the chest full of copper came to him; if he struck it twice, the dog that watched over the silver answered his summons; and if he struck it three times, he was forthwith attended by the monstrous guardian of the golden treasure.

The soldier could now remove back to his princely apartments, he bought himself an entirely new suit of clothes, and all his friends remembered him again, and loved him as much as ever. But one evening the thought occurred to him, "How truly ridiculous it is that no one should be allowed to see this Princess! They all say she is so very beautiful; what a shame it is that she should be shut up in that great copper palace with the towers guarding it round! And I do so want to see her—where's my tinder-box, by-the-bye?" He struck the flint, and lo! before him stood the dog with eyes as large as teacups.

"It is rather late, I must own," began the soldier; "but I do want to see the Princess so much, only for one minute, you know!"

And the dog was out of the door, and, before the soldier had time to think of what he should say or do, he was back again with the Princess sitting asleep on his back. A real Princess was this, so beautiful, so enchantingly beautiful! the soldier could not help himself, he knelt down and kissed her hand.

The dog ran back to the palace with the Princess that very minute; however, next morning while she was at breakfast with the King and Queen, the Princess said that she had had such a strange dream during the past night. She had dreamt that she was riding on a dog, an enormously large dog, and that a soldier had knelt down to her, and kissed her hand.

"A pretty sort of a dream, indeed!" exclaimed the Queen.

And she insisted that one of the old ladies of the court should watch by the Princess's bedside on the following night, in case she should again be disturbed by dreams.

The soldier longed so exceedingly to see the fair Princess of the copper palace again; accordingly, next evening, the dog was summoned to fetch her. So he did, and ran as fast as he could; however, not so fast but that the ancient dame watching at the Princess's couch found time to put on a pair of waterproof boots before running after them. She saw the dog vanish in a large house; then, thinking to herself, "Now I know what to do," she took out a piece of chalk and made a great white cross on the door. She then went home and betook herself to rest, and the Princess was home almost as soon. But on his way the dog chanced to observe the white cross on the door of the hotel where the soldier lived; so he immediately took another piece of chalk and set crosses on every door throughout the town. And this was wisely done on his part.

Early in the morning came out the King, the Queen, the old Court dame, and all the officers of the royal household, every one of them curious to see where the Princess had been.

"Here it is!" exclaimed the King, as soon as he saw the first street-door with a cross chalked on it.

"My dear, where are your eyes?—this is the house," cried the Queen, seeing the second door bear a cross.

"No, this is it surely—why, here's a cross too!" cried all of them together, on discovering that there were crosses on all the doors. It was evident that their search would be in vain, and they were obliged to give it up.

But the Queen was an exceedingly wise and prudent woman; she was good for something besides sitting in a state carriage, and looking very grand and condescending. She now took her gold scissors, cut a large piece of silk stuff into strips and sewed these strips together, to make a pretty, neat little bag. This bag she filled with the finest, whitest flour, and with her own hands tied it to the Princess's waist, and when this was done, again took up

18

her golden scissors and cut a little hole in the bag, just large enough to let the flour drop out gradually all the time the Princess was moving.

That evening the dog came again, took the Princess on his back, and ran away with her to the soldier. Oh, how the soldier loved her, and how he wished he were a prince, that he might have this beautiful Princess for his wife!

The dog never perceived how the flour went drip, drip, dripping, all the way from the palace to the soldier's room, and from the soldier's room back to the palace. So next morning the King and Queen could easily discover where their daughter had been carried, and they took the soldier and cast him into prison.

And now he sat in the prison. Oh! how dark it was, and how wearisome! and the turnkey kept coming in to remind him that tomorrow he was to be hanged. This piece of news was by no means agreeable; and the tinder-box had been left in his lodgings at the hotel.

When morning came, he could, through his narrow iron grating, watch the people all hurrying out of the town to see him hanged; he could hear the drums beating, and presently, too, he saw the soldiers marching to the place of execution. What a crowd there was rushing by! among the rest was a shoemaker's apprentice in his leathern apron and slippers; he bustled on with such speed that one of his slippers flew off and bounded against the iron staves of the soldier's prison window.

"Stop, stop, little 'prentice!" cried the soldier; "it's of no use for you to be in such a hurry, for none of the fun will begin till I come, but if you'll oblige me by running to my lodgings and fetching me my tinder-box, I'll give you twopence. But you must run for your life!" The shoemaker's boy liked the idea of earning twopence, so away he raced after the tinder-box, returned, and gave it to the soldier, and then—ah, yes, now we shall hear what happened then.

Outside the city a gibbet had been erected; round it were marshalled the soldiers with many hundred thousand people, men, women, and children; the King and Queen were seated on magnificent thrones, exactly opposite the judges and the whole assembled council.

Already had the soldier mounted the topmost step of the ladder; already was the executioner on the point of fitting the rope round his neck, when, turning to their Majesties, he began to entreat most earnestly that they would suffer a poor criminal's innocent fancy to be gratified before he underwent his punishment. He wished so much, he said, to smoke a pipe of tobacco, and as it was the last pleasure he could enjoy in this world, he hoped it would not be denied him.

The King could not refuse this harmless request, accordingly the soldier took out his tinder-box and struck the flint—once he struck it, twice he struck it, three times he struck it!—and lo! all the three wizard dogs stood before him, the dog with eyes as large as teacups, the dog with eyes as large as mill-wheels, and the dog with eyes each as large as the Round Tower!

"Now, help me, don't let me be hanged!" cried the soldier. And forthwith the three terrible dogs fell upon the judges and councillors, tossing them high into the air, so high that on falling down to the ground again they were broken in pieces.

"We will not——" began the king, but the monster dog with eyes as large as the Round Tower did not wait to hear what his Majesty would not; he seized both him and the Queen, and flung them up into the air after the councillors. And the soldiers were all desperately frightened, and the people shouted out with one voice, "Good soldier, you shall be our King, and the beautiful Princess shall be your wife, and our Queen!"

So the soldier was conducted into the royal carriage, and all the three dogs bounded to and fro in front, little boys whistled upon their fingers, and the guards presented arms. The Princess was forthwith sent for and made Queen, which she liked much better than living a prisoner in the copper palace. The bridal festivities lasted for eight whole days, and the three wizard dogs sat at the banquet table, staring about them with their great eyes.

THE SHEPHERDESS AND THE CHIMNEY-SWEEPER

Have you never seen an old-fashioned oaken-wood cabinet, quite black with age and covered with varnish and carving work? Just such a piece of furniture, an old heirloom that had been the property of its present mistress's great-grandmother, once stood in a parlour. It was carved from top to bottom—roses, tulips, and little stags' heads with long, branching antlers, peering forth from the curious scrolls and foliage surrounding them. Moreover, in the centre panel of the cabinet was carved the full-length figure of a man, who seemed to be perpetually grinning, perhaps at himself, for in truth he was a most ridiculous figure; he had crooked legs, small horns on his forehead, and a long beard. The children of the house used to call him "the crooked-legged Field-marshal-Major-General-Corporal-Sergeant," for this was a long, hard name, and not many figures, whether carved in wood or in stone, could boast of such a title. There he stood, his eyes always fixed upon the table under the pier-glass, for on this table stood a pretty little porcelain shepherdess, her mantle gathered gracefully round her, and fastened with a red rose; her shoes and hat were gilt, her hand held a crook—oh, she was charming! Close by her stood a little chimney-sweeper, likewise of porcelain. He was as clean and neat as any of the other figures, indeed, the manufacturer might just as well have made a prince as a chimney-sweeper of him, for though elsewhere black as a coal, his face was as fresh and rosy as a girl's, which was certainly a mistake,—it ought to have been black. His ladder in his hand, there he kept his station, close by the little shepherdess; they had been placed together from the first, had always remained on the same spot, and had thus plighted their troth to each other; they suited each other so well, they were both young people, both of the same kind of porcelain, both alike fragile and delicate.

Not far off stood a figure three times as large as the others. It was an old Chinese mandarin who could nod his head; he too was of porcelain, and declared that he was grandfather to the little shepherdess. He could not prove his assertion; however, he insisted that he had authority over her, and so, when "the crooked-legged Field-marshal-Major-General-Corporal-Sergeant" made proposals to the little shepherdess, he nodded his head in token of his consent.

"Now, you will have a husband," said the old mandarin to her, "a husband who, I verily believe, is of mahogany wood; you will be the wife of a Field-marshal-Major-General-Corporal-Sergeant, of a man who has a whole cabinet full of silver plate, besides a store of no one knows what in the secret drawers!"

"I will not go into that dismal cabinet!" declared the little shepherdess. "I have heard say that eleven porcelain ladies are already imprisoned there."

"Then you shall be the twelfth, and you will be in good company!" rejoined the mandarin. "This very night, when the old cabinet creaks, your nuptials shall be celebrated, as sure as I am a Chinese mandarin!"

Whereupon he nodded his head and fell asleep.

But the little shepherdess wept, and turned to the beloved of her heart, the porcelain chimney-sweep.

"I believe I must ask you," said she, "to go out with me into the wide world, for here we cannot stay."

"I will do everything you wish," replied the little chimney-sweeper; "let us go at once. I think I can support you by my profession."

"If you could but get off the table!" sighed she; "I shall never be happy till we are away, out in the wide world."

And he comforted her, and showed her how to set her little foot on the carved edges and gilded foliage twining round the leg of the table, till at last they reached the floor. But turning to look at the old cabinet, they saw everything in a grand commotion, all the carved stags putting their little heads farther out, raising their antlers, and moving their throats, whilst the crooked-legged Field-marshal-Major-General-Corporal-Sergeant sprang up, and shouted out to the old Chinese mandarin, "Look, they are eloping! they are eloping!" They were not a little frightened, and quickly jumped into an open drawer for protection.

In this drawer there were three or four incomplete packs of cards, and also a little puppet-theatre; a play was being performed, and all the queens, whether of diamonds, hearts, clubs or spades, sat in the front row fanning themselves with the flowers they held in their hands; behind them stood the knaves, showing that they had each two heads, one above and one below, as most cards have. The play was about two persons who were crossed in love, and the sherpherdess wept over it, for it was just like her own history.

"I cannot bear this!" said she. "Let us leave the drawer." But when they had again reached the floor, on looking up at the table, they saw that the old Chinese mandarin had awakened, and was rocking his whole body to and fro with rage.

"Oh, the old mandarin is coming!" cried the little shepherdess, and down she fell on her porcelain knees in the greatest distress. "A sudden thought has struck me," said the chimney-sweeper, "suppose we creep into the large pot-pourri vase that stands in the corner: there we can rest upon roses and lavender, and throw salt in his eyes if he comes near us."

"That will not do at all," said she: "besides, I know that the old mandarin was once betrothed to the pot-pourri vase, and no doubt there is still some slight friendship existing between them. No, there is no help for it, we must wander forth together into the wide world."

"Hast thou indeed the courage to go with me into the wide world?" asked the chimney-sweeper. "Hast thou considered how large it is, and that we may never return home again?"

"I have," replied she.

And the chimney-sweeper looked keenly at her, and then said, "My path leads through the chimney; hast thou indeed the courage to creep with me through the stove, through the flues and the tunnel? Well do I know the way! We shall mount up so high that they cannot come near us, and at the top there is a cavern that leads into the wide world."

And he led her to the door of the stove.

"Oh, how black it looks!" sighed she; however, she went on with him, through the flues and through the tunnel, where it was dark, pitch dark.

"Now we are in the chimney," said he; "and look, what a lovely star shines above us!"

And there was actually a star in the sky, shining right down upon them, as if to show them the way. And they crawled and crept—a fearful path was theirs—so high, so very high! but he guided and supported her, and showed her the best places whereon to plant her tiny porcelain feet, till they reached the edge of the chimney, where they sat down to rest, for they were very tired, and indeed not without reason.

Heaven with all its stars was above them, and the town with all its roofs lay beneath them; the wide, wide world surrounded them. The poor shepherdess had never imagined all this; she leant her little head on her chimney-sweeper's arm, and wept so vehemently that the gilding broke off from her waistband.

"This is too much!" exclaimed she. "This can I not endure! The world is all too large! Oh that I were once more upon the little table under the pier-glass! I shall never be happy till I am there again. I have followed thee out into the wide world, surely thou canst follow me home again, if thou lovest me!"

And the chimney-sweeper talked very sensibly to her, reminding her of the old Chinese mandarin and "the crooked-legged Field-marshal-Major-General-Corporal-Sergeant," but she wept so bitterly, and kissed her little chimney-sweeper so fondly, that at last he could not but yield to her request, unreasonable as it was.

So with great difficulty they crawled down the chimney, crept through the flues and the tunnel, and at length found themselves once more in the dark stove; but they still lurked behind the door, listening, before they would venture to return into the room. Everything was quite still; they peeped out: also! on the ground lay the old Chinese mandarin. In attempting to follow the runaways, he had fallen down off the table and had broken into three pieces; his head lay shaking in a corner; "the crooked-legged Field-marshal-Major-General-Corporal-Sergeant" stood where he had always stood, thinking over what had happened.

"Oh, how shocking!" exclaimed the little shepherdess, "old grandfather is broken in pieces, and we are the cause! I shall never survive it!" and she wrung her delicate hands.

"He can be put together again," replied the chimney-sweeper. "He can very easily be put together; only be not

25

so impatient! If they glue his back together, and put a strong rivet in his neck, then he will be as good as new again, and will be able to say plenty of unpleasant things to us."

"Do you really think so?" asked she. And then they climbed up the table to the place where they had stood before.

"See how far we have been!" observed the chimney-sweeper, "we might have spared ourselves all the trouble."

"If we could but have old grandfather put together!" said the shepherdess. "Will it cost very much?"

And he was put together; the family had his back glued and his neck riveted; he was as good as new, but could no longer nod his head.

"You have certainly grown very proud since you broke in pieces!" remarked the crooked-legged Field-marshal-Major-General-Corporal-Sergeant, "but I must say, for my part, I do not see that there is anything to be proud of. Am I to have her or am I not? Just answer me that!"

And the chimney-sweeper and the little shepherdess looked imploringly at the old mandarin; they were so afraid lest he should nod his head, but nod he could not, and it was disagreeable to him to tell a stranger that he had a rivet in his neck, so the young porcelain people always remained together, they blessed the grandfather's rivet, and loved each other till they broke in pieces.

THE CONSTANT TIN SOLDIER

There were once five-and-twenty tin soldiers, all brothers, for they had all been made out of one old tin spoon. They carried muskets in their hands, and held themselves very upright, and their uniforms were red and blue—very gay indeed. The first word that they heard in this world, when the lid was taken off the box wherein they lay, was "Tin soldiers!" It was a little boy who made this exclamation, clapping his hands at the same time. They had been given to him because it was his birthday, and he now set them out on the table. The soldiers resembled each other to a hair, one only was rather different from the rest; he had but one leg, for he had been made last, when there was not quite tin enough left; however, he stood as firmly upon his one leg as the others did upon their two; and this identical tin soldier it is whose fortunes seem to us worthy of record.

On the table where the tin soldiers were set out were several other playthings, but the most charming of them all was a pretty pasteboard castle. Through its little windows one could look into the rooms. In front of the castle stood some tiny trees, clustering round a little mirror intended to represent a lake, and waxen swans swam in the lake and were reflected on its surface. All this was very pretty, but prettiest of all was a little damsel standing in the open doorway of the castle; she, too, was cut out of pasteboard, but she had on a frock of the clearest muslin, a little sky-blue riband was flung across her shoulders like a scarf, and in the midst of this scarf was set a bright gold wing. The little lady stretched out both her arms, for she was a dancer, and raised one of her legs so high in the air that the tin soldier could not find it, and fancied that she had, like him, only one leg.

"That would be just the wife for me," thought he, "but then, she is of rather too high rank; she lives in a castle. I have only a box, besides, there are all our five-and-twenty men in it; it is no place for her! However, there will be no harm in my making acquaintance with her!" and so he stationed himself behind a snuff-box that stood on the table; from this place he had a full view of the delicate little lady, who still remained standing on one leg, yet without losing her balance.

When evening came, all the other tin soldiers were put away into the box, and the people of the house went to bed. The playthings now began to play in their turn; they pretended to visit, to fight battles, and give balls. The tin soldiers rattled in the box, for they wanted to play too, but the lid would not come off. The nutcrackers cut capers, and the slate-pencil played at commerce on the slate; there was such a racket that the canary bird waked up, and began to talk, too, but he always talked in verse. The only two who did not move from their places were the tin soldier and the little dancer; she constantly remained in her graceful position, standing on the point of her foot, with outstretched arms; and, as for him, he stood just as firmly on his one leg, never for one moment turning his eyes away from her.

Twelve o'clock struck. Crash! Open sprang the lid of the snuff-box, but there was no snuff inside it! no, out jumped a little black conjuror, in fact it was a Jack-in-the-box. "Tin soldier!" said the conjuror, "wilt thou keep thine eyes to thyself?"

But the tin soldier pretended not to hear.

"Well, only wait till tomorrow!" quoth the conjuror.

When the morrow had come, and the children were out of bed, the tin soldier was placed on the window-ledge, and, whether the conjuror or the wind occasioned it, all at once the window flew open, and out fell the tin soldier, head foremost, from the third storey to the ground. A dreadful fall was that! His one leg turned over and over in the air, and at last he rested, poised on his soldier's cap, with his bayonet between two paving-stones.

The maid-servant and the little boy immediately came down to look for him; but although they very nearly trod on him, they could not see him. If the tin soldier had but called out "Here I am!" they might easily have found him; but he thought it would not be becoming for him to cry out, as he was in uniform.

It now began to rain; every drop fell heavier than the last; there was a regular shower. When it was over, two boys came by. "Look," said one, "here is a tin soldier, he shall have a sail for once in his life."

So they made a boat out of an old newspaper, put the tin soldier into it, and away he sailed down the gutter, both the boys running along by the side and clapping their hands. The paper boat rocked to and fro, and every now and then veered round so quickly that the tin soldier became quite giddy; still he moved not a muscle, looked straight before him, and held his bayonet tightly clasped.

All at once the boat sailed under a long gutter-board; he found it as dark here as at home in his own box.

"Where shall l get to next?" thought he; "yes, to be sure, it is all that conjuror's doing! Ah, if the little maiden were but sailing with me in the boat I would not care for its being twice as dark!"

Just then a great water-rat that lived under the gutter-board darted out.

"Have you a passport?" asked the rat. "Where is your passport?"

But the tin soldier was silent, and held his weapon with a still firmer grasp. The boat sailed on, and the rat followed. Oh! how furiously he showed his teeth, and cried out to sticks and straws, "Stop him, stop him! he has not paid the toll, he has not shown his passport!" But the stream grew stronger and stronger. The tin soldier could already catch a glimpse of the bright daylight before the boat came from under the tunnel, but at the same time he heard a roaring noise, at which the boldest heart might well have trembled. Only fancy! where the tunnel ended, the water of the gutter fell perpendicularly into a great canal; this was as dangerous for the tin soldier as sailing down a mighty waterfall would be for us.

He was now so close that he could no longer stand upright; the boat darted forwards, the poor tin soldier held himself as stiff and immovable as possible, no one could accuse him of having even blinked. The boat spun round and round three, nay, four times, and was filled with water to the brim; it must sink. The tin soldier stood up to his neck in water, deeper and deeper sank the boat, softer and softer grew the paper; the water went over the soldier's head, he thought of the pretty little dancer whom he should never see again, and these words rang in his ears:

> "Wild adventure, mortal danger,
> Be thy portion, valiant stranger!"

The paper now tore asunder, the tin soldier fell through the rent; but, in the same moment, he was swallowed up by a large fish. Oh, how dark it was! worse even than under the gutter-board, and so narrow, too! but the tin soldier's resolution was as constant as ever; there he lay, at full length, shouldering his arms.

The fish turned and twisted about, and made the strangest movements. At last he became quite still; a flash of lightning, as it were, darted through him. The daylight shone brightly, and some one exclaimed, "Tin soldier!" The fish had been caught, taken to the market, sold, and brought home into the kitchen, where the servant-girl was cutting him up with a large knife. She seized the tin soldier by the middle with two of her fingers, and took him into the parlour, where every one was eager to see the wonderful man who had travelled in the maw of a fish; however, our little warrior was by no means proud. They set him on the table, and there—no, how could anything so extraordinary happen in this world?—the tin soldier was in the very same room in which he had been before; he saw the same children, the same playthings stood on the table, among them the beautiful castle with the pretty little dancing maiden, who was still standing upon one leg, whilst she held the other high in the air; she too was constant. It quite affected the tin soldier; he could have found it in his heart to weep tin tears, but such weakness would have been unbecoming in a soldier. He looked at her and she looked at him, but neither of them spoke a word.

And now one of the little boys took the soldier and threw him without ceremony into the stove. He did not give any reason for so doing, but no doubt the conjuror in the snuff-box must have had a hand in it.

The tin soldier now stood in a blaze of red light; he felt extremely hot. Whether this heat were the result of the actual fire or of the flames of love within him, he knew not. He had entirely lost his colour. Whether this change had happened during his travels, or were the effect of strong emotion, I know not. He looked upon the little damsel, she looked upon him, and he felt that he was melting; but, constant as ever, he still stood shouldering his arms. A door opened, the wind seized the dancer, and, like a sylph, she flew straightway into the stove, to the tin soldier; they both flamed up into a blaze, and were gone. The soldier was melted to a hard lump, and when the maid took out the ashes the next day she found his remains in the shape of a little tin heart; of the dancer there remained only the gold wing, and that was burnt black as coal.

THE LITTLE MERMAID

Far out in the wide sea,—where the water is blue as the loveliest cornflower, and clear as the purest crystal, where it is so deep that very, very many church-towers must be heaped one upon another, in order to reach from the lowest depth to the surface above,—dwell the Mer-people.

Now you must not imagine that there is nothing but sand below the water: no, indeed, far from it! Trees and plants of wondrous beauty grow there, whose stems and leaves are so light, that they are waved to and fro by the slightest motion of the water, almost as if they were living beings. Fishes, great and small, glide in and out among the branches, just as birds fly about among our trees.

Where the water is deepest, stands the palace of the Mer-king. The walls of this palace are of coral, and the high, pointed windows are of amber; the roof, however, is composed of mussel-shells, which, as the billows pass over them, are continually opening and shutting. This looks exceedingly pretty, especially as each of these mussel-shells contains a number of bright, glittering pearls, one only of which would be the most costly ornament in the diadem of a king in the upper world.

The Mer-king, who lived in this palace, had been for many years a widower; his old mother managed the household affairs for him. She was, on the whole, a sensible sort of a lady, although extremely proud of her high birth and station, on which account she wore twelve oysters on her tail, whilst the other inhabitants of the sea, even those of distinction, were allowed only six. In every other respect she merited unlimited praise, especially for the affection she showed to the six little princesses, her granddaughters. These were all very beautiful children; the youngest was, however, the most lovely; her skin was as soft and delicate as a rose-petal, her eyes were of as deep a blue as the sea, but like all other mermaids, she had no feet; her body ended in a tail like that of a fish.

The whole day long the children used to play in the spacious apartments of the palace, where beautiful flowers grew out of the walls on all sides around them. When the great amber windows were opened, fishes would swim into these apartments as swallows fly into our rooms; but the fishes were bolder than the swallows;

they swam straight up to the little princesses, ate from their hands, and allowed themselves to be caressed.

In front of the palace there was a large garden, full of fiery red and dark blue trees, whose fruit glittered like gold, and whose flowers resembled a bright, burning sun. The sand that formed the soil of the garden was of a bright blue colour, something like flames of sulphur; and a strangely beautiful blue was spread over the whole so that one might have fancied oneself raised very high in the air, with the sky at once above and below, certainly not at the bottom of the sea. When the waters were quite still the sun might be seen looking like a purple flower, out of whose cup streamed forth the light of the world.

Each of the little princesses had her own plot in the garden, where she might plant and sow at her pleasure. One chose hers to be made in the shape of a whale, another preferred the figure of a mermaid, but the youngest had hers quite round like the sun, and planted in it only those flowers that were red, as the sun seemed to her. She was certainly a singular child, very quiet and thoughtful. Whilst her sisters were adorning themselves with all sorts of gay things that came out of a ship which had been wrecked, she asked for nothing but a beautiful white marble statue of a boy, which had been found in it. She put the statue in her garden, and planted a red weeping willow by its side. The tree grew up quickly, and let its long boughs fall upon the bright blue ground, where ever-moving shadows played in violet hues, as if boughs and root were embracing.

Nothing pleased the little princess more than to hear about the world of human beings living above the sea. She made her old grandmother tell her everything she knew about ships, towns, men, and land animals, and was particularly pleased when she heard that the flowers of the upper world had a pleasant fragrance (for the flowers of the sea are scentless), and that the woods were green, and the fishes fluttering among the branches of various gay colours, and that they could sing with a loud clear voice. The old lady meant birds, but she called them fishes, because her grandchildren, having never seen a bird, would not otherwise have understood her.

"When you have attained your fifteenth year," added she, "you will be permitted to rise to the surface of the sea; you will then sit by moonlight in the clefts of the rocks, see the ships sail by, and learn to distinguish towns and men."

The next year the eldest of the sisters reached this happy age, but the others—alas! the second sister was a year younger than the eldest, the third a year younger than the second, and so on; the youngest had still five whole years to wait till that joyful time should come when she also might rise to the surface of the water and see what was going on in the upper world; however, the eldest promised to tell the others of everything she might see, when the first day of her being of age arrived; for the grandmother gave them but little information, and there was so much that they wished to hear.

But none of all the sisters longed so ardently for the day when she should be released from childish restraint as the youngest: she who had longest to wait, and was so quiet and thoughtful. Many a night she stood by the open window, looking up through the clear blue water, whilst the fishes were leaping and playing around her. She could see the sun and the moon; their light was pale, but they appeared larger than they do to those who live in the upper world. If a shadow passed over them, she knew it must be either a whale or a ship sailing by full of human beings, who indeed little thought that, far beneath them, a little mermaiden was passionately stretching forth her white hands towards their ship's keel.

The day had now arrived when the eldest princess had attained her fifteenth year, and was therefore allowed to rise up to the surface of the sea.

When she returned she had a thousand things to relate. Her chief pleasure had been to sit upon a sandbank in the moonlight, looking at the large town which lay on the coast, where lights were beaming like stars, and where music was playing; she had heard the distant noise of men and carriages, she had seen the high church-towers, had listened to the ringing of the bells; and just because she could not go there she longed the more after all these things.

How attentively did her youngest sister listen to her words. And when she next stood at night-time, by her open window, gazing upwards through the blue waters, she thought so intensely of the great noisy city that she fancied she could hear the church-bells ringing.

Next year the second sister received permission to swim wherever she pleased. She rose to the surface of the sea, just when the sun was setting; and this sight so delighted her, that she declared it to be more beautiful than anything else she had seen above the waters.

"The whole sky seemed tinged with gold," said she, "and it is impossible for me to describe to you the beauty of the clouds. Now red, now violet, they glided over me; but still more swiftly flew over the water a flock of white swans, just where the sun was descending; I looked after them, but the sun disappeared, and the bright rosy light on the surface of the sea and on the edges of the clouds was gradually extinguished."

It was now time for the third sister to visit the upper world. She was the boldest of the six, and ventured up a river. On its shores she saw green hills covered with woods and vineyards, from among which arose houses and castles; she heard the birds singing, and the sun shone with so much power, that she was continually obliged to plunge below, in order to cool her burning face. In a little bay she met with a number of children, who were bathing and jumping about; she would have joined in their gambols, but the children fled back to land in great terror, and a little black animal barked at her in such a manner, that she herself was frightened at last, and swam back to the sea. She could not, however, forget the green woods, the verdant hills, and the pretty children, who, although they had no fins, were swimming about in the river so fearlessly.

The fourth sister was not so bold; she remained in the open sea, and said on her return home, she thought nothing could be more beautiful. She had seen ships sailing by, so far off that they looked like seagulls; she had watched the merry dolphins gambolling in the water, and the enormous whales, sending up into the air a thousand sparkling fountains.

The year after, the fifth sister attained her fifteenth year. Her birthday happened at a different season to that of her sisters; it was winter, the sea was of a green colour, and immense icebergs were floating on its surface. These, she said, looked like pearls; they were, however, much larger than the church-towers in the land of human beings. She sat down upon one of these pearls, and let the wind play with her long hair, but then all the ships hoisted their sails in terror and escaped as quickly as possible. In the evening the sky was covered with sails; and whilst the great mountains of ice alternately sank and rose again, and beamed with a reddish glow, flashes of lightning burst forth from the clouds, and the thunder rolled on, peal after peal. The sails of all the ships were instantly furled, and horror and fear reigned on board, but the princess sat still on the iceberg, looking unconcernedly at the blue zigzag of the flashes.

The first time that any of these sisters rose out of the sea, she was quite enchanted at the sight of so many new and beautiful objects, but the novelty was soon over, and it was not long ere their own home appeared more attractive than the upper world, for there only did they find everything agreeable.

Many an evening would the five sisters rise hand in hand from the depths of the ocean. Their voices were far sweeter than any human voice, and when a storm was coming on, they would swim in front of the ships, and sing,—oh! how sweetly did they sing!—describing the happiness of those who lived at the bottom of the sea, and entreating the sailors not to be afraid, but to come down to them.

The mariners, however, did not understand their words; they fancied the song was only the whistling of the wind, and thus they lost the hidden glories of the sea; for if their ships were wrecked, all on board were drowned, and none but dead men ever entered the Mer-king's palace.

Whilst the sisters were swimming at evening time, the youngest would remain motionless and alone, in her father's palace, looking up after them. She would have wept, but mermaids cannot weep, and therefore, when they are troubled, suffer infinitely more than human beings do.

"Oh! if I were but fifteen!" sighed she, "I know that I should love the upper world and its inhabitants so much."

At last the time she had so longed for arrived.

"Well, now, it is your turn," said the grandmother, "come here that I may adorn you like your sisters." And she wound around her hair a wreath of white lilies, whose every petal was the half of a pearl, and then commanded eight large oysters to fasten themselves to the princess's tail, in token of her high rank.

"But that is so very uncomfortable!" said the little princess.

"One must not mind slight inconveniences when one wishes to look well," said the old lady.

How willingly would the princess have given up all this splendour, and exchanged her heavy crown for the red flowers of her garden, which were so much more becoming to her. But she dared not do so. "Farewell," said she; and she rose from the sea, light as a flake of foam.

When, for the first time in her life, she appeared on the surface of the water, the sun had just sunk below the horizon, the clouds were beaming with bright golden and rosy hues, the evening star was shining in the pale western sky, the air was mild and refreshing, and the sea as smooth as a looking-glass. A large ship with three masts lay on the still waters; one sail only was unfurled, but not a breath was stirring, and the sailors were quietly seated on the cordage and ladders of the vessel. Music and song resounded from the deck, and after it grew dark hundreds of lamps all of a sudden burst forth into light, whilst innumerable flags were fluttering overhead. The little mermaid swam close up to the captain's cabin, and every now and then when the ship was raised by the motion of the water, she could look through the clear window panes. She saw within many richly-dressed men; the handsomest among them was a young prince with large black eyes. He could not certainly be more than sixteen years old, and it was in honour of his birthday that a grand festival was being celebrated. The crew were dancing on the deck, and when the young prince appeared among them, a hundred rockets were sent up into the air, turning night into day, and so terrifying the little mermaid, that for some minutes she plunged beneath the water. However, she soon raised her little head again, and then it seemed as if all the stars were falling down upon her. Such a fiery shower she had never even seen before, never had she heard that men possessed such wonderful powers. Large suns revolved around her, bright fishes swam in the air, and everything was reflected perfectly on the clear surface of the sea. It was so light in the ship, that everything could be seen distinctly. Oh! how happy the young prince was! He shook hands with the sailors, laughed and jested with them, whilst sweet notes of music mingled with the silence of night.

It was now late, but the little mermaid could not tear herself away from the ship and the handsome young prince. She remained looking through the cabin window, rocked to and fro by the waves. There was a foaming and fermentation in the depths beneath, and the ship began to move on faster, the sails were spread, the waves rose high, thick clouds gathered over the sky, and the noise of distant thunder was heard. The sailors perceived that a storm was coming on, so they again furled the sails. The great vessel was tossed about on the tempestuous ocean like a light boat, and the waves rose to an immense height, towering over the ship, which alternately sank beneath and rose above them. To the little mermaid this seemed most delightful, but the ship's crew thought very differently. The vessel cracked, the stout masts bent under the violence of the billows, the waters rushed in. For a minute the ship tottered to and fro, then the mainmast broke as if it had been a reed; the ship turned over, and was filled with water. The little mermaid now perceived that the crew was in danger, for she herself was forced to beware of the beams and splinters torn from the vessel, and floating about on the waves. But at the same time it became pitch dark so that she could not distinguish anything; presently, however, a dreadful flash of lightning disclosed to her the whole of the wreck. Her eyes sought the young prince—the same instant the ship sank to the bottom. At first she was delighted, thinking that the prince must now come to her abode, but she soon remembered that man cannot live in water, and that therefore if the prince ever entered her palace, it would be as a corpse.

"Die! no, he must not die!" She swam through the fragments with which the water was strewn regardless of the danger she was incurring, and at last found the prince all but exhausted, and with great difficulty keeping his head above water. He had already closed his eyes, and must inevitably have been drowned, had not the little mermaid come to his rescue. She seized hold of him and kept him above water, suffering the current to bear them on together.

Towards morning the storm was hushed; no trace, however, remained of the ship. The sun rose like fire out of the sea; his beams seemed to restore colour to the prince's cheeks, but his eyes were still closed. The mermaid kissed his high forehead and stroked his wet hair away from his face. He looked like the marble statue in her garden; she kissed him again and wished most fervently that he might recover.

She now saw the dry land with its mountains glittering with snow. A green wood extended along the coast, and at the entrance of the wood stood a chapel or convent, she could not be sure which. Citron and lemon trees grew in the garden adjoining it, an avenue of tall palm trees led up to the door. The sea here formed a little bay, in which the water was quite smooth but very deep, and under the cliffs there were dry firm sands. Hither swam the little mermaid with the seemingly dead prince; she laid him upon the warm sand, and took care to place his head high, and to turn his face to the sun.

The bells began to ring in the large white building which stood before her, and a number of young girls came out to walk in the garden. The mermaid went away from the shore, hid herself behind some stones, covered her head with foam, so that her little face could not be seen, and watched the prince with unremitting attention.

It was not long before one of the young girls approached. She seemed quite frightened at finding the prince in this state apparently dead; soon, however, she recovered herself, and ran back to call her sisters. The little mermaid saw that the prince revived, and that all around smiled kindly and joyfully upon him—for her, however, he looked not, he knew not that it was she who had saved him, and when the prince was taken into the house, she felt so sad, that she immediately plunged beneath the water, and returned to her father's palace.

If she had been before quiet and thoughtful, she now grew still more so. Her sisters asked her what she had seen in the upper world, but she made no answer.

Many an evening she rose to the place where she had left the prince. She saw the snow on the mountains melt, the fruits in the garden ripen and gathered, but the prince she never saw, so she always returned sorrowfully to her subterranean abode. Her only pleasure was to sit in her little garden gazing on the beautiful statue so like the prince. She cared no longer for her flowers; they grew up in wild luxuriance, covered the steps, and entwined their long stems and tendrils among the boughs of the trees, so that her whole garden became a bower.

At last, being unable to conceal her sorrow any longer, she revealed the secret to one of her sisters, who told it to the other princesses, and they to some of their friends. Among them was a young mermaid who recollected the prince, having been an eye-witness herself to the festivities in the ship; she knew also in what country the prince lived, and the name of its king.

"Come, little sister!" said the princesses, and embracing her, they rose together arm in arm, out of the water, just in front of the prince's palace.

This palace was built of bright yellow stones, a flight of white marble steps led from it down to the sea. A gilded cupola crowned the building, and white marble figures, which might almost have been taken for real men and women, were placed among the pillars surrounding it. Through the clear glass of the high windows one might look into magnificent apartments hung with silken curtains, the walls adorned with magnificent paintings. It was a real treat to the little royal mermaids to behold so splendid an abode; they gazed through the windows of one of the largest rooms, and in the centre saw a fountain playing, whose waters sprang up so high as to reach the glittering cupola above, through which the sunbeams fell dancing on the water, and brightening the pretty plants which grew around it.

The little mermaid now knew where her beloved prince dwelt, and henceforth she went there almost every evening. She often approached nearer the land than her sisters had ventured, and even swam up the narrow channel that flowed under the marble balcony. Here on a bright moonlight night, she would watch the young prince who believed himself alone.

Sometimes she saw him sailing on the water in a gaily-painted boat with many coloured flags waving above. She would then hide among the green reeds which grew on the banks, listening to his voice, and if any one in the boat noticed the rustling of her long silver veil, which was caught now and then by the light breeze, they only fancied it was a swan flapping his wings.

Many a night when the fishermen were casting their nets by the beacon's light, she heard them talking of the prince, and relating the noble actions he had performed. She was then so happy, thinking how she had saved his life when struggling with the waves, and remembering how his head had rested on her bosom, and how she had kissed him when he knew nothing of it, and could never even dream of such a thing.

Human beings became more and more dear to her every day; she wished that she were one of them. Their world seemed to her much larger than that of the mer-people; they could fly over the ocean in their ships, as well as climb to the summits of those high mountains that rose above the clouds; and their wooded domains extended much farther than a mermaid's eye could penetrate.

There were many things that she wished to hear explained, but her sisters could not give her any satisfactory answer; she was again obliged to have recourse to the old queen-mother, who knew a great deal about the upper world, which she used to call "the country above the sea."

"Do men live for ever when they are not drowned?" she asked one day. "Do they not die as we do, who live at the bottom of the sea?"

"Yes," was the grandmother's reply, "they must die like us, and their life is much shorter than ours. We live to the age of three hundred years, but when we die, we become foam on the sea, and are not allowed even to share a grave among those that are dear to us. We have no immortal souls, we can never live again, and are like the grass which, when once cut down, is withered for ever. Human beings, on the contrary, have souls that continue to live when their bodies become dust, and as we rise out of the water to admire the abode of man, they ascend to glorious unknown dwellings in the skies which we are not permitted to see."

"Why have not *we* immortal souls?" asked the little mermaid. "I would willingly give up my three hundred years to be a human being for only one day, thus to become entitled to that heavenly world above."

"You must not think of that," answered her grandmother, "it is much better as it is; we live longer and are far happier than human beings."

"So I must die, and be dashed like foam over the sea, never to rise again and hear the gentle murmur of the ocean, never again see the beautiful flowers and the bright sun! Tell me, dear grandmother, are there no means by which I may obtain an immortal soul?"

"No!" replied the old lady. "It is true that if thou couldst so win the affections of a human being as to become dearer to him than either father or mother; if he loved thee with all his heart, and promised whilst the priest joined his hands with thine to be always faithful to thee; then his soul would flow into thine, and thou wouldst then become partaker of human bliss. But that can never be! for what in our eyes is the most beautiful part of our body, the tail, the inhabitants of the earth think hideous; they cannot bear it. To appear handsome to them, the body must have two clumsy props which they call legs."

The little mermaid sighed and looked mournfully at the scaly part of her form, otherwise so fair and delicate.

"We are happy," added the old lady, "we shall jump and swim about merrily for three hundred years; that is a long time, and afterwards we shall repose peacefully in death. This evening we have a court ball."

The ball which the queen-mother spoke of was far more splendid than any that earth has ever seen. The walls of the salon were of crystal, very thick, but yet very clear; hundreds of large mussel-shells were planted in rows along them; these shells were some of rose-colour, some green as grass, but all sending forth a bright light, which not only illuminated the whole apartment, but also shone through the glassy walls so as to light up the waters around for a great space, and making the scales of the numberless fishes, great and small, crimson and purple, silver and gold-coloured, appear more brilliant than ever.

Through the centre of the salon flowed a bright, clear stream, on the surface of which danced mermen and mermaids to the melody of their own sweet voices, voices far sweeter than those of the dwellers upon earth. The little princess sang more harmoniously than any other, and they clapped their hands and applauded her. She was pleased at this, for she knew well that there was neither on earth nor in the sea a more beautiful voice than hers. But her thoughts soon returned to the world above her; she could not forget the handsome prince; she could not control her sorrow at not having an immortal soul. She stole away from her father's palace, and whilst all was joy within, she sat alone lost in thought in her little neglected garden. Suddenly she heard the tones of horns resounding over the water far away in the distance, and she said to herself, "Now he is going out to hunt, he whom I love more than my father and my mother, with whom my thoughts are constantly occupied, and to whom I would so willingly trust the happiness of my life! All! all, will I risk to win him—and an immortal soul! Whilst my sisters are still dancing in the palace, I will go to the enchantress whom I have hitherto feared so much, but who is, nevertheless, the only person who can advise and help me."

So the little mermaid left the garden, and went to the foaming whirlpool beyond which dwelt the enchantress. She had never been this way before—neither flowers nor sea-grass bloomed along her path; she had to traverse an extent of bare grey sand till she reached the whirlpool, whose waters were eddying and whizzing like mill-wheels, tearing everything they could seize along with them into the abyss below. She was obliged to make her way through this horrible place, in order to arrive at the territory of the enchantress. Then she had to pass through a boiling, slimy bog, which the enchantress called her turf-moor: her house stood in a wood beyond this, and a strange abode it was. All the trees and bushes around were polypi, looking like hundred-headed serpents shooting up out of the ground; their branches were long slimy arms with fingers of worms, every member, from the root to the uttermost tip, ceaselessly moving and extending on all sides. Whatever they seized they fastened upon so that it could not loosen itself from their grasp. The little mermaid stood still for a minute looking at this horrible wood; her heart beat with fear, and she would certainly have returned without attaining her object, had she not remembered the prince—and immortality. The thought gave her new courage, she bound up her long waving hair, that the polypi might not catch hold of it, crossed her delicate arms over her bosom, and, swifter than a fish can glide through the water, she passed these unseemly trees, who stretched their eager arms after her in vain. She could not, however, help seeing that every polypus had something in his grasp, held as firmly by a thousand little arms as if enclosed by iron bands. The whitened skeletons of a number of human beings who had been drowned in the sea, and had sunk into the abyss, grinned horribly from the arms of these polypi; helms, chests, skeletons of land animals were also held in their embrace; among other things might be seen even a little mermaid whom they had seized and strangled! What a fearful sight for the unfortunate princess!

But she got safely through this wood of horrors, and then arrived at a slimy place, where immense, fat snails were crawling about, and in the midst of this place stood a house built of the bones of unfortunate people who had been shipwrecked. Here sat the witch caressing a toad in the same manner as some persons would a pet bird. The ugly fat snails she called her chickens, and she permitted them to crawl about her.

"I know well what you would ask of me," said she to the little princess. "Your wish is foolish enough, yet it shall be fulfilled, though its accomplishment is sure to bring misfortune on you, my fairest princess. You wish to get rid of your tail, and to have instead two stilts like those of human beings, in order that a young prince may fall in love with you, and that you may obtain an immortal soul. Is it not so?" Whilst the witch spoke these words, she laughed so violently that her pet toad and snails fell from her lap. "You come just at the right time," continued she; "had you come after sunset, it would not have been in my power to have helped you before another year. I will prepare for you a drink with which you must swim to land, you must sit down upon the shore and swallow it, and then your tail will fall and shrink up to the things which men call legs. This transformation will, however, be very painful; you will feel as though a sharp knife passed through your body. All who look on you after you have been thus changed will say that you are the loveliest child of earth they have ever seen; you will retain your peculiar undulating movements, and no dancer will move so lightly, but every step you take will cause you pain all but unbearable; it will seem to you as though you were walking on the sharp edges of swords, and your blood will flow. Can you endure all this suffering? If so, I will grant your request."

"Yes, I will," answered the princess, with a faltering voice; for she remembered her dear prince, and the immortal soul which her suffering might win.

"Only consider," said the witch, "that you can never again become a mermaid, when once you have received a human form. You may never return to your sisters, and your father's palace; and unless you shall win the prince's love to such a degree that he shall leave father and mother for you, that you shall be mixed up with all his thoughts and wishes, and unless the priest join your hands, so that you become man and wife, you will never obtain the immortality you seek. The morrow of the day on which he is united to another will see your death; your heart will break with sorrow, and you will be changed to foam on the sea."

"Still I will venture!" said the little mermaid, pale and trembling as a dying person.

"Besides all this, I must be paid, and it is no slight thing that I require for my trouble. Thou hast the sweetest voice of all the dwellers in the sea, and thou thinkest by its means to charm the prince; this voice, however, I demand as my recompense. The best thing thou possessest I require in exchange for my magic drink; for I shall be obliged to sacrifice my own blood, in order to give it the sharpness of a two-edged sword."

"But if you take my voice from me," said the princess, "what have I left with which to charm the prince?"

"The graceful form," replied the witch, "the modest gait, and speaking eyes. With such as these, it will be easy to infatuate a vain human heart. Well now! hast thou lost courage? Put out thy little tongue, that I may cut it off, and take it for myself, in return for my magic drink."

"Be it so!" said the princess, and the witch took up her cauldron, in order to mix her potion. "Cleanliness is a good thing," remarked she, as she began to rub the cauldron with a handful of toads and snails. She then scratched her bosom, and let the black blood trickle down into the cauldron, every moment throwing in new ingredients, the smoke from the mixture assuming such horrible forms as were enough to fill beholders with terror, and a moaning and groaning proceeding from it, which might be compared to the weeping of crocodiles. The magic drink at length became clear and transparent as pure water; it was ready.

"Here it is!" said the witch to the princess, cutting out her tongue at the same moment. The poor little mermaid was now dumb: she could neither sing nor speak.

"If the polypi should attempt to seize you, as you pass through my little grove," said the witch, "you have only to sprinkle some of this magic drink over them, and their arms will burst into a thousand pieces." But the princess had no need of this counsel, for the polypi drew hastily back, as soon as they perceived the bright phial that glittered in her hand like a star; thus she passed safely through the formidable wood over the moor, and across the foaming mill-stream.

She now looked once again at her father's palace; the lamps in the salon were extinguished, and all the family were asleep. She would not go in, for she could not speak if she did; she was about to leave her home for ever; her heart was ready to break with sorrow at the thought; she stole into the garden, plucked a flower from the bed of each of her sisters as a remembrance, kissed her hand to them again and again, and then rose through the dark blue waters to the world above.

The sun had not yet risen when she arrived at the prince's dwelling, and ascended those well-known marble steps. The moon still shone in the sky when the little mermaid drank the wonderful liquid contained in her phial—she felt it run through her like a sharp knife, and she fell down in a swoon. When the sun rose she awoke, and felt a burning pain in all her limbs, but—she saw standing close to her the object of her love, the handsome young prince, whose coal-black eyes were fixed inquiringly upon her. Full of shame she cast down her own, and perceived, instead of the long fish-like tail she had hitherto borne, two slender legs; but she was quite naked, and tried in vain to cover herself with her long thick hair. The prince asked who she was, and how she had got there; and she, in reply, smiled and gazed upon him with her bright blue eyes, for alas! she could not speak. He then led her by the hand into the palace. She found that the witch had told her true; she felt as though she were walking on the edges of sharp swords, but she bore the pain willingly; on she passed, light as a zephyr, and all who saw her wondered at her light undulating movements.

When she entered the palace, rich clothes of muslin and silk were brought to her; she was lovelier than all who dwelt there, but she could neither speak nor sing. Some female slaves, gaily dressed in silk and gold brocade, sang before the prince and his royal parents; and one of them distinguished herself by her clear sweet voice, which the prince applauded by clapping his hands. This made the little mermaid very sad, for she knew that she used to sing far better than the young slave. "Alas!" thought she, "if he did but know that, for his sake, I have given away my voice for ever."

The slaves began to dance; our lovely little mermaiden then arose, stretched out her delicate white arms, and hovered gracefully about the room. Every motion displayed more and more the perfect symmetry and elegance of her figure; and the expression which beamed in her speaking eyes touched the hearts of the spectators far more than the song of the slaves.

All present were enchanted, but especially the young prince, who called her his dear little foundling. And she danced again and again, although every step cost her excessive pain. The prince then said she should always be with him; and accordingly a sleeping place was prepared for her on velvet cushions in the ante-room of his own apartment.

The prince caused a suit of riding apparel to be made for her, in order that she might accompany him in his rides; so together they traversed the fragrant woods, where green boughs brushed against their shoulders, and the birds sang merrily among the fresh leaves. With him she climbed up steep mountains, and although her tender feet bled, so as to be remarked by the attendants, she only smiled, and followed her dear prince to the heights, whence they could see the clouds chasing each other beneath them, like a flock of birds migrating to other countries.

During the night she would, when all in the palace were at rest, walk down the marble steps, in order to cool her feet in the deep waters; she would then think of those beloved ones who dwelt in the lower world.

One night, as she was thus bathing her feet, her sisters swam together to the spot, arm in arm and singing, but alas! so mournfully! She beckoned to them, and they immediately recognised her, and told her how great was the mourning in her father's house for her loss. From this time the sisters visited her every night; and once they brought with them the old grandmother, who had not seen the upper world for a great many years; they likewise brought their father, the Mer-king, with his crown on his head; but these two old people did not venture near enough to land to be able to speak to her.

The little mermaiden became dearer and dearer to the prince every day; but he only looked upon her as a sweet, gentle child; and the thought of making her his wife never entered his head. And yet his wife she must be, ere she could receive an immortal soul; his wife she must be, or she would change into foam, and be driven restlessly over the billows of the sea!

"Dost thou not love me above all others?" her eyes seemed to ask, as he pressed her fondly in his arms, and kissed her lovely brow.

"Yes," the prince would say, "thou art dearer to me than any other, for no one is as good as thou art! Thou lovest me so much; and thou art so like a young maiden, whom I have seen but once, and may never see again. I was on board a ship, which was wrecked by a sudden tempest; the waves threw me on the shore, near a holy temple, where a number of young girls are occupied constantly with religious services. The youngest of them found me on the shore, and saved my life. I saw her only once, but her image is vividly impressed upon my memory, and her alone can I love. But she belongs to the holy temple; and thou who resemblest her so much hast been given to me for consolation; never will we be parted!"

"Alas! he does not know that it was I who saved his life," thought the little mermaiden, sighing deeply; "I bore him over the wild waves, into the wooded bay, where the holy temple stood; I sat behind the rocks, waiting till some one should come. I saw the pretty maiden approach, whom he loves more than me,"—and again she heaved a deep sigh, for she could not weep,—"he said that the young girl belongs to the holy temple; she never comes out into the world, so they cannot meet each other again—and I am always with him, and see him daily; I will love him, and devote my whole life to him."

"So the prince is going to be married to the beautiful daughter of the neighbouring king," said the courtiers, "that is why he is having that splendid ship fitted out. It is announced that he wishes to travel, but in reality he goes to see the princess; a numerous retinue will accompany him." The little mermaiden smiled at these and similar conjectures, for she knew the prince's intentions better than any one else.

"I must go," he said to her, "I must see the beautiful princess; my parents require me to do so; but they will not compel me to marry her, and bring her home as my bride. And it is quite impossible for me to love her, for she cannot be so like the beautiful girl in the temple as thou art; and if I were obliged to choose, I should prefer thee, my little silent foundling, with the speaking eyes." And he kissed her rosy lips, played with her locks, and folded her in his arms, whereupon arose in her heart a sweet vision of human happiness, and immortal bliss.

"Thou art not afraid of the sea, art thou, my sweet silent child?" asked he tenderly, as they stood together in the splendid ship, which was to take them to the country of the neighbouring king. And then he told her of the storms that sometimes agitate the waters; of the strange fishes that inhabit the deep, and of the wonderful things seen by divers. But she smiled at his words, for she knew better than any child of earth what went on in the depths of the ocean.

At night-time, when the moon shone brightly, and when all on board were fast asleep, she sat in the ship's gallery, looking down into the sea. It seemed to her, as she gazed through the foamy track made by the ship's keel, that she saw her father's palace, and her grand-mother's silver crown. She then saw her sisters rise out of the water, looking sorrowful and stretching out their hands towards her. She nodded to them, smiled, and would have explained that everything was going on quite according to her wishes; but just then the cabin boy approached, upon which the sisters plunged beneath the water so suddenly that the boy thought what he had seen on the waves was nothing but foam.

The next morning the ship entered the harbour of the king's splendid capital. Bells were rung, trumpets sounded, and soldiers marched in procession through the city, with waving banners, and glittering bayonets. Every day witnessed some new entertainments, balls and parties followed each other; the princess, however, was not yet in the town; she had been sent to a distant convent for education, and had there been taught the practice of all royal virtues. At last she arrived at the palace.

The little mermaid had been anxious to see this unpar-alleled princess; and she was now obliged to confess that she had never before seen so beautiful a creature.

The skin of the princess was so white and delicate, that the veins might be seen through it, and her dark eyes sparkled beneath a pair of finely formed eyebrows.

"It is herself!" exclaimed the prince, when they met; "it is she who saved my life, when I lay like a corpse on the seashore!" and he pressed his blushing bride to his beating heart.

"Oh, I am all too happy!" said he to his dumb foundling. "What I never dared to hope for has come to pass. Thou must rejoice in my happiness, for thou lovest me more than all others who surround me." And the little mermaid kissed his hand in silent sorrow; it seemed to her as if her heart was breaking already, although the morrow of his marriage day, which must inevitably see her death, had not yet dawned.

Again rang the church-bells, whilst heralds rode through the streets of the capital, to announce the approaching wedding. Flames burned in silver candlesticks on all the altars; the priests swung their golden censers; and the bride and bridegroom joined hands, whilst the holy words that united them were spoken. The little mermaid, clad in silk and cloth of gold, stood behind the princess, and held the train of the bridal dress; but her ear heard nothing of the solemn music; her eye saw not the holy ceremony; she remembered her approaching end, she remembered that she had lost both this world and the next.

That very same evening, bride and bridegroom went on board the ship; cannons were fired, flags waved with the breeze, and in the centre of the deck stood a magnificent pavilion of purple and cloth of gold, fitted up with the richest and softest couches. Here the princely pair were to spend the night. A favourable wind swelled the sails, and the ship glided lightly over the blue waters.

As soon as it was dark, coloured lamps were hung out and dancing began on the deck. The little mermaid was thus involuntarily reminded of what she had seen the first time she rose to the upper world. The spectacle that now presented itself was equally splendid—and she was obliged to join in the dance, hovering lightly as a bird over the shipboards. All applauded her, for never had she danced with more enchanting grace. Her little feet suffered extremely, but she no longer felt the pain; the anguish her heart suffered was much greater. It was the last evening she might see him, for whose sake she had forsaken her home and all her family, had given away her beautiful voice, and suffered daily the most violent pain— all without his having the least suspicion of it. It was the last evening that she might breathe the same atmosphere in which he, the beloved one, lived; the last evening when she might behold the deep blue sea, and the starry heavens—an eternal night, in which she might neither think nor dream, awaited her. And all was joy in the ship; and she, her heart filled with thoughts of death and annihilation, smiled and danced with the others, till past midnight. Then the prince kissed his lovely bride, and arm in arm they entered the magnificent tent, prepared for their repose.

All was now still; the steersman alone stood at the ship's helm. The little mermaid leaned her white arms on the gallery, and looked towards the east, watching for the dawn; she well knew that the first sunbeam would witness her dissolution. She saw her sisters rise out of the sea; deadly pale were their features, and their long hair no more fluttered over their shoulders, it had all been cut off.

"We have given it to the witch," said they, "to induce her to help thee, so that thou mayest not die. She has given to us a knife: here it is! before the sun rises, thou must plunge it into the prince's heart; and when his warm blood trickles down upon thy feet they will again be changed to a fish-like tail; thou wilt once more become a mermaid, and wilt live thy full three hundred years, ere thou changest to foam on the sea. But hasten! either he or thou must die before sunrise. Our aged mother mourns for thee so much, her grey hair has fallen off through sorrow, as ours fell before the scissors of the witch. Kill the prince, and come down to us! hasten! hasten! dost thou not see the red streaks on the eastern sky, announcing the near approach of the sun? A few minutes more and he rises, and then all will be over with thee." At these words they sighed deeply and vanished.

The little mermaid drew aside the purple curtains of the pavilion, where lay the bride and bridegroom; bending over them, she kissed the prince's forehead, and then glancing at the sky, she saw that the dawning light became every moment brighter. The prince's lips unconsciously murmured the name of his bride—he was dreaming of her, and her only, whilst the fatal knife trembled in the hand of the unhappy mermaid. All at once, she threw far out into the sea that instrument of death; the waves rose like bright blazing flames around, and the water where it fell seemed tinged with blood. With eyes fast becoming dim and fixed, she looked once more at her beloved prince; then plunged from the ship into the sea, and felt her body slowly but surely dissolving into foam.

The sun rose from his watery bed; his beams fell so softly and warmly upon her, that our little mermaid was scarcely sensible of dying. She still saw the glorious sun; and over her head hovered a thousand beautiful, transparent forms; she could still distinguish the white sails of the ship, and the bright red clouds in the sky; the voices of those airy creatures above her had a melody so sweet and soothing that a human ear would be as little able to catch the sound as her eye was capable of distinguishing their forms; they hovered around her without wings, borne by their own lightness through the air. The little mermaid at last saw that she had a body as transparent as theirs; and felt herself raised gradually from the foam of the sea to higher regions.

"Where are they taking me?" asked she, and her words sounded just like the voices of those heavenly beings.

"Speak you to the daughters of air?" was the answer. "The mermaid has no immortal soul, and can only acquire that heavenly gift by winning the love of one of the sons of men; her immortality depends upon union with man. Neither do the daughters of air possess immortal souls, but they can acquire them by their own good deeds. We fly to hot countries, where the children of earth are sinking under sultry pestilential breezes—our fresh cooling breath revives them. We diffuse ourselves through the atmosphere; we perfume it with the delicious fragrance of flowers; and thus spread delight and health over the earth. By doing good in this manner for three hundred years, we win immortality, and receive a share of the eternal bliss of human beings. And thou, poor little mermaid! who, following the impulse of thine own heart, hast done and suffered so much, thou art now raised to the airy world of spirits, that by performing deeds of kindness for three hundred years, thou mayest acquire an immortal soul."

The little mermaid stretched out her transparent arms to the sun; and, for the first time in her life, tears moistened her eyes.

And now again all were awake and rejoicing in the ship; she saw the prince, with his pretty bride; they had missed her; they looked sorrowfully down on the foamy waters, as if they knew she had plunged into the sea; unseen she kissed the bridegroom's forehead, smiled upon him, and then, with the rest of the children of air, soared high above the rosy cloud which was sailing so peacefully over the ship.

"After three hundred years we shall fly in the kingdom of Heaven!"

"We may arrive there even sooner," whispered one of her sisters. "We fly invisibly through the dwellings of men, where there are children; and whenever we find a good child, who gives pleasure to his parents and deserves their love, the good God shortens our time of probation. No child is aware that we are flitting about his room; and that whenever joy draws from us a smile, a year is struck out of our three hundred. But when we see a rude naughty child, we weep bitter tears of sorrow, and every tear we shed adds a day to our time of probation."

GREAT CLAUS AND LITTLE CLAUS

Once upon a time there lived in the same village two men bearing the very same name. One of them chanced to possess four horses, the other had only one horse, so, by way of distinguishing them from each other, the proprietor of four horses was called "Great Claus," and he who owned but one horse was known as "Little Claus". And now we shall relate their true and veritable history.

All the week long Little Claus had to plough for Great Claus, and to lend him his one horse, and in return Great Claus lent him his four horses, but only for one day in the week, and that day was Sunday. Hurrah! a proud man then was little Claus, and how he brandished his whip over his five horses, for all five were his, he thought, for this one day at least. And the sun shone so brightly, and all the bells in the church-tower were ringing; the people were dressed in their best and walking to church, and as they passed they looked at Little Claus, who was driving his five horses, and he was so pleased that he kept cracking his whip again and again, crying out the while, "Hip, hip, hurrah! five fine horses, and all of them mine!"

"You must not say that," observed Great Claus; "only one of the horses is yours, you know that well enough."

But when another party of church-goers passed close by him, Little Claus quite forgot that he had been told he must not say so, and cried out again, "Hip, hip, hurrah! five fine horses, all mine!"

"Did not I tell you to hold your tongue?" exclaimed Great Claus, very angrily. "If you say that again, I'll give your one horse such a blow on the forehead as shall strike him dead on the spot, and then there'll soon be an end to your boasting about your five fine horses."

"Oh, but I'll never say it again, indeed I won't!" said Little Claus, and he quite intended to keep his word. But presently some more people came by, and when they nodded a friendly "good-morning" to him, he was so delighted, and it seemed to him such a grand thing to have five horses to plough his bit of a field, that he really could not contain himself, he flourished his whip aloft, and shouted out, "Hip, hip, hurrah! five fine horses, every one of them mine!"

"I'll soon cure you of that!" cried Great Claus, in a fury, and, taking up a large stone, he flung it at the head of Little Claus' horse—so heavy was the stone that the poor creature fell down dead.

"Alas, now I have no horses at all!" cried Little Claus, and he began to weep. As soon as he had recovered himself a little, he set to work to flay the skin off his dead horse, dried the skin thoroughly in the air, and then putting it into a sack, he slung the sack across his shoulders, and set out on his way to the nearest town, intending to sell the skin. He had a long way to go, and the road led him through a large and thickly-grown wood. And here a violent tempest burst forth; the clouds, the rain, and the dark firs, bowed to and fro by the wind, so bewildered poor Claus that he lost his path, and before he could recover it, evening had darkened into night; he could neither return homewards nor get on to the town. However, not far off stood a large farmhouse; the window-shutters were closed, but Little Claus could see lights shining out through the cracks. "Perhaps I may get shelter there," thought he, so he went up to the house, and knocked at the door. The farmer's wife came and opened it to him, but when she heard what he wanted, she very obligingly told him he must go and ask elsewhere; he shouldn't come into her house; her good man was from home, and she couldn't be receiving strangers in his absence.

"Well then, I must sleep outside, under this stormy sky," replied Little Claus, and the farmer's wife shut the door in his face.

Close by stood a haystack, and between it and the house there was a little penthouse with a flat straw roof.

"I'll get up there," said Little Claus to himself, on perceiving this; "it will make me a capital bed—only I do hope the stork yonder may not take it into his head to fly down and bite my legs," for a stork had made his nest on the roof, and had mounted guard beside the nest, as wide-awake as could be, although it was night.

So Little Claus crept up on the penthouse, and there he turned and twisted about till he had made himself a right comfortable couch. The window-shutters did not close properly at the top, so that from his high and airy position he could see all that went on in the room.

There he saw a large table spread with bread and wine, roast meat and fried fish. The farmer's wife and the sexton sat at table; no one else was there; the farmer's wife was pouring out a glass of wine for the sexton, who, meantime, was eagerly helping himself to a large slice of the fish—he happened to be particularly fond of fish.

"Too bad, really, to keep it all to themselves!" sighed Little Claus. "If they would but give me a little, wee morsel!" and he stretched out his head as near to the window as he could. Oh, what a magnificent cake he could see now! Why, this was quite a banquet!

Presently he heard the sound of hoof-tramps approaching from the road. It was the farmer riding home.

A regularly good-hearted fellow was this farmer, but he had one peculiar weakness, namely that he never could endure to see a sexton; the sight made him half mad. Now, the sexton of the neighbouring town happened to be first cousin to his wife, and they were old playmates and good friends, so, this evening, knowing that the farmer would be from home, he came to pay his cousin a visit, and the good woman, being very pleased to see him, had brought out all the choice things in her larder, wherewith to regale him. But now, while they were sitting together so comfortably, they heard the tramp of the farmer's horse; they both started up, and the woman bade the sexton creep into a large empty chest that stood in a corner of the room. He did so, for he knew that the poor farmer would be almost driven wild if he came in and saw a sexton standing unexpectedly before him. And the farmer's wife then made a bustle to hide all the wine and the dishes inside her baking-oven, for fear her husband, if he saw the table spread with them, should ask for whom she had been preparing such a grand entertainment.

"Oh dear, oh dear!" sighed Little Claus from his couch on the penthouse, when he saw the feast all put on one side.

"Anybody up there?" inquired the farmer, on hearing the voice; and he looked up and perceived Little Claus. "Why are you lying there? Come down into the house with me."

And Little Claus explained that he had lost his way, and asked the farmer if he would not give him shelter for the night.

"To be sure I will," replied the good-natured man. "Come in quickly, and let's have something to eat."

The woman received them both with a great show of welcome, covered one end of the long table, and brought out a large dish of oatmeal. The farmer set to with a capital appetite, but Little Claus could not eat for thinking of the good roast meat, the fish, the wine, and the delicious cake which he had seen stowed away inside the oven.

He put his sack containing the horse's skin under the table, and now, as he could not relish the oatmeal porridge, he began trampling the sack under his feet till the dry skin creaked aloud.

"Hush! " muttered Little Claus, as if speaking to his sack, but at the same moment he trod upon it again, so as to make it creak louder than before.

"What have you got in your sack?" asked the farmer.

"Oh! I've got a little conjuror there," replied Little Claus, "and he says we are not to be eating oatmeal porridge any longer, for he has conjured a feast of beef-steak, fried fish, and cake, into the oven on purpose for us."

"A conjuror, did you say?" exclaimed the farmer, and up he got in a vast hurry to look into the oven and see whether the conjuror had spoken truly. And there, to be sure, were fish, and steak, and cake; the conjuror had been as good as his word. The farmer's wife durst not utter a syllable of explanation; almost as much bewildered as her husband, she set the viands on the table, and the farmer and his guest began with a hearty appetite to eat of the good cheer before them.

Presently Little Claus trampled on his sack again, and again made the skin creak.

"What does your conjuror say now?" asked the farmer.

"He says," replied Little Claus, "that he has also conjured three bottles of wine here for us; you will find them standing just in the corner of the oven." So the woman was now obliged to bring out the wine that she had concealed, and the farmer poured himself out a glass and began to think it would be a fine thing to have such a capital conjuror as this.

"A right proper sort of conjuror this of yours!" observed he at last. "I should rather like to see him; will he let me, do you think?"

"Oh, of course," returned Little Claus; "my conjuror will do anything I ask him. That you will, won't you?" asked he, again treading on his sack. "Didn't your hear him say 'Yes'? But I warn you he will look somewhat dark and unpleasing; after all, it is scarcely worth while to see him!"

"Oh, I shall not be afraid. What will he look like?"

"Why, he will appear for all the world just like a sexton."

"A sexton!" repeated the farmer, "that is a pity! You must know that I cannot endure the sight of a sexton; but no matter, since I shall know that it is not a real sexton, but only your conjuror, I shall not care about it. Oh, I've plenty of courage, only don't let him come too near me!"

"Well, I'll speak to my conjuror about it again," said Little Claus, and he trod on his skin till it went "creak, creak, creak," and bent his ear down as though to listen.

"What does he say now?"

"He says he will transport himself into yonder chest in the corner; you have only to lift up the lid, and there you will see him, but you must mind and shut the lid close down again."

"Will you help me to hold up the lid? it is very heavy," said the farmer, and he went up to the chest wherein his wife had concealed the real sexton, who sat with his limbs huddled up, trembling, and holding his breath, lest he should be discovered; certainly in no very comfortable state.

The farmer gently raised the lid of the chest and peeped under it. "Ugh!" cried he, and immediately started back in affright. "Oh dear, oh dear! I saw him; he looked exactly like our sexton in the town— oh, how horrible!"

However, he sat down at table again, and began to drink glass after glass of wine, by way of recovering from the shock. The wine soon revived his fallen courage. Neither he nor his guest ever thought of going to bed; there they sat, talking and feasting, till late in the night.

"Did you ever see your conjuror before?" inquired the farmer of Claus.

"Not I," replied Little Claus, "I should never have thought of asking him to show himself, if you had not proposed it. He knows he is not handsome—he does not wish to obtrude himself into any company; he talks to me, and I to him, and isn't that enough?"

"Oh, indeed, it is!" rejoined the farmer quickly. Then after a minute's hesitation he went on, "Do you know, I should like very much to have your conjuror; would you mind selling him to me? Name your own price; I don't care if I give you a whole bushelful of silver on the spot if only you'll give him to me."

"Oh, how can you ask such a thing?" exclaimed Little Claus; "such a useful, such a faithful servant as he is to me, how could I think of parting with him? Why, he's worth his weight in gold ten times over."

"I can't offer you gold," replied the farmer, "but I should like so very much to have him! that is, provided he would never show his ugly self to me again."

"Oh, no fear of that," said Little Claus; "and really, since you have been so kind as to give me shelter tonight, I do not think I can refuse you any request. I will let you have my conjuror for a bushel of silver—only the bushel must be crammed full, you know."

"Certainly it shall," answered the farmer, "and the chest yonder too, you shall have that into the bargain; I don't want it to remain an hour longer in the house, it will always be reminding me of the odious sexton-face I saw inside it."

So the bargain was struck, and Little Claus gave the farmer his sack, with the dry skin in it, and received instead a whole bushelful of silver. The farmer also gave him a large wheelbarrow wherewith to convey home his money and his chest.

"Farewell!" said Little Claus, and away he drove the wheelbarrow, the unfortunate sexton still lying concealed in the chest.

On the opposite side of the wood flowed a broad, deep river: the current was so strong that no one could swim against it, so a bridge had lately been built over it. Little

Claus took his way over the bridge, but stopped short in the middle of it, saying very loud, on purpose that the man in the chest might hear him, "Now, what on earth can be the use of this great tumbledown chest to me? and it's as heavy, too, as if it were filled with stones; it quite tires me out. I'll fling it out into the river; if it chooses to float it homewards to me, well and good, if not, it may let it alone; all the same to me."

And he lifted the chest as though intending to throw it into the water.

"Oh, pray don't do that," cried the sexton in the chest; "let me out first, pray."

"Holloa!" exclaimed Little Claus; "is the chest bewitched? If so, the sooner it's off my hands the better."

"Oh, no, no, no," cried the sexton; "let me out, and I'll give you another whole bushelful of money."

"Ah, that's quite another matter," said Little Claus; and he immediately set down the chest, and lifted the lid. Out crept the sexton, greatly to his own satisfaction. He kicked the empty chest into the water, and then took Little Claus to his house with him, where he gave him the bushelful of money, as agreed. Little Claus had now a wheelbarrow full of money.

"Certainly, I must own I have been well paid for my horse's skin," said he to himself, as he entered his own little room, and overturned all his money in a great heap on the floor. "It will vex Great Claus, I'm afraid, when he finds out how rich my horse's skin has made me."

And now he sent a little boy to Great Claus to borrow a measure of him.

"What can he want with a measure, I wonder?" thought Great Claus, and he cunningly smeared the bottom of the measure with clay, hoping that some part of whatever was measured might cleave to the clay. And accordingly, when the measure was returned to him, he discovered three silver coins sticking to the bottom. "Fine doings, upon my word," exclaimed Great Claus, in amazement; and off he set forthwith to the house of his namesake. "Where did you get all that money?" thundered he.

"Oh, I got it by my horse's skin, which I sold yesterday," was the reply.

"Really?" exclaimed Great Claus; "what, are horses' skins so dear as that? Who would have thought it?" And he ran quickly home, took an axe, and struck all his four horses on the head with it, then flayed off the skins, and drove into the town. "Skins, skins, who will buy skins?" cried he, as he passed through the streets.

All the shoemakers and tanners in the town came running up to him, and asked his price.

"I will have a bushelful of money for each," replied Great Claus.

"Are you mad?" cried they. "Do you think we reckon our money by bushels?"

"Skins, fresh skins, who will buy skins?" shouted he again; and still to all who asked how much he wanted for them, he replied, "A bushelful of money."

"The rude boor! he is trying to make fools of us," declared one of his customers at last in very great wrath.

"Skins, fresh skins, fine fresh skins," cried they all, mimicking him. "Out of the town with him, the great ass! or he shall have no skin left on his own shoulders." And Great Claus was ignominiously thrust out of the town, and returned home in no very good humour.

"Little Claus shall pay for this," muttered he. "Sleep soundly this night, Little Claus, for thou shalt hardly wake again."

It so chanced that Little Claus' grandmother died that same evening; she had always been very cross and ill-natured to him in her lifetime, but now, on finding her dead, he felt really sorry for her. He laid the dead woman in his own warm bed in hopes that the warmth might bring her to life again; for his own part, he thought he could spend the night in a chair in a corner of the room; he had often done so before. About midnight the door opened, and Great Claus, his axe in his hand, came in. He knew well where Little Claus' bed was wont to stand; he went straight up to it, and struck the dead grandmother a violent blow on the forehead.

"There's for you," cried he, "now you'll never make a fool of me again," and herewith he went out of the room and returned home.

"What a very wicked man he is," sighed Little Claus. "So he wanted to kill me; it was a good thing that old grandmother was dead already, or that blow would have hurt her very much."

The next day, in the evening, he met Great Claus in a lane near the village. Great Claus started back and stared at him. "What, aren't you dead? I thought I killed you last night."

"Yes, you wicked man," replied Little Claus; "I know you came into my room intending to kill me, but my grandmother, not I, was lying in bed; it was she that you struck with your pickaxe, and you deserve to be hanged for it."

"And are you going to tell people about it?" said Great Claus; "that you never shall!" He was carrying a very large sack; he seized Little Claus by the waist and thrust him into the sack, crying out, "I will drown thee at once, and that will be the end of thy tale-telling."

But he had a long way to walk before he reached the river, and Little Claus was by no means a light burden. The road led past the church, the organ was playing, for the service had just begun. Among the congregation Great Claus saw a man he wanted to speak to; "Little Claus cannot get out of the sack by himself," thought he, "and no one can help him, for all the people are in church. I can just go in and call that man back into the porch for a minute." So he set down the heavy sack and ran into church.

"Oh dear, oh dear!" sighed Little Claus inside the sack; he turned and twisted in vain, it was not possible for him to get the string loose. Just then a very, very old cattle-driver passed by, his hair white as snow, and with a stout staff in his hand; he was driving a large herd of cows and bullocks before him, many more than he, feeble as he was, could manage. One of them rushed up against the sack, and turned it over and over. "Oh, help me, pray!" cried Little Claus, "I am so young to die; help me out of the sack."

"What, is there a man in the sack?" And the ancient cattle-driver bent down, though with some difficulty, and untied the string. "The bullock has not hurt you, I hope?" But Little Claus sprang out so briskly as showed he was not hurt, and set himself immediately to rooting up the withered stump of a tree which stood by the roadside, and which he rolled into the sack, then tying the string he placed the sack exactly as Great Claus had left it. The cattle had, meantime, passed on.

"Will you not drive these cattle home to the village for me?" asked the old man. "I am so weary, and I want to go into church so much."

"Right gladly will I help you since you have helped me," replied Little Claus, and he took the cattle-driver's goad from his hand, and followed the herd in his stead.

Presently Great Claus cane running back again. He took up the sack, and again flung it across his shoulders, thinking, "How much lighter the burden seems now; it always does one good to rest for ever so short a time." So on he trudged to the river, flung the sack out into the water, and shouted after it, "There now, Little Claus, you shall never cheat me any more!" He then turned homewards, but on passing a spot where several roads crossed, who should he meet but Little Claus himself with his herd of cattle.

"How comes this?" exclaimed Great Claus; "is it really you? Did I not drown you then, after all?"

"I believe you meant to drown me," said Little Claus; "you threw me into the river just half-an-hour ago, did you not?"

"But how did you come by all these beautiful cattle?" asked Great Claus, in utter amazement, his eyes wandering admiringly from one to another of the herd.

"These are sea-cattle," said Little Claus. "Ah, I'll tell you the whole story! I am really much obliged to you for drowning me; it has made me richer than ever, as you may see. I was so frightened when I lay in the sack, and the wind whistled so uncomfortably into my ears when you threw me down from the bridge into the cold water! I sank to the bottom at once, but I was not hurt, for I was received by the softest, freshest grass. Immediately the sack was opened, and the most beautiful young girl you can imagine, clad in snow-white robes, and with a green wreath in her wet hair, took me by the hand, saying, 'Art thou Little Claus? Here are some cattle of thine, and a mile farther up the road, another and larger herd is grazing, and I will give thee that herd also!' And then I understood that the river was a sort of high-road for the people of the sea, and that on it they walked and drove to and fro from the sea far up into the land where the river rises, and thence back to the sea again. And no place can be more beautiful than it is at the bottom of the water. The prettiest flowers and the freshest grass grow there, and the fishes swimming in the water slipped to and fro about my ears just as birds flutter about us up here in the air. And such gaily-dressed people I saw there, and such a multitude of cattle grazing in pastures enclosed with hedges and ditches!"

"Then why were you in such a hurry to come up again?" inquired Great Claus. "I shouldn't have done so, not I, when I found it so pleasant there."

"Ah," rejoined Little Claus; "that was so cleverly done on my part! Did not I tell you that the sea-lady told me that a mile up the road—and by the road she could only mean the river, she can't come onto our land roads—there was another and larger herd of cattle for me? But I knew that the river makes a great many turns and windings, and therefore I thought I'd just spare myself half a mile of the way by taking the short cut across the land. So here I am, you see, and I shall soon get to my sea-cattle!"

"Oh, what a lucky fellow you are!" exclaimed Great Claus. "Don't you think that I might have some cattle given to me, too, if I went down to the bottom of the river?"

"How can I tell?" asked Little Claus, in reply.

"You envious scoundrel! you want to keep all the beautiful sea-cattle for yourself, I warrant!" cried Great Claus. "Either you will carry me to the water's edge, and throw me over, or I will take out my great knife and kill you! Make your choice!"

"Oh no, please don't be so angry!" entreated Little Claus. "I cannot carry you in the sack to the river, you are too heavy for me; but if you will walk there yourself, and then creep into the sack, I will throw you over with all the pleasure in the world!"

"But if, when I get to the bottom, I find no sea-cattle for me, I shall kill you all the same when I come back, remember that!" said Great Claus; and to this arrangement Little Claus made no objection.

They walked together to the river. As soon as the thirsty cattle saw the water, they ran on as fast as they could, eagerly crowding against each other, and all wanting to drink first.

"Only look at my sea-cattle!" said Little Claus; "see how they are longing to be at the bottom of the river."

"That's all very well," said Great Claus, "but you must help me first." And he quickly crept into the great sack which had lain stretched across the shoulders of one of the oxen. "Put a heavy stone in with me," said Great Claus, "else, perhaps, I shall not sink to the bottom."

"No fear of that!" replied Little Claus. However, he put a large stone into the sack, tied the strings, and pushed the sack into the water—plump! there it fell, straight to the bottom.

"I am much afraid he will not find his sea-cattle!" observed Little Claus, and he drove his own herd quietly home to the village.

TOMMELISE

Once upon a time there lived a young wife who longed exceedingly to possess a little child of her own, so she went to an old witch-woman and said to her, "I wish so very much to have a child, a little tiny child, won't you give me one, old mother?"

"Oh, with all my heart!" replied the witch. "Here is a barley-corn for you; it is not exactly of the same sort as those that grow on the farmer's fields, or that are given to the fowls in the poultry yard, but do you sow it in a flowerpot, and then you shall see what you shall see!"

"Thank you, thank you! " cried the woman, and she gave the witch a silver sixpence, and then having returned home sowed the barley-corn as she had been directed, whereupon a large and beautiful flower immediately shot forth from the flowerpot. It looked like a tulip, but the petals were tightly folded up; it was still in bud.

"What a lovely flower!" exclaimed the peasant woman, and she kissed the pretty red and yellow leaves, and as she kissed them the flower gave a loud report and opened. It was indeed a tulip, but on the small green pointal in the centre of the flower there sat a little tiny girl, so pretty and delicate, but her whole body scarcely bigger than the young peasant's thumb. So she called her Tommelise.

A pretty varnished walnut-shell was given her as a cradle, blue violet leaves served as her mattresses, and a rose-leaf was her coverlet; here she slept at night, but in the daytime she played on the table. The peasant-wife had filled a plate with water, and laid flowers in it, their blossoms bordering the edge of the plate, while the stalks lay in the water; on the surface floated a large tulip-leaf, and on it Tommelise might sit and sail from one side of the plate to the other, two white horse hairs having been given her for oars. That looked quite charming! And Tommelise could sing too, and she sang in such low sweet tones as never were heard before.

One night, while she was lying in her pretty bed, a great ugly toad came hopping in through the broken window-pane. The toad was such a great creature, old and withered-looking, and wet too; she hopped at once down upon the table where Tommelise lay sleeping under the red rose-petal.

"That is just the wife for my son," said the toad; and she seized hold of the walnut-shell, with Tommelise in it, and hopped away with her through the broken pane down into the garden. Here flowed a broad stream; its banks were muddy and swampy, and it was amongst this mud that the old toad and her son dwelt. Ugh, how hideous and deformed he was! just like his mother.

"Coax, coax, brekke-ke-kex!" was all he could find to say on seeing the pretty little maiden in the walnut-shell.

"Don't make such a riot, or you'll wake her!" said old mother toad. "She may easily run away from us, for she is as light as a swan-down feather. I'll tell you what we'll do; we'll take her out into the brook, and set her down on one of the large water-lily leaves; it will be like an island to her, who is so light and small. Then she cannot run away from us, and we can go and get ready the state-rooms down under the mud, where you and she are to dwell together."

72

Out in the brook there grew many water-lilies, with their broad green leaves, each of which seemed to be floating over the water. The leaf which was the farthest from the shore was also the largest; to it swam old mother toad, and on it she set the walnut-shell, with Tommelise.

The poor little tiny creature awoke quite early next morning, and, when she saw where she was, she began to weep most bitterly, for there was nothing but water on all sides of the large green leaf, and she could in no way reach the land.

Old mother toad was down in the mud, decorating her apartments with bulrushes and yellow buttercups, so as to make them quite gay and tidy to receive her new daughter-in-law. At last, she and her frightful son swam together to the leaf where she had left Tommelise; they wanted to fetch her pretty cradle, and place it for her in the bridal chamber before she herself was conducted into it. Old mother toad bowed low in the water, and said to her, "Here is my son, he is to be thy husband, and you will dwell together so comfortably down in the mud!"

"Coax, coax, brekk-ke-kex!" was all that her son could say.

Then they took the neat little bed and swam away with it, whilst Tommelise sat alone on the green leaf, weeping, for she did not like the thought of living with the withered old toad, and having her ugly son for a husband. The little fishes that were swimming to and fro in the water beneath had heard what mother toad had said, so they now put up their heads—they wanted to see the little maid. And when they saw her, they were charmed with her delicate beauty, and it vexed them very much that the hideous old toad should carry her off. No, that should never be! They surrounded the green stalk in the water, whereon rested the water-lily leaf and gnawed it asunder with their teeth, and then the leaf floated away down the brook, with Tommelise on it; away, far away, where the old toad could not follow.

Tommelise sailed past so many places, and the wild birds among the bushes saw her and sang, "Oh, what a sweet little maiden!" On and on, farther and farther, floated the leaf: Tommelise was on her travels.

A pretty little white butterfly kept fluttering round and round her, and at last settled down on the leaf, for he loved Tommelise very much, and she was so pleased. There was nothing to trouble her now that she had no fear of the old toad pursuing her, and wherever she sailed everything was so beautiful, for the sun shone down on the water, making it bright as liquid gold. And now she took off her sash, and tied one end of it round the butterfly, fastening the other end firmly into the leaf. On floated the leaf, faster and faster, and Tommelise with it.

Presently a great cockchafer came buzzing past; he caught sight of her, and immediately fastening his claw round her slender waist, flew up into a tree with her. But the green leaf still floated down the brook, and the butterfly with it; he was bound to the leaf and could not get loose.

Oh, how terrified was poor Tommelise when the cockchafer carried her up into the tree, and how sorry she felt, too, for the darling white butterfly which she had left tied fast to the leaf; she feared that if he could not get away, he would perish of hunger. But the cockchafer cared nothing for that. He settled with her upon the largest leaf in the tree, gave her some honey from the flowers to eat, and hummed her praises, telling her she was very pretty, although she was not at all like a henchafer. And by-and-by all the chafers who lived in that tree came to pay her a visit; they looked at Tommelise, and one Miss Henchafer drew in her feelers, saying, "She has only two legs, how miserable that looks!" "She has no feelers," cried another. "And see how thin and lean her waist is; why, she is just like a human being!" observed a third. "How very, very ugly she is!" at last cried all the ladychafers in chorus. The chafer who had carried off Tommelise still could not persuade himself that she was otherwise than pretty, but, as all the rest kept repeating and insisting that she was ugly, he at last began to think they must be in the right, and determined to have nothing more to do with her; she might go whenever she would, for aught he cared, he said. And so the whole swarm flew down from the tree with her, and set her on a daisy; then she wept because she was so ugly that the ladychafers would not keep company with her, and yet Tommelise was the prettiest little creature that could be imagined, soft and delicate and transparent as the loveliest rose-leaf.

All the summer long poor Tommelise lived alone in the wide wood. She wove herself a bed of grass-straw, and hung it under a large burdock-leaf which sheltered her from the rain; she dined off the honey from the flowers, and drank from the dew that every morning spangled the leaves and herblets around her. Thus passed the summer and autumn, but then came winter, the cold, long winter. All the birds who had sung so sweetly to her flew away, trees and flowers withered, the large burdock-leaf under which Tommelise had lived, rolled itself up, and became a dry, yellow stalk, and Tommelise was fearfully cold, for her clothes were wearing out, and she herself was so slight and frail, poor little thing! she was nearly frozen to death. It began to snow, and every light flake that fell upon her made her feel as we should if a whole shovel-ful of snow were thrown upon us, for we are giants in comparison with a little creature only an inch long. She wrapped herself up in a withered leaf, but it gave her no warmth; she shuddered with cold.

Close outside the wood, on the skirt of which Tommelise had been living, lay a large cornfield, but the corn had been carried away long ago, leaving only the dry, naked stubble standing up from the hard-frozen earth. It was like another wood to Tommelise, and oh, how she shivered with cold as she made her way through. At last she came past the field-mouse's door; for the field-mouse had made herself a little hole under the stubble, and there she dwelt snugly and comfortably, having a room full of corn, and a neat kitchen and store-chamber besides. And poor Tommelise must now play the beggar-girl; she stood at the door and begged for a little piece of a barley-corn, for she had had nothing to eat during two whole days.

"Thou poor little thing!" said the field-mouse, who was indeed a thoroughly good-natured old creature, "come into my warm room and dine with me."

And as she soon took a great liking to Tommelise, she proposed to her to stay. "You may dwell with me all the winter if you will, but keep my room clean and neat, and tell me stories, for I love stories dearly."

And Tommelise did all that the kind old field-mouse required of her, and was made very comfortable in her new abode.

"We shall have a visitor presently," observed the field-mouse; "my next-door neighbour comes to see me once every week. He is better off than I am, has large rooms in his house, and wears a coat of such beautiful black velvet. It would be a capital thing for you if you could secure him for your husband, but unfortunately he is blind, he cannot see you. You must tell him the prettiest stories you know."

But Tommelise did not care at all about pleasing their neighbour Mr. Mole, nor did she wish to marry him. He came and paid a visit in his black-velvet suit, he was so rich and so learned, and the field-mouse declared his domestic offices were twenty times larger than hers; but the sun and the pretty flowers he could not endure, he was always abusing them, though he had never seen either. Tommelise was called upon to sing for his amusement, and by the time she had sung "Ladybird, ladybird, fly away home!" and "The Friar of Orders Grey," the mole had quite fallen in love with her through the charm of her sweet voice; however, he said nothing, he was such a prudent, cautious animal.

He had just been digging a long passage through the earth from their house to his, and he now gave permission to the field-mouse and Tommelise to walk in it as often as they liked; however, he bade them not be afraid of the dead bird that lay in the passage; it was a whole bird, with beak and feathers entire, and therefore he supposed it must have died quite lately, at the beginning of the winter, and had been buried just in the place where he had dug his passage.

The mole took a piece of tinder, which shines like fire in the dark, in his mouth, and went on first to light his friends through the long dark passage, and when they came to the place where the dead bird lay, he thrust his broad nose up against the ceiling and pushed up the earth, so as to make a great hole for the light to come through. In the midst of the floor lay a swallow, his wings clinging firmly to his sides, his head and legs drawn under the feathers; the poor bird had evidently died of cold. Tommelise felt so very sorry, for she loved all the little birds, who had sung and chirped so merrily to her the whole summer long; but the mole kicked it with his short legs, saying, "Here's a fine end to all its whistling! a miserable thing it must to be to be born a bird. None of my children will be birds, that's a comfort! Such creatures have nothing but their 'quivit,' and must be starved to death in the winter."

"Yes, indeed, a sensible animal like you may well say so," returned the field-mouse; "what has the bird got by all his chirping and chirruping? when winter comes it must starve and freeze; and it is such a great creature too!"

Tommelise said nothing, but when the two others had

turned their backs upon the bird, she bent over it, smoothed down the feathers that covered its head, and kissed the closed eyes. "Perhaps it was this one that sang so delightfully to me in the summer-time," thought she; "how much pleasure it has given me, the dear, dear bird!"

The mole now stopped up the hole through which the daylight had pierced, and then followed the ladies home. But Tommelise could not sleep that night, so she got out of her bed, and wove a carpet out of hay, and then went out and spread it round the dead bird; she also fetched some soft cotton from the field-mouse's room, which she laid over the bird, that it might be warm amid the cold earth.

"Farewell, thou dear bird," said she; "farewell, and thanks for thy beautiful song in the summer-time, when all the trees were green, and the sun shone so warmly upon us!" And she pressed her head against the bird's breast, but was terrified to feel something beating within it. It was the bird's heart, the bird was not dead; it had lain in a swoon, and now that it was warmer its life returned.

Every autumn all the swallows fly away to warm countries; but if one of them lingers behind, it freezes and falls down as though dead, and the cold snow covers it.

Tommelise trembled with fright, for the bird was very large compared with her, who was only an inch in length. However, she took courage, laid the cotton more closely round the poor swallow, and fetching a leaf which had served herself as a coverlet, spread it over the bird's head.

The next night she stole out again, and found that the bird's life had quite returned, though it was so feeble that only for one short moment could it open its eyes to look at Tommelise, who stood by with a piece of tinder in her hand—she had no other lantern.

"Thanks to thee, thou sweet little child!" said the sick swallow. "I feel delightfully warm now; soon I shall recover my strength, and be able to fly again, out in the warm sunshine."

"Oh no," she replied, "it is too cold without, it snows and freezes! thou must stay in thy warm bed, I will take care of thee."

She brought the swallow water in a flower-petal and he drank, and then he told her how he had torn one of his wings in a thorn bush, and therefore could not fly fast enough to keep up with the other swallows who were all migrating to the warm countries. He had at last fallen to the earth, and more than that he could not remember; he did not at all know how he had got underground.

However, underground he remained all the winter long, and Tommelise was kind to him, and loved him dearly, but she never said a word about him either to the mole or the field-mouse, for she knew they could not endure the poor swallow.

As soon as the spring came and the sun's warmth had penetrated the earth, the swallow said farewell to Tommelise, and she opened for him the covering of earth which the mole had thrown back before. The sun shone in upon them so deliciously, and the swallow asked whether she would not go with him; she might sit upon his back, and then they would fly together far out into the greenwood. But Tommelise knew it would vex the old field-mouse if she were to leave her.

"No, I cannot, I must not go," said Tommelise.

"Fare thee well, then, thou good and pretty maiden," said the swallow, and away he flew into the sunshine. Tommelise looked after him and the tears came into her eyes, for she loved the poor swallow so much.

"Quivit, quivit," sang the bird, as he flew into the greenwood. And Tommelise was now sad indeed. She was not allowed to go out into the warm sunshine; the wheat that had been sown in the field above the field-mouse's house grew up so high that it seemed a perfect forest to the poor little damsel who was only an inch in stature.

"This summer you must work at getting your wedding clothes ready," said the field-mouse, for their neighbour, the blind dull mole in the black-velvet suit, had now made his proposals in form to Tommelise. "You shall have worsted and linen in plenty; you shall be well provided with all manner of clothes and furniture before you become the mole's wife." So Tommelise was obliged to work hard at the distaff, and the field-mouse hired four spiders to spin and weave night and day. Every evening came the mole, and always began to talk about the summer soon coming to an end, and that then, when the sun would no longer shine so warmly, scorching the earth till it was as dry as a stone, yes, then, his nuptials with Tommelise should take place. But this sort of conversation did not please her at all, she was thoroughly wearied of his dullness and his prating. Every morning when the sun rose, and every evening when it set, she used to steal out at the door, and when the wind blew the tops of the corn aside, so that she could see the blue sky through the opening, she thought how bright and beautiful it was out here, and wished most fervently to see the dear swallow once more; but he never came, he must have been flying far away in the beautiful greenwood.

Autumn came, and Tommelise's wedding clothes were ready.

"Four weeks more, and you shall be married!" said the field-mouse. But Tommelise wept, and said she would not marry the dull mole.

"Fiddlestick!" exclaimed the field-mouse; "don't be obstinate, child, or I shall bite thee with my white teeth! Is he not handsome, pray? Why, the queen has not got such a black-velvet dress as he wears! And isn't he rich? rich both in kitchens and cellars? Be thankful to get such a husband!"

So Tommelise must be married. The day fixed had arrived, the mole had already come to fetch his bride, and she must dwell with him, deep under the earth, never again to come out into the warm sunshine which she loved so much, and which he could not endure. The poor child was in despair at the thought that she must now bid farewell to the beautiful sun of which she had at least been allowed to catch a glimpse every now and then while she lived with the field-mouse.

"Farewell, thou glorious sun!" she cried, throwing her arms up into the air, and she walked on a little way beyond the field-mouse's door; the corn was already reaped, and only the dry stubble surrounded her. "Farewell, farewell!" repeated she, as she clasped her tiny arms round a little red flower that grew there. "Greet the dear swallow from me, if thou shouldst see him."

"Quivit! quivit!"—there was a fluttering of wings just over her head; she looked up, and behold! the little swallow was flying past. And how pleased he was when he perceived Tommelise! She told how that she had been obliged to accept the disagreeable mole as a husband, and that she would have to dwell deep underground where the sun never pierced. And she could not help weeping as she spoke.

"The cold winter will soon be here!" said the swallow; "I shall fly far away to the warm countries. Wilt thou go with me? Thou canst sit on my back, and tie thyself firmly to me with thy sash, and thus we shall fly away from the stupid mole and his dark room, far away over the mountains to those countries where the sun shines so brightly, where it is always summer, and flowers blossom all the year round. Come and fly with me, thou sweet little Tommelise, who didst save my life when I lay frozen in the dark cellars of the earth!"

"Yes, I will go with thee!" said Tommelise. And she seated herself on the bird's back, her feet resting on the outspread wings, and tied her girdle firmly round one of the strongest feathers, and then the swallow soared high into the air, and flew away over forest and over lake, over mountains whose crests are covered with snow all the year round. How Tommelise shivered as she breathed the keen frosty air! However, she soon crept down under the bird's warm feathers, her head still peering forth, eager to behold all the glory and beauty beneath her. At last they reached the warm countries. There the sun shone far more brightly than in her native clime. The heavens seemed twice as high, and twice as blue; and ranged along the sloping hills grew, in rich luxuriance, the loveliest green and purple grapes. Citrons and melons were seen in the groves, the fragrance of myrtles and balsams filled the air, and by the wayside gambolled groups of pretty merry children, chasing large bright-winged butterflies.

But the swallow did not rest here; still he flew on; and still the scene seemed to grow more and more beautiful. Near a calm, blue lake, overhung by lofty trees, stood a half-ruined palace of white marble, built in times long past; vine-wreaths trailed up the long slender pillars, and on the capitals, among the green leaves and waving tendrils, many a swallow had built his nest, and one of these nests belonged to the swallow on whose back Tommelise was riding.

"This is my house," said the swallow, "but if thou wouldst rather choose for thyself one of the splendid flowers growing beneath us, and thou shalt make thy home in the loveliest of them all."

"That will be charming!" exclaimed she, clapping her tiny hands.

On the green turf beneath there lay the fragments of a white marble column which had fallen to the ground, and around these fragments twined some beautiful large white flowers. The swallow flew down with Tommelise, and set her on one of the broad petals. But what was her surprise when she saw sitting in the very heart of the flower a little mannikin, fair and transparent as though he were made of glass! wearing the prettiest gold crown on his head, and the brightest, most delicate wings on his shoulders, yet scarcely one whit larger than Tommelise herself. He was the spirit of the flower. In every blossom there dwelt one such faery youth or maiden, but this one was the king of all these flower-spirits.

"Oh, how handsome he is, this king!" whispered Tommelise to the swallow. The faery prince was quite startled at the sudden descent of the swallow, who was a sort of giant compared with him; but when he saw Tommelise he was delighted, for she was the very loveliest maiden he had ever seen. So he took his gold crown off his own head and set it upon hers, asked her name, and whether she would be his bride, and reign as queen over all the flower-spirits. This, you see, was quite a different bridegroom from the son of the ugly old toad, or the blind mole with his black-velvet coat. So Tommelise replied "Yes" to the beautiful prince, and then the lady and gentlemen faeries came out, each from a separate flower, to pay their homage to Tommelise; so gracefully and courteously they paid their homage! and every one of them brought her a present.

But the best of all the presents was a pair of transparent wings; they were fastened on Tommelise's shoulders, and enabled her to fly from flower to flower.

That was the greatest of pleasures; and the little swallow sat in his nest above and sang to her his sweetest song; in his heart, however, he was very sad, for he loved Tommelise, and would have wished never to part from her.

"Thou shalt no longer be called Tommelise," said the king of flowers to her, "for it is not a pretty name, and thou art so lovely! We will call thee Maia."

"Farewell! farewell!" sang the swallow, and away he

flew from the warm countries, far away back to Denmark. There he had a little nest just over the window of the man who writes stories for children. "Quivit, quivit, quivit!" he sang to him, and from him we have learned this history.

THE SNOW QUEEN

Part One
Which treats of the mirror and its fragments

Listen! We are beginning our story! When we arrive at the end of it we shall, it is to be hoped, know more than we do now. There was once a magician! a wicked magician!! a most wicked magician!!! Great was his delight at having constructed a mirror possessing this peculiarity, viz.:—that everything good and beautiful, when reflected in it, shrank up almost to nothing, whilst those things that were ugly and useless were magnified, and made to appear ten times worse than before. The loveliest landscapes reflected in this mirror looked like boiled spinach; and the handsomest persons appeared odious, or as if standing upon their heads, their features being so distorted that their friends could never have recognised them. Moreover, if one of them had a freckle, he might be sure that it would seem to spread over the nose and mouth; and if a good or pious thought glanced across his mind, a wrinkle was seen in the mirror. All this the magician thought highly entertaining, and he chuckled with delight at his own clever invention. Those who frequented the school of magic where he taught, spread abroad the fame of this wonderful mirror, and declared that by its means the world and its inhabitants might be seen now for the first time as they really were. They carried the mirror from place to place, till at last there was no country nor person that had not been misrepresented in it. Its admirers now must needs fly up to the sky with it, to see if they could not carry on their sport even there. But the higher they flew the more wrinkled did the mirror become; they could scarcely hold it together. They flew on and on, higher and higher, till at last the mirror trembled so fearfully that it escaped from their hands, and fell to the earth, breaking into millions, billions, and trillions of pieces. And then it caused far greater unhappiness than before, for fragments of it, scarcely as large as a grain of sand, would be flying about in the air, and sometimes get into people's eyes, causing them to view everything the wrong way, or to have eyes only for what was perverted and corrupt; each little fragment having retained the peculiar properties of the entire mirror. Some people were so unfortunate as to receive a little splinter into their hearts—that was terrible! The heart became cold and hard, like a lump of ice. Some pieces were large enough to be used as window panes, but it was of no use to look at one's friends through such panes as those. Other fragments were made into spectacles, and then what trouble people had with setting and re-setting them!

The wicked magician was greatly amused with all this, and he laughed till his sides ached.

There are still some little splinters of this mischievous mirror flying about in the air. We shall hear more about them very soon.

Part Two
A little boy and a little girl

In a large town, where there are so many houses and inhabitants that there is not room enough for all the people to possess a little garden of their own, and therefore many are obliged to content themselves with keeping a few plants in pots, there dwelt two poor children, whose garden was somewhat larger than a flowerpot. They were not brother and sister, but they loved each other as much as if they had been, and their parents lived in two attics exactly opposite. The roof of one neighbour's house nearly joined the other, the gutter ran along between, and there was in each roof a little window, so that you could stride across the gutter from one window to the other. The parents of each child had a large wooden box in which grew herbs for kitchen use, and they had placed these boxes upon the gutter, so near that they almost touched each other. A beautiful little rose-tree grew in each pot, scarlet runners entwined their long shoots over the windows, and, uniting with the branches of the rose-trees, formed a flowery arch across the street. The boxes were very high, and the children knew that they might not climb over them, but they often obtained leave to sit on their little stools, under the rose-trees, and thus they passed many a delightful hour.

But when winter came there was an end to these pleasures.

The windows were often quite frozen over, and then they heated halfpence on the stove, held the warm copper against the frozen pane, and thus made a little round peep-hole, behind which would sparkle a bright gentle eye, one from each window.

The little boy was called Kay, the little girl's name was Gerda. In summer-time they could get out of the window and jump over to each other; but in winter there were stairs to run down, and stairs to run up, and sometimes the wind roared, and the snow fell outdoors.

"Those are the white bees swarming there!" said the old grandmother.

"Have they a Queen bee?" asked the little boy, for he knew that the real bees have one.

"They have," said the grandmother. "She flies yonder where they swarm so thickly; she is the largest of them, and never remains upon the earth, but flies up again into the black cloud. Sometimes on a winter's night she flies through the streets of the town, and breathes with her frosty breath upon the windows, and then they are covered with strange and beautiful forms, like trees and flowers."

"Yes, I have seen them!" said both the children—they knew that this was true.

"Can the Snow Queen come in here?" asked the little girl.

"If she does come in," said the boy, "I will put her on the warm stove and then she will melt."

And the grandmother stroked his hair and told him some stories.

That same evening, after little Kay had gone home, and was half undressed, he crept upon the chair by the window and peeped through the little round hole. Just then a few snowflakes fell outside, and one, the largest of them, remained lying on the edge of one of the flower-pots. The snowflake appeared larger and larger, and at last took the form of a lady dressed in the finest white crêpe, her attire being composed of millions of starlike particles. She was exquisitely fair and delicate, but entirely of ice, glittering, dazzling ice; her eyes gleamed like two bright stars, but there was no rest or repose in them. She nodded at the window, and beckoned with her hand. The little boy was frightened and jumped down from the chair; he then fancied he saw a large bird fly past the window.

There was a clear frost next day, and soon afterwards came spring; the trees and flowers budded, the swallows built their nests, the windows were opened, and the little children sat once more in their little garden upon the gutter that ran along the roof of the houses.

The roses blossomed beautifully that summer, and the little girl had learned a hymn in which there was something about roses; it reminded her of her own. So she sang it to the little boy, and he sang it with her.

> "Our roses bloom and fade away,
> Our Infant Lord abides alway;
> May we be blessed His face to see,
> And ever little children be!"

And the little ones held each other by the hand, kissed the roses, and looked up into the blue sky, talking away all the time. What glorious summer days were those! how delightful it was to sit under those rose-trees which seemed as if they never intended to leave off blossoming! One day Kay and Gerda were sitting looking at their picture-book full of birds and animals, when suddenly— the clock on the old church tower was just striking five— Kay exclaimed, "Oh, dear! what was that shooting pain in my heart? And now again, something has certainly got into my eye!"

The little girl turned and looked at him. He winked his eyes; no, there was nothing to be seen.

"I believe it is gone," said he; but gone it was not. It was one of those glass splinters from the Magic Mirror, the wicked glass which bade everything great and good reflected in it to appear little and hateful, and which magnified everything ugly and mean. Poor Kay had also received a splinter in his heart; it would now become hard and cold like a lump of ice. He felt the pain no longer, but the splinter was there.

"Why do you cry?" asked he; "you look so ugly when you cry! There is nothing the matter with me. Fie!" exclaimed he again, "this rose has an insect in it, and just look at this! after all, they are ugly roses! and it is an ugly box they grow in!" Then he kicked the box, and tore off the roses.

"O Kay, what are you doing?" cried the little girl, but

when he saw how it grieved her, he tore off another rose, and jumped down through his own window, away from his once dear little Gerda.

Ever afterwards when she brought forward the picture-book, he called it a baby's book, and when her grand-mother told stories, he interrupted her with a "but," and sometimes, whenever he could manage it, he would get behind her, put on her spectacles, and speak just as she did; he did this in a very droll manner, and so people laughed at him. Very soon he could mimic everybody in the street. All that was singular and awkward about them could Kay imitate, and his neighbours said, "What a remarkable head that boy has!" But no, it was the glass splinter which had fallen into his eye, the glass splinter which had pierced into his heart—it was these which made him regardless whose feelings he wounded, and even made him tease the Gerda who loved him so fondly.

His games were now quite different from what they used to be, they were so rational! One winter's day when it was snowing, he came out with a large burning-glass in his hand, and, holding up the skirts of his blue coat, let the snowflakes fall upon them. "Now look through the glass, Gerda!" said he, returning to the house. Every snowflake seemed much larger, and resembled a splendid flower, or a star with ten points; they were quite beauti-ful. "See, how curious!" said Kay, "these are far more interesting than real flowers, there is not a single blemish in them; they would be quite perfect if only they did not melt."

Soon after this Kay came in again, with thick gloves on his hands, and his sledge slung across his back. He called out to Gerda, "I have got leave to drive on the great square where the other boys play!" and away he went.

The boldest boys in the square used to fasten their sledges firmly to the wagons of the county people, and thus drive a good way along with them; this they thought particularly pleasant. Whilst they were in the midst of their play a large sledge, painted white, passed by; in it sat a person wrapped in a rough white fur, and wearing a rough white cap. When the sledge had driven twice round the square, Kay bound to it his little sledge, and was carried on with it. On they went, faster and faster, into the next street. The person who drove the large sledge turned round and nodded kindly to Kay, just as if they had been old acquaintances, and every time Kay was going to loose his little sledge, turned and nodded again, as if to signify that he must stay. So Kay sat still, and they passed through the gates of the town. Then the snow began to fall so thickly that the little boy could not see his own hand, but he was still carried on. He tried hastily to unloose the cords and free himself from the large sledge, but it was of no use; his little carriage could not be unfastened, and glided on swift as the wind. Then he cried out as loud as he could, but no one heard him; the snow fell and the sledge flew; every now and then it made a spring as if driving over hedges and ditches. He was very much frightened; he would have repeated "Our Father," but he could remember nothing but the multiplication table.

The snowflakes seemed larger and larger; at last they looked like great white birds. All at once they fell aside, the large sledge stopped, and the person who drove it arose from the seat. He saw that the cap and coat were entirely of snow; that it was a lady, tall and slender, and dazzlingly white—it was the Snow Queen!

"We have driven fast!" said she, "but no one likes to be frozen; creep under my bear-skin," and she seated him in the sledge by her side, and spread her cloak around him— he felt as if he were sinking into a drift of snow.

"Are you still cold?" asked she, and then she kissed his brow. Oh! her kiss was colder than ice. It went to his heart, although that was half frozen already; he thought he should die. It was, however, only for a moment;

directly afterwards he was quite well, and no longer felt the intense cold around.

"My sledge! do not forget my sledge!"—he thought first of that—it was fastened to one of the white birds, which flew behind with it on his back. The Snow Queen kissed Kay again, and he entirely forgot little Gerda, her grandmother, and all at home.

"Now you must have no more kisses!" said she, "else I should kiss thee to death."

Kay looked at her, she was so beautiful; a more intelligent, more lovely countenance, he could not imagine; she no longer appeared to him ice, cold ice, as at the time when she sat outside the window and beckoned to him; in his eyes she was perfect; he felt no fear. He told her how well he could reckon in his head, even fractions; that he knew the number of square miles of every country, and the number of the inhabitants contained in different towns. She smiled, and then it occurred to him that, after all, he did not yet know so very much. He looked up into the wide, wide space, and she flew with him high up into the black cloud while the storm was raging.

They flew over woods and over lakes, over sea and over land; beneath them the cold wind whistled, the wolves howled, the snow glittered, and the black crow flew cawing over the plain, whilst above them shone the moon, so clear and tranquil.

Thus did Kay spend the long, long winter night; all day he slept at the feet of the Snow Queen.

Part Three
The enchanted flower garden

But how fared it with little Gerda when Kay never returned? Where could he be? No one knew, no one could give any account of him. The boys said that they had seen him fasten his sledge to another larger and very handsome one which had driven into the street, and thence through the gates of the town. No one knew where he was, and many were the tears that were shed; little Gerda wept much and long, for the boys said he must be dead, he must have been drowned in the river that flowed not far from the town. Oh, how long and dismal the winter days were now! At last came the spring, with its warm sunshine.

"Alas, Kay is dead and gone," said little Gerda.

"That I do not believe," said the sunshine.

"He is dead and gone," said she to the swallows.

"That we do not believe," returned they, and at last little Gerda herself did not believe it.

"I will put on my new red shoes," said she one morning, "those which Kay has never seen, and then I will go down to the river and ask after him."

It was quite early. She kissed her old grandmother, who was still sleeping, put on her red shoes, and went alone through the gates of the town towards the river.

"Is it true," said she, "that thou hast taken my little playfellow away? I will give thee my red shoes if thou wilt restore him to me!"

And the wavelets of the river flowed towards her in a manner which she fancied was unusual; she fancied that they intended to accept her offer, so she took off her red shoes—though she prized them more than anything else she possessed—and threw them into the stream; but they fell near the shore, and the little waves bore them back to her, as though they would not take from her what she most prized, as they had not got little Kay. However, she thought she had not thrown the shoes far enough, so she stepped into a little boat which lay among the reeds by the shore, and, standing at the farthest end of it, threw them from thence into the water. The boat was not fastened, and her movements in it caused it to glide away from the shore. She saw this, and hastened to get out, but, by the time she reached the other end of the boat, it was more than a yard distant from the land; she could not escape, and the boat glided on.

Little Gerda was much frightened and began to cry, but no one besides the sparrows heard her, and they could not carry her back to the land; however, they flew along the banks, and sang, as if to comfort her, "Here we are, here we are!" The boat followed the stream. Little Gerda sat in it quite still; her red shoes floated behind her, but they could not overtake the boat, which glided along faster than they did.

Beautiful were the shores of that river; lovely flowers, stately old trees, and bright green hills dotted with sheep and cows, were seen in abundance, but not a single human being.

"Perhaps the river may bear me to my dear Kay," thought Gerda, and then she became more cheerful, and amused herself for hours with looking at the lovely country around her. At last she glided past a large cherry garden, wherein stood a little cottage with thatched roof and curious red and blue windows; two wooden soldiers stood at the door, who presented arms when they saw the little vessel approach.

Gerda called to them, thinking they were alive; but they, naturally enough, made no answer. She came close up to them, for the stream drifted the boat to the land.

Gerda called still louder, whereupon an old lady came out of the house, supporting herself on a crutch; she wore a large hat, with most beautiful flowers painted on it.

"Thou poor little child!" said the old woman, "the mighty flowing river has indeed borne thee a long, long way," and she walked right into the water, seized the boat with her crutch, drew it to land, and took out the little girl.

Gerda was glad to be on dry land again, although she was a little afraid of the strange old lady.

"Come and tell me who thou art, and how thou camest hither," said she.

And Gerda told her all, and the old lady shook her head, and said, "Hem! hem!" And when Gerda asked if she had seen little Kay, the lady said that he had not arrived there yet, but that he would be sure to come soon, and that in the meantime Gerda must not be sad; that she might stay with her, might eat her cherries, and look at her flowers, which were prettier than any picture-book, and could each tell her a story.

She then took Gerda by the hand; they went together into the cottage, and the old lady shut the door. The windows were very high and their panes of different coloured glass, red, blue, and yellow, so that when the bright daylight streamed through them, various and beautiful were the hues reflected upon the room. Upon a table in the centre was placed a plate of very fine cherries, and of these Gerda was allowed to eat as many as she liked. And whilst she was eating them, the old dame combed her hair with a golden comb, and the bright flaxen ringlets fell on each side of her pretty, gentle face, which looked as round and as fresh as a rose.

"I have long wished for such a dear little girl," said the old lady. "We shall see if we cannot live very happily together." And, as she combed little Gerda's hair, the child thought less and less of her foster-brother Kay, for the old lady was an enchantress. She did not, however, practise magic for the sake of mischief, but merely for her own amusement. And now she wished very much to keep little Gerda, to live with her; so, fearing that if Gerda saw her roses, she would be reminded of her own flowers and of little Kay, and that then she might run away, she went out into the garden, and extended her crutch over all her rose-bushes, upon which, although they were full of leaves and blossoms, they immediately sank into the black earth, and no one would have guessed that such plants had ever grown there.

Then she led Gerda into this flower-garden. Oh, how beautiful and how fragrant it was! Flowers of all seasons and all climes grew there in fullness of beauty—certainly no picture-book could be compared with it. Gerda bounded with delight, and played among the flowers till the sun set behind the tall cherry-trees; after which a pretty little bed, with crimson silk cushions, stuffed with blue violet leaves, was prepared for her, and here she slept as sweetly and had such dreams as a queen might have on her bridal eve.

The next day she again played among the flowers in the warm sunshine, and many more days were spent in the same manner. Gerda knew every flower in the garden, but, numerous as they were, it seemed to her that one was wanting, she could not tell which. She was sitting one day, looking at her hostess's hat, which had flowers painted on it, and, behold, the loveliest among them was a rose! The old lady had entirely forgotten the painted rose on her hat, when she made the real roses disappear from her garden and sink into the ground. This is often the case when things are done hastily.

"What," cried Gerda, "are there no roses in the garden?" And she ran from one bed to another, sought and sought again, but no rose was to be found. She sat down and wept, and it so chanced that her tears fell on a spot where a rose-tree had formerly stood, and as soon as her warm tears had moistened the earth, the bush shot up anew, as fresh and as blooming as it was before it had sunk into the ground; and Gerda threw her arms around it, kissed the blossoms, and immediately recalled to memory the beautiful roses at home, and her little playfellow Kay. "Oh, how could I stay here so long!" exclaimed the little maiden. "I left my home to seek for Kay. Do you know where he is?" she asked of the roses; "think you that he is dead?"

"Dead he is not," said the roses. "We have been down in the earth; the dead are there, but not Kay."

"I thank you," said little Gerda, and she went to the other flowers, bent low over their cups, and asked, "Know you not where little Kay is?"

But every flower stood in the sunshine dreaming its own little tale. They related their stories to Gerda, but none of them knew anything of Kay.

"And what, think you?" said the tiger-lily.

"Listen to the drums beating, boom! boom! They have but two notes, always boom! boom! Listen to the dirge the women are singing! Listen to the chorus of priests! Enveloped in her long red robes stands the Hindoo wife on the funeral pile, the flames blaze around her and her dead husband, but the Hindoo wife thinks not of the dead. She thinks only of the living, and the anguish which consumes her spirit is keener than the fire which will soon reduce her body to ashes. Can the flame of the heart expire amid the flames of the funeral pile?"

"I do not understand that at all!" said little Gerda.

"That is my tale!" said the tiger-lily.

"What says the convolvulus?"

"Hanging over a narrow mountain causeway, behold an ancient, baronial castle. Thick evergreens grow amongst the time-stained walls, their leafy branches entwine about the balcony, and there stands a beautiful maiden; she bends over the balustrades and fixes her eyes with eager expectation on the road winding beneath. The rose hangs not fresher and lovelier on its stem than she; the apple-blossom which the wind threatens every moment to tear from its branch is not more fragile and trembling. Listen to the rustling of her rich silken robe! Listen to her half-whispered words, 'He comes not!'"

"Is it Kay you mean?" asked little Gerda.

"I do but tell you my tale—my dream," replied the convolvulus.

"What says the little snowdrop?"

"Between two trees hangs a swing. Two pretty little maidens, their dress as white as snow, and long green ribands fluttering from their hats, sit and swing themselves in it. Their brother stands up in the swing, he has thrown his arms round the ropes to keep himself steady, for in one hand he holds a little cup, in the other a pipe made of clay; he is blowing soap bubbles. The swing moves and the bubbles fly upwards with bright, ever-changing colours; the last hovers on the edge of the pipe, and moves with the wind. The swing is still in motion, and the little black dog, almost as light as the soap bubbles, rises on his hind feet and tries to get into the swing also; away goes the swing, the dog falls, is out of temper, and barks; he is laughed at, and the bubbles burst. A swinging board, a frothy, fleeting image is my song."

"What you describe may all be very pretty, but you speak so mournfully, and there is nothing about Kay."

"What say the hyacinths?"

"There were three fair sisters, transparent and delicate they were; the kirtle of the one was red, that of the second blue, of the third pure white; hand in hand they danced in the moonlight beside the quiet lake; they were not faeries, but daughters of men. Sweet was the fragrance when the maidens vanished into the wood; the fragrance grew stronger; three biers, whereon lay the fair sisters, glided out from the depths of the wood, and floated upon the lake; the glow-worms flew shining around like little hovering lamps. Sleep the dancing maidens, or are they dead? The odour from the flowers tells us they are corpses, the evening bells peal out their dirge."

"You make me quite sad," said little Gerda. "Your fragrance is so strong I cannot help thinking of the dead maidens. Alas! and is little Kay dead? The roses have been under the earth, and they say no!"

"Ding dong! ding dong!" rang the hyacinth bells. "We toll not for little Kay, we know him not! We do but sing our own song."

And Gerda went to the buttercup, which shone so yellow and so brightly from among her smooth green leaves.

"Thou art like a little bright sun," said Gerda; "tell me, if thou canst, where I may find my playfellow."

And the buttercup glittered so brightly, and looked at Gerda. What song could the buttercup sing? Neither was hers about Kay. "One bright spring morning, the sun shone warmly upon a little courtyard, the bright beams streamed down the white walls of a neighbouring house, and close by grew the first yellow flower of spring, glittering like gold in the warm sunshine. An old grandmother sat without in her armchair; her granddaughter, a pretty, lowly maiden, had just returned home from a short visit, she kissed her grandmother; there was gold, pure gold, in that loving kiss:

"Gold was the flower!
Gold the fresh, bright, morning hour!"

"That is my little story," said the buttercup.

"My poor old grandmother!" sighed Gerda; "yes, she must be wishing for me, just as she wished for little Kay. But I shall soon go home again, and take Kay with me. It is of no use to ask the flowers about him; they only know their own song, they can give me no information." And she folded her little frock round her, that she might run the faster; but, in jumping over the narcissus, it caught her foot, as if wishing to stop her, so she turned and looked at the tall yellow flower.

"Have you any news to give me?" She bent over the narcissus, waiting for an answer.

And what said the narcissus?

"I can look at myself!—I can see myself! Oh, how sweet is my fragrance! Up in the little attic-chamber stands a little dancer. She rests sometimes on one leg, sometimes on two. She has trampled the whole world under her feet; she is nothing but an illusion. She pours water from a tea-pot upon a piece of cloth she holds in her hand—it is her bodice; cleanliness is a fine thing! Her white dress hangs on the hook, that has also been washed by the water from the tea-pot, and dried on the roof of the house. She puts it on, and wraps a saffron-coloured handkerchief round her neck; it makes the dress look all the whiter. With one leg extended, there she stands, as though on a stalk. I can look at myself!—I see myself!"

"I don't care if you do!" said Gerda. "You need not have told me that!" and away she ran to the end of the garden.

The gate was closed, but she pressed upon the rusty lock till it broke. The gate sprang open, and little Gerda, with bare feet, ran out into the wide world. Three times she looked back, there was no one following her; she ran till she could run no longer, and then sat down to rest upon a large stone.

Casting a glance around, she saw that the summer was past, that it was now late in the autumn. Of course, she had not remarked this in the enchanted garden, where there were sunshine and flowers all the year round.

"How long I must have stayed there!" said little Gerda. "So it is now autumn! Well then, there is no time to lose!" and she rose to pursue her way.

Oh, how sore and weary were her little feet! and all around looked so cold and barren. The long willow-leaves had already turned yellow, and the dew trickled down from them like water. The leaves fell off the trees, one by one; the sloe alone bore fruit, and its berries were so sharp and bitter! Cold, and grey, and sad seemed the world to her that day.

Part Four
The prince and the princess

Gerda was again obliged to stop and take rest. Suddenly a large raven hopped upon the snow in front of her, saying, "Caw!—Caw!— Good-day!—Good-day!" He sat for some time on the withered branch of a tree just opposite, eyeing the little maiden, and wagging his head, and he now came forward to make acquaintance and to ask her whither she was going all alone. That word "alone" Gerda understood right well—she felt how sad a meaning it had. She told the raven the history of her life and fortunes, and asked if he had seen Kay.

And the raven nodded his head, half doubtfully, and said, "That is possible—possible."

"Do you think so?" exclaimed the little girl, and she kissed the raven so vehemently that it is a wonder she did not squeeze him to death.

"More moderately!—moderately!" said the raven. "I think I know. I think it may be little Kay; but he has certainly forsaken thee for the princess."

"Dwells he with a princess?" asked Gerda.

"Listen to me," said the raven, "but it is so difficult to speak your language! Do you understand Ravenish? If so, I can tell you much better."

"No! I have never learned Ravenish," said Gerda, "but my grandmother knew it, and Pye-language also. Oh, how I wish I had learned it!"

"Never mind," said the raven, "I will relate my story in the best manner I can, though bad will be the best;" and he told all he knew.

"In the kingdom wherein we are now sitting there dwells a princess, a most uncommonly clever princess. All the newspapers in the world has she read, and forgotten them again, so clever is she. It is not long since she ascended the throne, which I have heard is not quite so

100

agreeable a situation as one would fancy; and immediately after she began to sing a new song, the burden of which was this, 'Why should I not marry me?' 'There is some sense in this song!' said she, and she determined she would marry, but at the same time declared that the man whom she would choose must be able to answer sensibly whenever people spoke to him, and must be good for something else besides merely looking grand and stately. The ladies of the court were then all drummed together, in order to be informed of her intentions, whereupon they were highly delighted, and one exclaimed, 'That is just what I wish;' and another, that she had lately been thinking of the very same thing. Believe me." continued the raven, "every word I say is true, for I have a tame beloved who hops at pleasure about the palace, and she has told me all this."

‑ Of course the "beloved" was also a raven, for birds of a feather flock together.

"Proclamations, adorned with borders of hearts, were immediately issued, wherein, after enumerating the style and titles of the princess, it was set forth that every well-favoured youth was free to go to the palace and converse with the princess, and that whoever should speak in such wise as showed that he felt himself at home, there would be the one the princess would choose for her husband.

"Yes, indeed," continued the raven, "you may believe me; all this is as true as that I sit here. The people all crowded to the palace; there was famous pressing and squeezing; but it was all of no use, either the first or the second day; the young men could speak well enough while they were outside the palace gates, but when they entered, and saw the royal guard in silver uniform, and the lackeys on the staircase in gold, and the spacious saloon, all lighted up, they were quite confounded. They stood before the throne where the princess sat, and when she spoke to them, they could only repeat the last word she had uttered, which, you know, it was not particularly interesting for her to hear over again. It was just as though they had been struck dumb the moment they entered the palace, for as soon as they got out, they could talk fast enough. There was a regular procession constantly moving from the gates of the town to the gates of the palace. I was there, and saw it with my own eyes," said the raven. "They grew both hungry and thirsty whilst waiting at the palace, but no one could get even so much as a glass of water; to be sure, some of them, wiser than the rest, had brought with them slices of bread and butter, but none would give any to his neighbour, for he thought to himself 'Let him look hungry, and then the princess will be sure not to choose him.'"

"But Kay, little Kay, when did he come?" asked Gerda; "was he among the crowd?"

"Presently, presently; we have just come to him. On the third day arrived a youth with neither horse nor carriage; gaily he marched up to the palace; his eyes sparkled like yours; he had long beautiful hair, but was very meanly clad."

"That was Kay!" exclaimed Gerda. "Oh then I have found him," and she clapped her hands with delight.

"He carried a knapsack on his back," said the raven.

"No, not a knapsack," said Gerda, "a sledge, for he had a sledge with him when he left home."

"It is possible," rejoined the raven, "I did not look very closely; but this I heard from my beloved, that when he entered the palace gates and saw the royal guard in silver, and the lackeys in gold upon the staircase, he did not seem in the least confused, but nodded pleasantly and said to them, 'It must be very tedious standing out here, I prefer going in.' The halls glistened with light, cabinet councillors and excellencies were walking about bare-footed and carrying golden keys—it was just a place to make a man solemn and silent—and the youth's boots creaked horribly, yet he was not at all afraid."

"That most certainly was Kay!" said Gerda; "I know he had new boots; I have heard them creak in my grandmother's room."

"Indeed they did creak," said the raven; "but merrily went he up to the princess, who was sitting upon a pearl as large as a spinning-wheel, whilst all the ladies of the court, with the maids of honour and their handmaidens, ranged in order, stood on one side, and all the gentlemen in waiting, with their gentlemen, and their gentlemen's gentlemen, who also kept pages, stood ranged in order on the other side, and the nearer they were to the door the prouder they looked. The gentlemen's gentlemen's page, who always wears slippers, one dare hardly look at, so proudly he stands at the door."

"That must be dreadful!" said little Gerda. "And has Kay really won the princess?"

"Had I not been a raven I should have won her myself, notwithstanding my being betrothed. The young man spoke as well as I speak when I converse in Ravenish; that I have heard from my tame beloved. He was handsome and lively—'He did not come to woo her,' he said, 'he had only come to hear the wisdom of the princess,' and he liked her much, and she liked him in return."

"Yes, to be sure, that was Kay," said Gerda; "he was so clever, he could reckon in his head, even fractions! Oh, will you not take me into the palace?"

"Ah! that is easily said," replied the raven, "but how is it to be done? I will talk it over with my tame beloved; she will advise us what to do, for I must tell you that such a little girl as you are will never gain permission to enter publicly."

"Yes, I shall!" cried Gerda. "When Kay knows that I am here, he will immediately come out and fetch me."

"Wait for me at the trellis yonder," said the raven. He wagged his head and away he flew.

The raven did not return till late in the evening. "Caw,

caw," said he. "My tame beloved greets you kindly, and sends you a piece of bread which she took from the kitchen; there is plenty of bread there, and you must certainly be hungry. It is not possible for you to enter the palace, for you have bare feet; the royal guard in silver uniform, and the lackeys in gold, would never permit it; but do not weep, thou shalt go there. My beloved knows a little back staircase leading to the sleeping apartments, and she knows also where to find the key."

And they went into the garden, down the grand avenue, where the leaves dropped upon them as they passed along, and, when the lights in the palace one by one had all been extinguished, the raven took Gerda to a back-door which stood half open. Oh, how Gerda's heart beat with fear and expectation! It was just as though she was about to do something wrong, although she only wanted to know whether Kay was really there—yes, it must be he, she remembered so well his bright eyes and long hair. She would see if his smile were the same as it used to be when they sat together under the rose-trees. He would be so glad to see her, to hear how far she had come for his sake, how all at home mourned his absence. Her heart trembled with fear and joy.

They went up the staircase. A small lamp placed on a cabinet gave a glimmering light; on the floor stood the tame raven, who first turned her head on all sides, and then looked at Gerda, who made her curtsey, as her grandmother had taught her.

"My betrothed has told me much about you, my good young maiden," said the tame raven; "your adventures, too, are extremely interesting! If you will take the lamp, I will show you the way. We are going straight on, we shall not meet any one now."

"It seems me as if some one were behind us," said Gerda; and in fact there was a rushing sound as of something passing; strange-looking shadows flitted rapidly along the wall, horses with long, slender legs and fluttering manes, huntsmen, knights, and ladies.

"These are only Dreams!" said the raven; "they come to amuse the great personages here at night; you will have a better opportunity of looking at them when you are in bed. I hope that when you arrive at honours and dignities you will show a grateful heart."

"Do not talk of that!" said the wood-raven.

They now entered the first saloon; its walls were covered with rose-coloured satin, embroidered with gold flowers. The Dreams rustled past them, but with such rapidity that Gerda could not see them. The apartments through which they passed vied with each other in splendour, and at last they reached the sleeping-hall. In the centre of this room stood a pillar of gold resembling the stem of a large palm-tree, whose leaves of glass, costly glass, formed the ceiling, and depending from the tree, hung near the door, on thick golden stalks, two beds in the form of lilies—the one was white, wherein reposed the princess, the other was red, and here must Gerda seek her playfellow, Kay. She bent aside one of the red leaves and saw a brown neck. Oh, it must be Kay! She called him by his name aloud, held the lamp close to him, the Dreams again rushed by—he awoke, turned his head, and behold! it was not Kay.

The prince resembled him only about the throat; he was, however, young and handsome; and the princess looked out from the white lily petals, and asked what was the matter. Then little Gerda wept and told her whole story, and what the ravens had done for her. "Poor child!" said the prince and princess; and they praised the ravens, and said they were not at all angry with them. Such liberties must never be taken again in their palace, but this time they should be rewarded.

"Would you like to fly away free to the woods?" asked the princess, addressing the ravens, "or to have the appointment secured to you as Court-Ravens, with the perquisites belonging to the kitchen, such as crumbs and leavings?"

And both the ravens bowed low and chose the appointment at Court, for they thought of old age, and said it would be so comfortable to be well provided for in their declining years. Then the prince arose and made Gerda sleep in his bed; and she folded her little hands, thinking, "How kind both men and animals are to me!" She closed her eyes and slept soundly and sweetly, and all the Dreams flitted about her, they looked like angels from heaven, and seemed to be drawing a sledge whereon Kay sat and nodded to her; but this was only fancy, for as soon as she awoke all the beautiful visions had vanished.

The next day she was dressed from head to foot in silk and velvet. She was invited to stay at the palace and enjoy all sorts of diversions, but she begged only for a little carriage and a horse, and a pair of little boots,—to go again into the wide world to seek Kay.

And they gave her the boots and a muff besides, she was dressed so prettily. And as soon as she was ready there drove up to the door a new carriage of pure gold with the arms of the prince and princess glittering upon it like a star, the coachman, the footman, and outriders all wearing gold crowns. The prince and princess themselves helped her into the carriage and wished her success. The wood-raven, who was now married, accompanied her the first three miles; he sat by her side, for riding backwards was a thing he could not bear; the other raven stood at the door flapping her wings; she did not go with them on account of a headache she had felt ever since she had received her appointment, in consequence of eating too much. The carriage was well provided with sugar-plums, fruit, and gingerbread nuts.

"Farewell! farewell!" cried the prince and princess. Little Gerda wept, and the raven wept out of sympathy;

but his farewell was a far sorer trial; he flew up to the branch of a tree and flapped his black wings at the carriage till it was out of sight.

Part Five
The little robber maiden

They drove through the dark, dark forest; the carriage shone like a torch. Unfortunately its brightness attracted the eyes of the robbers who dwelt in the forest-shades; they could not bear it.

"That is gold! gold!" cried they. Forward they rushed, seized the horses, stabbed the outriders, coachman, and footmen to death, and dragged little Gerda out of the carriage.

"She is plump, she is pretty, she has been fed on nut kernels," said the old robber-wife, who had a long, bristly beard, and eyebrows hanging like bushes over her eyes. "She is like a little fat lamb, and how smartly she is dressed!" and she drew out her bright dagger, glittering most terribly.

"Oh, oh!" cried the woman, for at the very moment she had lifted her dagger to stab Gerda, her own wild and wilful daughter jumped upon her back and bit her ear violently. "You naughty child!" said the mother.

"She shall play with me," said the little robber-maiden, "she shall give me her muff and her pretty frock, and sleep with me in my bed!" And then she bit her mother again, till the robber-wife sprang up and shrieked with pain, whilst the robbers all laughed, saying, "Look at her playing with her young one!"

"I will get into the carriage," said the little robber-maiden, and so spoiled and wayward was she that she always had her own way, and she and Gerda sat together in the carriage, and drove over stock and stone farther and farther into the wood. The little robber-maiden was about as tall as Gerda, but much stronger; she had broad shoulders, and a very dark skin; her eyes were quite black, and had an expression almost melancholy. She put her arm round Gerda's waist, and said, "She shall not kill thee so long as I love thee! Art thou not a princess?"

"No!" said Gerda; and then she told her all that had happened to her, and how much she loved little Kay.

The robber-maiden looked earnestly in her face, shook her head, and said, "She shall not kill thee even if I do quarrel with thee; then, indeed, I would rather do it myself!" And she dried Gerda's tears, and put both her hands into the pretty muff that was so soft and warm.

The carriage at last stopped in the middle of the court-yard of the robbers castle. This castle was half-ruined; crows and ravens flew out of the openings, and some fearfully large bulldogs, looking as if they could devour a man in a moment, jumped round the carriage; they did not bark, for that was forbidden.

The maidens entered a large, smoky hall, where a tremendous fire was blazing on the stone floor; the smoke rose up to the ceiling, seeking a way of escape, for there was no chimney; a large cauldron full of soup was boiling over the fire, whilst hares and rabbits were roasting on the spit.

"Thou shalt sleep with me and my little pets tonight!" said the robber-maiden. Then they had some food, and afterwards went to the corner wherein lay straw and a piece of carpet. Nearly a hundred pigeons were perched on staves and laths around them; they seemed to be asleep, but were startled when the little maidens approached.

"These all belong to me," said Gerda's companion, and seizing hold of one of the nearest, she held the poor bird by the feet and swung it. "Kiss it," said she, flapping it into Gerda's face. "The rabble from the wood sit up there," continued she, pointing to a number of laths fastened across a hole in the wall; "those are wood-pigeons, they would fly away if I did not keep them shut up. And here is my old favourite!" She pulled forward by the horn a reindeer who wore a bright copper ring round his neck, by which he was fastened to a large stone. "We are obliged to chain him up, or he would run away from us; every evening I tickle his neck with my sharp dagger; it makes him fear so much!" and the robber-maiden drew out a long dagger from a gap in the wall, and passed it over the reindeer's throat; the poor animal struggled and kicked, but the girl laughed, and then she pulled Gerda into bed with her.

"Will you keep the dagger in your hand whilst you sleep?" asked Gerda, looking timidly at the dangerous plaything.

"I always sleep with my dagger by my side," replied the little robber-maiden, "one never knows what may happen. But now tell me all over again what you told me before about Kay, and the reason of your coming into the wide world all by yourself."

And Gerda again related her history, and the wood-pigeons imprisoned above listened, but the others were fast asleep. The little robber-maiden threw one arm round Gerda's neck, and holding the dagger with the other, was also soon asleep; one could hear her heavy breathing, but Gerda could not close her eyes throughout the night— she knew not what would become of her, whether she would even be suffered to live. The robbers sat round the fire drinking and singing. Oh, it was a dreadful night for the poor little girl!

Then spoke the wood-pigeons, "Coo, coo, coo! we have seen little Kay. A white fowl carried his sledge, he himself was in the Snow Queen's chariot, which passed through the wood whilst we sat in our nest. She breathed upon us young ones as she passed, and all died of her breath excepting us two,—coo, coo, coo!"

"What are you saying?" cried Gerda. "Where was the Snow Queen going? Do you know anything about it?"

"She travels most likely to Lapland, where ice and snow abide all the year round. Ask the reindeer bound to the rope there."

"Yes, ice and snow are there all through the year, it is a glorious land!" said the reindeer. "There, free and happy, one can roam through the wide, sparkling valleys! There the Snow Queen has her summer-tent; her strong castle is very far off, near the North Pole, on the island called Spitsbergen."

"Oh, Kay, dear Kay!" sighed Gerda.

"You must lie still," said the robber-maiden, "or I will thrust my dagger into your side."

When morning came Gerda repeated to her what the wood-pigeons had said, and the little robber-maiden looked grave for a moment, then nodded her head, saying, "No matter! no matter! Do you know where Lapland is?" asked she of the reindeer.

"Who should know but I?" returned the animal, his eyes kindling. "There was I born and bred, there how often have I bounded over the wild icy plains!"

"Listen to me!" said the robber-maiden to Gerda. "You see all our men are gone, my mother is still here and will remain, but towards noon she will drink a little out of the great flask, and after that she will sleep—then I will do something for you!" And so saying she jumped out of bed, sprung upon her mother, pulled her by the beard, and said, "My own dear mam, good-morning!" and the mother caressed her so roughly that she was red and blue all over; however, it was from pure love for her daughter.

When her mother was fast asleep, the robber-maiden went up to the reindeer, and said, "I should have great pleasure in stroking you a few more times with my sharp dagger, for then you look so droll; but never mind, I will unloose your chain and help you to escape, on condition that you run as fast as you can to Lapland, and take this little girl to the castle of the Snow Queen, where her playfellow is. You must have heard her story, for she speaks loud enough, and you know well how to listen."

The reindeer bounded with joy, and the robber-maiden lifted Gerda on his back, taking the precaution to bind her on firmly, as well as to give her a little cushion to sit on. "And here," said she, "are your fur boots, you will need them in that cold country; the muff I must keep myself, it is too pretty to part with; but you shall not be frozen. Here are my mother's huge gloves; they reach up to the elbow, put them on—now your hands look as clumsy as my old mother's!"

And Gerda shed tears of joy.

"I cannot bear to see you crying!" said the little robber-maiden, "you ought to look glad; see, here are two loaves and a piece of bacon for you, that you may not be hungry on the way." She fastened this provender also on the reindeer's back, opened the door, called away the great dogs, and then cutting asunder with her dagger the rope which bound the reindeer, shouted to him, "Now then, run! but take good care of the little girl."

And Gerda stretched out her hands to the robber-maiden and bade her farewell, and the reindeer fleeted through the forest, over stock and stone, over desert and heath, over meadow and moor. The wolves howled and the ravens shrieked. "Isch! Isch!" A red light flashed—one might have fancied the sky was sneezing.

"Those are my dear old Northern Lights!" said the reindeer; "look at them, how beautiful they are!" And he ran faster than ever—the loaves were eaten, so was the bacon—at last they were in Lapland.

Part Six
The Lapland woman and the Finland woman

They stopped at a little hut, a wretched hut it was; the roof very nearly touched the ground, and the door was so low that whoever wished to go either in or out was obliged to crawl upon hands and knees. No one was at home except an old Lapland woman who was busy boiling fish over a lamp filled with train oil. The reindeer related to her Gerda's whole history, not, however, till after he had made her acquainted with his own, which appeared to him of much more importance. Poor Gerda, meanwhile, was so overpowered by the cold that she could not speak.

"Ah, poor things!" said the Lapland woman, "you have still a long way before you! You have a hundred miles to run before you can arrive in Finland: the Snow Queen dwells there, and burns blue lights every evening. I will write for you a few words on a piece of dried stock-fish—paper I have none—and you may take it with you to the wise Finland woman who lives there; she will advise you better than I can."

So when Gerda had well warmed herself and taken some food, the Lapland woman wrote a few words on a dried stock-fish, bade Gerda take care of it, and bound her once more firmly on the reindeer's back.

Onwards they sped; the wondrous Northern Lights, now of the loveliest, brightest blue colour, shone all through the night, and amidst these splendid illuminations they arrived in Finland, and knocked at the chimney of the wise woman, for she had no door to her house.

Hot, very hot was it within—so much so that the wise woman wore scarcely any clothing; she was low in stature and very dirty. She immediately loosened little Gerda's dress, took off her fur boots and thick gloves, laid a piece of ice on the reindeer's head, and then read what was written on the stock-fish. She read it three times. After the third reading she knew it by heart, and threw the fish into the porridge-pot, for it might make a very excellent supper, and she never wasted anything.

The reindeer then repeated his own story, and when that was finished he told of little Gerda's adventures, and the wise woman twinkled her wise eyes, but spoke not a word.

"Thou art so powerful," continued the reindeer, "that I know thou canst twist all the winds of the world into a thread, of which if the pilot loosen one knot he will have a favourable wind; if he loosen the second it will blow sharp, and if he loosen the third, so tremendous a storm will arise that the trees of the forest will be uprooted, and the ship wrecked. Wilt thou not mix for this little maiden that wonderful draught which will give her the strength of twelve men, and thus enable her to overcome the Snow Queen?"

"The strength of twelve men!" repeated the wise woman, "that would be of much use to be sure!" and she walked away, drew forth a large parchment roll from a shelf and began to read. What strange characters were seen inscribed on the scroll as the wise woman slowly unrolled it! She read so intently that the perspiration ran down her forehead.

But the reindeer pleaded so earnestly for little Gerda, and Gerda's eyes were raised so entreatingly and tearfully, that at last the wise woman's eyes began to twinkle again out of sympathy, and she drew the reindeer into a corner, and putting a fresh piece of ice upon his head, whispered thus:

"Little Kay is still with the Snow Queen, in whose abode everything is according to his taste, and therefore he believes it to be the best place in the world. But that is because he has a glass splinter in his heart, and a glass splinter in his eye—until he has got rid of them he will never feel like a human being, and the Snow Queen will always maintain her influence over him."

"But canst thou not give something to little Gerda whereby she may overcome all these evil influences?"

"I can give her no power so great as that which she already possesses. Seest thou not how strong she is? Seest thou not that both men and animals must serve her—a poor little girl wandering barefoot through the world? Her power is greater than ours, it proceeds from her heart, from her being a loving and innocent child. If this power which she already possesses cannot give her access to the Snow Queen's palace, and enable her to free Kay's eye and heart from the glass fragment, we can do nothing for her! Two miles hence is the Snow Queen's garden; thither thou canst carry the little maiden. Put her down close by the bush bearing red berries and half covered with snow: lose no time, and hasten back to this place!"

And the wise woman lifted Gerda on the reindeer's back, and away they went.

"Oh, I have left my boots behind! I have left my gloves behind!" cried little Gerda, when it was too late. The cold was piercing, but the reindeer dared not stop; on he ran until he reached the bush with the red berries. Here he set Gerda down, kissed her, the tears rolling down his cheeks the while, and ran fast back again—which was the best thing he could do. And there stood poor Gerda, without shoes, without gloves, alone in that barren region, that terrible icy-cold Finland.

She ran on as fast as she could; a whole regiment of snowflakes came to meet her. They did not fall from the sky, which was cloudless and bright with the Northern Lights, they ran straight along the ground, and the farther Gerda advanced the larger they grew. Gerda then remembered how large and curious the snowflakes had appeared to her when one day she had looked at them through a burning-glass; these, however, were very much larger, they were living forms, they were in fact the Snow Queen's guards. Their shapes were the strangest that could be imagined; some looked like great ugly porcupines, others like snakes rolled into knots with their heads peeping forth, and others like little fat bears with bristling hair—all, however, were alike dazzlingly white—all were living snowflakes. Little Gerda began to repeat "Our Father"; meanwhile, the cold was so intense that she could see her own breath, which, as it escaped her mouth, ascended into the air like vapour; the cold grew intense, the vapour more dense, and at length took the forms of little bright angels which, as they touched the earth, became larger and more distinct. They wore helmets on their heads, and carried shields and spears in their hands; their number increased so rapidly that, by the time Gerda had finished her prayer, a whole legion stood around her. They thrust with their spears against the horrible snowflakes, which fell into thousands of pieces, and little Gerda walked on unhurt and undaunted. The angels touched her hands and feet, and then she scarcely felt the cold, and boldly approached the Snow Queen's palace.

But before we accompany her there, let us see what Kay is doing. He is certainly not thinking of little Gerda, least of all can he imagine that she is now standing at the palace gate.

Part Seven
Which treats of the Snow Queen's palace, and of what came to pass therein

The walls of the palace were formed of the driven snow; its doors and windows of the cutting winds. There were above a hundred halls, the largest of them many miles in extent, all illuminated by the Northern Lights, all alike vast, empty, icily cold, and dazzlingly white. No sounds of mirth ever resounded through these dreary spaces; no cheerful scene refreshed the sight—not even so much as a bear's ball, such as one might imagine sometimes takes place, the tempest forming a band of musicians, and the polar bears standing on their hind paws and exhibiting themselves in the oddest positions. Nor was there ever a card-assembly, wherein the cards might be held in the mouth and dealt out by paws; nor even a small select coffee party for the white young lady foxes. Vast, empty, and cold were the Snow Queen's chambers, and the Northern Lights flashed, now high, now low, in regular gradations. In the midst of the empty, interminable snow saloon lay a frozen lake; it was broken into a thousand pieces, but these pieces so exactly resembled each other, that the breaking of them might well be deemed a work of more than human skill. The Snow Queen, when at home, always sat in the centre of this lake; she used to say that she was then sitting on the Mirror of Reason, and that hers was the best, indeed, the only one, in the world.

Little Kay was quite blue, nay, almost black with cold, but he did not observe it, for the Snow Queen had kissed away the shrinking feeling he used to experience, and his heart was like a lump of ice. He was busied among the sharp icy fragments, laying and joining them together in every possible way, just as people do with what are called Chinese puzzles. Kay could form the most curious and complete figures—this was the ice-puzzle of reason—and in his eyes these figures were of the utmost importance. He often formed whole words, but there was one word he could never succeed in forming—it was Eternity. The Snow Queen had said to him, "When thou canst put that figure together, thou shalt become thine own master, and I will give thee the whole world, and a new pair of skates besides."

But he could never do it.

116

"Now I am going to the warm countries," said the Snow Queen. "I shall flit through the air, and look into the black cauldrons"—she meant the burning mountains, Etna and Vesuvius. "I shall whiten them a little; that will be good for the citrons and vineyards." So away flew the Snow Queen, leaving Kay sitting all alone in the large empty hall of ice. He looked at the fragments, and thought and thought till his head ached. He sat so still and so stiff that one might have fancied that he too was frozen.

Cold and cutting blew the winds when little Gerda passed through the palace gates, but she repeated her evening prayer, and they immediately sank to rest. She entered the large, cold, empty hall: she saw Kay, she recognised him, she flew upon his neck, she held him fast, and cried, "Kay! dear, dear Kay! I have found thee at last!"

But he sat still as before, cold, silent, motionless; his unkindness wounded poor Gerda deeply. Hot and bitter were the tears she shed, they fell upon his breast, they reached his heart, they thawed the ice and dissolved the tiny splinter of glass within it. He looked at her whilst she sang her hymn—

"Our roses bloom and fade away,
Our Infant Lord abides alway;
May we be blessed His face to see,
And ever little children be!"

Then Kay burst into tears. He wept till the glass splinter floated in his eye and fell with his tears; he knew his old companion immediately, and exclaimed with joy, "Gerda, my dear little Gerda, where hast thou been all this time?—and where have I been?"

He looked around him. "How cold it is here! how wide and empty!" and he embraced Gerda, whilst she laughed and wept by turns. Even the pieces of ice took part in their joy; they danced about merrily, and when they were wearied and lay down they formed of their own accord the mystical letters of which the Snow Queen had said that when Kay could put them together he should be his own master, and that she would give him the whole world, with a new pair of skates besides.

And Gerda kissed his cheeks, whereupon they became fresh and glowing as ever; she kissed his eyes, and they sparkled like her own; she kissed his hands and feet, and he was once more healthy and merry. The Snow Queen might now come home as soon as she liked— it mattered not; Kay's charter of freedom stood written on the mirror in bright icy characters.

They took each other by the hand, and wandered forth out of the palace, talking meanwhile about the aged grandmother and the rose-trees on the roof of their houses; and as they walked on, the winds were hushed into a calm, and the sun burst forth in splendour from among the dark storm-clouds. When they arrived at the bush with the red berries, they found the reindeer standing by awaiting their arrival; he had brought with him another and younger reindeer, whose udders were full, and who gladly gave her warm milk to refresh the young travellers.

The old reindeer and the young hind now carried Kay and Gerda on their backs, first to the little hot room of the wise woman of Finland, where they warmed themselves, and received advice how to proceed in their journey home, and afterwards to the abode of the Lapland woman, who made them some new clothes and provided them with a sledge.

The whole party now ran on together till they came to the boundary of the country; but just where the green leaves began to sprout, the Lapland woman and the two reindeers took their leave. "Farewell! farewell!" said they all. And the first little birds they had seen for many a long day began to chirp, and warble their pretty songs; and the trees of the forest burst upon them full of rich and variously tinted foliage. Suddenly the green boughs parted asunder, and a spirited horse galloped up. Gerda knew it well, for it was the one which had been harnessed to her gold coach; and on it sat a young girl wearing a bright scarlet cap, and with pistols on the holster before her. It was indeed no other than the robber-maiden, who, weary of her home in the forest, was going on her travels, first to the north and afterwards to other parts of the world. She at once recognised Gerda, and Gerda had not forgotten her. Most joyful was their greeting.

"A fine gentleman you are, to be sure, you graceless young truant!" said she to Kay. "I should like to know if you deserved that anyone should be running to the end of the world on your account!"

But Gerda stroked her cheeks, and asked after the prince and princess and their whereabouts.

"They are gone travelling into foreign countries," replied the robber-maiden.

"And the raven?" asked Gerda.

"Ah! the raven is dead," returned she. "The tame beloved has become a widow; so she hops about with a piece of worsted wound round her leg; she moans most piteously, and chatters more than ever! But tell me now all that has happened to you, and how you managed to pick up your old playfellow."

And Gerda and Kay told their story.

"Snip-snap-snurre-basselurre!" said the robber-maiden. She pressed the hands of both, promised that if ever she passed through their town she would pay them a visit, and then bade them farewell, and rode away out into the wide world.

Kay and Gerda walked on hand in hand, and wherever they went it was spring, beautiful spring, with its bright flowers and green leaves.

119

They arrived at a large town; the church bells were ringing merrily, and they immediately recognised the high towers rising into the sky—it was the town wherein they had lived. Joyfully they passed through the streets, joyfully they stopped at the door of Gerda's grandmother. They walked up the stairs and entered the well-known room. The clock said "Tick, tick!" and the hands moved as before. Only one alternation could they find, and that was in themselves, for they saw that they were now full-grown persons. The rose-trees on the roof blossomed in front of the open window, and there beneath them stood the children's stools. Kay and Gerda went and sat down upon them, still holding each other by the hands; the cold, hollow splendour of the Snow Queen's palace they had forgotten, it seemed to them only an unpleasant dream. The grandmother meanwhile sat amid God's bright sunshine, and read from the Bible these words: "Unless ye become as little children, ye shall not enter into the kingdom of heaven."

And Kay and Gerda gazed on each other; they now understood the words of their hymn—

> "Our roses bloom and fade away,
> Our Infant Lord abides alway;
> May we be blessed His face to see,
> And ever little children be!"

There they sat, those two happy ones, grown-up and yet children—children in heart, while all around them glowed bright summer—warm, glorious summer.

THE FIR-TREE

Far away in the deep forest there once grew a pretty Fir-Tree: the situation was delightful, the sun shone full upon him, the breeze played freely around him, and in the neighbourhood grew many companion fir-trees, some older, some younger. But the little Fir-Tree was not happy: he was always longing to be tall; he thought not of the warm sun and the fresh air; he cared not for the merry, prattling peasant children who came to the forest to look for strawberries and raspberries. Except indeed, sometimes, when after having filled their pitchers, or threaded the bright berries on a straw, they would sit down near the little Fir-Tree, and say, "What a pretty little tree this is;" and then the Fir-Tree would feel very much vexed.

Year by year he grew, a long green shoot sent he forth every year; for you may always tell how many years a fir-tree has lived by counting the number of joints in its stem.

"Oh, that I was as tall as the others are," sighed the little Tree; "then I should spread out my branches so far, and my crown should look out over the wide world around! The birds would build their nests among my branches, and when the wind blew I should bend my head so grandly, just as the others do!" He had no pleasure in the sunshine, in the song of the birds, or in the red clouds that sailed over him every morning and evening.

In the winter-time when the ground was covered with the white glistening snow, there was a hare that would come continually scampering about, and jumping right over the little Tree's head—and that was most provoking! However, two winters passed away, and by the third the Tree was so tall that the hare was obliged to run round it. "Oh! to grow, to grow, to become tall and old, that is the only thing in the world worth living for;" so thought the Tree.

The wood-cutters came in the autumn and felled some among the largest of the trees; this happened every year, and our young fir, who was by this time a tolerable height, shuddered when he saw those grand, magnificent trees fall with a tremendous crash crackling to the earth; their boughs were then all cut off; terribly naked and lanky and long did the stem look after this—they could hardly be recognised. They were laid one upon another in wagons, and horses drew them away, far, far away from the forest.

Where could they be going? What might be their fortunes?

So next spring, when the swallows and the storks had returned from abroad, the Tree asked them, saying, "Know you not whither they are taken? Have you not met them?"

The swallows knew nothing about the matter, but the stork looked thoughtful for a moment, then he nodded his head, and said, "Yes, I believe I have seen them! As I was flying from Egypt to this place I met several ships; those ships had splendid masts. I have little doubt that they were the trees that you speak of; they smelled like fir-wood. I may congratulate you, for they sailed gloriously, quite gloriously!"

"Oh, that I too were tall enough to sail upon the sea! Tell me what it is, this sea! and what it looks like."

"Thank you, it would take too long, a great deal!" said the stork, and away he stalked.

"Rejoice in thy youth!" said the sunbeams; "rejoice in thy luxuriant youth, in the fresh life that is within thee!"

And the wind kissed the Tree, and the dew wept tears over him, but the Fir-Tree understood them not.

When Christmas approached, many quite young trees were felled, trees which were some of them not so tall or of just the same height as the young restless Fir-Tree who was always longing to be away; these young trees were chosen from the most beautiful, their branches were not cut off, they were laid in a wagon, and horses drew them away, far, far away from the forest.

"Where are they going?" asked the Fir-Tree. "They are

not larger than I am, indeed one of them was much less; why do they keep all their branches? Where can they be gone?"

"We know! we know!" twittered the sparrows. "We peeped in through the windows of the town below! We know where they are gone. Oh, you cannot think what honour and glory they receive! We looked through the window-panes and saw them planted in a warm room, and decked out with such beautiful things, gilded apples, sweetmeats, playthings, and hundreds of bright candles!"

"And then?" asked the Fir-Tree, trembling in every bough; "and then? What happened then?"

"Oh! we saw no more. That was beautiful, beautiful, beyond compare!"

"Is this glorious lot destined to be mine?" cried the Fir-Tree with delight. "This is far better than sailing over the sea. How I long for the time. Oh, that Christmas were come! I am now tall and full of branches, like the others which last year were carried away. Oh, that I were even now in the wagon! that I were in the warm room, honoured and adorned! and then—yes, then, something still better must happen, else why should they take the trouble to decorate me? It must be that something still greater, still more splendid, must happen—but what? Oh, I suffer, I suffer with longing! I know not what it is that I feel."

"Rejoice in our love," said the air and the sunshine. "Rejoice in thy youth and thy freedom!"

But rejoice he never would. He grew and grew, in winter as in summer; he stood there clothed in green, dark green foliage; the people that saw him said, "That is a beautiful tree!" and, next Christmas, he was the first that was felled. The axe struck sharply through the wood, the Tree fell to the earth with a heavy groan; he suffered an agony, a faintness that he had never expected; he quite forgot to think of his good fortune, he felt such sorrow at being compelled to leave his home, the place whence he had sprung; he knew that he should never see again those dear old comrades, or the little bushes and flowers that had flourished under his shadow, perhaps not even the birds. Neither did he find the journey by any means pleasant.

The Tree first came to himself when, in the courtyard to which he was first taken with the other trees, he heard a man say, "This is a splendid one, the very thing we want!"

Then came two smartly-dressed servants, and carried the Fir-Tree into a large and handsome saloon. Pictures hung on the walls, and on the mantelpiece stood large Chinese vases with lions on the lids; there were rocking-chairs, silken sofas, tables covered with picture-books, and toys that had cost a hundred times a hundred dollars, at least, so said the children. And the Fir-Tree was planted in a large cask filled with sand; but no one could know that it was a cask, for it was hung with green cloth and placed upon a carpet woven of many gay colours. Oh, how the Tree trembled! What was to happen next? A young lady, assisted by the servants, now began to adorn him. Upon some branches they hung little nets cut out of coloured paper, every net filled with sugar-plums; from others gilded apples and walnuts were suspended, looking just as if they had grown there, and more than a hundred little wax tapers, red, blue, and white, were placed here and there among the boughs. Dolls that looked almost like men and women—the Tree had never seen such things before— seemed dancing to and fro among the leaves, and highest, on the summit, was fastened a large star of gold tinsel; this was indeed splendid, splendid beyond compare.

"This evening," they said, "this evening it will be lighted up."

"Would that it were evening," thought the Tree.

"Would that the lights were kindled, for then—what will happen then? Will the trees come out of the forest to see me? Will the sparrows fly here and look in through the window-panes? Shall I stand here adorned both winter and summer?"

He thought much of it; he thought till he had barkache with longing, and barkaches with trees are as bad as headaches with us.

The candles were lighted—oh, what a blaze of splendour! The Tree trembled in all its branches so that one of them caught fire. "Oh dear!" cried the young lady, and it was extinguished in great haste.

So the Tree dared not tremble again; he was so fearful of losing something of his splendour, he felt almost bewildered in the midst of all this glory and brightness. And now, all of a sudden, both folding-doors were flung open, and a troop of children rushed in as if they had a mind to jump over him; the older people followed more quietly; the little ones stood quite silent, but only for a moment. Then their jubilee burst forth afresh, they shouted till the walls re-echoed, they danced round the Tree, one present after another was torn down.

"What are they doing?" thought the Tree; "what will happen now?" And the candles burnt down to the branches, so they were extinguished—and the children were given leave to plunder the Tree. Oh! they rushed upon him in such riot that the boughs all crackled; had not his summit been festooned with the gold star to the ceiling he would have been overturned.

The children danced and played about with their beautiful playthings; no one thought any more of the Tree except the old nurse, who came and peeped among the boughs, but it was only to see whether perchance a fig or an apple had not been left among them.

"A story! a story!" cried the children, pulling a short, thick man towards the Tree. He sat down, saying, "It is pleasant to sit under the shade of green boughs; besides, the tree may benefit by hearing my story. But I shall only tell you one. Would you like to hear about Ivedy Avedy, or about Humpty Dumpty, who fell downstairs, and yet came to the throne and won the Princess?"

"Ivedy Avedy!" cried some! "Humpty Dumpty!" cried others; there was a famous uproar. The Fir-Tree alone was silent, thinking to himself, "Ought I to make a noise as they do? or ought I to do nothing at all?" for he most certainly was one of the company, and had done all that had been required of him.

And the short, thick man told the story of Humpty Dumpty, who fell downstairs and yet came to the throne and won the Princess. And the children clapped their hands and called out for another; they wanted to hear the story of Ivedy Avedy also, but they did not get it. The Fir-Tree stood meanwhile quite silent and thoughtful, the birds in the forest had never related anything like this. "Humpty Dumpty fell downstairs, and yet was raised to the throne and won the Princess! Yes, yes, strange things come to pass in the world!" thought the Fir-Tree, who believed it must all be true, because such a pleasant man had related it. "Ah, ah! who knows but I may fall downstairs and win a Princess!" And he rejoiced in the expectation of being next day again decked out with candles and playthings, gold and fruit. "Tomorrow I will not tremble," thought he. "I will rejoice in my magnificence. Tomorrow I shall again hear the story of Humpty Dumpty, and perhaps that about Ivedy Avedy likewise." And the Tree mused thereupon all night.

In the morning the maids came in.

"Now begins my state anew!" thought the Tree. But they dragged him out of the room, up the stairs, and into an attic chamber, and there thrust him into a dark corner where not a ray of light could penetrate. "What can be the meaning of this?" thought the Tree. "What am I to do here? What shall I hear in this place?" And he leant against the wall, and thought, and thought. And plenty of time he had for thinking it over, for day after day, and night after night passed away, and yet no one ever came into the room. At last somebody did come in, but it was only to push into the corner some old trunks. The Tree was now entirely hidden from sight and apparently entirely forgotten.

"It is now winter," thought the Tree. "The ground is hard and covered with snow; they cannot plant me now, so I am to stay here in shelter till the spring. Men are so clever and prudent! I only wish it were not so dark and so dreadfully lonely; not even a little hare! Oh, how pleasant it was in the forest, when the snow lay on the ground and the hare scampered about, yes, even when he jumped over my head, though I did not like it then. It is so terribly lonely here."

"Squeak! squeak! " cried a little mouse, just then gliding forward. Another followed; they snuffed about the Fir-Tree, and then slipped in and out among the branches.

"It is horribly cold!" said the little mice. "Otherwise it is very comfortable here. Don't you think so, you old Fir-Tree?"

"I am not old," said the Fir-Tree; "there are many who are much older than I am."

"How came you here?" asked the mice, "and what do you know?" They were most uncommonly curious. "Tell us about the most delightful place on earth? Have you ever been there? Have you been into the storeroom, where cheeses lie on the shelves, and bacon hangs from the ceiling; where one can dance over tallow-candles; where one goes in thin and comes out fat?"

"I know nothing about that," said the Tree; "but I know the forest, where the sun shines and where the birds sing!" and then he spoke of his youth and its pleasures. The little mice had never heard anything like it before;

they listened so attentively and said, "Well, to be sure! how much you have seen! how happy you have been!"

"Happy!" repeated the Fir-Tree, in surprise, and he thought a moment over all that he had been saying. "Yes, on the whole those were pleasant times!" He then told them about the Christmas Eve when he had been decked out with cakes and candles.

"Oh!" cried the little mice, "how happy you have been, you old Fir-Tree!"

"I am not old at all!" returned the Fir; "it is only this winter that I have left the forest. I am just in the prime of life!"

"How well you can talk!" said the little mice, and the next night they came again and brought with them four other little mice, who wanted also to hear the Tree's history; and the more the Tree spoke of his youth in the forest, the more vividly he remembered it, and said, "Yes, those were pleasant times! but they may come again, they may come again! Humpty Dumpty fell downstairs, and yet for all that he won the Princess; perhaps I, too, may win a princess!" And then the Fir-Tree thought of a pretty little delicate birch-tree that grew in the forest—a real princess, a very lovely princess was she to the Fir-Tree.

"Who is this Humpty Dumpty?" asked the little mice. Whereupon he related the tale; he could remember every word of it perfectly: and the little mice were ready to jump to the top of the Tree for joy. The night following several more mice came, and on Sunday came also two rats; they, however, declared that the story was not at all amusing, which much vexed the little mice, who, after hearing their opinion, could not like it so well either.

"Do you know only that one story?" asked the rats.

"Only that one!" answered the Tree; "I heard it on the happiest evening of my life, though I did not then know how happy I was."

"It is a miserable story; do you know none about pork and tallow? No storeroom story?"

"No," said the Tree.

"Well, then, we have heard enough of it!" returned the rats, and they went their ways.

The little mice, too, never came again. The Tree sighed, "It was pleasant when they sat round me, those busy little mice, listening to my words. Now that, too, is all past! However, I shall have pleasure in remembering it, when I am taken from this place."

But when would that be? One morning, people came and routed out the lumber-room; the trunks were taken away, the Tree, too, was dragged out of the corner; they threw him carelessly on the floor, but one of the servants picked him up and carried him downstairs. Once more he beheld the light of day. "Now life begins again!" thought the Tree. He felt the fresh air, the warm sunbeams—he was out in the court. All happened so quickly that the Tree quite forgot to look at himself—there was so much to look at all around. The court joined a garden, everything was so fresh and blooming, the roses clustered so bright and so fragrant round the trellis-work, the lime-trees were in full blossom, and the swallows flew backwards and forwards, twittering, "Quirri-virri, vit, my beloved is come!" But it was not the Fir-Tree whom they meant.

"I shall live! I shall live!" He was filled with delightful hope; he tried to spread out his branches, but alas! they were all dried up and yellow. He was thrown down upon a heap of weeds and nettles. The star of gold tinsel that had been left fixed on his crown now sparkled brightly in the sunshine. Some merry children were playing in the court, the same who at Christmas-time had danced round the Tree. One of the youngest now perceived the gold star, and ran to tear it off.

"Look at it, still fastened to the ugly old Christmas Tree!" cried he, trampling upon the boughs till they broke under his boots.

And the Tree looked on all the flowers of the garden now blooming in the freshness of their beauty; he looked upon himself, and he wished from his heart that he had been left to wither alone in the dark corner of the lumber-room: he called to mind his happy forest-life, the merry Christmas Eve, and the little mice who had listened so eagerly when he related the story of Humpty Dumpty.

"Past, all past!" said the poor Tree. "Had I but been happy, as I might have been! Past, all past!"

And the servant came and broke the tree into small pieces, heaped them up and set fire to them. And the Tree groaned deeply, and every groan sounded like a little shot. The children all ran up to the place and jumped about in front of the blaze, looking into it and crying, "Piff! piff!" But at each of those heavy groans, the Fir-Tree thought of a bright summer's day, or a starry winter's night in the forest, of Christmas Eve, or of Humpty Dumpty, the only story that he knew and could relate. And at last the Tree was burned.

The boys played about in the court; on the bosom of the youngest sparkled the gold star that the Tree had worn on the happiest evening of his life; but that was past, and the story also, past, past, for all stories must come to an end, some time or other.

THE EMPEROR'S NEW CLOTHES

Many years ago, there was an Emperor, who was so excessively fond of new clothes that he spent all his money on dress. He did not trouble himself in the least about his soldiers; nor did he care to go either to the theatre or the chase, except for the opportunities then afforded him for displaying his new clothes. He had a different suit for each hour of the day; and as of any other king or emperor, one is accustomed to say, "He is sitting in council," it was always said of him. "The Emperor is sitting in his wardrobe."

Time passed away merrily in the large town which was his capital; strangers arrived every day at the court. One day, two rogues, calling themselves weavers, made their appearance. They gave out that they knew how to weave stuffs of the most beautiful colours and elaborate patterns, the clothes manufactured from which should have the wonderful property of remaining invisible to every one who was unfit for the office he held, or who was extraordinarily simple in character.

"These must indeed be splendid clothes!" thought the Emperor. "Had I such a suit, I might, at once, find out what men in my realms are unfit for their office, and also be able to distinguish the wise from the foolish! This stuff must be woven for me immediately." And he caused large sums of money to be given to both the weavers, in order that they might begin their work directly.

So the two pretended weavers set up two looms, and affected to work very busily, though in reality they did nothing at all. They asked for the most delicate silk and the purest gold thread; put both into their own knapsacks; and then continued their pretended work at the empty looms until late at night.

"I should like to know how the weavers are getting on with my cloth," said the Emperor to himself, after some little time had elapsed; he was, however, rather embarrassed, when he remembered that a simpleton, or one unfit for his office, would be unable to see the manufacture. "To be sure," he thought, "I have nothing to risk in my own person; but yet, I would prefer sending somebody else, to bring me intelligence about the weavers, and their work, before I trouble myself in the affair." All the people throughout the city had heard of the wonderful property the cloth was to possess; and all

131

were anxious to learn how wise, or how ignorant, their neighbours might prove to be.

"I will send my faithful old minister to the weavers," said the Emperor at last, after same deliberation, "he will be best able to see how the cloth looks; for he is a man of sense, and no one can be more suitable for his office than he is."

So the faithful old minister went into the hall, where the knaves were working with all their might at their empty looms. "What can be the meaning of this?" thought the old man, opening his eyes very wide. "I cannot discover the least bit of thread on the looms!" However, he did not express his thoughts aloud.

The impostors requested him very courteously to be so good as to come nearer their looms; and then asked him whether the design pleased him, and whether the colours were not very beautiful; at the same time pointing to the empty frames. The poor old minister looked and looked; he could not discover anything on the looms, for a very good reason, viz.: there was nothing there. "What!" thought he again, "is it possible that I am a simpleton? I have never thought so myself; and no one must know it now if I am so. Can it be that I am unfit for my office? No, that must not be said either. I will never confess that I could not see the stuff."

"Well, sir Minister!" said one of the knaves, still pretending to work, "you do not say whether the stuff pleases you."

"Oh, it is excellent!" replied the old minister, looking at the loom through his spectacles. "This pattern, and the colours—yes, I will tell the Emperor without delay how very beautiful I think them."

"We shall be much obliged to you," said the impostors, and then they named the different colours and described the pattern of the pretended stuff. The old minister listened attentively to their words, in order that he might repeat them to the Emperor; and then the knaves asked for more silk and gold, saying that it was necessary to complete what they had begun. However, they put all that was given them into their knapsacks; and continued to work with as much apparent diligence as before at their empty looms.

The Emperor now sent another officer of his court to see how the men were getting on, and to ascertain whether the cloth would soon be ready. It was just the same with this gentleman as with the minister; he surveyed the looms on all sides, but could see nothing at all but the empty frames.

"Does not the stuff appear as beautiful to you as it did to my lord the minister?" asked the impostors of the Emperor's second ambassador; at the same time making the same gestures as before, and talking of the design and colours which were not there.

"I certainly am not stupid!" thought the messenger. "It must be that I am not fit for my good profitable office! That is very odd; however, no one shall know anything about it." And accordingly he praised the stuff he could not see, and declared that he was delighted with both colours and patterns. "Indeed, please your Imperial Majesty," said he to his sovereign, when he returned, "the cloth which the weavers are preparing is extraordinarily magnificent."

The whole city was talking of the splendid cloth which the Emperor had ordered to be woven at his own expense.

And now the Emperor himself wished to see the costly manufacture whilst it was still on the loom. Accompanied by a select number of officers of the court, among whom were the two honest men who had already admired the cloth, he went to the crafty impostors, who as soon as they were aware of the Emperor's approach, went on working more diligently than ever; although they still did not pass a single thread through the looms.

"Is not the work absolutely magnificent?" said the two officers of the crown, already mentioned. "If your Majesty will only be pleased to look at it! what a splendid design! what glorious colours!" and, at the same time, they pointed to the empty frames; for they imagined that every one else could see this exquisite piece of workmanship.

"How is this?" said the Emperor to himself. "I can see nothing! this is indeed a terrible affair! Am I a simpleton, or am I unfit to be an Emperor? that would be the worst thing that could happen—oh! the cloth is charming," said he, aloud. "It has my complete approbation." And he smiled most graciously, and looked closely at the empty looms; for on no account would he say that he could not see what two of the officers of his court had praised so much. All his retinue now strained their eyes, hoping to discover something on the looms, but they could see no more than the others; nevertheless, they all exclaimed, "Oh, how beautiful!" and advised his Majesty to have some clothes made from this splendid material, for the approaching procession. "Magnificent! charming! excellent!" resounded on all sides; and every one was uncommonly gay. The Emperor shared in the general satisfaction; and presented the impostors with the riband of an order of knighthood, to be worn in their button-holes, and the title of "Gentlemen Weavers."

The rogues sat up the whole of the night before the day on which the procession was to take place, and had sixteen lights burning, so that every one might see how anxious they were to finish the Emperor's new suit. They pretended to roll the cloth off the looms; cut the air with their scissors; and sewed with needles without any thread in them. "See!" cried they at last, "the Emperor's new clothes are ready!"

And now the Emperor, with all the grandees of his court, came to the weavers; and the rogues raised their arms, as if in the act of holding something up, saying,

"Here are your Majesty's trousers! here is the scarf! here is the mantle! The whole suit is as light as a cobweb; one might fancy one has nothing at all on, when dressed in it; that, however, is the great virtue of this delicate cloth."

"Yes, indeed!" said all the courtiers, although not one of them could see anything of this exquisite manufacture.

"If your Imperial Majesty will be graciously pleased to take off your clothes, we will fit on the new suit, in front of the looking-glass."

The Emperor was accordingly undressed, and the rogues pretended to array him in his new suit; the Emperor turning round, from side to side, before the looking-glass.

"How splendid his Majesty looks in his new clothes! and how well they fit!" everyone cried out. "What a design! what colours! these are indeed royal robes!"

"The canopy which is to be borne over your Majesty in the procession is waiting," announced the chief master of the ceremonies.

"I am quite ready," answered the Emperor. "Do my new clothes fit well?" asked he, turning himself round again before the looking-glass, in order that he might appear to be examining his handsome suit.

The lords of the bed-chamber, who were to carry his Majesty's train, felt about on the ground, as if they were lifting up the ends of the mantle; and pretended to be carrying something; for they would by no means betray anything like simplicity or unfitness for their office.

So now the Emperor walked under his high canopy in the midst of the procession, through the streets of his capital; and all the people standing by, and those at the windows, cried out, "Oh! how beautiful are our Emperor's new clothes! what a magnificent train there is to the mantle; and how gracefully the scarf hangs!" In short, no one would allow that he could not see these much-admired clothes; because, in doing so, he would have declared himself either a simpleton or unfit for his office. Certainly, none of the Emperor's various suits had ever made so great an impression as these invisible ones.

"But the Emperor has nothing at all on!" said a little child.

"Listen to the voice of innocence!" exclaimed his father; and what the child had said was whispered from one to another.

"But he has nothing at all on!" at last cried out all the people. The Emperor was vexed, for he knew that the people were right; but he thought the procession must go on now: And the lords of the bed-chamber took greater pains than ever, to appear holding up a train, although, in reality, there was no train to hold.

THE SWINEHERD

There was once a poor Prince, who had a kingdom; his kingdom was very small, but still quite large enough to marry upon; and he wished to marry.

It was certainly rather cool of him to say to the Emperor's daughter, "Will you have me?" But so he did; for his name was renowned far and wide; and there were a hundred princesses who would have answered "Yes!" and "Thank you kindly." We shall see what this Princess said.

Listen!

It happened that where the Prince's father lay buried, there grew a rose-tree—a most beautiful rose-tree, which blossomed only once in every five years, and even then bore only one flower, but that was a rose! It smelt so sweet, that all cares and sorrows were forgotten by him who inhaled its fragrance.

And furthermore, the Prince had a nightingale, who

could sing in such a manner that it seemed as though all sweet melodies dwelt in her little throat. So the Princess was to have the rose, and the nightingale; and they were accordingly put into large silver caskets, and sent to her.

The Emperor had them brought into a large hall, where the Princess was playing at "Visiting," with the ladies of the court; and when she saw the caskets with the presents, she clapped her hands for joy.

"Ah, if it were but a little pussy-cat!" said she—but the rose-tree with its beautiful rose came to view.

"Oh, how prettily it is made!" said all the court ladies.

"It is more than pretty," said the Emperor, "it is charming!"

But the Princess touched it, and was almost ready to cry.

"Fie, papa!" said she, "it is not made at all, it is natural!"

"Let us see what is in the other casket, before we get into a bad humour," said the Emperor. So the nightingale came forth, and sang so delightfully that no one could say anything ill-humoured of her.

"*Superbe! charmante!*" exclaimed the ladies; for they all used to chatter French, each one worse than her neighbour.

"How much the bird reminds me of the musical box that belonged to our blessed Empress," said an old knight. "Oh yes! these are the same tones, the same execution."

"Yes! yes!" said the Emperor, and he wept like a child at the remembrance.

"I will still hope that it is not a real bird," said the Princess.

"Yes, it is a real bird," said those who had brought it.

"Well, then, let the bird fly," said the Princess; and she positively refused to see the Prince.

However, he was not to be discouraged; he daubed his face over brown and black; pulled his cap over his ears, and knocked at the door.

"Good day to my lord the Emperor!" said he. "Can I have employment at the palace?"

"Why, yes," said the Emperor, "I want someone to take care of the pigs, for we have a great many of them."

So the Prince was appointed "Imperial Swineherd." He had a dirty little room close by the pigsty; and there he sat the whole day, and worked. By the evening he had made a pretty little kitchen-pot. Little bells were hung all around it; and when the pot was boiling, these bells tinkled in the most charming manner, and played the old melody:

> *"Ach! du lieber Augustin,*
> *Alles ist weg, weg, weg!"*[1]

But what was still more curious, whoever held his finger in the smoke of the kitchen-pot, immediately smelt all the dishes that were cooking on every hearth in the city—this, you see, was something quite different from the rose.

Now the Princess happened to walk that way; and when she heard the tune she stood quite still, and seemed pleased; for she could play "Lieber Augustin"; it was the only piece she knew; and she played it with one finger.

"Why, there is my piece," said the Princess, "that swineherd must certainly have been well educated! go in and ask him the price of the instrument."

So one of the court-ladies must run in; however, she drew on wooden slippers first.

"What will you take for the kitchen-pot?" said the lady.

"I will have ten kisses from the Princess," said the swineherd.

"Yes, indeed!" said the lady.

"I cannot sell it for less," rejoined the swineherd.

1 *"Ah! dear Augustine!*
"All is gone, gone, gone!"

"He is an impudent fellow!" said the Princess, and she walked on—but when she had gone a little way, the bells tinkled so prettily—

> *"Ach! du lieber Augustin,*
> *Alles ist weg, weg, weg!"*[1]

"Stay," said the Princess. "Ask him if he will have ten kisses from the ladies of my court."

"No, thank you!" said the swineherd, "ten kisses from the Princess, or I keep the kitchen-pot myself."

"That must not be either!" said the Princess; "but do you all stand before me that no one may see us."

And the court-ladies placed themselves in front of her, and spread out their dresses—the swineherd got ten kisses, and the Princess— the kitchen-pot.

That was delightful! the pot was boiling the whole evening, and the whole of the following day. They knew perfectly well what was cooking at every fire throughout the city, from the chamberlain's to the cobbler's: the court-ladies danced, and clapped their hands.

"We know who has soup, and who has pancakes for dinner today; who has cutlets, and who has eggs. How interesting!"

"Yes, but keep my secret, for I am an Emperor's daughter."

The swineherd—that is to say, the Prince, for no one knew that he was other than an ill-favoured swineherd—let not a day pass without working at something; he at last constructed a rattle, which, when it was swung round, played all the waltzes and jig-tunes which have ever been heard since the creation of the world.

"Ah, that is *superbe!*" said the Princess when she passed by. "I have never heard prettier compositions! Go in and ask him the price of the instrument; but mind, he shall have no more kisses!"

"He will have a hundred kisses from the Princess!" said the lady who had been to ask.

"I think he is not in his right senses!" said the Princess, and walked on; but when she had gone a little way, she stopped again. "One must encourage art," said she. "I am the Emperor's daughter. Tell him he shall, as on yesterday, have ten kisses from me, and may take the rest from the ladies of the court."

"Oh!—but we should not like that at all!" said they. "What are you muttering?" asked the Princess; "if I can kiss him, surely you can! Remember that you owe everything to me. So the ladies were obliged to go to him again."

"A hundred kisses from the Princess!" said he, "or else let every one keep his own."

"Stand round!" said she; and all the ladies stood round her whilst the kissing was going on.

"What can be the reason for such a crowd close by the pigsty?" said the Emperor, who happened just then to step out on the balcony. He rubbed his eyes and put on his spectacles. "They are the ladies of the court; I must go down and see what they are about!" So he pulled up his slippers at the heel, for he had trodden them down.

As soon as he had got into the courtyard, he moved very softly, and the ladies were so much engrossed with counting the kisses that all might go on fairly that they did not perceive the Emperor. He rose on his tip-toes.

"What is all this?" said he, when he saw what was going on, and he boxed the Princess's ears with his slipper, just as the swineherd was taking the eighty-sixth kiss.

"March out!" said the Emperor, for he was very angry.; and both Princess and swineherd were thrust out of the city.

The Princess now stood and wept, the swineherd scolded, and the rain poured down.

"Alas! unhappy creature that I am!" said the Princess. "If I had but married the handsome young Prince! Ah! how unfortunate I am!"

And the swineherd went behind a tree, washed the black and brown colour from his face, threw off his dirty clothes, and stepped forth in his princely robes; he looked so noble that the Princess could not help bowing before him.

"I am come to despise thee," said he. "Thou wouldst not have an honourable prince! thou couldst not prize the rose and the nightingale, but thou wast ready to kiss the swineherd for the sake of a trumpery plaything. Thou art rightly served."

He then went back to his own little kingdom, and shut the door of his palace in her face. Now she might well sing

> *"Ach! du lieber Augustin,*
> *Alles ist weg, weg, weg!"*

THE NIGHTINGALE

In China, as you well know, the Emperor is Chinese, and all around him are Chinese also.—Now what I am about to relate, happened many years ago, but even on that very account it is the more important that you should hear the story now, before it is forgotten.

The Emperor's palace was the most magnificent palace in the world; it was made entirely of fine porcelain, exceedingly costly; but at the same time so brittle that it was dangerous even to touch it.

The choicest flowers were to be seen in the garden; and to the most splendid of all these little silver bells were fastened, in order that their tinkling might prevent any one from passing by without noticing them. Yes! everything in the Emperor's garden was excellently well arranged; and the garden extended so far that even the gardener did not know the end of it; whoever walked beyond it, however, came to a beautiful wood, with very high trees; and beyond that, to the sea. The wood went down quite to the sea, which was very deep and blue; large ships could sail close under the branches; and among the branches dwelt a nightingale, who sang so sweetly, that even the poor fisherman, who had so much else to do, when he came out at night-time to cast his nets, would stand still and listen to her song. "Oh! how pretty that is!" he would say—but then he was obliged to mind his work, and forget the bird; yet the following night, if again the nightingale sang, and the fisherman came out, again he would say, "Oh! how pretty that is!"

Travellers came from all parts of the world to the Emperor's city; and they admired the city, the palace, and the garden; but if they heard the nightingale, they all said, "This is the best." And they talked about her after they went home, and learned men wrote books about the city, the palace, and the garden; nor did they forget the nightingale: she was extolled above everything else; and poets wrote the most beautiful verses about the nightingale of the wood near the sea.

These books went round the world, and one of them at last reached the Emperor. He was sitting in his golden armchair; he read and read, and nodded his head every moment; for these splendid descriptions of the city, the palace, and the garden, pleased him greatly. "But the nightingale is the best of all," was written in the book.

"What in the world is this?" said the Emperor. "The nightingale! I do not know it at all! Can there be such a bird in my empire, in my garden even, without my having even heard of it? Truly one may learn something from books."

So he called his Cavalier[1]; now this was so grand a personage that no one of inferior rank might speak to him; and if one did venture to ask him a question, his only answer was "Pish!" which has no particular meaning.

"There is said to be a very remarkable bird here, called the nightingale," said the Emperor; "her song, they say, is worth more than anything else in all my dominions; why has no one ever told me of her?"

"I have never before heard her mentioned," said the Cavalier: "she has never been presented at court."

"I wish her to come, and sing before me this evening," said the Emperor. "The whole world knows what I have, and I do not know it myself!"

"I have never before heard her mentioned," said the Cavalier; "but I will seek her, I will find her."

But where was she to be found? The Cavalier ran up one flight of steps, down another, through halls, and through passages; not one of all whom he met had ever heard of the nightingale; and the Cavalier returned to the Emperor, and said, "It must certainly be an invention of the man who wrote the book. Your Imperial Majesty must not believe all that is written in books; much of them is pure invention, and there is what is called the Black Art."

"But the book in which I have read it," said the Emperor, "was sent me by the high and mighty Emperor of Japan, and therefore it cannot be untrue. I wish to hear the nightingale; she must be here this evening, and if she do not come, after supper the whole court shall be flogged."

"Tsing-pe!" said the Cavalier; and again he ran up stairs, and down stairs, through halls, and through passages, and half the court ran with him; for not one would have relished the flogging. Many were the questions asked respecting the wonderful nightingale, whom the whole world talked of, and about whom no one at court knew anything.

1 Gentleman in waiting.

At last they met a poor little girl in the kitchen, who said "Oh yes! the nightingale! I know her very well. Oh! how she can sing! Every evening I carry the fragments left at table to my poor sick mother. She lives by the sea-shore; and when I am coming back, and stay to rest a little in the wood, I hear the nightingale sing; it makes the tears come into my eyes! it is just as if my mother kissed me."

"Little kitchen-maiden," said the Cavalier, "I will procure for you a sure appointment in the kitchen, together with permission to see His Majesty the Emperor dine, if you will conduct us to the nightingale, for she is expected at court this evening."

So they went together to the wood, where the nightingale was accustomed to sing; and half the court went with them. Whilst on their way, a cow began to low.

"Oh!" said the court pages "now we have her! It is certainly an extraordinary voice for so small an animal; surely I have heard it somewhere before."

"No, those are cows you hear lowing," said the little kitchen-maid, "we are still far from the place."

The frogs were now croaking in the pond.

"That is famous!" said the chief court-preacher, "now I hear her; it sounds just like little church bells."

"No, those are frogs," said the little kitchen-maid, "but now I think we shall soon hear her."

Then the nightingale began to sing.

"There she is!" said the little girl, "listen! listen! There she sits!" and she pointed to a little grey bird up in the branches.

"Is it possible?" said the Cavalier. "I should not have thought it. How simple she looks! she must certainly have changed colour at the sight of so many distinguished personages."

"Little nightingale!" called out the kitchen-maid, "our gracious Emperor wishes you to sing something to him."

"With the greatest pleasure," said the nightingale, and

she sang in such a manner that it was delightful to hear her.

"It sounds like glass bells," said the Cavalier. "And look at her little throat, how it moves! It is singular that we should never have heard her before; she will have great success at court."

"Shall I sing again to the Emperor?" asked the nightingale, for she thought the Emperor was among them.

"Most excellent nightingale!" said the Cavalier, "I have the honour to invite you to a court festival, which is to take place this evening, when his Imperial Majesty will be enchanted with your delightful song."

"My song would sound far better among the green trees," said the nightingale; however she followed willingly when she heard that the Emperor wished it.

There was a regular trimming and polishing at the palace; the walls and the floors, which were all of porcelain, glittered with a thousand gold lamps; the loveliest flowers, with the merriest tinkling bells, were placed in the passages; there was a running to and fro, which made all the bells ring, so that one could not hear his own words.

In the midst of the grand hall where the Emperor sat, a golden perch was erected, on which the nightingale was to sit. The whole court was present, and the little kitchen-maid received permission to stand behind the door, for she had now actually the rank and title of "Maid of the Kitchen." All were dressed out in their finest clothes; and all eyes were fixed upon the little grey bird, to whom the Emperor nodded as a signal for her to begin.

And the nightingale sang so sweetly, that tears came into the Emperor's eyes, tears rolled down his cheeks; and the nightingale sang more sweetly still, and touched the hearts of all who heard her; and the Emperor was so merry, that he said, "The nightingale should have my golden slippers, and wear them round her neck." But the

nightingale thanked him, and said she was already sufficiently rewarded.

"I have seen tears in the Emperor's eyes, that is the
greatest reward I can have. The tears of an Emperor have
a particular value. Heaven knows I am sufficiently
rewarded."

And then she sang again with her sweet, lovely voice.
"It is the most amiable coquetry ever known," said the
ladies present; and they put water into their mouths, and
tried to move their throats as she did, when they spoke;
they thought to become nightingales also. Indeed even the
footmen and chamber-maids declared that they were
quite contented; which was a great thing to say, for of all
people they are the most difficult to satisfy. Yes, indeed,
the nightingale's success was complete. She was now to
remain at court to have her own cage; with permission to
fly out twice in the day and once in the night. Twelve
attendants were allotted her who were to hold a silken
band, fastened round her foot: and they kept good hold.
There was no pleasure in excursions made in this manner.

All the city was talking of the wonderful bird; and
when two persons met, one would say only "night," and
the other "gale," and then they sighed, and understood
each other perfectly; indeed eleven of the children of the
citizens were named after the nightingale, but none of
them had her tones in their throats.

One day a large parcel arrived for the Emperor, on
which was written "Nightingale."

"Here we have another new book about our far-famed
bird," said the Emperor. But it was not a book; it was a
little piece of mechanism, lying in a box; an artificial
nightingale, which was intended to look like the living
one, but was covered over with diamonds, rubies, and
sapphires. When this artificial bird had been wound up,
it could sing one of the tunes that the real nightingale
sang; and its tail all glittering with silver and gold, went

up and down all the time. A little band was fastened round its neck, on which was written, "The nightingale of the Emperor of China is poor compared with the nightingale of the Emperor of Japan."

"That is famous!" said every one; and he who had brought the bird, obtained the title of "Chief Imperial Nightingale Bringer." "Now they shall sing together; we will have a duet."

And so they must sing together; but it did not succeed, for the real nightingale sang in her own way, and the artificial bird produced its tones by wheels. "It is not his fault," said the artist, "he keeps exact time and quite according to method."

So the artificial bird must now sing alone; he was quite as successful as the real nightingale; and then he was so much prettier to look at; his plumage sparkled like jewels.

Three and thirty times he sang one and the same tune, and yet he was not weary; every one would willingly have heard him again; however, the Emperor now wished the real nightingale should sing something—but where was she? No one had remarked that she had flown out of the open window; flown away to her own green wood.

"What is the meaning of this?" said the Emperor; and all the courtiers abused the nightingale, and called her a most ungrateful creature. "We have the best bird at all events," said they, and for the four-and-thirtieth time they heard the same tune, but still they did not quite know it, because it was so difficult. The artist praised the bird inordinately; indeed he declared it was superior to the real nightingale, not only in its exterior, all sparkling with diamonds, but also intrinsically.

"For see, my noble lords, His Imperial Majesty especially, with the real nightingale, one could never reckon on what was coming; but everything is settled with the artificial bird; he will sing in this one way, and no other: this can be proved, he can be taken to pieces, and the works can be shown, where the wheels lie, how they move, and how one follows from another."

"That is just what I think," said everybody; and the artist received permission to show the bird to the people on the following Sunday. "They too should hear him sing," the Emperor said. So they heard him, and were as well pleased as if they had all been drinking tea; for it is tea that makes Chinese merry, and they all said "Oh!" and raised their forefingers, and nodded their heads.

But the fisherman, who had heard the real nightingale, said, "It sounds very pretty, almost like the real bird; but yet there is something wanting; I do not know what."

The real nightingale was, however, banished from the empire.

The artificial bird had his place on a silken cushion, close to the Emperor's bed; all the presents he received, gold and precious stones, lay around him; he had obtained the rank and title of "High Imperial Dessert Singer," and, therefore, his place was number one on the left side; for the Emperor thought that the side where the heart was situated must be the most honourable, and the heart is situated on the left side of an Emperor, as well as with other folks.

And the artist wrote five-and-twenty volumes about the artificial bird, with the longest and most difficult words that are to be found in the Chinese language. So, of course, all said they had read and understood them, otherwise they would have been stupid, and perhaps would have been flogged.

Thus it went on for a year. The Emperor, the court, and all the Chinese knew every note of the artificial bird's song by heart; but that was the very reason they enjoyed it so much, they could now sing with him. The little boys in the street sang "zizizi, cluck, cluck, cluck!" and the Emperor himself sang too—yes, indeed, that was charming!

But one evening, when the bird was in full voice, and the Emperor lay in bed, and listened, there was suddenly a noise, "bang," inside the bird, then something sprang "fur-r-r-r," all the wheels were running about, and the music stopped.

The Emperor jumped quickly out of bed, and had his chief physician called; but of what use could he be? Then a clockmaker was fetched, and at last, after a great deal of discussion and consultation, the bird was in some measure put to rights again; but the clockmaker said, he must be spared much singing, for the pegs were almost worn out, and it was impossible to renew them, at least so that the music should be correct.

There was great lamentation, for now the artificial bird was allowed to sing only once a year, and even then there were difficulties; however, the artist made a short speech full of his favourite long words, and said the bird was as good as ever; so then, of course, it was as good as ever.

When five years were passed away, a great affliction visited the whole empire, for in their hearts the people thought highly of their Emperor; and now he was ill, and it was reported that he could not live. A new Emperor had already been chosen, and the people stood in the street, outside the palace, and asked the Cavalier how the Emperor was?

"Pish!" said he, and shook his head.

Cold and pale lay the Emperor in his magnificent bed; all the court believed him to be already dead, and every one had hastened away to greet the new Emperor; the men ran out for a little gossip on the subject, and the maids were having a grand coffee party.

The floors of all the rooms and passages were covered with cloth, in order that not a step should be heard—it was everywhere so still! so still! But the Emperor was not yet dead; stiff and pale he lay in his splendid bed, with the long velvet curtains and heavy gold tassels. A window was opened above, and the moon shone down on the Emperor and the artificial bird.

The poor Emperor could scarcely breathe; it appeared to him as though something was sitting on his chest; he opened his eyes, and saw that it was Death, who had put on the Emperor's crown, and with one hand held the golden scimitar, with the other the splendid imperial banner; whilst, from under the folds of the thick velvet hangings, the strangest-looking heads were seen peering forth; some with an expression absolutely hideous, and others with an extremely gentle and lovely aspect: they were the bad and good deeds of the Emperor, which were now all fixing their eyes upon him, whilst Death sat on his heart.

"Dost thou know this?" they whispered one after another. "Dost thou remember that?" And they began reproaching him in such a manner that the sweat broke out upon his forehead.

"I have never known anything like it," said the Emperor. "Music, music, the great Chinese drum!" cried he, "let me not hear what they are saying."

They went on, however; and Death, quite in the Chinese fashion, nodded his head to every word.

"Music, music!" cried the Emperor. "Then dear little artificial bird! sing, I pray thee, sing!—I have given thee gold and precious stones, I have even hung my golden slippers round thy neck—sing, I pray thee, sing!"

But the bird was silent; there was no one there to wind him up, and he could not sing without this. Death continued to stare at the Emperor with his great hollow eyes! and everywhere it was still, fearfully still!

All at once the sweetest song was heard from the window; it was the little living nightingale who was sitting on a branch outside—she had heard of her Emperor's severe illness, and was come to sing to him of comfort and hope. As she sang, the spectral forms became

150

paler and paler, the blood flowed more and more quickly through the Emperor's feeble members, and even Death listened and said, "Go on, little nightingale, go on."

"Wilt thou give me the splendid gold scimitar? Wilt thou give me the gay banner, and the Emperor's crown?"

And Death gave up all these treasures for a song; and the nightingale sang on: she sang of the quiet churchyard, where white roses blossom, where the lilac sends forth its fragrance, and the fresh grass is bedewed with the tears of the sorrowing friends of the departed. Then Death was seized with a longing after his garden, and like a cold white shadow, flew out at the window.

"Thanks, thanks," said the Emperor, "thou heavenly little bird, I know thee well. I have banished thee from my realm, and thou hast sung away those evil faces from my bed, and death from my heart; how shall I reward thee?"

"Thou hast already rewarded me," said the nightingale, "I have seen tears in thine eyes, as when I sang to thee for the first time: those I shall never forget, they are jewels which do so much good to a minstrel's heart! but sleep now, and wake fresh and healthy; I will sing thee to sleep."

And she sang—and the Emperor fell into a sweet sleep. Oh, how soft and kindly was that sleep!

The sun shone in at the window when he awoke, strong and healthy. Not one of his servants had returned, for they all believed him dead; but the nightingale still sat and sang.

"Thou shalt always stay with me," said the Emperor, "thou shalt only sing when it pleases thee, and the artificial bird I will break into a thousand pieces."

"Do not so," said the nightingale; "truly he has done what he could; take care of him. I cannot stay in the palace; but let me come when I like: I will sit on the branches close to the window, in the evening, and sing to thee, that thou mayest become happy and thoughtful. I will sing to thee of the joyful and the sorrowing, I will sing to thee of all that is good or bad, which is concealed from thee. The little minstrel flies afar to the fisherman's hut, to the peasant's cottage, to all who are far distant from thee and thy court. I love thy heart more than thy crown, and yet the crown has an odour of something holy about it. I will come, I will sing. But thou must promise me one thing."

"Everything," said the Emperor. And now he stood in his imperial splendour, which he had put on himself, and held the scimitar so heavy with gold to his heart.—"One thing I beg of thee: let no one know that thou hast a little bird, who tells thee everything, then all will go on well." And the nightingale flew away.

The attendants came in to look at their dead Emperor—lo! there they stood—and the Emperor said, "Good-morning."

THE UGLY DUCKLING

It was beautiful in the country; it was summer-time, the wheat was yellow, the oats were green, the hay was stacked up in the green meadows, and the stork paraded about on his long red legs, discoursing in·Egyptian, which language he had learned from his mother. The fields and meadows were skirted by thick woods, and a deep lake lay in the midst of the woods.—Yes, it was indeed beautiful in the country! The sunshine fell warmly on an old mansion, surrounded by deep canals, and from the walls down to the water's edge there grew large burdock-leaves, so high that children could stand upright among them without being perceived. This place was as wild and unfrequented as the thickest part of the wood, and on that account a duck had chosen to make her nest there. She was sitting on her eggs; but the pleasure she had felt at first was now almost gone, because she had been there so long, and had so few visitors, for the other ducks preferred swimming on the canals to sitting among the burdock-leaves gossiping with her.

At last the eggs cracked one after another, "Tchick, tchick!" All the eggs were alive, and one little head after another appeared. "Quack, quack," said the duck and all got up as well as they could; they peeped about from under the green leaves, and as green is good for the eyes, their mother let them look as long as they pleased.

"How large the world is!" said the little ones, for they found their present situation very different to their former confined one, while yet in the eggshells.

"Do you imagine this to be the whole of the world?" said the mother! "it extends far beyond the other side of the garden, to the pastor's field; but I have never been there. Are you all here?" And then she got up. "No, I have not got you all, the largest egg is still here. How long will this last?" And then she sat down again.

"Well, and how are you getting on?" asked an old duck.

"This one egg keeps me so long," said the mother, "it will not break; but you should see the others! -they are the prettiest little ducklings I have seen in all my days; they are all like their father,—the good-for-nothing fellow! he has not been to visit me once."

"Let me see the egg that will not break," said the old duck, "depend upon it, it is a turkey's egg. I was cheated in the same way once myself, and I had such trouble with the young ones; for they were afraid of the water, and I could not get them there. I called and scolded, but it was all of no use. But let me see the egg—ah yes! to be sure, that is a turkey's egg. Leave it, and teach the other little ones to swim."

"I will sit on it a little longer," said the duck. "I have been sitting so long, that I may as well spend the harvest here."

"It is no business of mine," said the old duck, and away she waddled.

The great egg burst at last, "Tchick, tchick," said the little one, and out it tumbled—but oh! how large and ugly it was! The duck looked at it, "That is a great, strong creature," said she, "none of the others are at all like it, can it be a young turkey-cock? well, we shall soon find out, it must go into the water, though I push it in myself."

The next day there was delightful weather, and the sun shone warmly upon all the green leaves when mother duck with all her family went down to the canal; plump she went into the water, "quack, quack," cried she, and one duckling after another jumped in. The water closed over their heads, but all came up again, and swam together in the pleasantest manner; their legs moved without effort. All were there, even the ugly, grey one.

"No! it is not a turkey," said the old duck; "only see how prettily it moves its legs, how upright it holds itself, it is my own child, it is also really very pretty when one looks more closely at it; quack, quack, now come with me. I will take you into the world, introduce you in the duckyard; but keep close to me, or someone may tread on you, and beware of the cat."

So they came into the duckyard. There was a horrid noise; two families were quarreling about the remains of an eel, which in the end was secured by the cat.

"See, my children, such is the way of the world," said the mother duck, wiping her beak for she too was fond of roasted eels. "Now use your legs," said she, "keep together, and bow to the old duck you see yonder. She is the most distinguished of all the fowls present, and is of Spanish blood, which accounts for her dignified appearance and manners. And look, she has a red rag on her leg; that is considered extremely handsome, and is the greatest distinction a duck can have.

Don't turn your feet inwards, a well-educated duckling

always keeps his legs far apart, like his father and mother, just so—look! now bow your necks, and say 'quack.' "

And they did as they were told. But the other ducks who were in the yard looked at them and said aloud, "Only see, now we have another brood, as if there were not enough of us already, and fie! how ugly that one is, we will not endure it," and immediately one of the ducks flew at him, and bit him in the neck.

"Leave him alone," said the mother, "he is doing no one any harm."

"Yes, but he is so large, and so strange-looking, and therefore he shall be teased."

"Those are fine children that our good mother has," said the old duck with the red rag on her leg. "All are pretty except one, and that has not turned out well; I almost wish it could be hatched over again."

"That cannot be, please your highness," said the mother. "Certainly he is not handsome, but he is a very good child, and swims as well as the others, indeed rather better. I think he will grow like the others all in good time, and perhaps will look smaller. He stayed so long in the eggshell, that is the cause of the difference," and she scratched the duckling's neck, and stroked his whole body. "Besides," added she, "he is a drake; I think he will be very strong, therefore it does not matter so much, he will fight his way through."

"The other ducks are very pretty," said the old duck; "pray make yourselves at home, and if you find an eel's head you can bring it to me."

And accordingly they made themselves at home.

But the poor little duckling, who had come last out of its eggshell, and who was so ugly, was bitten, pecked, and teased by both ducks and hens. "It is so large," said they all. And the turkey-cock, who had come into the world with spurs on, and therefore fancied he was an emperor, puffed himself up like a ship in full sail, and marched up to the duckling quite red with passion. The poor little thing scarcely knew what to do; he was quite distressed, because he was so ugly, and because he was the jest of the poultry yard.

So passed the first day, and afterwards matters grew worse and worse; the poor duckling was scorned by all. Even his brothers and sisters behaved unkindly, and were constantly saying, "The cat fetch thee, thou nasty creature!" The mother said, "Ah, if thou wert only far away!" The ducks bit him, the hens pecked him, and the girl who fed the poultry kicked him. He ran over the hedge; the little birds in the bushes were terrified. "That is because I am so ugly," thought the duckling, shutting his eyes, but he ran on. At last he came to a wide moor, where lived some wild ducks; here he lay the whole night so tired and so comfortless. In the morning the wild ducks flew up, and perceived their new companion. "Pray who are you?" asked they; and our little duckling turned himself in all directions, and greeted them as politely as possible.

"You are really uncommonly ugly," said the wild duck; "however that does not matter to us, provided you do not marry into our families." Poor thing! he had never thought of marrying; he only begged permission to lie among the reeds, and drink the water of the moor.

There he lay for two whole days—on the third day there came two wild geese, or rather ganders, who had not been long out of their eggshells, which accounts for their impertinence.

"Hark-ye," said they, "you are so ugly that we like you infinitely well; will you come with us, and be a bird of passage? On another moor, not far from this, are some dear, sweet, wild geese, as lovely creatures as have ever said 'hiss, hiss.' You are truly in the way to make your fortune, ugly as you are."

Bang! a gun went off all at once, and both wild geese

were stretched dead among the reeds, the water became red with blood;—bang! a gun went off again, whole flocks of wild geese flew up from among the reeds, and another report followed.

There was a grand hunting party: the hunters lay in ambush all around; some were even sitting in the trees, whose huge branches stretched far over the moor. The blue smoke rose through the thick trees like a mist, and was dispersed as it fell over the water; the hounds splashed about in the mud, the reeds and rushes bent in all directions—how frightened the poor little duck was! he turned his head, thinking to hide it under his wings, and in a moment a most formidable-looking dog stood close to him, his tongue hanging out of his mouth, his eyes sparkling fearfully. He opened wide his jaws at the sight of our duckling, showed him his sharp white teeth, and, splash, splash! he was gone, gone without hurting him.

"Well! let me be thankful," sighed he, "I am so ugly, that even the dog will not eat me."

And now he lay still, though the shooting continued among the reeds, shot following shot.

The noise did not cease till late in the day, and even then the poor little thing dared not stir; he waited several hours before he looked around him, and then hastened away from the moor as fast as he could. He ran over fields and meadows, though the wind was so high that he had some difficulty in proceeding.

Towards evening he reached a wretched little hut, so wretched that it knew not on which side to fall, and therefore remained standing. The wind blew violently, so that our poor little duckling was obliged to support himself on his tail, in order to stand against it; but it became worse and worse. He then remarked that the door had lost one of its hinges, and hung so much awry that he could creep through the crevice into the room, which he did.

In this room lived an old woman, with her tom-cat and her hen; and the cat, whom she called her little son, knew how to set up his back and purr; indeed he could even emit sparks when stroked the wrong way. The hen had very short legs, and was therefore called "Cuckoo Shortlegs;" she laid very good eggs, and the old woman loved her as her own child.

The next morning the new guest was perceived; the cat began to mew, and the hen to cackle.

"What is the matter?" asked the old woman, looking round; however, her eyes were not good, so she took the young duckling to be a fat duck who had lost her way. "This is a capital catch," said she, "I shall now have ducks' eggs, if it be not a drake: we must try."

And so the duckling was put to the proof for three weeks, but no eggs made their appearance.

Now the cat was the master of the house, and the hen was the mistress, and they used always to say, "We and the world," for they imagined themselves to be not only the half of the world, but also by far the better half. The duckling thought it was possible to be of a different opinion, but that the hen would not allow.

"Can you lay eggs?" asked she.

"No."

"Well, then, hold your tongue."

And the cat said, "Can you set up your back? can you purr?"

"No."

"Well, then, you should have no opinion when reasonable persons are speaking."

So the duckling sat alone in the corner, and was in a very bad humour; however, he happened to think of the fresh air and bright sunshine, and these thoughts gave him such a strong desire to swim again that he could not help telling it to the hen.

"What ails you?" said the hen. "You have nothing to

158

do, and, therefore, brood over these fancies; either lay eggs, or purr, then you will forget them."

"But it is so delicious to swim," said the duckling, "so delicious when the waters close over your head, and you plunge to the bottom."

"Well, that is a queer sort of a pleasure!" said the hen. "I think you must be crazy. Not to speak of myself, ask the cat—he is the most sensible animal I know—whether he would like to swim or to plunge to the bottom of the water. Ask our mistress, the old woman— there is no one in the world wiser than she—do you think she would take pleasure in swimming, and in the waters closing over her head?"

"You do not understand me," said the duckling.

"What, we do not understand you! so you think yourself wiser than the cat, and the old woman, not to speak of myself. Do not fancy any such thing, child, but be thankful for all the kindness that has been shown you. Are you not lodged in a warm room, and have you not the advantage of society from which you can learn something? But you are a simpleton, and it is wearisome to have anything to do with you. Believe me, I wish you well. I tell you unpleasant things, but it is thus that real friendship is shown. Come, for once give yourself the trouble to learn to purr, or to lay eggs."

"I think I will go out into the wide world again," said the duckling.

"Well, go," answered the hen.

So the duckling went. He swam on the surface of the water, he plunged beneath, but all animals passed him by, on account of his ugliness. And the autumn came, the leaves turned yellow and brown, the wind caught them and danced them about, the air was very cold, the clouds were heavy with hail or snow, and the raven sat on the hedge and croaked:—the poor duckling was certainly not very comfortable!

One evening, just as the sun was setting with unusual brilliancy, a flock of large beautiful birds rose from out of the brushwood; the duckling had never seen anything so beautiful before; their plumage was of a dazzling white, and they had long, slender necks. They were swans; they uttered a singular cry, spread out their long, splendid wings, and flew away from these cold regions to warmer countries, across the open sea. They flew so high, so very high! and the little ugly duckling's feelings were so strange; he turned round and round in the water like a mill-wheel, strained his neck to look after them, and sent forth such a loud and strange cry, that it almost frightened himself.—Ah! he could not forget them, those noble birds! those happy birds! When he could see them no longer, he plunged to the bottom of the water, and when he rose again, was almost beside himself. The duckling knew not what the birds were called, knew not whither they were flying, yet he loved them as he had never before loved anything; he envied them not, it would never have occurred to him to wish such beauty for himself; he would have been quite contented if the ducks in the duckyard had but endured his company—the poor ugly animal!

And the winter was so cold, so cold! The duckling was obliged to swim round and round in the water, to keep it from freezing; but every night the opening in which he swam became smaller and smaller; it froze so that the crust of ice crackled; the duckling was obliged to make good use of his legs to prevent the water from freezing entirely; at last, wearied out, he lay stiff and cold in the ice.

Early in the morning there passed by a peasant, who saw him, broke the ice in pieces with his wooden shoe, and brought him home to his wife.

He now revived; the children would have played with him, but our duckling thought they wished to tease him, and in his terror jumped into the milk-pail, so that the milk was spilled about the room: the good woman screamed and clapped her hands; he flew thence into the pan where the butter was kept, and thence into the meal-barrel, and out again, and then how strange he looked!

The woman screamed, and struck at him with the tongs, the children ran races with each other trying to catch him, and laughed and screamed likewise. It was well for him that the door stood open; he jumped out among the bushes into the new fallen snow and lay there as in a dream.

But it would be too melancholy to relate all the trouble and misery that he was obliged to suffer during the severity of the winter—he was lying on a moor among the reeds, when the sun began to shine warmly again, the larks sang, and beautiful spring had returned.

And once more he shook his wings. They were stronger than formerly, and bore him forwards quickly, and before he was well aware of it, he was in a large garden where the apple-trees stood in full bloom, where the syringas sent forth their fragrance and hung their long green branches down into the winding canal. Oh! everything was so lovely, so full of the freshness of spring! And out of the thicket came three beautiful white swans. They displayed their feathers so proudly, and swam so lightly, so lightly! The duckling knew the glorious creatures, and was seized with a strange melancholy.

"I will fly to them, those kingly birds!" said he. "They will kill me, because ugly as I am, I have presumed to approach them; but it matters not; better to be killed by them than to be bitten by the ducks, pecked by the hens, kicked by the girl who feeds the poultry, and to have so much to suffer during the winter!" He flew into the water, and swam towards the beautiful creatures—they saw him and shot forward to meet him. "Only kill me," said the poor animal, and he bowed his head low, expecting death,—but what did he see in the water?—he saw beneath him his own form, no longer that of a plump, ugly, grey bird—it was that of a swan.

It matters not to have been born in a duckyard, if one has been hatched from a swan's egg.

The good creature felt himself really elevated by all the troubles and adversities he had experienced. He could now rightly understand his own happiness, and the larger swans swam round him, and stroked him with their beaks.

Some little children were running about in the garden; they threw grain and bread into the water, and the youngest exclaimed, "There is a new one!" The others also cried out, "Yes, there is a new swan come!" and they clapped their hands, and danced around. They ran to their father and mother, bread and cake were thrown into the water, and every one said, "The new one is the best, so young, and so beautiful!" and the old swans bowed before him. The young swan felt quite ashamed, and hid his head under his wings; he scarcely knew what to do, he was all too happy, but still not proud, for a good heart is never proud.

He remembered how he had been persecuted and derided, and he now heard every one say he was the most beautiful of all beautiful birds. The syringas bent down their branches towards him low into the water, and the sun shone so warmly and brightly—he shook his feathers, stretched his slender neck, and in the joy of his heart said, "How little did I dream of so much happiness when I was the ugly duckling!"

THE WILD SWANS

Far hence, in a country whither the Swallows fly in our winter-time, there dwelt a King who had eleven sons and one daughter, the beautiful Elise. The eleven brothers (they were princes) went to school with stars on their breasts and swords by their sides; they wrote on golden tablets with diamond pens, and could read either with a book or without one; in short, it was easy to perceive that they were princes. Their sister Elise used to sit upon a little glass stool, and had a picture-book which had cost the half of a kingdom. Oh! the children were so happy! But happy they were not to remain always.

Their father the King married a very wicked Queen, who was not at all kind to the poor children; they found this out on the first day after the marriage, when there was a grand gala at the palace; for when the children played at receiving company, instead of having as many cakes and sweetmeats as they liked, the Queen gave them only some sand in a little dish, and told them to imagine that was something nice.

The week after, she sent the little Elise to be brought up by some peasants in the country, and it was not long before she told the King so many falsehoods about the poor princes that he would have nothing more to do with them at all.

"Away, out into the world, and take care of yourselves," said the wicked Queen; "fly away in the form of great speechless birds." But she could not make their transformation so disagreeable as she wished,—the Princes were changed into eleven white swans. Sending forth a strange cry, they flew out of the palace windows, over the park and over the wood.

It was still early in the morning when they passed by the place where Elise lay sleeping in the peasant's cottage; they flew several times round the roof, stretched their long necks, and flapped their wings, but no one either heard or saw them, they were forced to fly away, up to the clouds and into the wide world; so on they went to the forest which extended as far as the seashore.

The poor little Elise stood in the peasant's cottage amusing herself with a green leaf, for she had no other plaything. She pricked a hole in the leaf and peeped through it at the sun, and then she fancied she saw her brothers' bright eyes, and whenever the warm sunbeams shone full upon her cheeks, she thought of her brothers' kisses.

One day passed exactly like the other. When the wind blew through the thick hedge of rose-trees in front of the house, she would whisper to the roses, "Who is more beautiful than you?" but the roses would shake their heads and say, "Elise." And when the peasant's wife sat on Sundays at the door of her cottage reading her hymn-book, the wind would rustle in the leaves and say to the book, "Who is more pious than thou?"—"Elise," replied the hymn-book. And what the roses and the hymn-book said, was no more than the truth.

Elise was now fifteen years old; she was sent for home; but when the Queen saw how beautiful she was, she hated her the more, and would willingly have transformed her like her brothers into a wild swan, but she dared not do so, because the King wished to see his daughter.

So the next morning the Queen went into a bath which was made of marble, and fitted up with soft pillows and the gayest carpets; she took three toads, kissed them, and said to one, "Settle thou upon Elise's head that she may become dull and sleepy like thee."—"Settle thou upon her forehead," said she to another, "and let her become ugly like thee, so that her father may not know her again."— And "Do thou place thyself upon her bosom," whispered she to the third, "that her heart may become corrupt and evil, a torment to herself." She then put the toads into the clear water, which was immediately tinted with a green colour, and having called Elise, took off her clothes and made her get into the bath—one toad settled among her

164

hair, another on her forehead, and the third upon her bosom, but Elise seemed not at all aware of it, she rose up and three poppies were seen swimming on the water. Had not the animals been poisonous and kissed by a witch, they would have been changed into roses whilst they remained on Elise's head and heart,—she was too good for magic to have any power over her. When the Queen perceived this, she rubbed walnut juice all over the maiden's skin, so that it became quite swarthy, smeared a nasty salve over her lovely face, and entangled her long thick hair,—it was impossible to recognise the beautiful Elise after this.

When her father saw her, he was shocked and said she could not be his daughter; no one would have anything to do with her but the mastiff and the swallows; but they, poor things, could not say anything in her favour.

Poor Elise wept, and thought of her eleven brothers, not one of whom she saw at the palace. In great distress she stole away and wandered the whole day over fields and moors, till she reached the forest. She knew not where to go, but she was so sad, and longed so much to see her brothers, who had been driven out into the world, that she determined to seek and find them.

She had not been long in the forest when night came on, and she lost her way amid the darkness. So she lay down on the soft moss, said her evening prayer, and leaned her head against the trunk of a tree. It was so still in the forest, the air was mild, and from the grass and moss around gleamed the green light of many hundred glow-worms, and when Elise lightly touched one of the branches hanging over her, bright insects fell down upon her like falling stars.

All the night long she dreamed of her brothers. They were all children again, played together, wrote with diamond pens upon golden tablets, and looked at the pictures in the beautiful book which had encountered, and in the picture-book everything seemed alive, straight strokes and pothooks upon the tablets; no, they wrote of the bold actions they had performed, and the strange adventures they had encountered, and in the picture-book everything seemed alive, the birds sang, then men and women stepped from the book and talked to Elise and her brothers; however, when she turned over the leaves, they jumped back into their places, so that the pictures did not get confused together.—

When Elise awoke the sun was already high in the heavens. She could not see it certainly, for the tall trees of the forest entwined their thickly-leaved branches closely together, which, as the sunbeams played upon them, looked like a golden veil waving to and fro. And the air was so fragrant, and the birds perched upon Elise's shoulders. She heard the noise of water; there were several springs forming a pool, with the prettiest pebbles at the bottom, bushes were growing thickly round, but the deer had trodden a broad path through them, and by this path Elise went down to the water's edge. The water was so clear that had not the boughs and bushes around been moved to and fro by the wind, you might have fancied they were painted upon the smooth surface, so distinctly was each little leaf mirrored upon it, whether glowing in the sunlight or lying in the shade.

As soon as Elise saw her face reflected in the water she was quite startled, so brown and ugly did it look; however, when she wetted her little hand, and rubbed her brow and eyes, the white skin again appeared.—So Elise took off her clothes, stepped into the fresh water, and in the whole world there was not a king's daughter more beautiful than she then appeared.

After she had again dressed herself, and had braided her long hair, she went to the bubbling spring, drank out of the hollow of her hand, and then wandered further into the forest. She knew not where she was going, but she thought of her brothers, and of the good God who, she felt, would never forsake her. He it was who made the wild crab-trees grow in order to feed the hungry, and who showed her a tree whose boughs bent under the weight of their fruit. She made her noonday meal under its shade, propped up the boughs, and then walked on amid the dark twilight of the forest. It was so still that she could hear her own footsteps, and the rustling of each little withered leaf that was crushed beneath her feet; not a bird was to be seen, not a single sunbeam penetrated through the thick foliage, and the tall stems of the trees stood so close together, that when she looked straight before her, she seemed enclosed by trellis-work upon trellis-work. Oh! there was a solitariness in this forest such as Elise had never known before.

And the night was so dark! not a single glow-worm sent forth its light. Sad and melancholy she lay down to sleep, and then it seemed to her as though the boughs above her opened, and that she saw the Angel of God looking down upon her with gentle aspect, and a thousand little cherubs all around him. When she awoke in the morning she could not tell whether this was a dream, or whether she had really been so watched.

She walked on a little farther and met an old woman with a basket full of berries; the old woman gave her some of them, and Elise asked if she had not seen eleven princes ride through the wood.

"No," said the old woman, "but I saw yesterday eleven swans with golden crowns on their heads swim down the brook near this place."

And she led Elise on a little farther to a precipice, the base of which was washed by a brook; the trees on each side stretched their long leafy branches towards each other, and where they could not unite, the roots had disengaged themselves from the earth and hung their interlaced fibres over the water.

Elise bade the old woman farewell, and wandered by the side of the stream till she came to the place where it reached the open sea.

The great, the beautiful sea lay extended before the maiden's eyes, but not a ship, not a boat was to be seen; how was she to go on? She observed the numberless little stones on the shore, all of which the waves had washed into a round form; glass, iron, stone, everything that lay scattered there, had been moulded into shape, and yet the water which had effected this was much softer than Elise's delicate, little hand. "It rolls on unweariedly," said she, "and subdues what is so hard; I will be no less unwearied! Thank you for the lesson you have given me, ye bright rolling waves; some day, my heart tells me, you shall carry me to my dear brothers!"

There lay upon the wet sea-grass eleven white swan feathers; Elise collected them together; drops of water hung about them, whether dew or tears she could not tell. She was quite alone on the sea-shore, but she did not care for that, the sea presented an eternal variety to her, more indeed in a few hours than the gentle inland waters would have offered in a whole year. When a black cloud passed over the sky, it seemed as if the sea would say, "I too can look dark," and then the wind would blow and the waves fling out their white foam, but when the clouds shone with a bright red tint, and the winds were asleep, the sea also became like a rose-leaf in hue; it was now green, now white, but as it reposed peacefully, a slight breeze on the shore caused the water to heave gently like the bosom of a sleeping child.

At sunset Elise saw eleven wild swans with golden crowns on their heads fly towards the land; they flew one behind another, looking like a streaming white ribbon. Elise climbed the precipice, and concealed herself behind a bush; the swans settled close to her, and flapped their long white wings.

As the sun sank beneath the water, the swans also vanished, and in their place stood eleven handsome princes, the brothers of Elise. She uttered a loud cry, for although they were very much altered, Elise knew that they were, felt that they must be, her brothers; she ran into their arms, called them by their names—and how happy were *they* to see and recognise their sister, who was now grown so tall and so beautiful! They laughed and wept, and soon told each other how wickedly their step-mother had acted towards them.

"We," said the eldest of the brothers, "fly or swim as long as the sun is above the horizon, but when it sinks below, we appear again in our human form; we are therefore obliged to look out for a safe resting-place, for if at sunset we were flying among the clouds, we should fall down as soon as we resumed our own form. We do not dwell here, a land quite as beautiful as this lies on the opposite side of the sea, but it is far off,—to reach it, we have to cross the deep waters, and there is no island midway on which we may rest at night; one little solitary rock rises from the waves, and upon it we only just find room enough to stand side by side. There we spend the night in our human form, and when the sea is rough, we are sprinkled by its foam; but we are thankful for this resting-place, for without it we should never be able to visit our dear native country. Only once in the year is this visit to the home of our fathers permitted; we require two of the longest days for our flight, and can remain here only eleven days, during which time we fly over the large forest, whence we can see the palace in which we were born, where our father dwells, and the tower of the church in which our mother was buried. Here even the trees and bushes seem of kin to us, here the wild horses still race over the plains, as in the days of our childhood, here the charcoal-burner still sings the same old tunes to which we used to dance in our youth, here we are still attracted, and here we have found thee, thou dear little sister! We have yet two days longer to stay here, then we must fly over the sea to a land beautiful indeed, but not our fatherland. How shall we take thee with us? we have neither ship nor boat!"

"How shall I be able to release you?" said the sister. And so they went on talking almost the whole of the night. They slumbered only a few hours.

Elise was awakened by the rustling of swans' wings which were fluttering above her. Her brothers were again transformed, and for some time flew around in large circles. At last they flew far, far away; one of them remained behind; it was the youngest. He laid his head in her lap and she stroked his white wings; they remained the whole day together. Towards evening the others came back, and when the sun was set, again they stood on the firm ground in their natural form.

"Tomorrow we shall fly away, and may not return for a year, but we cannot leave thee; hast thou courage to accompany us? My arm is strong enough to bear thee through the forest; shall we not have sufficient strength in our wings to transport thee over the sea?"

"Yes, take me with you," said Elise. They spent the whole night in weaving a mat of the pliant willow bark and the tough rushes, and their mat was thick and strong. Elise lay down upon it, and when the sun had risen, and the brothers were again transformed into wild swans, they seized the mat with their beaks and flew up high among the clouds with their dear sister who was still sleeping. The sunbeams shone full upon her face, so one of the swans flew over her head, and shaded her with his broad wings.

They were already far from land when Elise awoke: she thought she was still dreaming, so strange did it appear to her to be travelling through the air, and over the sea. By her side lay a cluster of pretty berries, and a handful of savoury roots. Her youngest brother had collected and laid them there; and she thanked him with a smile, for she knew him as the swan who flew over her head and shaded her with his wings.

They flew so high, that the first ship they saw beneath them seemed like a white sea-gull hovering over the water. Elise saw behind her a large cloud; it looked like a mountain, and on it she saw the gigantic shadows of herself and the eleven swans—it formed a picture more splendid than any she had ever yet seen; soon, however, the sun rose higher, the cloud remained far behind, and then the floating shadowy picture disappeared.

The whole day they continued flying with a whizzing noise somewhat like an arrow, but yet they went slower than usual—they had their sister to carry. A heavy tempest was gathering, the evening approached; anxiously did Elise watch the sun, it was setting, still the solitary rock could not be seen; it appeared to her that the swans plied their wings with increasing vigour. Alas! it would be her fault if her brothers did not arrive at the place in time! they would become human beings when the sun set, and if this happened before they reached the rock, they must fall into the sea and be drowned. She prayed to God most fervently; still no rock was to be seen, the black clouds drew nearer, violent gusts of wind announced the approach of a tempest, the clouds rested perpendicularly upon a fearfully large wave which rolled quickly forwards, and one flash of lightning rapidly succeeded another.

The sun was now on the rim of the sea. Elise's heart beat violently; the swans shot downwards so swiftly that she thought she must fall, but again they began to hover; the sun was half sunk beneath the water, and at that moment she saw the little rock below her; it looked like a seal's head when he raises it just above the water. And the sun was sinking fast,—it seemed scarcely larger than a star,—her foot touched the hard ground, and it vanished altogether, like the last spark on a burnt piece of paper. Arm in arm stood her brothers around her; there was only just room for her and them—the sea beat tempestuously against the rock, flinging over them a shower of foam; the sky seemed in a continual blaze with the fast-succeeding flashes of fire that lightened it, and peal after peal rolled on the thunder, but sister and brothers kept firm hold of each other's hands. They sang a psalm, and their psalm gave them comfort and courage.

By daybreak the air was pure and still, and as soon as the sun rose, the swans flew away with Elise from the rock. The waves rose higher and higher, and when they looked from the clouds down upon the blackish-green sea, covered as it was with white foam, they might have fancied that millions of swans were swimming on its surface.

As day advanced, Elise saw floating in the air before her a land of mountains intermixed with glaciers, and in the centre a palace a mile in length, with splendid colonnades, surrounded by palm-trees and gorgeous-looking flowers as large as mill-wheels. She asked if this were the country to which they were flying, but the swans shook their heads, for what she saw was the beautiful airy castle of the fairy Morgana, where no human being was admitted; and whilst Elise still bent her eyes upon it, mountains, trees, and castle all disappeared, and in their place stood twelve churches with high towers and pointed windows—she fancied she heard the organ play, but it was only the murmur of the sea. She was now close to these churches, but behold! they had changed into a large fleet sailing under them; she looked down and saw it was only a sea mist passing rapidly over the water. An eternal variety floated before her eyes, till at last the actual land to which she was going appeared in sight. Beautiful blue mountains, cedar woods, towns, and castles rose to view.

172

Long before sunset Elise sat down among the mountains, in front of a large cavern; delicate young creepers grew around so thickly that it appeared covered with gay embroidered carpets.

"Now we shall see what thou wilt dream of tonight!" said her youngest brother, as he showed her the sleeping chamber destined for her.

"Oh that I could dream how you might be released from the spell!" said she; and this thought completely occupied her; she prayed most earnestly for God's assistance, nay, even in her dreams she continued praying, and it appeared to her that she was flying up high in the air towards the castle of the fairy Morgana. The fairy came forward to meet her, radiant and beautiful, and yet she fancied she resembled the old woman who had given her berries in the forest, and told her of the swans with golden crowns.

"Thou *canst* release thy brothers," said she, "but hast thou courage and patience sufficient? The water is indeed softer than thy delicate hands, and yet can mould the hard stones to its will, but then it cannot feel the pain which thy tender fingers will feel; it has no heart, and cannot suffer the anxiety and grief which thou must suffer. Dost thou see these stinging-nettles which I have in my hand? There are many of the same kind growing round the cave where thou art sleeping; only those that grow there or on the graves in the churchyard are of use, remember that! Thou must pluck them, although they will sting thy hand, thou must trample on the nettles with thy feet, and get yarn from them, and with this yarn thou must weave eleven shirts with long sleeves;—throw them over the eleven wild swans, and the spell is broken. But mark this: from the moment that thou beginnest thy work till it is completed, even should it occupy thee for years, thou must not speak a word; the first syllable that escapes thy lips will fall like a dagger into the hearts of thy brothers; on thy tongue depends their life. Mark well all this!"

173

And at the same moment the fairy touched Elise's hands with a nettle, which made them burn like fire, and Elise awoke. It was broad daylight, and close to her lay a nettle like the one she had seen in her dream. She fell upon her knees, thanked God, and then went out of the cave in order to begin her work. She plucked with her own delicate hands the disagreeable stinging-nettles; they burned large blisters on her hands and arms, but she bore the pain willingly in the hope of releasing her dear brothers. She trampled on the nettles with her naked feet, and spun the green yarn.

At sunset came her brothers. Elise's silence quite frightened them, they thought it must be the effect of some fresh spell of their wicked stepmother, but when they saw her blistered hands, they found out what their sister was doing for their sakes. The youngest brother wept, and when his tears fell upon her hands, Elise felt no more pain; the blisters disappeared.

The whole night she spent in her work, for she could not rest till she had released her brothers. All the following day she sat in her solitude, for the swans had flown away; but never had time passed so quickly. One shirt was ready; she now began the second.

Suddenly a hunting horn resounded among the mountains. Elise was frightened. The noise came nearer, she heard the hounds barking; in great terror she fled into the cave, bound up the nettles which she had gathered and combed into a bundle, and sat down upon it.

In the same moment a large dog sprang out from the bushes; two others immediately followed, they barked loudly, ran away and then returned. It was not long before the hunters stood in front of the cave; the handsomest among them was the King of that country; he stepped up to Elise. Never had he seen a lovelier maiden.

"How camest thou here, thou beautiful child?" said he. Elise shook her head, she dared not speak, for a word might have cost her the life of her brothers, and she hid her hands under her apron lest the King should see how she was suffering.

"Come with me," said he, "thou must not stay here! If thou art good as thou art beautiful, I will dress thee in velvet and silk, I will put a gold crown upon thy head, and thou shalt dwell in my palace!" So he lifted her upon his horse, while she wept and wrung her hands; but the King said, "I only desire thy happiness! thou shalt thank me for this some day!" and away he rode over mountains and valleys, holding her on his horse in front, whilst the other hunters followed. When the sun set, the King's magnificent capital with its churches and cupolas lay before them, and the King led Elise into the palace, where, in a high marble hall, fountains were playing, and the walls and ceiling displayed the most beautiful paintings. But Elise cared not for all this splendour, she wept and mourned in silence, even whilst some female attendants dressed her in royal robes, wove costly pearls in her hair, and drew soft gloves over her blistered hands.

And now she was fully dressed, and as she stood in her splendid attire, her beauty was so dazzling, that the courtiers all bowed low before her, and the King chose her for his bride, although the Archbishop shook his head, and whispered that the "beautiful lady of the wood must certainly be a witch, who had blinded their eyes, and infatuated the King's heart."

But the King did not listen, and ordered that music should be played. A sumptuous banquet was served up, and the loveliest maidens danced round the bride; she was led through fragrant gardens into magnificent halls, but not a smile was seen to play upon her lips or beam from her eyes. The King then opened a small room next her sleeping apartment; it was adorned with costly green tapestry, and exactly resembled the cave in which she had been found; upon the ground lay the bundle of yarn which she had spun from the nettles, and by the wall hung the shirt she had completed. One of the hunters had brought all this, thinking there must be something wonderful in it.

"Here thou mayest dream of thy former home," said the King; "here is the work which employed thee; amidst all thy present splendour it may sometimes give thee pleasure to fancy thyself there again."

When Elise saw what was so dear to her heart, she smiled, and the blood returned to her cheeks; she thought her brothers might still be released, and she kissed the King's hand; he pressed her to his heart and ordered the bells of all the churches in the city be rung, to announce the celebration of their wedding. The beautiful dumb maiden of the wood was to become Queen of the land.

The Archbishop whispered evil words in the King's ear, but they made no impression upon him; the marriage was solemnised, and the Archbishop himself was obliged to put the crown upon her head. In his rage he pressed the narrow rim so firmly on her forehead that it hurt her; but a heavier weight (sorrow for her brothers) lay upon her heart; she did not feel bodily pain. She was still silent, a single word would have killed her brothers; her eyes, however, beamed with heartfelt love to the King, so good and handsome, who had done so much to make her happy. She became more warmly attached to him every day. Oh! how much she wished she might confide to him all her sorrows! but she was forced to remain silent, she could not speak until her work was completed! To this end she stole away every night, and went into the little room that was fitted up in imitation of the cave; there she worked at her shirts, but by the time she had begun the seventh, all her yarn was spent.

She knew that the nettles she needed grew in the churchyard, but she must gather them herself; how was she to get them?

"Oh, what is the pain in my fingers compared to the anguish my heart suffers!" thought she. "I must venture to the churchyard; the good God will not withdraw His protection from me!"

Fearful as though she was about to do something wrong, one moonlight night she crept down to the garden, and through the long avenues got into the lonely road leading to the churchyard. She saw sitting on one of the broadest tombstones a number of ugly old witches. They took off their ragged clothes as if they were going to bathe, and digging with their long lean fingers into the fresh grass, drew up the dead bodies and devoured the flesh. Elise was obliged to pass close by them, and the witches fixed their wicked eyes upon her; but she repeated her prayer, gathered the stinging-nettles, and took them back with her into the palace. One person only had seen her; it was the Archbishop, who was awake when others slept; now he was convinced that all was not right about the Queen; she must be a witch, who had through her enchantments infatuated the King, and all the people.

In the Confessional he told the King what he had seen, and what he feared; and when the slanderous words came from his lips, the sculptured images of the saints shook their heads as though they would say, "It is untrue, Elise is innocent!" But the Archbishop explained the omen quite otherwise; he thought it was a testimony against her that the holy images shook their heads at hearing of her sin.

Two large tears rolled down the King's cheeks; he returned home in doubt, he pretended to sleep at night, though sleep never visited him; and he noticed that Elise rose from her bed every night, and every time he followed her secretly and saw her enter her little room.

His countenance became darker every day; Elise perceived it, though she knew not the cause. She was much pained, and besides, what did she not suffer in her heart for her brothers! Her bitter tears ran down on the royal velvet and purple; they looked like bright diamonds, and all who saw the magnificence that surrounded her, wished themselves in her place. She had now nearly finished her work, only one shirt was wanting; unfortunately, yarn was wanting also, she had not a single nettle left. Once more, only this one time, she must go to the churchyard and gather a few handfuls. She shuddered when she thought of the solitary walk and of the horrid witches, but her resolution was as firm as her trust in God.

Elise went, the King and the Archbishop followed her; they saw her disappear at the churchyard door, and when they came nearer, they saw the witches sitting on the tombstones as Elise had seen them, and the King turned away, for he believed her whose head had rested on his bosom that very evening to be amongst them. "Let the people judge her!" said he. And the people condemned her to be burnt.

She was now dragged from the King's sumptuous apartments into a dark, damp prison, where the wind whistled through the grated window. Instead of velvet and silk, they gave her the bundle of nettles she had gathered; on that must she lay her head, the shirts she had woven must serve her as mattress and counterpane;—but they could not have given her anything she valued so much; and she continued her work, at the same time praying earnestly to her God. The boys sang scandalous songs about her in front of her prison; not a soul comforted her with one word of love.

Towards evening she heard the rustling of a swan's wings at the grating. It was the youngest of her brothers, who had at last found his sister, and she sobbed aloud for joy although she knew that the coming night would probably be the last of her life; but then her work was almost finished and her brother was near.

The Archbishop came in order to spend the last hour with her; he had promised the King he would; but she shook her head and entreated him with her eyes and gestures to go—this night she must finish her work, or all she had suffered, her pain, her anxiety, her sleepless nights, would be in vain. The Archbishop went away with many angry words, but the unfortunate Elise knew herself to be perfectly innocent, and went on with her work.

Little mice ran busily about and dragged the nettles to her feet, wishing to help her; and the thrush perched on the iron bars of the window, and sang all night as merrily as he could, that Elise might not lose courage.

It was still twilight, just one hour before sunrise, when the eleven brothers stood before the palace gates, requesting an audience with the King; but it could not be, they were told, it was still night, the King was asleep, and they dared not wake him. They entreated, they threatened, the guard came up, the King himself at last stepped out to ask what was the matter—at that moment the sun rose, the brothers could be seen no longer, and eleven white Swans flew away over the palace.

The people poured forth from the gates of the city; they wished to see the witch burnt. One wretched horse drew the cart in which Elise was placed. A coarse frock of sackcloth had been put on her, her beautiful long hair hung loosely over her shoulders, her cheeks were of a deadly paleness, her lips moved gently, and her fingers wove the green yarn: even on her way to her cruel death she did not give up her work; the ten shirts lay at her feet, she was now labouring to complete the eleventh. The rabble insulted her.

"Look at the witch, how she mutters! she has not a hymn book in her hand, no, there she sits with her accursed hocus-pocus. Tear it from her, tear it into a thousand pieces!"

And they all crowded about her, and were on the point

of snatching away the shirts, when eleven white swans came flying towards the cart; they settled all round her, and lapped their wings. The crowd gave way in terror.

"It is a sign from Heaven; she is certainly innocent!" whispered some; they dared not say so aloud.

The Sheriff now seized her by the hand—in a moment she threw the eleven shirts over the Swans, and eleven handsome Princes appeared in their place. The youngest had, however, only one arm, and a wing instead of the other, for one sleeve was deficient in his shirt; it had not been quite finished.

"Now I may speak," said she: "I am innocent!"

And the people who had seen what had happened bowed before her as before a saint. She, however, sank lifeless in her brothers' arms; suspense, fear, and grief had quite exhausted her.

"Yes, she is innocent," said her eldest brother, and he now related their wonderful history. Whilst he spoke a fragrance as delicious as though it proceeded from millions of roses diffused itself around, for every piece of wood in the funeral pile had taken root and sent forth branches, a hedge of blooming red roses surrounded Elise, and above all the others blossomed a flower of dazzling white colour, bright as a star; the King plucked it and laid it on Elise's bosom, whereupon she awoke from her trance with peace and joy in her heart.

And all the church-bells began to ring of their own accord, and birds flew to the spot in swarms, and there was a festive procession back to the palace, such as no King has ever seen equalled.